Everyone LOVES *Summer Strawberries at Swallowtail Bay*!

'So beautifully written. It made me want to move house right now and set up by the sea!'
Tilly Tenant

'Simply delicious – summer escapes don't come any more tasty!'
Jane Linfoot

'Seaside, strawberries and a sexy hero – what's not to love?'
Mandy Baggot

'A hilarious romantic comedy that left me with a big smile on my face and longing for the seaside'
Holly Martin

'A delightful and delicious read for hopeful romantics everywhere'
Sandy Barker

'Hetty is the kind of plucky heroine I love – with big dreams and the tenacity to achieve them.'
Susan Mallery

'My first Katie Ginger book and it was wonderful! It was a BERRY special book!'
Christie Barlow

'What a gorgeous book!… It made me laugh out loud, snort, smile, and finally cry at the perfect ending. A charming romantic read that I didn't want to put down!'
Jaimie Admans

Summer Strawberries at Swallowtail Bay

KATIE GINGER

ONE PLACE. MANY STORIES

HQ
An imprint of HarperCollins*Publishers* Ltd
1 London Bridge Street
London SE1 9GF

First published by HQ 2020

This edition published in Great Britain by
HQ, an imprint of HarperCollins*Publishers* Ltd 2020

Copyright © Katie Ginger 2020

Katie Ginger asserts the moral right to be
identified as the author of this work.
A catalogue record for this book is
available from the British Library.

ISBN: 9780008380564

MIX
Paper from
responsible sources
FSC www.fsc.org FSC® C007454

This book is produced from independently certified FSC™ paper
to ensure responsible forest management.

For more information visit: www.harpercollins.co.uk/green

Printed and bound in Great Britain by
CPI Group (UK) Ltd, Melksham, SN12 6TR

To the best (and craziest) sisters-in-law
I could ever have hoped for,
Carla and BB!

Chapter 1

A small child charged passed Hetty, wielding fake green fists and shouting at his twin brother that he was going to smash him good just as soon as he got his hands on him. The twin brother replied by turning around and pretending to shoot him with something imaginary coming from the palms of his hands. Hetty smiled at them both, happy they were enjoying their birthday party.

Approximately two minutes before, the garden had been wonderfully silent and still, the quiet punctuated by an occasional buzzing of a bee as it flew from flower to flower, or the chirrup of a bird hiding in the mature trees. You could even hear the gentle murmur of the sea just a few streets away and the air carried a slight salty sting if you inhaled deeply enough. Now though, the children's party was well and truly underway and Hetty stood back to enjoy the fruits of her labour.

'Oh, Hetty,' the birthday boys' mother said. 'You've done such a fantastic job. I can't believe you managed to do all this in just a week. It's amazing.'

'Well, that's what I'm here for,' Hetty replied, with a grin. Mrs Silverman had come to her last Saturday in a complete panic because she'd left it too late to organise her twin boys' birthday party and had no idea where to even start. As a local event planner with a multitude of contacts, and seeing as Mrs Silverman lived down the road, Hetty had been only too happy to step in. After a couple of hours, she'd had everything sorted and in place for a superhero birthday party.

Hetty brushed a hand through her short blonde hair and shoved her hands into the pockets of her favourite dungarees. 'The boys seem happy,' she said, as Hector, wearing the green fists, began pummelling his brother who he'd pinned to the ground and was now sat on.

'They're absolute terrors,' Mrs Silverman said fondly. 'Hector, Lucas, come here and say thank you to Hetty for your party.'

The boys ran over.

'Is that what you want to be when you grow up?' Hetty asked, pointing to their Hulk and Spiderman costumes. 'Superheroes?'

Hector shook his head. 'I want to be an arse-ologist—'

'Archaeologist, dear,' Mrs Silverman cut in quickly. 'Like his father.'

'What about you, Lucas?' Hetty asked the other twin, enjoying this conversation immensely.

'I want to be an arsonist too.'

Hetty bit back the laugh that was forcing its way out. 'Sounds fabulous. I hope you enjoy your party.'

The boys ran away as more of their friends arrived, shepherded in by Mr Silverman who already looked in desperate need of a drink.

The huge back garden had been decorated with brightly coloured bunting, balloons were hung everywhere and several garden tables had been laid together and covered in a red chequered cloth to hold the party food. Naively, Mrs Silverman had requested celery sticks and rice cakes, but Hetty applauded the effort nonetheless. You never knew, she might get lucky and some child would eat one by mistake.

The strong midday sun beat down into the garden, warming

them all and casting shadows as it dappled through the leafy branches of the trees. It had been one of the best summers on record, so when Mrs Silverman turned up on Hetty's doorstep, distraught and virtually hyperventilating, it had seemed the easiest solution to hold the party in their back garden. Hetty's own back garden was much smaller as she lived in one of the smaller fisherman's cottages, rather than the larger houses that made up the conservation area of Swallowtail Bay. It was only just big enough for a little table and the two chairs she and Macie, her assistant, often sat at when they were planning.

From across the table, a slightly muffled voice said, 'These sausage rolls are lush.' Hetty looked up to see Macie stuffing two into her mouth at once.

'Try and leave some for the kids, won't you? But don't worry, I've already snaffled us a little treat tray. And Mrs Silverman's promised us a piece of cake too. I know how you love birthday cake.'

'Kids' birthday cake is the best,' Macie replied. 'It's pretty much one hundred per cent sugar with a bit of buttercream added for good measure. And jam. I love jam.' Her long, cinnamon-coloured hair hung down in a plait, and the freckles on her nose disappeared as it crinkled from her mischievous grin.

A little girl came and tugged on Macie's arm. She'd been crying and Hetty was suddenly on high alert. Macie knelt down to ensure she was eye-level with the girl. 'Hey, poppet, what's wrong?'

The little one mumbled something but neither of them caught it, and Macie asked her again as the girl's mum came over.

'Don't worry, she's not upset with the party. She's got the hump with me.'

'Oh no, why's that?' asked Hetty.

'I got her costume wrong. She wanted to come as a parrot, but I thought she said carrot, so that's what I ordered online and by the time it came it was too late to send it back.' The little girl, complete with bright orange carrot costume and a little green hat with sticky out bits, wiped her eyes and stared sullenly at her mother.

'I think you look smashing,' said Hetty. 'Here, why don't you come and have one of my extra special sweets?' The little girl immediately brightened, even though the sweet Hetty gave her was the same as all the ones on the table. The girl's mum mouthed a thank-you as, cheered, the little girl ran off to join her friends.

So far, things were going well for a kids' party. There was always some disaster or other. The key was how you handled it. As an event organiser, Hetty was incredibly experienced, having run every sort of event you could imagine. Yet, for a while now, she had hoped to extend the reach of her business beyond the borders of her sweet hometown of Swallowtail Bay. With its pebbly beach and boutique shops it was a wonderful place to live – peaceful, beautiful – but she desperately wanted to attract clientele from the wider area and the bigger towns nearby. Pulling her mind back to the task at hand, she checked her watch. 'Ten minutes and the entertainment will be here.'

'I can't believe you managed to get them at such short notice,' Macie said. 'They're normally booked up months in advance.'

'They owed me a favour.'

'Miss,' a little girl dressed as a Disney princess said, 'Tommy was just sick behind a bush.'

Hetty smiled, knowing this would happen at some point. 'Whereabouts, darling? Can you show me?' As the girl led her by the hand to a disgruntled hydrangea, Hetty called over her shoulder to Macie. 'Can you bring the cat litter please, Macie?' Though sawdust was traditional in these circumstances, after years of hosting kids' parties, Hetty had found that cat litter was much better at dealing with these sorts of incidents. Moving some branches out of the way, she was slightly surprised to find a pirate hidden behind it, weeing. 'Do you think you could do that in the toilet, please, sweetheart? I don't think hydrangeas respond very well to that sort of watering.'

4

As soon as she'd sorted that, the entertainment arrived. The boys had requested Superman and Batman attend their birthday party and fight to the death. While she couldn't promise that exactly, she had managed to get two trained karate masters who ran a sideline in dressing-up as superheroes and play-fighting at kid's parties. They had another booking straight after but had squeezed in Hector and Lucas as a special favour to Hetty.

'They've got bulges in all the right places,' Macie commented. To which Hetty gave an I'm-too-grown-up-to-comment eye-roll but let her grin show that she hadn't missed that observation either.

The kids adored them and cheered as the battle played out. All was going swimmingly until near the end of their set when Superman threw out a foot rather too enthusiastically and hit Batman square in the privates. Poor Batman quickly lost his superhero status as he crumpled to the ground holding the damaged area and taking deep breaths.

'Ouch,' commented Macie. 'I don't think his manly bulge is going to be quite so bulgy now.'

Hetty leapt into the fray. 'Time for some food, everyone! I bet I can beat you to the cupcakes.'

As expected, the kids left Batman and Superman to recuperate and charged at the food table. Watching them eat was like watching monkeys in a zoo. Food was suddenly everywhere, drinks were knocked over as arms went flailing around for sausage rolls, jam sandwiches and chocolate biscuits, but the smiles and the giggles made it all worthwhile.

Once the food was eaten, Hetty signalled to Mrs Silverman to bring out the cake and kept everyone seated and quiet, ready to sing 'Happy Birthday'. Mr Silverman, who still looked like he needed a shot of whisky, circled with his phone, desperately trying to catch every moment as the candles were blown out.

Content with how everything was going, the remaining hour flew by for Hetty, with only minor hiccups. A toilet roll was discovered and used as a streamer, another had been stuffed down the loo, and overwrought with the whole affair, the birthday boys collapsed into sobs when Mrs Silverman told them they couldn't have a fourth slice of cake. Overall though, it had been one of the less traumatic children's parties she'd organised and Hetty was thankful when the children left and the clear-up began.

She and Macie had it down to a fine art by now and were sorted within half an hour. Hetty put the last black sack into the bin as Mrs Silverman came over with an envelope and a bottle of wine. 'Here,' she said to Hetty.

'What's this?'

'For you and Macie. You've been absolutely brilliant, and I can't thank you enough. I was going completely mental and you took all the stress off me. I don't know how you do this for a living. It would kill me.'

Hetty graciously accepted the gifts and after splitting the generous tip with Macie, they were on their way.

'Well, that went well,' Macie said, stretching her arms above her head and bashing the roof of Myrtle, Hetty's Mini.

'It did, didn't it.' Hetty circled her neck, easing her shoulders, but it didn't alleviate the feeling that lingered more and more with each passing day. A fidgety feeling. A feeling of expectancy and restlessness. 'I love doing the kids' parties – and all the other things we do – but I really want to try something different.'

'Like what?' Macie asked.

'Oh, I don't know.' Hetty searched for the right word but was unable to fix on anything specific. 'Just something bigger – something more challenging.'

As much as she loved the bay, she felt somewhat limited by the repetitive nature of her job which mainly involved birthday, anniversary or retirement parties, and the odd funeral. 'I just feel like there's a lot more we could be doing and we're not. It's always the same old, same old. I'd like something meatier to get my teeth into.'

'Don't say *meatier*, you're making me hungry.'

Hetty glanced over. 'How can you possibly be hungry? You ate a gazillion sausage rolls *and* all that cake.'

'I was chasing around after twenty 7-year-olds, it works up quite an appetite you know.' Macie grinned. 'I don't know about you, but my feet are killing me. If something more challenging means more ache in my feet, I might have to resign.'

'No, you won't, you love this job too much.' But it was true, the soles of Hetty's feet were throbbing too. 'Do you want me to drop you home or do you fancy sharing this bottle of wine in my back garden with our feet up?'

'Will Stanley be there?' Stanley was the limpy seagull Hetty had adopted and fed regularly from a special little plate. They'd both grown very fond of him as they imagined his deformed foot meant all the other seagulls teased him and wouldn't let him join their gangs.

'He will.'

'In that case, it's a definite yes. I think I've got a spare sausage roll somewhere about my person,' said Macie with a chuckle, feeling her pockets to locate it. 'He'll like that.'

Hetty grinned too. 'As long as it's not in your bra. If it is, I might have to stage an intervention.' Pushing her restless feelings back down, she turned up the air-con. 'Right, mine it is, then.'

Chapter 2

The monthly meeting of the Swallowtail Bay business forum was about to get underway. Glancing down at her favourite crimson silk shirt, Hetty saw that the stick-on label with her name on it was already peeling off in the dense summer heat and she wondered if it would last through what was bound to be a lengthy, hot meeting.

Hetty smiled politely at the lithe and toned woman in front of her merrily chatting away about the weight-loss benefits of detox teas and waving a pain au chocolat in the air. Considering that Hetty's figure was curvy – a fact that she was entirely comfortable with now she'd reached her late thirties – and that Hetty herself was brandishing a half-eaten mini croissant, it seemed an odd conversation to be having. But then the local business forum often ended up in odd conversations. Last time, Hetty had talked to a woman who made bath soap with avocado milk and spent the following day wondering how on earth one milked an avocado.

'Shall we begin?' asked Bob, the chairman of the forum, a man in his fifties with grey hair that fluffed out over his temples.

The woman in front of her paused mid-sentence at the words 'ginkgo biloba' – which for some reason made Hetty laugh – and excitedly went to sit down.

Hetty tactically chose a seat that would remain in the shade as it was already getting stuffy and the windows were cast wide open to let in as much air as possible. The tiniest of breezes fluttered the blue blinds sending dust motes into the air. Hetty watched them float lazily in the sun's rays, landing unseen on people's shoulders.

The forum was attended by many of the businesses in Swallowtail Bay and Hetty enjoyed the monthly get-together, finding out about upcoming events and promotion opportunities.

'Right,' said Bob, 'you've all had time to network, now down to business.'

Despite the forum not having yielded any tangible results so far, Hetty believed it was time well spent. Running her own business, Simply Fantastic Events, had taught her you have to seek out new opportunities rather than just wait for them to land in your lap. People had to know who you were – especially as an event organiser. Waiting for opportunities to magically appear meant missed mortgage payments, worry lines and stress. All of which Hetty had enough of already.

'Now,' said Bob, 'you all know that a new bakery has opened in town.' He checked his notes. 'Fairy Cakes, down the other end of the high street. The new owner's assured me she'll be here next time, so that's another member of the forum. Good news all round, I'd say.'

Another baker's? Hetty wondered if they'd prove a rival to The Bake House. But Hetty refused to let her thoughts linger on that subject.

'Our first order of business for today is the strawberry festival—'

'What strawberry festival?' asked Stella, a new resident of Swallowtail Bay and owner of Old Herbert's Shop. She'd moved in earlier in the year and had worked hard to turn around the fortunes of the strange old shop that had sold such a random assortment of goods no one was quite sure what to call it.

'Oh, it used to be brilliant,' said Lexi, who worked at Raina's Café and was here to represent her. Lexi always wore vintage clothes and had attended today's meeting in an amazing spaghetti-strapped Fifties-style dress that flared out at the waist. Hetty couldn't wear anything with spaghetti straps. She usually had to wear a bra with straps as wide as scaffolding planks. 'Swallowtail Bay used to be the strawberry-growing capital of Britain and we'd have a festival every year to celebrate. Stalls lined every single street up and down the high street and sold every type of straw-berry thing you can think of. There were jams, scones, wines, soaps – anything and everything. Do you remember it, Hetty?' Her bright green eyes – with a slick of thick black liner – turned to Hetty full of excitement.

'I do. It really used to be something.' Underneath the soft sleeves of her shirt, the hairs on Hetty's arms stood on end.

Gwen, owner of Snip-It, the hairdresser's, scoffed. 'It *used* to be a festival many moons ago, but now it's nothing more than a church jumble sale.'

'There aren't many venues available anymore,' answered Mary, who alongside Gwen was part of the festival committee. No one really knew why Gwen was so depressed about the whole thing. They just assumed it was part of her normal approach to life, or maybe she resented doing any work for it when no one turned out. 'And no one wants to take part. As everyone has lost interest it's shrunk, and we've had to find smaller venues that don't charge. We're very lucky to use St John's Church Hall. And we all still do our best.'

Reluctantly, Hetty had to admit that miserable Gwen's state-ment was true. The strawberry festival had, at one time, when she was little, been a huge event. There'd been the stalls that Lexi mentioned, plus games, puppet shows, street entertainers – so much to grab your attention, no matter what your taste. It had been the highlight of the summer holidays when bunting lined the streets and everyone came together. When Hetty thought back to the bank holiday weekends spent there, all she could remember was laughter and a strange buzz in the air. The reminiscence brought a smile to her face. But these days the strawberry festival was held in a small church hall and comprised a few tables set out with a handful of homemade cakes, bric-a-brac and a tombola. Not a strawberry in sight. And outside, in the church car park, second-hand clothes would be piled up on wobbly tables. It really was such a shame it had died. It had been a great Swallowtail Bay tradition.

'We used to have awards for the best strawberry product,' Mary continued. 'A strawberry trail to find a big stuffed strawberry toy, and a strawberry-eating competition. Oh, it was so lovely.'

'Yes, well …' Bob tried to bring them to order but the two older ladies were off.

'People used to come from everywhere,' Gwen agreed. 'All the neighbouring towns turned out.' Hetty cocked her head, listening with interest. 'Now it's an embarrassment to the word festival.' Poor Mary blushed at Gwen's harsh words, but she carried on regardless. 'We used to have to squeeze the stalls in wherever we could – it was so popular. Now we're lucky if we make twenty pounds from donations.'

'It is a bit of a shame it's not as popular anymore,' said Bob. 'But it's still a great opportunity for us all to promote our businesses. I was thinking we could have a stand of leaflets or something like that.'

Sparks began to fire in Hetty's brain and intuition tied a knot in her stomach. Her body was telling her something. And if there was one thing Hetty Colman always did, it was listen to her intuition. Her brain quickly made a list of pros and cons, tallied costs against potential profit, calculated the work involved and went through a million and one other things, then she opened her mouth to speak.

'I've a suggestion about the strawberry festival, actually.' All eyes turned to her. 'You all know how I've been looking for opportunities to expand my business, well, I've a gut feeling this is just the chance I've been looking for.'

'Go on,' said Bob with genuine interest. Gwen and Mary had gone quiet and everyone else waited for her to speak.

'I think we should revamp the strawberry festival and bring it back to its former glory.' Eyes widened a little but with Lexi and Stella's encouraging expressions, Hetty confidently continued. 'I think we should turn it into a giant food festival that lasts the whole of the bank holiday weekend.'

'What?' asked Gwen, the scornful tone returning to her voice. 'You? Run a great big food festival? It's a lot more complicated than a kid's birthday party or ordering sandwiches for a wake.'

Hetty simply smiled in response. She didn't take Gwen's remarks personally, she was always like this. It was a wonder Gwen had any customers left with her gloomy, glass-half-empty attitude. And Hetty was incredibly thick-skinned. 'As I said,' she replied cheerfully, 'this is just the challenge I'm looking for to boost my business. Strawberries would remain a focus, but I think if it's expanded to other things too, we could have a really big food festival attracting regional, maybe even national attention. And we all know how business slows in the winter without the tourists. This would give us a final boost before the drop.'

Nell, the owner of a boutique bed and breakfast, Holly Lodge, nodded along. 'I could definitely do with the boost, so anything that brings in the visitors is good with me.'

'Still held in the town?' asked Bob. 'It's in four weeks, though, Hetty. If you plan to keep it to the bank holiday weekend, I'm not sure we'd get permission from the council by then.'

It was true that time was short, but even though she was excited, Hetty's logical and practical mind had, in the few minutes available, already mulled over several possibilities for locations. Bob was quite right that getting permission from the council to close roads, divert traffic and all that faff for the August bank holiday weekend was most likely not going to happen in the time she had available. To attract stalls and entertainment on the scale she was thinking of, she needed a firm location before approaching vendors, so the town was definitely out. That left two other options as far as she could see: the first was a large sports field on the east side of the bay, but it was owned and operated by a private leisure facility and they'd be unlikely to give permission at such short notice. The other was a difficult option too but more likely to succeed, and one that could turn out to be beneficial to both parties, if local rumours were anything to go by.

'I was actually thinking of Thornhill Hall,' Hetty said confidently.

The full tables surrounding her erupted into low mumbles and the incredulous shaking of heads. When they fell silent, Hetty again watched the dust motes dance down the shafts of light.

'Thornhill Hall?' asked Gwen, returning to her sarcastic tone. 'You're having a laugh, aren't you? There's absolutely no way John Thornhill will let you use his family's land for a food festival. The Thornhills keep themselves to themselves these days.'

'If rumour is to be believed,' said Hetty, adopting her best don't-mess-with-me voice and tucking her blonde pixie-cropped hair behind her ear, 'he needs the money. If I offer him a share of the profits in exchange for use of his land, what has he got to lose? He hasn't got to do anything. I'm going to do all the organising.'

'And what about the costs?' countered Gwen. 'Who's going to stump up for all this? As much as we love Swallowtail Bay, we can't all volunteer, or pay for pitches. Or move our businesses to a different location for the day, hiring extra staff so we can have one of those pop-up shop type things. Then there are stewards and all that what-not.'

A few people nodded support then regarded Hetty with apologetic expressions. The meeting room suddenly seemed stuffy under everyone's gaze and Hetty felt an uncharacteristic moment of self-doubt. Adjusting her glasses, she pushed it down; it was a moment's nerves, that was all. And nerves were a good thing. They kept you focused.

While Hetty's dislike for Gwen was growing by the second, she had to concede that, again, Gwen had a valid point. With safety and security to think about, and stewards and equipment hire, there were going to be a lot of expenses, but grumpy Gwen had underestimated her. Hetty relaxed. To make this work she was going to have to use the capital from her own business, and as scary as that was, it was an investment in her future. One that she was more than willing to make. Hetty didn't normally commit to things without a lot of forethought but something about this opportunity felt right deep down in her bones. She knew this was the right thing to do, the right step for her career. It was a cliché, but sometimes you really did have to speculate to accumulate.

'Well?' said Gwen again. 'Who do you propose will pay for it all? You haven't got time to find sponsors, have you?'

Matching Gwen's gaze, with a carefree shrug Hetty answered. 'I will.'

'Are you sure, Hetty?' asked Lexi, her forehead creasing in concern.

'Absolutely. I really think this could be a great way for Swallowtail Bay to get back on the map. After all, we have some of the best food around. We have artisan bakers, cheese makers, vineyards, not to mention the best fish and chips in the land. By turning the food festival into a big weekend event, we could really get people coming back to Swallowtail Bay.'

'It'll be a lot of work,' said Bob. 'Especially with such a tight timescale.'

'I think it's a fabulous idea,' said Lexi.

Stella nodded too. 'I'd definitely be interested in having a stall.'

Hetty couldn't help feeling like she was in a job interview under everyone's expectant gaze. 'I know this seems like a big deal, and it is. But I'm ready for the challenge. More than ready.'

Adrenalin was already pumping through her veins and she had a sudden urge to leave the meeting, grab a new notebook and get started. From the corner of her eye she caught sight of Mary, the member who'd spoken earlier and was on the festival committee. Her head was bowed, but Hetty couldn't quite make out her expression. Realising she may have overstepped the mark by getting too carried away, she said, 'Mary, do you think the committee would agree to this? I don't want to step on anyone's toes or make any enemies. I just thought it would be a solution that worked for everyone.'

Mary's head lifted and Hetty saw her face suddenly relax into a smile. 'Thank you for asking, Hetty. While I'm sure they'd be relieved to have it off their hands, I think you'd better talk to the festival committee when we're all together. I can't agree to it on my own.'

'Okay, Mary. Perhaps we can get something set up over the next few days?'

Gwen snorted. 'Don't jump the gun, Hetty. You still need to get John Thornhill on board first and there's about as much chance of him agreeing to this as there is of me winning Miss World.'

Resisting the urge to stick her tongue out, Hetty hid the feeling of dread that was creeping up her spine with a confident beam. There was only one thing for it. Straight after the meeting Hetty would make a trip to Thornhill Hall and face the scary – and scarily handsome – lord of the manor. She had to convince him to agree.

***

Filled with excitement, Hetty didn't waste any time after the forum finished, pausing only to steal a couple more mini croissants on her way out. Once outside, she swapped her glasses for sunglasses, jumped into Myrtle and drove to Thornhill Hall.

John Thornhill very rarely came into town but from the few visits he'd made he had gathered quite a reputation for himself. Insanely handsome, with green-blue eyes and thick dark hair, but with a rather too entitled and forbidding attitude, Mr Thornhill was known for being rude, irascible and a complete stick-in-the-mud who also happened to be stuck in the past, obsessed with his ancestral home. Unlike a lot of country houses that were open to the public for at least a few days a year, the Thornhills kept themselves locked away and rarely mixed with the local riffraff. It hadn't gone down well with the residents of Swallowtail Bay.

The slightest of sea breezes blew through the open window as Hetty drove the long road that ran along the seafront. Once she'd left the town centre and the boutique shops that lined the front, the bay opened up onto a wonderful pebbly beach. A long green ran parallel with the road and weather-beaten and well-used fishing boats sat between small white beach huts. At this time of year the huts were well used and doors hung open while children ran in and out.

When finally the pebble beach curved away to the left and the road she was on took her to the right, Hetty drove until she reached the outskirts of town to be surrounded by fields and winding country lanes. Though the salt air faded, overtaken by the strong aroma of manure, if she looked in the rear-view mirror, she could see the bright blue of the sea on the horizon. Hetty watched as the fields rolled by, dotted here and there with enormous circular hay bales. Closing the window but cranking up the air-con, Hetty swung Myrtle past a tractor and down the road to Thornhill Hall. Though it was such a large country house, it nestled amid such sprawling acres of land that made it seem small by comparison.

According to the town gossips, John's father, Rupert, had expensive tastes which had lost most of the family fortune and now the place was falling into disrepair. As excited as she was to get the festival planning underway in earnest, Hetty was also keen to see if any of the rumours were true. No one got to see Thornhill Hall up close, only sighting its beautiful columned façade from gaps in the hedges lining the roads.

As a child she'd imagined what it would be like to live there, running its lengthy halls like an orphan in a Victorian gothic novel. There'd be butlers, cooks, maids and governesses – a house full of staff serving the masters of the house. At one point, before she started grammar school, Hetty had decided that one day she'd live in a house like this. The thought made her chuckle now as she adjusted the sun visor. Obviously, that hadn't happened, but she loved the small cottage by the sea she'd ended up in, with its rickety front gate and tiny kitchen. From the seat in her bay window she could sit and watch the tide – strong and fierce in the winter and serene and calm in summer.

Finally reaching the boundary of the grand estate, Hetty pulled off the single-track country lane into the drive, surprised to see the large wrought-iron gates had been left open. Her rickety front gate paled in comparison to the eight-foot tall, dark black metal with gold patterning at the top. The long gravel drive lay before her, lined on either side with mature trees whose verdant haws offered only a little shade on this hot, cloudless day. The light shone through onto her windscreen and she drove slowly, following the winding path towards the house. About halfway down the drive, the mature trees were replaced with formal gardens. High, unkept privet hedges now lined the driveway but what lay behind them, Hetty couldn't see.

Behind her owl-like sunglasses, Hetty felt her eyes widen at the enormity of the house as it finally came into view. She slowed the car. She'd always imagined seeing Thornhill Hall up close for the first time as something akin to the moment Elizabeth Bennett first sees Pemberley. But somehow, up close, it managed to be even grander than she had thought. The great grey Palladian façade was a mass of windows, covered in wisteria. Though not a gardener, wisteria was one plant Hetty knew the name of. Even in winter it made a house look enchanting and magical. The pale brown vines reached out over the front of Thornhill Hall in long winding fingers, and a few spring blooms dotted the front, hanging down here and there like lilac lanterns. She wasn't exactly boned-up on architectural design, but Hetty supposed the house would be called Neo-classical in style. The two recessed wings on either side of the main building housed six windows each and the front door, which was in fact enormous, appeared small nestled behind four columns on top of which stood a large vaulted gable. Behind the house, great swathes of fields spread out and the sea became a vista of hazy lines of blue.

The drive ended in a turning circle, in the middle of which was a massive stone vase overflowing with flowers. Hetty parked just down from the front door. As she climbed out of the car her eyes remained fixed on the house. It was utterly beautiful and perfectly situated in the middle of the overgrown ornate topiary that formed the formal gardens. They clearly weren't paying a gardener right now.

Being of a practical nature, Hetty could well see that as lovely as the place was, the heating bills alone would be astronomical. Would it really be wonderful to live somewhere like this, she thought, or more trouble than it was worth? Before her mind could answer, she spied the name sticker from the business forum just about holding on to her shirt and pulled it off, screwing it into a ball and stuffing it in her jeans pocket. Hetty suddenly wished she'd worn a skirt or shorts as the sun beat down on the backs of her legs. Though June had been a bit patchy, the sun had shone relentlessly since the beginning of July, causing hot, sticky days and long, frustratingly sleepless nights. Taking a deep breath and swapping her sunglasses back to normal glasses, Hetty rolled her shoulders and readied herself to face John Thornhill.

The deep stone steps that led to the front door were of the same grey as the house and seemed smooth, almost soft, worn by time and the feet that had trodden them over the years. A sense of history imparted with every step and Hetty was curious to know how long the Thornhills had owned the house. Picking up the heavy iron knocker on the large wooden door, a sudden rush of nerves swamped her normally confident demeanour. It was too late to go back now though, she thought, glancing back at the car. She'd committed herself at the forum and here she was on John Thornhill's doorstep. Hetty reminded herself that her business needed this boost, and as steely determination rose up, she tapped three times, hearing the deep bass note resonate around her.

Chapter 3

John sighed with relief when he heard the loud knock echo through the hall; the delivery was finally here. At least one thing was going right this morning. So far today he'd had another final demand, a row with his brother, Felix, over the best way to raise funds for the roof repairs, his mother was almost packing her bags, so utterly terrified of losing her home, and his dad – well, his dad had been pruning in the garden since 6 a.m. A completely unhelpful task and one he was performing with increasing regularity as a way of avoiding the mess he'd got the family into.

John ran a hand through his short dark hair, then down his chin, feeling the neat, trimmed beard beneath his fingertips. As the silent house filled with the echo of the knock, he made his way from the study to the front door in time to see Jaz, his PA, running down the stairs faster than a whippet to get there before him. Her black hair was tied in a tight high ponytail and bobbed as she descended. When he'd been her age, he'd had energy too.

'You beat me to it,' he said with a grin, his deep voice echoing almost as loud as the heavy lion-shaped knocker on the front door. She returned his smile with one of her own.

'I'm surprised you left the study. I thought you'd be waiting for that call from Christie's. Do you want me to ring them for you and chase them once I've dealt with this? Oh, and don't forget you've got Mr Stevens ringing at ten about that Ming vase. It might be best if I ring Christie's so you don't get stuck on another call.'

John was struck by his assistant's bright eyes and impressive organisation skills. He couldn't remember now how he'd managed to run his antiques business on his own. As it had grown, he'd found the admin side too much to handle but had resisted needing an assistant. He found it hard to delegate and give up control. Considering how reticent he'd originally been to hire someone, particularly someone so young, Jaz Simmons had more than proved herself capable. She'd been 24 when he'd hired her. Now, two years later, he had no idea what he'd do without her. 'If you could, that'd be great. I've still got fifteen minutes before Stevens though, which should be enough time to deal with this delivery.' Jaz took a step back, leaving John to answer.

Turning the handle, he pulled open the heavy oak door, beautifully weathered by time. At moments like this, the magnificence and history of the house would grab him, and he'd feel the hard work was all worthwhile. He shouldn't ever forget how much that meant to his family even though it was often the case that his ideas and the hours of work all came to nothing.

Expecting to see a middle-aged man in overalls delivering a large wooden crate, John was surprised to be faced with an attractive woman wearing a dark red shirt tucked into tight jeans and with pink ballet pumps on her small feet. Her pale blonde hair was cut short, which suited her gamine face which was made all the more attractive by a cute pair of spectacles. Momentarily lost for words – not a state of affairs he was used to and one that put him on his guard – he barked, 'How did you get in?'

However, the beautiful woman before him didn't seem in the least bit offended as she brushed her hair over her ear. 'The gates

21

were open, Mr Thornhill. I was quite surprised myself; I know you usually keep them shut, but I'm taking it as a sign.'

The gates *were* normally kept firmly shut so people didn't just randomly decide to visit the house. They used to be left unlocked all the time but then visitors would come and knock on the front door, asking to look around like their home was in some kind of estate agent's open-house session. His mother used to be terrified and over the years had become increasingly jumpy at the sound of a rat-a-tat-tat and would run upstairs like a frightened rabbit. Still, he didn't welcome this interruption to his day. 'A sign of what?'

Smiling, she replied confidently, 'You'll find out if you let me inside.'

A light warmth rose in him that he put down to the heat of the day. This woman probably just wanted a donation to some local charity event or other and they had nothing to give, even if they wanted to. The do-gooders they normally met were little old ladies with grey hair, not attractive self-assured women. He glanced around hoping to be saved by his delivery driver and the sun shone on his face making him hot. 'Listen, you can't just drive onto private land, this is trespassing.'

'Oh, hush, don't be so dramatic,' she said, laughing. 'I'm not doing anything of the kind. I've come to speak to you, Mr Thornhill.'

Taken aback, John tried to regain control of the conversation. 'How exactly can I help you?'

'Let's start again, shall we?' The woman thrust out a hand. 'Good morning, Mr Thornhill. My name's Hetty Colman and I have a business proposition for you.'

'Really?' Slightly amused but also conscious of the time and the calls he was expecting, not to mention the chaotic morning he'd endured so far, he scowled. He didn't have time for a 'proposition' that would inevitably be for a charity bake sale or some such local event. 'I don't have time right now, but if you'd like to make an appointment with my assistant, I'd be happy to speak to you another time.'

Disappointment and annoyance flashed over her features, but Miss Colman, it seemed, was not to be deterred. Her hand dropped back down to her side and he realised in his flustered state he hadn't taken it. A wave of embarrassment hit him. 'I'm afraid time is of the essence, Mr Thornhill and I'll only take a moment of your day.' She edged a little closer to the door, which irritated him even though the sparkling confidence in her eyes made him hesitate.

'I'm very sorry, Miss Colman.' He really didn't have time for this now. 'Another time.' John backed away from the door, leaving Jaz to speak to her, but the woman didn't move. Normally he'd consider it an admirable quality, but not today.

'What I'm proposing,' Hetty called out to him, 'could be of great financial benefit to you, just as much as me, Mr Thornhill. And I've heard that's something you require right now. I really would prefer to speak to you, rather than your assistant, if that's at all possible.'

The words 'great financial benefit' and 'heard' stopped him in his tracks and he turned, feeling his hackles rise. Had the town been gossiping about his family and their situation again? It was true that thanks to his father's obsession with French vineyards, the family fortune had been lost and, as a result, most of the paintings and anything made of precious metal had been sold to try to claw back some much-needed funds. Where they'd been removed from walls leaving squares of bright wallpaper, the rooms now looked bereft and sorry. Damp was creeping in everywhere, creating corners full of black mould and a general smell of dust. Now the roof of the east wing needed repairing, and some of the tapestries were in danger of being lost forever because they couldn't afford a conservator. The place was already re-mortgaged to the hilt and the chance of repaying anything other than a token amount that wouldn't even touch the interest was remote.

At 44, and with his own business going well, he should have been enjoying life. Maybe finding time for love and having a family, like Felix. Instead, half his time was spent researching possible income streams to raise money for the house, but with his mother against opening to the general public, and Felix always suggesting some outlandish scheme or other, it was proving virtually impossible.

Jaz was attempting to mollify the bossy woman, who from her polite, but dogged expression, wasn't having any of it, and he only had twelve minutes now until his ten o'clock call. Jaz's voice was harsh. 'Miss Colman, I assure you, as Mr Thornhill's assistant I'm quite capable of dealing with anything to do with his affairs.' Jaz flicked her ponytail over her shoulder, something she did, he'd noticed, when she was asserting her authority.

'I'm sure you can, Miss …?'

'Simmons.'

'Miss Simmons.' Miss Colman's voice was warm and friendly, not patronising, he noticed, just assured. 'But I really would prefer to speak to Mr Thornhill directly.'

'As Mr Thornhill has already explained, he has business to attend to this morning. But I can help you. Or we can arrange a more convenient time.'

'Miss Simmons—'

Jaz's voice took on a steely edge and for a second this battle of wills was far too close to call. 'Miss Colman, as I've already explained Mr Thornhill—'

'Mr Thornhill hasn't actually gone anywhere, Miss Simmons. I can see him quite clearly hiding in the hallway over there.' The woman pointed to him and met his gaze. 'So I can only assume he is in fact, still interested in what I have to say. Aren't you, Mr Thornhill?' She tipped her head slightly as she said his name and John turned away, hiding the smile that was pulling up the corner of his mouth.

He checked his watch and without quite knowing why, found

himself saying, 'I can give you five minutes. Follow me into the study.'

From the set of Jaz's shoulders, she was a little cross that he'd given in, but she stood aside to let Miss Hetty Colman enter Thornhill Hall. Jaz's eyes followed her as she walked into the house, the soles of her shoes tapping lightly on the tiled floor.

John stepped back and motioned for Hetty to go through to the study. It was, he felt, the grandest and least tatty room in the house these days. And for some reason, he didn't want Hetty Colman thinking badly of him or his home. Hetty peered around, taking in the décor, and John followed her gaze, appraising his own home once more.

Three of the four walls were lined with books: great old-fashioned tomes with green, brown and red leather bindings, half of which he'd never even touched let alone read. The fourth wall had a large window with a view out towards the front of the house and the grand driveway. As he glanced out of it now, he could just see, through the mass of wisteria vines (a pretty, yet invasive and costly plant), the bonnet of Hetty's car parked at the furthest end of the turning circle. Sitting down at his antique mahogany desk, he quickly brushed aside the large pile of unpaid bills and final demands taking centre stage and ran his fingers over the worn green leather inlay. He gestured for her to take the seat opposite, which she did, with a mesmerising grace he tried to ignore. For some reason, Jaz had followed them in.

'Thanks, Jaz. If Stevens calls early, can you come and get me please?' Not only was this an instruction for Jaz to leave but also a tactful reminder to this woman that she was only getting the five minutes he'd promised. However, Jaz didn't take the hint as she lingered and directed a sideways glance at Hetty. Hetty didn't seem to notice as she was still busy looking around. After a second of silence Jaz got the message and left.

25

'So, Miss Colman, you've managed to get your five minutes. What is it you want? What is this proposition that's going to be of great financial benefit to me?'

She smiled. 'I've come to talk to you about the Swallowtail Bay strawberry festival.'

He leaned forwards, his elbows resting on the desk. 'Hardly a festival, Miss Colman—'

'Yes, I know,' she replied, with a small shake of her head. 'More of a church jumble sale these days, but I'm happy to say, I plan to change all that.'

'Oh, you do, do you?' He sat back, amused at her confidence and the twinkle in her icy blue eyes.

Every so often a charity bod would come along full of new ideas that were going to raise millions to do this, that and the other, but it never happened. If she was looking to revamp the strawberry festival – an event he'd enjoyed as a child – it was going to take a lot of hard work. And he was sure she wouldn't have thought of half the things that needed to be considered with only four weeks to go. 'Whatever it is, you don't have much time.' Hetty raised her eyebrows in surprise. 'Oh, yes, I know when it is. Despite what people think, we do know what's happening in the town. And what's being said.' The bitterness he felt had crept out again, but she didn't comment and he moved the conversation along. 'So, what is it you're planning on doing, Miss Colman?'

'I'm a local event organiser and I plan to turn our current boring boot-fair type afternoon into a huge food festival, lasting the whole of the bank holiday weekend. I was hoping we could hold it in the grounds of Thornhill Hall.'

Now that was a surprise. John felt his mouth open slightly but didn't speak, wanting to consider his response. He needn't have worried as Hetty continued.

'Obviously I don't expect you to let us use your land for free, we'd either sell pitches for a flat rate or get a percentage of profits that you and I would then split. The more pitches, the more profit.'

So, she wasn't quite a charity do-gooder but a small-timer trying the big leagues. While John admired the spirit, his family had learned from bitter experience that these ventures rarely ended well. 'Unless it's a failure and no one comes.'

The instant he said it he felt a stab of regret. John knew his manner took some getting used to. A boarding school education had formed his direct way of speaking and even when he tried to soften it, it didn't come naturally. Constant concentration on not sounding like a sergeant major barking out orders gave him a headache and he'd long ago given up trying to correct it. The woman in front of him didn't seem to mind it as she gave a polite smile and adjusted her glasses.

'A, I don't think that's likely, and B, even if that is the case, as you haven't had to shell out any money upfront it won't be a problem, will it?'

Her confidence was astounding. The only person he'd met with confidence like it was Jaz, but that had grown over time. She'd been timid and worried of making mistakes at first, but with support and encouragement had grown into her role and John had watched on with almost brotherly affection. Miss Colman's confidence was much more … attractive – no, mature. That's the word he was looking for: mature. And impressive. Still, he wasn't convinced and there were many more questions to be answered. 'What exactly are you planning?'

'I'm planning on a huge number of food vendors showcasing different things as well as other local producers, entertainment and activities.'

'Why can't you hold it in town?' The idea of people running all over his land would send his mother into fits, not to mention cause him untold problems.

Miss Colman's hands were resting in her lap, one on top of the other and there wasn't an ounce of tension in her shoulders.

'You know as well as I do, Mr Thornhill, that to hold it in the town would require applying for road closures, the diversion of traffic, and a number of other licenses and permissions. All of which we're unlikely to get in the time we have available. Your land is the best option. We wouldn't be limited by size and I plan to make this a *big* event worthy of regional, if not national, coverage. Your fields are fairly flat and not currently growing crops.'

'No, they're not,' he said with a sigh. They hadn't been farmed for a long time, his family unable to pay the farmers, repair equipment or process the yields even if they had grown any. He was working on plans to sell more land, but the price wasn't what they needed to sell for and the solicitors said it really wasn't worth it. 'Will it still keep the strawberry theme?' he asked. He'd always enjoyed the festival and hoped that it would.

'Not entirely. I think to get the most vendors we need to broaden it. We'll certainly ask them to consider it as a theme but if people sell other things, that's fine too. We don't want to limit ourselves, but I am going to start some awards and we'll have a special one for strawberry-based products.'

'And what do you want me to do? Apart from let you use my land?' He waited for the catch. There was always a catch.

She lifted her delicate hands a fraction. 'As much or as little as you like, Mr Thornhill. You don't have to get involved at all if you don't want to.'

He had an idea that 'as little' was probably the way she wanted it. He doubted very much that this powerhouse would ever give up an inch of control, not unless she absolutely had to, and he couldn't imagine what catastrophic circumstance would require it. She seemed the sort of person who had contingency plans for contingency plans. It probably made her less than fun, though there was that mischievous glint in her eye which could mean otherwise. John took a moment to mull over everything she'd said.

It would cause untold disruption to the house and an insane amount of stress for his family. He had to admit the idea of additional income was appealing but these things were rarely as simple as this woman was making out. If any costs needed covering and she asked him to contribute, there was no way he'd be able to. They didn't have any spare money. What was left in the back was there for emergency repairs and right now, there wasn't even enough to cover that. John glanced at his watch. Impressively, she had only taken around five minutes. But he needed the loo before his ten o'clock call, and a coffee. After clearing his throat, he gave his reply.

'No.'

***

'No?' Hetty couldn't believe what she was hearing. He'd actually said no. *No!* What was wrong with the man? This was a brilliant idea and what's more, she wasn't asking him to do anything. It looked like he was living up to his reputation after all.

From the moment she'd entered the house after finally managing to get past that bulldog of an assistant with her mulish expression, she'd sensed trouble. In Hetty's mind, she'd seen the grandeur of a BBC costume drama. Though the exterior was incredibly beautiful, the small bit of the interior she'd seen so far showed signs of age and lack of care. The air smelt damp and musty, like soggy towels, tiles were cracked in the hall floor, and in the study, though he'd quickly swept them aside, she'd spotted the stack of unpaid bills on his desk. They clearly needed the money. She'd also imagined him opening the door wearing a Saville Row suit or something equally expensive, but his rumpled pale-blue shirt and faded denim jeans were a surprise, even if they did fit quite nicely on his muscular frame. Bringing her mind swiftly back to business, Hetty asked herself again how he could possibly think this was a bad idea. All Hetty could assume was that John Thornhill was an idiot with no business sense. As handsome as he was – and he was handsome, much more so than she'd imagined – he was looking a gift horse in the mouth then walking behind it and giving it a swift kick up the backside for good measure. Plus, he hadn't shaken her hand when she offered it. The height of rudeness in her opinion.

'No,' he said again. His voice was deep with authority, something Hetty found attractive, but his piercing and steady eyes were fixed. 'I'm afraid this isn't something we can support.'

Worryingly for Hetty, on seeing John Thornhill her stomach had tightened a little and it was doing the same thing now. Hetty hoped it was just her stubborn streak kicking in and nothing to do with the way his voice resonated in her head, or the way his shirt pulled slightly open across his broad chest. If it wasn't, this would be the first time in a long while she'd had a physical reaction to a man, and she couldn't have chosen a more stuffed-up grump if she'd put an ad on Craigslist. Plus, he had a beard and she didn't like beards.

'Mr Thornhill, I don't think you're quite grasping what an amazing opportunity this is. I'm planning on turning the food festival into a massive event and I'll be marketing it widely so there'll be a lot of attention. Don't you think it would be good to raise the profile of Thornhill Hall?'

'That depends on what's said about it.'

'Are you always so negative?' She couldn't help the challenging question.

He shrugged as if he didn't care what she thought, and it bothered her. 'I'm just being realistic, Miss Colman. If it's a whitewash it won't reflect well on either of us and Thornhill Hall has enough problems as it is.'

And you're one of them, she thought, but made sure the words didn't escape. 'What if I promise you it won't be?'

'I'm sure you can promise many things, Miss Colman, but that isn't one of them.'

When they'd been talking before, she hadn't felt tense or worried in the least, confident in her idea and that she could achieve it, but now she found herself leaning forward as John Thornhill's negative attitude frustrated her. 'Then perhaps you can tell me exactly what it is you're concerned about? We've already discussed the land isn't currently being used for anything helpful.' A slight tightening in his jaw showed the remark had stung and Hetty knew she had to bring this back around before she lost any chance of convincing him at all. 'All I mean is that the fields won't take any damage from our using it and I'll be covering the costs of setting up the festival.'

John eyed her for a moment and a slight tingle of hope rose within her only to be extinguished almost immediately. 'If you're planning on holding it on the bank holiday weekend, that's only four weeks away, which is clearly not enough time to do all the things you're saying you're going to do. Is it just you working on this?'

She lifted her head a little, offended at his saying it was too much for her to handle. He clearly didn't know her. 'It'll be myself and my assistant, Macie, which I can assure you is more than enough to get everything organised. We'll also have a number of volunteers for the weekend.'

'It's simply not enough people, Miss Colman, and I don't have the time to spend on this. As I'm sure you're aware from town gossip, Thornhill Hall has a number of concerns at present and they require my full attention.'

'I realise that, but—'

'I'm, sorry, Miss Colman. I'm afraid the house and the land surrounding it is private property and not open to the public. I won't consent to opening up the place for people to wander around willy-nilly.'

'But they won't be wandering around willy-nilly.' She didn't think people said willy-nilly anymore and the ancient phrase almost made her laugh. 'They'll be at the food festival which, if we hold it in a field, won't be anywhere near your house. And I'll have stewards to make sure people don't come near the hall if that's what you want.'

Outside they heard a van speed up the drive, and the sound of gravel flying as it parked. Mr Thornhill checked his watch and stood up behind his desk. 'Miss Colman, I've actually given you seven minutes and I thank you for considering Thornhill Hall, but the answer is no.'

The thought of Gwen's smug face at the next business forum made Hetty briefly consider planting herself in the chair and refusing to leave until he agreed, but John Thornhill was tall and broad and could probably lift her and carry her out. The idea of him doing so sent a small shiver through her body, and she looked up to see him staring at her.

Reluctantly, Hetty stood and found a business card in her back pocket. 'I have to say, Mr Thornhill, I think you're making a very big mistake, but here's my business card in case you change your mind.' She handed it over and watched a hint of a smile play at the corners of his mouth.

Mr Thornhill went to the study door and opened it for her, letting her through first. Jaz had helpfully opened the front door already and clearly couldn't be happier to watch her go. Hetty took the chance of a final look around before leaving. The hallway was massive, about the size of the entire ground floor of Hetty's cottage but it had a melancholy, almost broken feel to it. Faded wallpaper had begun to peel from the bottom of the walls and the giant chandelier that hung in the centre of the room was missing a number of drops.

'Thank you for your time, Mr Thornhill. Goodbye.' She held out her hand for him to shake and he took it in a strong grip.

'Goodbye, Miss Colman.'

As she walked down the steps back to her car, he spoke to the delivery driver. Climbing into Myrtle, she drove away as quickly as possible, her hopes crushed by his refusal. But she would not give up so easily. Winding the window down she took a moment to enjoy the warm sunny day and allowed the brightness of the world to refill her enthusiasm. She'd have to find another venue, that was all. She was determined not to be defeated by stubborn and stuffy John Thornhill. She'd organise the festival somewhere else and show him just what he was missing out on.

Chapter 4

'There isn't anywhere else,' Hetty exclaimed, throwing her hands in the air as her patience ran out. 'And I can't get people on board if I can't tell them where they're going to be. Urgh, I'm actually getting cross now at how stubborn John-bloody-Thornhill was in saying no. It's the perfect spot. He's being such an idiot. I mean, what will it take to convince that man? Do I need to show him projected profit? Detailed health and safety plans? My colour-coded spreadsheets? I don't understand how someone who runs a successful antiques business doesn't have enough business sense to see this is an excellent idea. And he didn't shake my hand. Did I tell you that?'

Down the other end of the phone, Macie giggled. 'Yes, you did. Twice. He's really got under your skin, hasn't he?'

Hetty's free hand rested on her hip as she paced around her living room. 'I just don't understand how he hasn't leapt at this chance. This is the most brilliant idea ever to walk up to his enormous, crumbly old house and fall into his lap.'

'Wait, did *you* fall into his lap? You didn't mention that before.'

'You know what I mean,' Hetty said, refusing to think about what that might be like. She flopped onto the sofa, then curled a leg underneath her.

With all the windows open, birdsong filled the late afternoon air and mixed with the constant hum of the sea. A wonderful breeze rustled the leaves of nearby trees, cooling the warm day. Her home had originally been part of a pair of fisherman's cottages, complete with flowering window baskets giving huge pops of colour against the bright white canvas of the walls. Across the road from her, the beach was so full she couldn't see anything except for a mass of heads and sunhats.

Though Hetty had originally called Macie to ensure everything was in place for the retirement party they were running that night, she hadn't been able to stop herself talking about the food festival and John's refusal to support it. After much research she hadn't come up with anywhere else that was suitable and had even made a tentative call to a contact in the council who'd confirmed everything she'd expected about the chances of getting the road closures to hold it in town. He'd actually laughed at her before giving a kinder answer of slim to none. The whole situation was frustrating and Hetty could feel it knotting her shoulders.

'So, what's the plan?' asked Macie. 'Oh, hang on a second.' In the background, Hetty heard Macie telling someone where a balloon display was supposed to go. 'I'm back,' she said, cheerfully. 'I take it we're not giving up.'

'Of course we're not,' Hetty replied. 'I'll keep researching and find somewhere else. There must a local farmer who'll let us have a field. I'm not letting this opportunity go, even if it means I work day and night between now and the bank holiday to get it done.'

'This is why I love you,' said Macie, sweetly. 'You're my hero.'

'Are you just saying that because they've got those mini spring rolls at this buffet tonight and you want me to turn a blind eye to you eating them all?'

'Something like that.'

With a giggle, Hetty signed off and tossed her mobile phone onto the seat beside her. That morning, she'd been checking the land registry to see who owned fields suitable for hosting the food festival, but there weren't actually that many that weren't growing crops. She didn't like the idea of having to tone down her plans and really couldn't stomach the picture of smug Gwen grinning as she admitted defeat. The thought made her uneasy and she went to the kitchen to get a drink of water. Stanley the seagull had returned to her garden after trying his luck on the beach and was hopping about on his one good foot, nibbling at the breakfast she'd put out for him.

Glancing at the kitchen table, the pine top of which was obliterated by random notes and bits of paper, Hetty went to it and stared at a plan of one of the Thornhill fields she'd sketched out earlier. She'd mapped out a number of pitches on the rough drawing, and again her excitement for the project and the gut instinct that told her it could be a huge success boiled up once more. The heat of the day and hot stuffy atmosphere inside made her eyelids heavy and she decided a walk would freshen her mind and wake her up enough to get through the busy evening ahead.

She quickly grabbed her keys and pulled the front door closed behind her before heading across the street to the beach. The breeze was usually a little stronger on the shore and she enjoyed the feel of it on her skin, blowing the cobwebs from her mind. There was something wonderful about being this close to nature. The sea was wild and uncontrollable at times – dangerous – but on days like this it was friendly and inviting. It made itself more a part of the bay in the summer, like an extra piece of land to be walked on and enjoyed. Hetty wondered why John Thornhill was so determined to keep his distance from them all. Riffraff he may consider them to be, but they didn't bite.

The difference in Swallowtail Bay in the summer compared to all the other months was unimaginable. The town was so much busier; the beach full of families lying out on blankets, shaded by big sun umbrellas; kids running around with buckets of water, couples walking hand in hand, carrying their shoes as the water lapped at their feet. Even the air was different, thick with the salt of the sea but mixed with the smell of sweet lollies, ice creams and sun lotion. In its stillness it carried the laughing and chattering voices all the way into town. Even if it rained, the sense of fun remained as everyone dived into coffee shops, pubs and restaurants for cover. And always, the ever greedy, overly confident seagulls hopped about, or circled in the sky waiting for their chance to strike and steal someone's lunch. Hetty put her hands in her pockets and took a moment to enjoy it all.

As she looked up to watch a small boy searching for shells, she spied a figure she recognised marching along the promenade: John Thornhill. His powerful legs made long strides as he headed to a car. Figuring she had no time to lose, Hetty quickened her pace. She wasn't letting him get away that easily.

'Mr Thornhill? Mr Thornhill?' He glanced around and though he clocked her, he dropped his eyes to his car and unlocked it. 'Mr Thornhill, what a surprise to see you in town.'

'Not really, Miss Colman. We'd run out of milk.' He held up the carrier bag for her to inspect. 'And like everyone else we have to shop, you know. We don't have staff to go out and get things for us.'

Hetty decided to ignore his bluntness and smiled instead. 'I didn't think you had, Mr Thornhill, unless you were hiding them all when I came to Thornhill Hall yesterday.'

'Was it only yesterday? It seems longer.' His voice carried a tiredness that surprised her, and he ran his other hand over his face and down his neatly trimmed beard.

'Well, I'm glad I caught you because I wanted to speak to you again about the food festival.' She switched immediately into business mode. 'I really think you need to understand more fully how it's going to benefit Thornhill Hall.'

'Miss Colman, I really don't have time for this right now—'

'Then when will you have time? Would you like me to show

you the more detailed plans I've been working on? Because if I could use the field nearest the road, we could fit in—'

'I've already said no and given you my reason. I don't think there's anything else you can tell me that will be convince me to change my mind. Once it's made up, it's made up.'

'Yes, you seem the type,' Hetty replied, her business persona falling away a little.

'What type?'

He'd got under her skin so much, her business persona fell away completely. 'Unmovable. Stubborn. The type that refuses to change their mind once they've said no because they're scared it'll make them look weak, when really it's a mark of strength to admit you got something wrong.' Though she admonished herself, her words at least seemed to have an impact on Mr Thornhill, who stared at her, taken aback. Hetty felt her cheeks redden.

'Right,' he said.

'Look around you, Mr Thornhill,' she said more softly. 'Look at how packed out the beach is. Look over at the Wild Goose, it's full.' The pub had even erected a few tables and chairs outside and they were overflowing with people. 'Look at the queue at the ice-cream trucks. Just *look* at this place.' Hetty motioned around her. 'It's full of tourists and all those tourists will come to our food festival.'

'Our?'

She couldn't quite catch his tone and was surprised when he seemed almost embarrassed. 'I'm afraid I have to go, Miss Colman. I've an important call first thing tomorrow morning I must prepare for. Good afternoon.'

Crossing her arms over her chest, Hetty watched him climb into his car and turned on her heel, marching back to her cottage. Whatever that last odd moment between them was, there'd been a flicker in his eye and a slight hesitation in his manner that she was sure meant she still had a chance of convincing him. It was time to pull out the big guns and try one last assault.

Chapter 5

'Jaz, can I have that letter ready before the phone auction please? I'd just like to check it through so that we're ready to go once I've secured this piece, okay?'

'No problem' she replied and made her way from the study to her own desk in one of the spare rooms upstairs. The house wasn't really designed for running a business from home and John felt a tinge of jealousy towards his brother who had a nice air-conditioned office. John went to the window and pulled it open. How could it be this hot at only just half past eight in the morning? He'd never known a summer like it.

As well as phoning into an auction at nine on behalf of a client, he needed to work on some calculations for the bank. John flopped into the chair, feeling the stifling heat, and pulled out the stack of unpaid bills from under a neat pile of paperwork. He eyed them like they were death threats. It was looking like they'd need a loan to clear the backlog of debts and buy them some breathing space while he tried to secure some income. He'd have to speak to the bank on Monday. If only his family weren't so resistant to every idea he put to them.

Tossing the letter aside, he let his head rest in his hands, but his mind wandered to the food festival idea. He was beginning to think it wouldn't be such a bad idea after all. They desperately needed something, and it had been presented to him by an extremely capable woman who clearly knew what she was doing. She'd even said he could do as much or as little as he liked. John knew he hadn't really given it the consideration it deserved and her words on the seafront yesterday had bitten deeply. He was slightly ashamed to admit that perhaps she was right. Was he now saying no simply because he'd said no in the first place? It wasn't the first time he'd been accused of that. He also had a feeling he'd used his family's ridiculous concerns as an excuse to say no because he simply couldn't deal with the additional work-load, but he might just have to. If the bank refused the loan, he had no idea what they'd do.

Raised voices from the hallways caught his attention and he lifted his head out of his hands. He could hear Jaz denying someone entry and then a voice he was beginning to recognise carried through the door.

'I only need a few minutes with Mr Thornhill, Miss Simmons. And I know he's here because yesterday—'

'You saw him yesterday?' There was a strange tone to Jaz's voice, and he went to help her.

Hetty continued. 'Yes. And he said he had a meeting this morning and I'm willing to bet it hasn't started yet because it's only eight-thirty. So, if you can let me in, I'll go and see him quickly and be out of your hair in no time.'

John found himself shaking his head as he walked to the study door. A strange smile was pulling at his lips. Hetty Colman was without doubt the most infuriating person he'd ever met, but he had to admit her audacity and tenaciousness were unparalleled.

When he opened the study door it was to see her with a large rolled sheet of paper tucked under her arm, and an enormous A4 folder chock full of papers cradled in the other. There was also that pretty grin on her face.

'How did you get in?' asked Jaz.

'Luckily for me the gate had been shut but not bolted. Otherwise I'd have had to climb it and I didn't really fancy that much.'

John did actually believe that she'd climb the eight-foot-tall iron gates if she had to and couldn't decide if that was a good or bad thing.

'Ah, Mr Thornhill, there you are. I thought you'd be in.' She shuffled everything about and pushed her cute glasses up the bridge of her nose. The folder looked like it was about to fall open and the papers fly everywhere. Instinctively, John went to help her. 'Oh, thank you. Do you have a moment?'

An incredulous chuckle escaped him. 'Yes, I suppose I must as you've gone to all this effort.'

Jaz interrupted. 'You've got that auction starting at nine, John.'

'I know, Jaz, thanks.' He quickly checked his watch. 'You'd best come through, Miss Colman.'

John closed the study door and put the folder down on the other side of his desk, near his visitor. 'Please take a seat.'

'Oh, no thank you.' Hetty immediately began to unroll the paper. 'Right. I'm here to show you that you really should say yes to the food festival.' He opened his mouth to speak but she held up her hand to silence him. 'Please, just hear me out. This is a map of that field of yours near the road. I've marked pitch sizes on it already and where the toilets will need to go, unless we can find somewhere else for them which means we could then get more stalls in. As you can see from the number I've marked out, this alone could spell a good profit for us and we can decide if we want to charge per pitch or take a percentage of profits made over the weekend. I personally think there's more money to be made in taking a percentage of profits. I already know a number of vendors who'd be interested, and I can guarantee you once I actually start rounding people up, we'll be inundated. People are already excited and talking about this idea. We can make it an amazing weekend—'

'Miss Colman?'

'There'll be a load more tourists around over the bank holiday weekend too because we always get weekend visitors and I've got a ton of ideas for other things we can have, and as you can see from my file ...' She opened it and began showing him printed documents in plastic wallets. 'I've already mapped out health and safety requirements, written risk assessments and contracts and—'

'Miss Colman?' he said again, a little more loudly this time.

'Yes?' She looked up, almost startled. Her eyes were an incredible pale blue.

It was time to admit that this was turning into quite a good idea and for some reason he felt a sense of trust deep down in his belly. Miss Colman was intelligent, focused, not in the least bit flighty or ditzy and he really did have faith she could pull this off. He desperately needed his share of the profits. And though his mother wouldn't like it much, it would only be for a weekend. There might even be other ways he could capitalise on this too, but he'd have to think about that later. 'Very well, Miss Colman. You can use our land. The lower field as you've already mapped it out.'

A wide grin spread across her face, lifting her cheeks, and her eyes twinkled once more. 'Perfect,' she said, with a bright cheery smile. 'You'll soon see what an amazing idea this is. In fact, can you meet me at Raina's Café on Tuesday at ten? Yes?' She didn't even wait for him to check his diary. 'Marvellous.' Hetty began collecting all her things. 'Just text me if you need to make it later, but there's a lot to do, so ten would be best. I'll even treat you to a coffee.' She was half out of the door when she suddenly spun on her heel. 'Actually, better keep the whole day free if you can.'

She flashed another brilliant smile, and like a whirlwind she was out of the door and gone before he knew it. John watched Miss Colman replace her glasses with large, elegant sunglasses then climb into her car. As soon as he'd met her, he should have known that, eventually, she'd leave having achieved exactly what she wanted.

***

That evening, the family gathered in the dining room which wasn't half as grand as everyone expected it to be. John glanced down the length of the long cherry wood table, easily big enough to seat thirty, though he and his family were settled around just one end. He studied the faded deep-red curtains and the patchy, peeling wallpaper. The only things that still seemed to belong were the antique sideboard and dusty chandelier. How much longer they would get to stay was another matter.

His mother brought in a tray bearing their dinners, with Jaz following, also carrying a fully laden tray. Despite what the town might think, they weren't sitting up here with butlers and maids. As in any house, the person nearest the front door answered it, and his mother did most of the cooking, though they all helped out when she was tired. Jaz lived in town, but as they'd ended up working late, he'd invited her to dinner. It was the least he could do considering her commitment to him and his family, and that he couldn't pay her half of what she deserved.

Thoughts of Hetty had lingered in his brain all afternoon, distracting him to the point that he'd thrown down his pen and gone for a walk. He wasn't looking forward to telling his family about the food festival and had waited till now, so everyone was together and it could all be over with in one go. It wasn't that he regretted his decision – if it was a success, it would definitely make life easier for them all – but his family would be reticent. How he wished there were easier ways of making money. With his family before him, he swallowed down his apprehension along with a mouthful of roast chicken, wiped his mouth with a napkin and made his announcement.

'You should all know I've agreed that the strawberry festival

43

can be held here this year. In the lower field. The woman organising it is turning it into a food festival.'

The responses came in exactly the order he'd anticipated and with the exact exclamations and protests, from everyone but his father who simply ignored things he didn't like. The only person he was surprised at was Jaz. She stared at him, disapprovingly, her upper lip curling a little. She was being less supportive than he'd expected. Once he'd told her of his and Miss Colman's agreement this morning, she'd asked a million and one questions, doubting if it would make any money at all and if anyone would come all the way out here just to eat. She wasn't normally this negative, and of all people, he'd thought she would see the financial benefits. At least now, whatever Jaz's concerns, she was keeping them to herself. His mother, Lucinda, was the first to speak.

'Why on earth did you do that, John?' Her long, thin face, drawn and tired from worry, had fixed in an expression of disappointment.

He decided not to say that Hetty Colman had impressed him with her clear-minded, business-like approach, or that there was something about the confident way she moved her body that had flitted in and out of his mind all afternoon. Instead he said, 'Because we're going to get a share of the profits and as that well-known advert says, "Every little helps". It'll give us some income. Income that we desperately need.'

'I can't believe,' began his brother, 'that you, the man who never agrees to anything on the spur of the moment, have agreed to this.' He gave a scornful, incredulous laugh and clenched his jaw.

'It wasn't on the spur of the moment. She actually approached me a few days ago. But regardless, it's a good idea and doesn't require us to really do anything.'

Lucinda delicately rested her fork on the edge of her plate. 'Oh, but it does sound awful, John. There'll be people everywhere' – her voice was rising with worry – 'so many people—'

'It'll be fine, Mother. They'll be in the lower field, they won't come up to the house at all.'

'But what if they wander about and get lost and end up on the doorstep? And how did this woman get in in the first place?'

'Mother, I promise, it'll be fine. Please trust me.' John took a sip of water from the chipped mug before him. 'And she only got in because I had the gates open for a delivery.' Lucinda looked to John's father, Rupert. He'd barely said a word and was scooping peas onto his fork with a finger.

Felix glared at John. 'It won't be enough to solve our problems, John. Just seems a lot of inconvenience for a pittance.'

John couldn't believe he was going through all this again. He and his brother had endured this conversation so many times before. It was all right for Felix who dipped in and out of the family's affairs when it suited him. John couldn't help the feeling of resentment that mounted when Felix became argumentative just for the sake of it. 'Felix, just because it won't wipe out all our debts in one go doesn't mean we shouldn't do it. As far as I can see, there's no one single way to pay it all off and make us financially sustainable. It's going to take time and lots of effort.'

'Well,' said Felix, 'I think you're wrong. I think we could make huge in-roads rather than taking tiny baby steps all the time if we invested what we have left.' Felix turned to their mother. He was tall and thin like her, but wiry – more like a pencil – especially as his hair was still very dark despite being five years older than John. He was also joining them for dinner as his wife, Elizabeth, was out at her book club and his twin girls had been deposited at dance club. They lived in Swallowtail Bay in a large new-build house that didn't have any of the problems their parents' house did. To make it all worse, because he worked as a finance manager for a local insurance firm, he thought he knew everything about money. John couldn't have disagreed more about investing the entirety of what little they had left, but Felix kept going on and on about it.

A few weeks ago, a colleague had tipped Felix off to a 'sound investment' and since then, he'd done nothing but nag their mother, hoping for her go-ahead to cast the deciding vote. No one bothered consulting their father anymore. You could never get a straight answer from him. And as John was against it from the moment it was nonchalantly dropped into conversation one morning at breakfast, Felix was now trying to get their mother onside in a bid to gang up on him.

John placed a forkful of food in his mouth but found it difficult to chew and swallow. Jaz's shoulders were tensed on his behalf and she threw reassuring glances his way. Lucinda had her head down nibbling delicately, ignoring the disagreement between her offspring.

'Felix,' he said sternly, 'you know full well I disagree with you on the investment. And even if this doesn't solve all our problems it will at least give us a little income. Maybe enough to make a full mortgage payment or hire a conservator so we can fix up the tapestries and sell them.'

Lucinda dropped her fork and inhaled sharply. 'John, do we have to?'

'I'm sorry, Mother, but you know how much they'd fetch if they were repaired.'

Felix leapt to her defence. 'I can't believe you'd say that, John. You know how much they mean to Mother.'

Making an effort to control his temper and enjoy his dinner, John replied. 'I don't enjoy it, Felix, but it's the truth.' He had no idea how much more needed to go wrong with the house for his mother to realise that they were verging on having to sell up and move if they couldn't come up with something viable. The carpets were threadbare, the paint peeling from the doorframes and windowsills, and the plaster cornicing falling from the ceiling. A clammy wetness pervaded the house from all the pin-mould that was finding its way inside and God only knew what that was doing to their lungs. The gardens were a mess and they'd yet to repair the windows that had cracked under the strain of last winter.

Jaz sipped her water and examined the tablecloth, keeping well and truly out of it. John was forever grateful for her discretion; it was a trait he didn't thank her for enough. Rupert also kept his head down merrily munching his dinner, pretending the argument going on around him wasn't happening. Lucinda wiped the corners of her mouth and laid down her napkin.

'Do you really think this food festival will bring in some money, John?'

The incredible Hetty Colman appeared in his brain. Not just her face, but the sound of her voice and the feeling of assurance she gave. She clearly had a great business sense and knew what she was doing. 'I do,' he said firmly. 'And even if it's not much, it'll be in the lower field with very little inconvenience to us. I can't see any reason why we shouldn't do it.'

'Very well then,' she replied with a sigh, earning John a scathing look from his brother. 'I'll just have to lock myself in my room until it's over.'

Chapter 6

Hetty moved the two coffee cups delivered by their fabulous waitress, Lexi, in one of her amazing Fifties outfits, out of the way of the mass of papers. John, she knew, had been watching her since the moment they'd arrived.

'Have you been here before?' she asked hoping to break the tension. Hetty was beginning to believe John Thornhill existed in a bubble of stress that followed him around everywhere he went like one of those cartoon rainclouds.

He shook his head. 'No. It's nice though. Food looks good.'

At odd times he looked around the room as if everyone was talking about him, which Hetty was sure they weren't. Well, possibly the old ladies over the other side of the café were, but she was sure they were only commenting on how handsome he was because she'd heard the words 'attractive' and 'knock-out' whispered far too loudly.

'Did you want anything to eat?'

'No, thank you.'

'I always have a piece of cake for elevenses when I'm working here. The chocolate mousse cake is delicious. Maybe I can tempt you in a bit.' The lyrical notes of Raina's Irish accent sounded out as she served a customer and as John didn't respond to Hetty's cake suggestion, she got started. 'I've already brainstormed and listed everything we need to do for the festival. And by *we*, you know I mean *I*, because I did say you didn't have to do anything.' After a full-on planning session, the likes of which NATO would have been impressed by, Hetty had organised her thoughts, and the small idea she'd begun with was growing magnificently.

John glanced nervously around and sipped his coffee, then eyed the cup in surprise. 'Wow, this is good.'

Hetty smiled. 'Raina's is the best in town.'

Across the road in the churchyard, the birds were merrily chirping away hidden in the dense leaves. The world seemed so much brighter in summer, Hetty mused. Like Swallowtail Bay had been painted in brighter and bolder colours. The town and the café were full of people she'd never seen before, tourists eager to find the best spot to eat. Hetty enjoyed the warmth of the sun through the window as it fell on her back. For some reason, she was feeling slightly nervous opposite John. It seemed to add to the pressure of the event somehow. But Hetty reminded herself it was like organising anything else. She just had to tackle it one step at a time.

'Right, Mr Thornhill. I've listed all the local businesses we'd like to attend, and any we'd prefer not to.'

'You should probably call me John.' He said it with only slight enthusiasm but given how tense he was, she took it as progress.

'Okay. Then I'm Hetty, not Miss Colman.'

'Hetty then. Are there some people we'd prefer not to come?'

'Basically, if they haven't got a good hygiene rating, I'm not trusting them at a festival.' John tilted his head and the angle showed off his strong Roman nose.

The Bake House was top of the list and looking at it, apprehension built in her stomach. She'd learned long ago to portion up her worries, putting them in little boxes and storing them away in her mind until she was ready to deal with them. It kept her focused on the task at hand and that was exactly what she was doing now. 'We'll also need some entertainment. I was going to ask the local radio station to come along, maybe some local bands, and there'll be things like guys making balloon animals, that sort of thing.'

John nodded and sipped his coffee again. 'Bouncy castle?'

'Yes, definitely.' Hetty waved the pen in excitement, happy that he was starting to participate in the meeting. She'd imagined this would be a very one-sided conversation with her simply stating what she was going to do and him scowling and reluctantly agreeing or out-and-out arguing. She hadn't anticipated him making suggestions or speaking in any helpful way. 'But I was thinking we could have something a bit different too, maybe a slip and slide.'

John shook his head. *Here we go*, thought Hetty. Just as she'd expected. He'd simply needed a coffee before he began in full grumpy lord-of-the-manor mode. If he was going to start pooh-poohing all her ideas, she'd have to have more than one piece of cake to keep her temper. 'That'll need a water supply and a lot of space. It'll be very messy too and require constant supervision.'

'Oh,' said Hetty, slightly taken aback. That was a valid point. 'Yes, that's true. What about a different shaped bouncy castle?'

'So … not a castle then?'

His tone was actually teasing, like he was enjoying himself. A cheeky grin grew on her face in response. 'Maybe something like a pirate ship, or an assault course?'

'Pirate ship would be good. What about a puppet show for the kids?'

Hetty nodded agreement. 'It's vintage and old-fashioned. I like it.'

'And a carousel? It's traditional and everyone loves them.'

Hetty sat straighter and put her pen down. 'Right, what's going on here?'

'What?'

'You seem far too happy to be doing this. And I know Raina's coffee is good, but I've never seen it have this effect on someone before.'

'Maybe I like your ideas,' he replied taking another sip as if to deliberately challenge her theory about the coffee.

What on earth was happening here? This wasn't the John Thornhill she'd met on previous occasions. 'Well, if you like those ones you're going to love this. I like to say go big or go home – so if you let me have another field, we could even have a whole funfair!'

John laughed and it brought a lightness to his features. 'Okay. Maybe we need to calm down a little.'

'No,' Hetty said, finally taking a sip of her own coffee. In all the list-making, she'd forgotten it was there. 'Now isn't the time to hold back, Mr Thornhill. Now's the time to make this the biggest event Swallowtail Bay has ever seen.'

'Are you always this convincing?' he teased.

'Convincing is my middle name,' she replied with a smile, surprised that he mirrored it.

After a second, the smile began to fade, and his voice became serious again. 'And how are all the set-up costs to be paid for? The bigger this is, the larger they'll be.'

Hetty sighed and brushed a hand through her short hair. 'It's going to use up all my available capital and possibly some of my own savings, but it's an investment in my future – one I'm happy to make, I might add. Which is why I have to make this work. The more stuff we have to attract people, the more successful it will be.'

'You're really committed to this, aren't you?'

'I am,' Hetty said confidently. 'Which is why my next idea might seem a bit out there and not something you usually find at a food festival, but I think it could be a brilliant way to keep people there literally all day on the Saturday.'

'What?' John's intrigued expression slid into a scowl.

'I'm thinking on the Saturday night we'll have a film screening.

We can hire a giant screen and people can have food they've bought from the food stalls and picnics on the grass.'

'Okay,' he replied reticently. 'But seeing as you now have a video screen and a funfair, how exactly are you going to fit all this in one or even two fields?'

Hetty bit the inside of her cheek and grabbed the Ordnance Survey map she'd stuffed down beside her.

'With all this you'll need a lot of facilities and parking space as well.'

Judging by the local funfair that visited once a year, they'd need a field to themselves for the rides, parking and facilities, and the screening and picnic space needed to be near enough to the food stalls that people could get something to eat during the performance. And John was right, they'd need a good number of toilets too. Hetty picked up her pen again and tapped it against her lip. This was all proving to be a bit of a jigsaw. Some of the larger parties she'd organised before had been like this, figuring out what had to go where. They were just on a slightly smaller scale. No, she would not be daunted, she could do this and then Simply Fantastic Events would really be on the map.

Hetty unfolded the sides of the map and studied the entirety of the Thornhill estate. John stood, walked behind her and leaned over her shoulder. Her heart gave an involuntary flutter as she smelt his aftershave. It was subtle and pleasant, carrying a depth that suited him. She glanced up and he ran a hand over his jaw.

'What about using these fields here?' he said, pointing to a large square of land.

'Four fields?' Had she heard right? He was now offering her even more space.

John re-took his seat so he was looking at her. 'Despite what you might think, I'm not the type to keep saying no just because I said it once before.' Hetty coloured, hearing her own words repeated back to her. She hadn't meant them to be so acerbic. 'These ideas' – he motioned to the table now covered in paper

– 'are good ideas, and as you said, we might as well make this as good as it can be.'

Hetty felt the tension ease from her shoulders. 'In that case, you'd better come with me this afternoon to sell this idea to the traders. Convincing is my middle name, but it'll help even more if you're there, lending support.' John shook his head as he smiled, but she could tell it wasn't a no. 'And we're stopping in at the town hall at four to convince the festival committee to hand over control to me. And you, it seems.'

This time, John fell back in his chair. 'Is that why you asked me to keep the whole day free?'

'Have you ever tried to get six retired or working people together at the same time, on the same day?' He shrugged a no. 'It's a nightmare. Trust me. It was the only time I could get, but please don't be cross. Anyway, after today, you won't need to do anything.'

A strange look passed over his face and Hetty couldn't figure out what it was before it disappeared, but it looked almost sad. 'Your middle name really is "convincing", isn't it?'

***

That afternoon, after stashing everything else in her car, Hetty and John, armed with her notebook and the list of vendors, began their quest to convince the shop owners of Swallowtail Bay to take a pitch at the food festival. The sun was shining brightly on the sea, the gentle waves sparkling as they rolled back and forth and a handful of clouds scudded across the sky. Unlike the recent stifling weather, today's breeze – just enough to lift the longer strands of her short hair – was perfect.

Starting at the top end of the high street where the taxis gathered, Hetty had decided they should focus on only food shops to begin with. If there were pitches left over after, she'd approach some of the nearby towns and ask different types of businesses if they wanted to attend. Miserable Gwen's hairdresser's was, naturally, out of the question, but the local bath bombe shop, and even Stella, with all the weird and wonderful things from Old Herbert's Shop, might be a good try if there were places to fill.

Hetty and John strolled down the grey-blue, uneven cobbles, admiring the vibrant window displays of the boutique shops and the stomach-rumbling smells coming from the restaurants and cafés. Everywhere people were smiling and chatting and bidding her good afternoon, laden with bags, pushing buggies or pulling along wheelie shopping trolleys. This was why she loved her hometown so much and why she'd never left for long. But there was no denying the shock on some people's faces when they saw her with John Thornhill. She wondered how he was feeling about it and cast a glance in his direction, but he was mostly watching his feet as he walked along. Replying to a friend of her mum's with a cheery hello, Hetty and John entered the first shop.

'Hi, Terry,' Hetty said to the owner of the fishmonger's. It always amazed Hetty that a good fishmonger's never smelt fishy, and as Swallowtail Bay's had the freshest fish around, you couldn't smell anything except for a woody scent from the locally made smoked salmon. John stared at the display like he'd never been in a shop before.

'Hello, Hetty love. What can I get for you today?'

'Me and Mr Thornhill here were wondering if you'd like to have a pitch at the food festival I'm organising.'

'Oh, yes,' he said with a chuckle. 'I heard Gwen having a moan about that. She does love a moan, that one.'

Hetty decided to ignore the fact that Gwen had already started moaning. She was only going to get worse as time wore on, and she'd be seeing her this afternoon on the festival committee, so she didn't want to bad-mouth her in public. 'What do you think, though, Terry? Interested?'

'Definitely,' he replied, cheerfully. 'Could sell some of our lovely smoked salmon, we could. Where's it to be?'

'Thornhill Hall.' Terry immediately looked at John in shock. 'Well, in the grounds anyway.'

'Thornhill Hall?' He studied John as if he was an alien from another planet having a quick daytrip to Swallowtail Bay. Then, with a sort of derisive snort, he dropped his head and began filleting a piece of fish. Hetty nudged John, urging him to speak up.

'We're very much looking forward to hosting it,' John said. 'It'll be wonderful to welcome everyone one.'

'Didn't think you Thornhills liked having people on your land.'

'We don't as a rule,' John said rather sharply and Hetty stepped on his foot. Thankfully, he took the hint. 'But we're very excited about the festival. We think it'll be really good for the Swallowtail Bay economy.'

Terry took a moment to consider John's response. 'Go on then. Sign me up.'

'Fabulous,' said Hetty, placing a giant tick on her list, next to the shop's name. 'I'll email you all the relevant information.'

Outside, she said, 'See, that wasn't so hard, was it?' With a shrug, John placed his hands in his pockets, seemingly happy to walk along beside her.

Half an hour later, they'd ticked off a number of businesses, all of whom had agreed to attend and been interested in the awards she was proposing to start. Hetty was grateful to be wearing her baggy dungarees because so far, everyone had been so excited at the prospect of the food festival, they'd forced a sample of their wares on her. Being too polite to refuse, she and John had eaten crostini with fresh tomato and balsamic vinegar from the local deli, a quarter of a pulled pork bap from The Pig and Pen, some weird seaweed crisps from The Veg Box vegan café, tabbouleh, patatas bravas from the tapas place, a lemon slice from the speciality cake makers, plus the chocolate mousse cake and coffees from Raina's that morning.

'Gosh, I'm stuffed,' she said to John as they walked on. 'If anyone else offers me anything, I'll have to ask for a doggy bag. I might explode.'

John's deep, hearty laugh reverberated around her. 'Yes, me too. We're on the last one though, aren't we?'

'I am,' she said, faking confidence. The Bake House was next.

'Am I not invited to this one?'

'I thought you might need to ring your assistant or check on the house or something?'

'No,' he answered slowly. 'I'm sure Jaz has everything under control. She'd ring me if there was a problem.'

'Right. Well,' Hetty hesitated. 'You can have half an hour off and amuse yourself while I tackle The Bake House. The owner can be a bit …' She searched for the right word. 'Funny. It really would be better if I did this one on my own.'

'Don't tell me, he's another one who hates us Thornhills and our pots of gold?'

'No, it's not that.' Hetty considered telling him the truth but quickly decided not to. 'I'll ring you as soon as I'm done.'

John clearly wasn't convinced. 'Look, Hetty, thanks for the support but I've faced enough people today who don't like us, I'm sure I can manage this last one.'

'Honestly, John it's fine, I—'

He walked past Hetty pausing in the doorway and motioning for her to enter first. Rather chivalrously he wasn't going anywhere. *Fabulous*, thought Hetty. This wouldn't be at all awkward would it? Pausing, Hetty straightened the straps of her dungarees, mussed up her short hair for added confidence, then stepped inside.

Chapter 7

The divine smell made her mouth water, despite being full to bursting.

The Bake House's specialty was bread and the air was heavy with yeast and all the things they flavoured the breads with: olives, tomato, goat's cheese. The shop was still packed as people tried to buy the last few things that were left. The constant slide of the till drawer and the beep of the card machine mixed with the voices of staff and customers. On the other side, a large glass counter was half empty except for a few cakes and pastries. Heat from the giant ovens made it feel close and humid, and Hetty hoped she wasn't going red.

Ben, artisan baker – and unfortunately, her ex-boyfriend – had started The Bake House around about the same time she'd started her business. Breaking up with Ben had been the hardest thing she'd ever had to do. They'd been together for nearly ten years and despite hinting at marriage, kids, and – gasp! – living together, nothing had happened. He'd never seemed that keen on moving their relationship forward or taking the next step commitment-wise. Then six months ago, having had enough of waiting, Hetty had made the difficult decision to tear her own heart in two and move on. Seeing him now, for the first time in months, she

57

tightened her grip on the notebook in her hand, willing herself to remain detached and business-like.

He'd had another good day's trading and many of the baskets and large wicker bowls used to display things were empty. Chatter filled the air as Ben, cheeky and cheerful as ever, made his customers laugh with gentle teasing and jokes at both his, and their, expense. Hearing his voice, Hetty's heart, which she liked to believe had mostly healed, gave a double beat. Memories of all the good times they'd had together flooded back into her brain sending a longing through her bones.

The split hadn't been exactly amicable, but for Hetty it had been resigned. He'd argued that it was an extreme and sudden reaction. She'd shouted back that she'd subtly let him know she needed real commitment – for their relationship to move forward as they got older – but that still hadn't prompted him to ask her to marry him, or even for them to move in together. Ben had stubbornly refused to be 'rushed' into doing anything, even though rushing wasn't exactly how Hetty would have put it. If he'd responded how she'd hoped, not necessarily going down on one knee but with something to show he thought they had a future, things would have been different. She'd loved being with him. They laughed constantly, he'd always been faithful, even if he did have a flirty nature, and he'd loved her. *Just not quite enough*, she thought with a sigh.

This meeting was going to be a test – the longest conversation they'd have had since the immediate aftermath of the break-up and with John Thornhill watching on, even more awkward than she'd ever imagined. Ben's light-brown hair, heavily peppered with grey, was sticking up in its naturally fluffy style, and deep laughter lines were visible as he smiled at his customer. 'What you do with your bread in the comfort of your own home, Mrs Wilson, is entirely your own business.'

Mrs Wilson, who was about 80 and shrunken with age, giggled. 'Oh, Ben, you are a treasure.'

'Kind of you to say so, Mrs Wilson. Have a great afternoon.'

Hetty smiled to herself just as Ben glanced up. Seeing her, a flicker of surprise washed over his face then he grinned. Hetty felt her eyes drawn to it. 'Hetty, hi. Err, what can I get you?' He planted both hands firmly on the counter and leaned forwards. His dark-blue T-shirt tightened over his biceps, muscles worked by the constant kneading of bread, and a sudden image of his back as she ran her hands over it flitted through her brain. Luckily, the rest of him was obscured by a bright white apron, the ties of which had been wrapped twice around his waist and fastened at the front, otherwise she might have ended up blushing.

'Nothing to eat, thanks,' she said, her head and heart full of confusion. It was good to see him again. Too good, maybe, and an ache of pain threatened to seize her. Cramming all her feelings into another little box in her brain, she ensured her emotions didn't come to the fore. She focused on the fact that if she ate any more she'd be sick. Suddenly remembering John was there too, she shuffled over a little, so he was visible as well. 'We came to ask if you'd consider having a stall at the food festival I'm organising.'

'We?' Ben's eyes suddenly focused on John who Hetty saw stood a little straighter, rolling his shoulders back.

'Yes, this is John Thornhill. He's agreed to us using some of the land around Thornhill Hall. John, this is Ben Jackson.'

'Ben Jackson, baker extraordinaire,' Ben replied. John acknowledged him with a slight raise of the head and Ben nodded. He didn't offer any more and after a second, her curiosity piqued.

'So, what do you think?' She hated herself for asking, but if Ben could be relied upon for anything, it was telling her what he really thought. She'd always admired his straight-talking because when he paid a compliment, he really meant it. He had a good business sense too.

'It's ambitious but – wait, hang on – Karen?' he called to one of his staff. 'Can you come and serve please?' Then he moved to the end of the counter to speak to Hetty. Hetty followed him to the gap in the worktop and felt that familiar pull of his charisma and charm beckoning her towards him both physically and emotionally. 'But if anyone can do it, you can. I used to love the strawberry festival.' There was a fondness in his voice that made her swallow hard. 'I think I had my first kiss at the strawberry festival. It should definitely be brought back. And, if you ask me, you're just the person to do it.'

She wondered how he'd fared over the last six months. Had he moved on or was he still hurting too? Was his confidence hiding any remaining pain, or was he really fine? Under his intoxicating gaze she pulled her mind back to business. 'I'm going to start some awards too. Taste of the Bay awards. Knowing your skill, you'd probably win. So, do you want a pitch?' She still wasn't sure what response she'd prefer. A yes would be a big draw for the locals; a no would be easier for her emotionally. As the business side of her brain kicked in, she found herself trying to convince him. 'There'll be a lot of people going.' *I hope*, she added internally. 'You could make a lot of money, and you know how trade drops in the winter.'

'Not for me,' he replied with a grin. 'I'm busier than I can handle anyway. And all year round too.' It was annoyingly true. His bread was so good that even in the depths of winter when the high street was dead, people came to his shop.

'But still, we think it's going to be very successful. Even if your business is doing well, it'll be worth you getting involved,' said John, trying to help in convincing him. Hetty admired the thought but was also surprised that he'd taken it upon himself.

'Maybe,' Ben answered with a slightly dismissive tone she knew to be teasing but probably hadn't come across that way to John. Ben turned to Hetty, inclining his head towards her and speaking in a low murmur. From the corner of her eye, she saw John bristle at being shut out of the conversation. 'Do *you* want me there?' His tone had that familiar teasing edge again and it felt like he was asking about a lot more than just the food festival.

Hetty suddenly realised the possibilities. If she said yes, she was planting the seed that they might get back together. There was clearly still an attraction between them. But could he give her what she wanted? The commitment she wanted? A tingle ran down her spine. 'You'd be a great draw, as you know.'

'That doesn't answer my question.' He folded his arms over his chest and cocked his head to the side.

Damn, his easy confidence still had a magnetic effect that was hard to resist, but she couldn't deal with that right now. She had other things on her mind, like the mountainous to-do list she needed to get through. Plus, she could feel deep down there was a danger of falling back in love with him if she stayed too long. John folded his arms over his chest and gave a heavy sigh; clearly Ben and his confident, cheeky manner was getting on his nerves. 'Well, it's the only answer you're going to get,' she said firmly. 'You've got my number. If you decide you want a pitch, call me, but they're selling out fast.' And with that she turned on her heel and sashayed out of the shop.

Hetty and John made their way back towards the promenade. As she made her way there, she took a moment to enjoy the salty sea air and let it cool her cheeks. Seeing Ben had been far more intense than she'd expected it to be. Having a real conversation with him and one in which she valued his opinion, had reminded her of all the conversations they'd had when they were together, both building up their fledgling businesses, and the evenings cuddled on the sofa, the Friday nights at the pub and holidays in Rome and Venice. It reminded her of all the things that had attracted her to him in the first place. And having John looking over her shoulder, stern and disapproving, hadn't helped either.

'He's quite full of himself, isn't he?' John said, thrusting his hands into his pockets as they strolled along.

'Not really,' she replied, defensive on Ben's behalf. 'Anyway, he kind of has a right to be. Everything he said was true. His is one of the best businesses in Swallowtail Bay and he is the best baker in the town, if not the county.'

'Right,' was all John said before training his eyes on the horizon.

At the promenade, she took a moment to watch a sandwich tern resting on the water's edge, its messy black head down as it gently hopped along. Before John could say anything more about Ben, her mobile rang in her pocket. It was her mum, Daisy. 'Sorry, John, I just need to take this.' Wandering a little away, Hetty took a deep breath, put on her cheerful voice, and answered. 'Hi, Mum, what's up?'

'Ugh, it's your dad again.'

Hetty rolled her eyes. 'What's he done now?'

There was a time, a year ago, when her mum would have answered with a smile and fondness in her voice, but her parents had made what had proved to be a catastrophic mistake by retiring at exactly the same time. The first few months had been fine, they'd loved being together and having days out here and there, but over the six months that followed they'd grown increasingly intolerant of each other to the point where they now irritated the other daily with their breathing, chewing and general existence.

'Oh, nothing out of the ordinary.' Hetty immediately picked up on the strange tone to her mum's voice. 'Just what he's done every day for the last few months. He's gone golfing with Tony Dean.'

John had wandered towards the pebbles and was absent-mindedly nudging them off the promenade and back onto the beach with his foot.

'Isn't that a good thing? It means he's out from under your feet. You can chill out by yourself. Grab a coffee, read a book in the garden.'

'He's always out these days, Hetty. I can't remember the last time we had a day together. But the worst thing is ...' Daisy was quickly finding her stride ... 'he comes home and does nothing but talk about bloody golf. I'm sick of the subject. Absolutely sick of it. If he tells me again what his handicap is and what Tony's putting is like, I'm going to scream – right in his face – and then—'

'All right, Mum,' Hetty interrupted, gazing out over the calm, clear water of the sea, trying to absorb some of its serenity. The breeze was dying again, and the water resembled a giant silver-blue jelly gently wobbling a little here and there. Hetty matched her breathing to the faint sound of the tide nudging the shingle back and forth. 'Do try and calm down, Mum. You'll give yourself a heart attack.'

'At least it would put me out of my misery as far as your dad is concerned, and then he might actually appreciate me. If he's not golfing or talking about golf, he's in his shed doing goodness knows what. I'm starting to wish I'd never blimmin' well retired.'

'You could start volunteering or something?' Hetty offered, hoping it might stem the flow of her mum's vitriol.

'Volunteer to murder your dad and bury him under the patio, maybe.' Hetty rolled her eyes. 'Come for lunch on Sunday.'

It was a demand, not a question. Hetty had a lot to do and as soon as possible, but she was getting more and more concerned as to where this new family dynamic was heading. 'All right then,' she agreed. 'Will you make trifle?'

For the first time in ages her mum chuckled. 'Just for you. Traditional or chocolate?'

'Umm … hard question. Traditional, I think.' Hearing the smile in her mum's voice was worth losing a day's work anytime. 'About one?'

'Yes. We'll eat at two.'

'Okay. See you then. Love you. Try not to kill Dad in the meantime.'

'I'll try but I'm not making any promises. Anyway, love you too, darling. Bye bye.'

As lovely as the prospect of a trifle was, Hetty couldn't help frowning. The way her mum had said goodbye in a despondent, unhappy tone was worrying. Was a life of leisure with her dad really that bad?

'Everything all right?' John asked.

'Yes fine. We've got just enough time to talk tactics before we meet with the festival committee. Don't look like that,' she said upon seeing his grumpy expression. 'Trust me, we need a plan.'

***

John sat down opposite the festival committee hoping the terror he felt inside wasn't visible on his face. He'd never before encountered six more frightening people. Hetty had described a lady called Gwen before they'd arrived. Their main opposition apparently, and he'd clocked her immediately. She sat scowling at him like he was something on the bottom of her shoe. This was precisely why his family didn't come into town unless they absolutely had to. The five other people looked equally terrifying but had slightly less aggressive eyes. The room was stuffy where the windows had been closed all day and he felt tiny beads of sweat form on his forehead. He shouldn't have been here today really. He should have been trying to find a piece for a client, and the old radiator in the kitchen had started coming off the wall. He had to fix that when he got back.

Hetty sat beside him, quietly composed in the face of her opposition. She was so serene. The complete opposite of him. His quiet world had been spun on its axis by this crazy whirlwind of a woman. It was like she'd walked into his silent, book-lined study, shattering the peace, grabbing him by the scruff of the neck and shaking him till his teeth rattled. He'd never known anyone like her. And now he was doing something for her he never envisioned doing for anyone – sitting opposite terrifying older ladies and one kind-looking older gentleman. But he was doing this for himself too, he remembered. One of the older ladies sipped a cup of tea and attempted to smile at him.

'That's Mary,' Hetty whispered. 'She's already on our side, I think. I've tried to scope out the others, but they could go either way. Don't forget, stick to the plan.'

The plan, hatched after they'd come out of The Bake House, was for John to remain silent in a speak-only-when-spoken-to fashion. He'd agreed, given that he didn't know any of these people and trusted Hetty's judgement, but she'd been different after visiting that last place. Her calm exterior seemed as if it had been tested and he wasn't surprised; the guy running the place was a bit too full of himself for his liking and very flirty with Hetty. That in itself hadn't surprised him; Hetty was a very pretty lady.

'So,' said Gwen, clasping her hands in front of her, enjoying this moment of power. 'Hetty, you've come to try and convince us to hand over the strawberry festival to you.'

'Yes,' she replied confidently. 'As I said at the business forum, this is just the opportunity I've been looking for and now I'm pleased to say that Mr Thornhill has agreed to us hosting the event at Thornhill Hall and in fact, to us using four of his fields.'

'Four?' Gwen almost shouted across the table. She had one of those piercing voices that carried. The remaining committee members looked on in surprise. 'What on earth do you need four fields for?'

Hetty calmly outlined the number of people who'd already agreed to have a stall, and all the additional things they'd discussed that morning.

'It doesn't sound like you're running a food festival anymore, you're running a – a – I don't know what.' Gwen was beginning to redden. 'But it doesn't sound like something the committee should be supporting.'

To John's horror, some of the heads nodded.

'I'll admit,' said Hetty, 'my original idea has grown—'

'It sounds like it's grown to more than just you and your assistant can handle.'

The older gentleman on the committee piped up. 'Ambition is to be applauded, but we don't want it to turn into an embarrassment. The strawberry festival we currently have might be small but it's manageable.'

More nodding of heads and John bit back the retort that it was more of an embarrassment as it presently was. Seeing the support she had, Gwen was back on the attack.

'And Thornhill Hall is famously anti the townsfolk going anywhere near the place. Do you think people will suddenly be brave enough to visit when you've made it clear you don't want us normal people anywhere near your house?'

A flash of apprehension and annoyance passed over Hetty's features and John decided it was time for him to speak. His own annoyance was mounting like steam inside a pressure cooker and needed to be released before it erupted into a response he might regret. A response that might cause Hetty even more problems.

'I understand your reticence,' he said calmly, rising out of his seat. 'I was resistant to the idea myself. But I've come to realise that this is a fabulous idea and I have every confidence Hetty can not only organise this, but that it will be a great success as well.' Gwen glanced at the other committee members and her mouth formed a tight angry line as their faces began to change, swaying away from her. 'As for people coming to Thornhill Hall …' He paused. 'It's true that we don't open up the house and the grounds for public viewing. There are a number of reasons for that which, quite frankly, are nobody's business but our own.'

Hetty's eyes had been following him and the corners tensed as he said this.

'But we're ready now to welcome anyone and everyone to the food festival. I'm happy to allow Hetty to use our land to organise what will undoubtedly be a fabulous event over one of the busiest summer weekends, so that everyone can capitalise on it and enjoy the financial benefits.'

As John sat down, he saw the look of confusion and approval on Hetty's face. She couldn't have thought that he'd speak so enthusiastically on her behalf. He found himself glad that he'd both surprised and impressed her.

'Right,' said Mary, speaking up for the first time. 'I don't know about anyone else, but I'm tired of organising an event everyone laughs at and only comes along to out of a sense of duty. If Hetty is happy to organise this amazing-sounding food festival, I think we should let her. Show of hands, please. All in favour?'

Four hands raised. Gwen and the older gentleman's arms stayed firmly by their sides, but it didn't matter because the motion was carried. The first Swallowtail Bay Food Festival was to be held on the August bank holiday weekend in just under four weeks' time.

As much as she'd impressed him, John really hoped Hetty and her assistant could pull it all off in time. His family didn't need any more egg on their faces. They had a whole omelette there already.

Chapter 8

Hetty pulled up outside her mum and dad's house and unclipped her seatbelt. The three-bedroom pebbledashed semi had been her home until she was 20 when she'd moved out to her own slightly grotty flat in a nearby town. She'd quickly found that being inland and away from the sea wasn't for her and had moved back to the bay as soon as possible. Walking along the shore had been a way of relieving stress and anxiety since she was little when they'd gone out as a family. Unbreakable habits had been formed in her childhood and Hetty hated not feeling the strong sea breeze on her face or seeing the constant ebb and flow of the tide. In times of trouble, it reminded her that life went on no matter what else had occurred.

There hadn't been any point in going to university and lumbering herself with a ton of debt for an education that couldn't provide the real-life skills required to run her own events management business – something she'd wanted since she was old enough to go to parties.

While all the other kids enjoyed running around like lunatics and stressed-out mums appeared with candle-covered birthday cakes, Hetty had loved helping out, giving out party bags, handing out balloons – making someone feel like the most important person in the whole entire world. It was still a feeling that gave her a buzz. The weird thing about the food festival was that when she thought about whom that special moment was for, she couldn't decide if it was herself or the town.

Eyeing the upstairs right-hand window, the window to what had been her room, Hetty thought back to all she had achieved and all she was now risking with the food festival. Nerves crashed together in her stomach, jostling around for space. She'd started the business at just 25 years old. Hetty was incredibly good at her job, as she always believed she would be. Not because she was big headed or more talented than anyone else, but because she put the work in. She slogged away, growing her business, seeking out new opportunities. She met Ben three years later at the grand old age of 28, and that was that.

He'd looked good when she'd seen him on Tuesday. And that cheeky grin still had the power to stir something inside her, but she pushed those feelings out of her mind. She had this lunch to get through first and hoped her mum's mood had brightened since their conversation on Tuesday.

Hetty strolled to the front door and placed her spare key in the lock, giving a knock to signal her arrival as she pushed it open. From the numerous phone calls she'd received recently, she'd expected to hear arguing, but instead the house was quiet. No voices sounded out, only Phil Collins singing from the ancient CD player her mum still used, his voice carrying towards her on the roast-beef-scented air. Her stomach was beginning to rumble and after shouting hello, Hetty walked down the hall towards the kitchen. The blue carpet, which had been in place since she was a teenager, was still immaculate and mirrored the pale-blue flowers of the wallpaper. The back door closed and Hetty heard her mum enter the kitchen with a huff and saw her begin to chop carrots.

'Hi, Mum,' Hetty said, placing an arm around her mum's shoulders. Being a good deal taller, she rested her head on top of Daisy's. Her mum's once-blonde hair, a darker blonde than Hetty's, was almost entirely grey and silver now, but it was still soft and pretty, and Hetty pressed her cheek against it, enjoying the familiar smell of her mum's perfume.

'Hello, darling. You okay?'

'Yes, I'm fine.'

'Been busy?'

Hetty thought about telling her about the food festival now but wanted to tell her mum and dad together. 'Yes, I have. I'll tell you about it in a bit.' From the large window they were in front of, Hetty could see her dad on his knees in the back garden, fiddling with a red flower. Hetty wasn't very good with flowers or gardening. She'd developed her mum's love of organisation and order, rather than her dad's laid-back attitude and green fingers. 'How're you, Mum?' She nicked a bit of raw carrot and popped it in her mouth as Daisy tutted.

'Hmm?' Her mum seemed far away and not quite with it which was worrying. She was normally happy to see her and chatty. And considering she'd invited Hetty for dinner it was odd that she wasn't more interested in their conversation. Hetty repeated the question. 'Oh, I'm fine, darling. Just busy with dinner.'

'Can I help?'

'No, it's all under control.' Her mum began attacking a head of broccoli with such force Hetty stepped backwards.

'Can I take some leftovers for Stanley?'

Her mum paused her chopping. 'You're not still feeding that awful seagull, are you? You shouldn't encourage them. They're just pests.'

'Stanley's not a pest. He's a good boy.' Daisy looked down her nose at Hetty. 'What?'

'Are you sure he even is a boy?'

'Well, no.' How did you tell if a seagull was a boy or a girl? She'd Google it later. 'He loves your Yorkshire puddings almost as much as I do.' Hetty looked up to see her dad was now on his back looking under the bush he'd been wrestling with moments before like a mechanic looking under a car. 'What's Dad up to?'

'Gardening.' Her mum's voice was cross, which didn't bode well for dinner.

'Well, I can see that, but is he doing anything in particular? I thought there were special gardening terms for things.' She popped another piece of carrot in her mouth and her mum narrowed her eyes again. 'You know pruning, composting … shearing.'

'That's for sheep.'

'Oh.' Hetty smiled, but Daisy didn't join her. 'You know what I mean.'

Her mum gave a great sigh and, picking up the chopping board, slid the knife down it to push the chopped carrots into a saucepan of water and the florets of broccoli into a steamer. 'If there is a term, I don't know it.'

Hetty eyed her mum suspiciously. This was all very unusual behaviour. First of all, she hadn't put the kettle on yet, which was always the first thing she did when a visitor stopped by. And then, Daisy was a sharer. Even when she was annoyed about something, she was more than happy to tell her daughter all about it. They had what Hetty considered to be a fantastic relationship, discussing everything from serious health worries and cancer scares to everyday chit-chat and town gossip. She wasn't normally this closed off, especially with Hetty. Taking the lead and filling the kettle for a cup of tea, Hetty asked, 'What's wrong, Mum?'

'It doesn't matter, sweetheart. Now come here.' She turned and gave her daughter a proper hug. When she spoke next, her voice was at its normal cheery level, but there was a tense undertone and her smile didn't reach her eyes. 'How are you really? How's Macie?'

'We're good thanks, Mum. I've got some news to tell you later, but I want to tell you both together.'

'Okay,' Daisy replied nervously, gathering cups and plopping teabags into the pot.

'Don't worry, it's good news.' At least she thought it was good news. Now she was getting into the nitty-gritty of the festival and shelling out her own money, she was beginning to wonder if she'd bitten off more than she could chew.

'And how's life without Ben?'

Hetty hesitated. This had been a standard question over the last six months and one she was usually happy to answer but since she'd seen him on Tuesday, old feelings had been creeping back into her heart and soul. Deciding she wasn't ready to talk about what seeing him had done to her, she settled on, 'Oh, it's fine. I'm moving on.'

The kettle boiled and Daisy began to talk about normal day-to-day things. After sharing a cup of tea, her dad having forgotten to come and get his, Hetty helped with the last-minute preparations for dinner and laid the table.

On her mum's command, Hetty went to the back door. 'Dad, dinner's ready.'

Jeff wandered in with an affectionate, 'Hello, darling. I didn't see you'd arrived. I'd have come in sooner.'

'That's okay, I could see you were busy. What were you doing?'

'Oh, just fiddling with my dahlias.'

'Fiddling? Is that a technical term?'

'It is,' he replied cheerfully. 'So, how's tricks?'

'Good thanks. I've got some good news to tell you over dinner.'

'Oh, good. I'll look forward to that.'

While her mum was petite, Hetty had inherited her dad's figure. He was tall and a bit softer around the middle. Not exactly overweight, but despite all the golf and gardening his tummy had grown a little rounder. With a smile at Hetty, he approached the sink where Daisy stood, gazing out of the window lost in her own world. She expected him to give her mum a kiss on the cheek and playfully shove her over – something she'd seen a million times before – but instead, in a very formal voice he said, 'Excuse me, please.' Begrudgingly, her mum moved aside, and he washed his hands before heading to the dining room and taking his place at the table.

Hetty felt like she'd entered an alternate reality. This wasn't the happy house she was used to. Even as things had become strained over the last few months, they'd never treated each other like this. How had she not seen things had reached this level of unhappiness? They'd always been so connected, so together. And in a way, she'd thought their recent arguments were just part of the post-retirement adjustment. After working full-time for so long, it was inevitable that suddenly being together 24/7 would cause some friction. She was sure that was why Dad had become a little golf-obsessed. But Hetty had been so sure the obsession would pass and they'd find a balance of being together and having their own hobbies.

Hetty had friends who had gone on maternity leave and they'd often talked about a loss of identity with not working. Perhaps her mum and dad were undergoing something similar and they needed time to find themselves again? The worrying thing was it had been a year now, and rather than being happy that the slog of work was over, they were unhappier than ever. Could it be money worries? She didn't think so. Her parents were comfortably off and had decent pensions; they'd also been keen savers and had imparted that lesson to Hetty. Hetty chewed the inside of her cheek. There must be something she could do. She'd have to think about it later. Maybe she could take her mum out for the day to cheer her up. Yes, she'd make the suggestion at dinner.

Daisy carried her and Jeff's plates through to the dining room and Hetty followed, carrying her plate and the gravy boat. Her stomach gave a loud gurgle and she realised how hungry she was, and there was her mum's amazing trifle to look forward to.

Unfortunately, dinner was a horrid, tortuous affair. Both her parents spoke to her but whenever they did and said something the other didn't like, there'd be sneers and huffs and dismissive sideways glances. Hetty felt more like she was running a nursery than having dinner with her mum and dad. Deciding the situation wasn't going to get any better and knowing just how to steer it to calmer waters, Hetty said, 'So, my good news is that I'm turning the old strawberry festival into a huge food festival.'

Jeff smiled at his daughter. 'Well done, you. What a great idea.'

Hetty grinned back and turned to her mum. 'What do you think, Mum?'

'It's a very good idea,' she agreed. *Hallelujah!* They'd agreed on something at last. 'What made you think of it?'

Hetty told them about the business forum and all the work she'd done so far in convincing John to let them use some land. She'd glossed over his contribution to the committee meeting, not quite sure what to make of it herself. 'Sorry I didn't tell you sooner, but I've been manic trying to get things organised. By the time I've sat down in the evenings I've been so wiped out I fall asleep. Yesterday I dozed off in front of *Casualty*.'

'You must look after yourself,' her mum chided.

'I know,' Hetty replied. 'I've had a great response but there's still so much to sort out. I need to organise volunteer stewards, the St John's Ambulance – all that stuff.' She loaded her fork with beef smothered in gravy and a large piece of Yorkshire pudding. 'John Thornhill's been surprisingly helpful now he's got on board with the idea.' She placed the food in her mouth and savoured the taste. Her mum made the best roast dinners.

'I always loved the strawberry festival when you were little,' Daisy said sounding wistful. 'The whole town came out for it and there were red banners everywhere, criss-crossing the high street—'

'And stalls,' her dad added.

A flicker of reminiscence passed over her parents' faces and they gazed at each other in a moment of fondness. Eager to keep the cessation of hostilities, Hetty said, 'Thornhill Hall's something special, isn't it? Have you guys ever been up to the house?'

Daisy sipped her water. 'I think we went once a few years ago, before Rupert Thornhill lost his marbles, poor thing. They had some sort of open day because they were showing off the produce from their vineyard.'

'Poor man,' offered her dad, pushing a piece of Yorkshire pudding around his plate so it soaked up all the gravy. 'He should have hired a financial adviser or something before agreeing to anything.'

Dribs and drabs of town gossip had come Hetty's way over the years, but the talk was unfailingly unsympathetic. Thinking of John's comment that despite what the town thought, they knew what was being said about them, Hetty suddenly felt a lot more kindly about the family. From his defensive tone, John clearly felt the barbs and digs. No wonder they kept themselves to themselves. 'Do you know what happened?'

'All I know,' her dad began, 'is that Rupert was a bit of a wine snob and sunk the whole of the family's money into a French vineyard. There was some sort of fire that ruined pretty much everything, and he lost the lot.'

'But why?' Hetty asked, sitting forwards. 'Surely they had insurance or something?'

Her dad shrugged. 'There must have been a reason they didn't pay out. But I don't know about that.'

'I don't think he could cope with the guilt,' added Daisy. 'He used to come into town and be all la-di-da but after that he apparently shut himself away and now barely speaks to anyone. Since then the family have been scratching around trying to make ends meet.'

Jeff nodded, placing his knife and fork down on his empty plate. 'They sold off a lot of land—'

'But the place is huge. How much bigger was it originally?'

He shrugged. 'I'm not sure exactly. But that money must be running out by now.'

Daisy began to clear the table. 'After that, according to Mrs

Porter who used to clean for them, Rupert Thornhill went a bit ga-ga and has even stopped talking to his own family.'

'How awful,' said Hetty. So John had been left to try and rectify his father's mistake. If Rupert had sunk the family's fortune then selling off land would help, but with a place like that having such high running costs it must be a constant battle to stay afloat. She could only imagine how much the heating bill was for somewhere so big. Hetty watched as her mum brought in the trifle she'd made for pudding and as she eyed the layers of custard, sponge, jelly and cream, she saw her dad's eyes light up. How would she feel if her dad suddenly shut down and stopped talking to them? A shudder shot down her spine. It would be awful. Almost like losing someone.

During pudding, which was as delicious as Hetty knew it would be, her dad started talking about golf and gardening and the sombre mood that Hetty had encountered when she first walked in fell on the house again. Afterwards, her dad disappeared back into the garden as her mum washed the plates and she dried them.

'Hetty,' her mum began cautiously, and Hetty hoped she'd finally find out what had been bothering her so much.

'Yes?' she answered, stacking the flower-patterned plates on the side.

'I want you to know something.'

'Oh yes?' She mentally crossed her fingers that there was nothing physically wrong with either of her parents.

'I'm going to see a solicitor tomorrow to ask how I get a divorce. And I've decided to move out.'

Hetty almost dropped the wet plate and caught it in the tips of her fingers. She leaned back against the counter as her heart squeezed. 'What? Why? Surely things aren't that bad, Mum?'

'I'm afraid they are, darling,' her mum said calmly, still washing plates as if they were talking about the weather. 'I'm afraid I've become very unhappy.'

76

'But why? What about Dad? Don't you love him anymore?' Hetty's voice was pleading and while she didn't want to guilt-trip her mum, she couldn't help but wish this conversation wasn't happening. The idea that her mum and dad might divorce was crazier than her organising a giant food festival, and she knew how bonkers everyone thought that one was. Hetty tried to control the faint trembling in her legs.

Her mum rested her rubber-gloved hands on the edge of the stainless-steel sink and watched Jeff through the window. He was struggling with a rose bush and from the way he was flapping his arms around and giving it angry looks, he was losing. Bubbles slid slowly down the cheerful yellow rubber of her gloves and into the water. 'I haven't been happy for months now.' She hadn't said whether she still loved him though and Hetty needed to know. Her dad would be devastated and the thought of it all broke her heart.

'But you do still love Dad, don't you? And I know it must be weird being retired, and I know he can be annoying but—'

The sigh that escaped her mum's mouth seemed to deflate her whole body. 'I think your dad's having an affair.' Tears misted Hetty's vision and her mum's.

'Mum, that's crazy. Why on earth would you think that?'

Daisy answered without looking at her as she picked up a dish and began scrubbing it clean. 'I have my reasons.'

'Mum, you can't not tell me.' Dropping a bomb like that and then refusing to give details was not on as far as Hetty was concerned.

'I'd prefer not to. You're just going to have to believe me.'

It suddenly occurred to Hetty that it might be to do with bedroom antics and chose not to press. She'd always trusted her mum and their honest relationship, and from Daisy's expression, now wasn't the time to press too hard for information. 'Anyway, I just wanted you to know. I'll let you know how I get on at the solicitor's.'

'So you haven't told Dad yet?' Hetty's voice was almost wild with shock. Daisy handed Hetty a clean dish and on autopilot she dried it.

'No, not yet.'

It was the faintest glimmer of hope but Hetty dug her fingernails in so it wouldn't slip away.

'But I will. Tonight. When I leave.' In an instant her hope was extinguished.

Hetty looked again at her completely oblivious dad. An image of him sat alone in the house this evening filled her mind and made her want to howl. 'Where are you going to stay? I mean, of course you can stay with me, but—'

'I'm going to stay at Aunt Anne's.'

At least that meant she'd still be in the bay. Hetty felt like her heart had been torn out of her chest. Her parents were going to be separated. They were having a trial separation – on the verge of divorce. How had this happened? She didn't believe for one minute her dad had been having an affair. They'd always been so devoted to one another, she was positive neither of them would have strayed. Whatever her mum's reasons were, Hetty was sure there'd been a misunderstanding. She watched her mum staring out at her dad battling away in the garden. If Hetty could find out more, she could show her what a mistake this all was. From her mum's forlorn expression there was still love in her heart somewhere, Hetty was sure of it. But now she had to handle this on top of organising the biggest event Swallowtail Bay had ever seen, and she wasn't one hundred per cent sure she could.

Chapter 9

John had a feeling that however Monday mornings should be spent, it wasn't like this. He gingerly placed his foot on the attic beam, hoping it would take his weight, and waved the torch around. Dipping his head to avoid a joist that was threatening to knock him over if he didn't pay attention, he cursed under his breath. He hadn't even had a coffee yet.

This morning, as soon as he'd sat down at the breakfast table, his mother had mentioned a drip-drip-drip that had kept her up half the night. She wasn't entirely sure where it was coming from, but as the attic was above her and his father's bedroom, it wasn't a complete leap of the imagination to assume that there was yet another hole in the roof. Typical that they'd have a leak in the middle of summer. Most houses saved leaks for winter, but not Thornhill Hall. Oh, no. His annoying home had to have leaks in the driest season they'd had in fifty years. There'd been no rain for ages, except for last night. He'd seen storm clouds gathering out of his bedroom window, rolling in across the sea. They'd slowly filled the sky, covering the stars and a beautifully bright moon. Then, the heavens opened.

As usual, John had been awake in the early hours, tossing and turning, his brain full of strange and worrying things. Money, of course, featured heavily but thoughts of Hetty kept wandering in, only to be snatched away by tiredness before he could really get a handle on why she was there in the first place. Eventually sleep found him as he listened to the rain clatter hard on the windowpanes.

Sometimes, John wished he hadn't agreed to move back in when the vineyard had burned down. If he hadn't, he'd have much more control over his time. But after his father had shut down so completely on the rest of the family – lost and ashamed – his mother had had to bear the brunt of the disaster, fearing not only losing her home but her husband too; John knew he didn't really have a choice. Felix and Elizabeth had 8-year-old twin girls and it would have been too disruptive for them to move back in. But still being single, he'd been the logical choice. It was probably his own fault for being a workaholic and prioritising his business over relationships.

The two long-term relationships he'd been in had fallen by the wayside, their success diminishing as his business thrived. The problem with being so focused was the tunnel vision that came with it. Both his partners had also mentioned (none too gently) that he had a habit of never backing down once he'd said something, and up until recently, he had seen changing his mind as a sign of weakness.

But here John was at 8.30 a.m., in the loft, having only eaten half a slice of buttered toast – he hadn't even had a chance to put marmalade on it – examining the inside of the roof with a torch. Spying the patch of wet, he ran his fingers over it. It was indeed another leak. Luckily, he'd brought a bucket up with him and placed it where the water was. At least it was a slow leak and the weather reports predicted sunny skies and hosepipe bans so there shouldn't be any more rain for a while. Now all he had to do was go outside and have a look at the roof. If his luck held, it would just be a loose tile or something he could fix himself rather than having to hire someone in. Hiring someone cost money and after dipping into the profits from his own business, even those funds were running low.

With a heavy sigh, John made his way back to the loft hatch. If this food festival was as successful as he hoped it would be, it might just supply enough money to repair some things and pay a few of those bills he was too afraid to open. Silly really. No grown man should be afraid of a small manilla envelope. Although it was the bright red letters spelling out final demand that scared him most. *If* the food festival was successful, he reminded himself. It wasn't a given. Though with Hetty Colman running the show, he was sure she'd do a good job. Whether it would be enough was another matter. For some strange, nebulous reason he couldn't quite pinpoint, she kept appearing in his brain when he was awake as well as half asleep, and their conversations would replay time and again.

In a moment of lost concentration John stumbled. His foot landed on the edge of a beam and his ankle turned, sending him crashing to the right. Immediately he dropped the torch, and just about managed to brush the roof joist with his fingertips, slowing his fall, but as his feet tried to plant themselves, one went through the ceiling of the upstairs landing and he crashed half onto the beam on his bum.

'Arrgh!' he shouted as he landed with one leg tucked behind him, the other sticking out through the gap in the ceiling. Tiny beams of light shot up from the hole into the dark and dusty attic and annoyance tightened his features. 'Damn it,' he blustered. He wasn't hurt physically, but his pride was more than a little bruised. He'd never live this down if Felix saw him in this state – one foot sticking out of the ceiling. Having to tell him later, when he asked why there was a size-eleven boot hole above his head, was going to be bad enough. John hoped he hadn't destroyed any of the crown moulding that had somehow remained intact despite the rest of the house falling to bits.

A wave of heat ran over the back of John's neck and he rolled his eyes. He had to get himself out of this mess and quickly before any more of the ceiling gave way and he went through the lot. Finding the beam with his hands, he lifted himself up and managed to rest his bum on the edge. It was incredibly uncomfortable, and he'd bruised his coccyx. John ran a hand down his beard, composing himself. Dust and debris were stuck to his fingers and he could smell the grime on them.

'John?' said his mother, her voice wafting up through the loft hatch. 'What on earth are you doing?'

'Mother,' he said, repressing a sigh, as if it wasn't perfectly obvious what had happened.

'Oh, were you looking for the leak? Did you find it? Or were you doing something else? I did mention it to you, didn't I? I'm sure I did at breakfast. Or did I tell Felix on the telephone last night? Sometimes I forget which one of you I've told about what. There's always something going wrong with this house.'

John threw his hands in the air in exasperation and then, wobbling, grabbed hold of the beam again before he could topple forwards and make the size-eleven hole a damn sight bigger. Had Lucinda not noticed a foot sticking out above her head? Had she not noticed that there were bits of plaster scattered all over the old worn carpet under her slippered feet? Did she not remember asking John to have a look at where the annoying leak was coming from only half an hour before? Just as he was about to give a rather sarcastic reply, through the gap he saw her step over the debris on the carpet and her kind voice wafted back up through the loft hatch. 'Would you like a cup of tea, John?'

At this there was no way he could repress the laughter that gurgled inside him. Her comment instantly lifted his mood and he was able to see the funny side.

'What are you laughing at up there? Have you found the old photo albums from when you were little? I'm sure there's one of Felix holding a hosepipe with no underpants on.'

'No, I haven't found those yet, Mother,' he replied, his voice light and chuckling. But he might have a sneaky look for them just to get back at Felix for always being such a bossy big brother. 'Tea would be wonderful though, please. Just give me five minutes to get myself out of this hole.' *Literally and metaphorically*, he thought.

'Right you are, dear,' Lucinda said and she padded away, back down the stairs.

With a small shake of the head, John wiggled his foot out and, carefully balancing, stood on the sturdy roof beam to make his way to the loft hatch. He felt like one of those Olympic gymnasts on the balance beam and had a newfound admiration for them. His ankle twinged a little as he put his weight on it; he'd have to check it out when he got down, sure that it was swelling. His feet found the comfort and security of the ladder, and he exhaled a long happy breath.

As he stepped off the final rung, from the corner of his eye he saw the landing window and found himself walking towards it. He never took the time anymore to enjoy the house's vantage point from the top of the hill. The sea was calm again after last night's rain, but seagulls were flying over, hoping to find something on the beach left there by the tide. He wished he wasn't so torn between hating his home and loving it. It was rather tiring.

'Morning, boss,' came a chirpy voice from behind him. He turned and saw Jaz looking pretty in skinny black trousers, brogues and a crisp white shirt. She had her hair down today and he noticed that her skin had tanned in the sun. The work diary was tucked in the crook of her arm and she was ready for the day, armed with black and red biros and a highlighter. A confused look shot across her face and her eyes scanned his body, resting on his trouser leg, still rucked up and covered in dust. A graze had appeared on his shin and little dots of red blood were pooling on the surface. He brushed himself clean and rolled his trouser leg down.

'Busy already?' Jaz asked in a cheeky voice.

'Not really. Just thought I'd start the day with a morning constitutional in the attic.'

She followed his gaze upwards. 'What were you looking for up there? I thought you said it was full of rubbish.'

'A leak.'

'Another one?' He nodded, resting his hands in his jeans pockets. 'And did you find it?'

'Yes. And I've put a bucket under it. Though I've created an even bigger problem now.'

She tipped her head in silent sarcasm. 'You could have just used the loft ladder you know. Trying to come through the ceiling is just lazy.'

John managed a small smile. 'Thanks for the advice. I might take it next time.' He scrubbed his hand over his short hair to remove the dust still clinging to him.

As he remembered his mother's reaction from a few moments before his smile grew wider. Lost in thought, he was taken aback when Jaz stepped closer, her body almost pressing against his. She reached up and picked a small piece of plaster from his beard, her eyes lingering on his. A massive warning light came on in his head and he immediately stepped back. As he did, a wave of pink rose up Jaz's face. What was that? She'd never stood so close to him before. Unsure what had just happened, he said, 'Come on, let's have a cup of tea. I've been promised one already.'

Jaz's eyes were now fixed on the carpet as she adjusted the grip on the diary in her arms. John hoped against hope she'd been picking the dust from his beard in a sisterly fashion. 'Who's promised you that?' she asked, her tone light but her cheeks still colouring as they walked together down the grand curving staircase.

'Mother did. What's on for today?' He wanted to bring the conversation round to business matters as soon as possible. 'I know I've got a couple of calls this morning, and there's an item I want to bid on at that auction in Halebury this afternoon, but

I'll phone that in.'

'Are you sure? I don't mind nipping out and making sure the car's got petrol if you wanted to go. It might do you good to get away from here for a bit.'

John gave her a sideways glance. She normally preferred him to be in the office rather than out of it so he could sign letters and things. Jaz never encouraged him to be away for entire afternoons. 'No, it's fine. I'd rather be here. I've got a lot of emails to answer anyway, and I thought I'd take a look around the fields, just to make sure they'll be fine for this food festival.'

'Oh, okay.' John glanced at Jaz again, unused to her odd tone. She must just still be embarrassed about the beard thing.

At times like this he wished he understood women better than he did. Some men had that gift, but it wasn't a skill he'd been able to master. He and his last girlfriend had been together for two years but parted ways a year ago and to be perfectly honest, he'd been fine about it. She'd blamed the fact he was always working but had thrown in a parting shot that for someone who overthought everything, he could never understand her or how she felt. It was true he was a planner, someone who thought through all possibilities before deciding on a course of action and she'd found it boring. He supposed he'd never found someone he connected with enough to prioritise them over his business. Either way, the result was he'd spent so long concentrating on work, he hadn't had time for relationships and then the house had taken over.

It was all right for Felix. He'd met his wife at university, and they'd been together ever since, growing up together, tackling life's obstacles side by side. Felix was the lucky one. He didn't even realise how lucky he was. Having his own life meant he wasn't here all the time to deal with the minutiae of problems the house brought with it. The responsibility fell to John who'd been tackling life alone for so long he had no idea how he'd fare in a serious relationship. And why was Hetty in his mind again?

A picture of her smile filled his head, warming every cell in his body, but before he could think any more on it, Jaz opened the diary and carried on.

'So, tea, then you've got …' John nodded his understanding as she listed the morning's tasks they'd already timetabled. Time to forget about this crumbling money-pit of a house and get on with his own job for a while.

***

After spending such a long time ignoring her mum's calls, it felt strange for Hetty to be eyeing her phone every two minutes, eager for her mum to ring. Yesterday, her mum had promised to ring straight after her appointment with the solicitor, but it was now well after lunch and Hetty was still to hear. She'd chosen not to chase. She'd been busy herself organising more things for the food festival and now she was on her way to the lower field to have a good look around.

Though Hetty would normally do a detailed site visit first before organising an event, she was having to catch up on a few things. If she was honest, the real reason she hadn't called her mum was fear of hearing how her dad was. He'd called last night when her mum had left to stay at Aunt Anne's, completely beside himself. Hetty could hear the strain in his voice as he tried not to cry, incredulous that his wife had left him. It hadn't seemed like her mum had told him the whole truth either. He'd made no mention of being accused of having an affair and Hetty was at a loss as to why her mum wouldn't have brought it up. Comforting her dad had been a disconcerting change in roles. She'd been powerless to say anything that might actually help. All she could do was tell her dad that they needed to talk and that he had to give Mum time to figure things out. The two things seemed so utterly at odds for her dad, he'd rung off in a state of panic and confusion. Dealing with this was proving too painful and clouding her judgement. Her only option was to place all those feelings at the back of mind and tackle them later.

Hopping over the turnstile in as graceful a fashion as she could manage in purple-spotted Wellington boots, she stared around her at the wide-open green space, determined to focus on this enormous task she'd set herself. The earth smelt damp from last night's rain, but the strong sun had already dried most of it and the ground was surprisingly solid underfoot.

The emails Hetty sent the other night to food shops in neighbouring villages had already been answered with mostly positive responses meaning nearly all the pitches were filled. It had given her confidence a huge boost and suppressed some of the niggling doubts that were starting to creep in. A couple of people had been humpy and blunt, saying it would be a waste of their time and it wasn't going to be a success, but Hetty wasn't going to listen to naysayers. When she felt something was right, she went for it and that's what she was doing now. She took a great big breath of the fresh clean air and placed her hands on her hips.

The grass had grown to knee-height in the lower field, and pretty flowers danced in the breeze all around her. Everywhere there were spots of red, yellow, blue and white. The warm summer air carried the gentle sound of birdsong and pale cream butterflies flitted here and there between the blooms. In contrast, speedy dragonflies in bright, jewelled colours darted about with urgency. The field would need a mow before the festival, which felt like a shame, but there was no way around it. It was certainly big enough to hold the food vendors who'd already signed up and she wanted to get more if she could.

As the fields rolled away before her, she could see so much of Swallowtail Bay. To her left, at the other end of the arc of coastline was the Langdon Mansion Hotel. It too had been a stately home but had been refurbished into a five-star hotel. Hetty wondered why John hadn't thought to do the same, but perhaps

Thornhill Hall had been too expensive. In between the two stately homes that sat either end of the bay was a vast expanse of pebble beach, a faraway wiggly line of foam marking the sea's edge like a child had drawn it with a piece of white chalk. It really was magnificent. And luckily, there were numerous bridleways across the fields that led into town, so people would be able to walk to the festival if they didn't want to drive.

Having researched whether to charge a fixed price per pitch, or charge a percentage of profits, Hetty had decided to go with the latter option. The gains stood to be bigger but as with most things it also carried a greater risk. As she was going to split the profits with Thornhill Hall, it was the best option for them both to make a decent amount of money. Right now, a profit was looking more likely than a loss, but there was a lot left to do and pay for, and every possibility of little to no profit if they didn't attract lots of visitors all eager to spend money. Pulling the Ordnance Survey map from her back pocket, she checked her position and studied the great green fields surrounding her. 'So, if this is the lower field,' she said out loud to herself, 'then that one must be the west field and this one is the north field—'

'Wrong, I'm afraid.'

Hetty spun to see John Thornhill striding towards her, his hands deep in the pockets of his jeans. A slight fizz in her stomach started at the sight of his broad chest clad in a khaki T-shirt. His eyes were sparkling as he approached, then he stopped behind her and looked over her shoulder to see the map. Immediately she could smell his aftershave again. She wasn't usually one to like beards, but his was nicely trimmed over his cheeks and jaw. His sea-green eyes fixed on her and she reminded herself to breathe given that her lungs had temporarily forgotten what they were supposed to do.

'It's actually the middle field. The north field is more north, north-east and …' He leaned over Hetty's shoulder and pointed to the map, his body brushing hers. Her eyes focused on the strong muscles of his arm. She had to stop having a thing about arms, she decided, as every nerve in her body awoke at once. 'There's another field in between the north field and the middle field called the far-middle field. My forebears clearly decided having the names of the fields actually follow a compass would be far too helpful and obvious.'

'It would, wouldn't it?' Hetty replied with a smile, turning to face him. The colour of his eyes seemed to change with the weather. They'd warmed today, losing their stern, cold edge. As he backed away, they flicked down the length of her body stopping on her spotty Wellington boots.

'Nice boots.' The teasing note in his voice was a surprising hint of personality she hadn't anticipated when she'd first met him at Thornhill Hall after the business forum. But over the day she'd spent with him visiting vendors, she'd seen it more and more.

'Thank you. I thought it was going to be wetter after last night's rain. What are you doing here? I wasn't expecting to see you this afternoon.'

'No reason why you shouldn't, is there?'

Confusion creased her brow. 'When I called earlier this morning, your assistant said you were out all afternoon.'

'Did she?'

John's face resumed its normal stern look, his eyes changing to a cold ice-blue and Hetty hoped she hadn't landed the assistant in any trouble. Perhaps Miss Simmons had made a mistake. Then his expression softened as he stepped closer to her, side-stepping a molehill. 'I had planned on attending an auction in Halebury but then I decided to call my bid in and stay here. I told Jaz this morning, but she must have forgotten.'

Hetty's trustworthy gut instinct sent a signal to her brain, not convinced it was a mistake at all. When she'd come to the house that first time, it was clear that Jaz felt threatened by her. To be honest, it was something Hetty was used to. Her extreme focus

89

often intimidated people – men and women in equal measure. Jaz had done that thing Hetty had experienced time and again and learned to ignore; she'd run her eyes up and down the length of Hetty's body. Hetty had also spied the puppy dog eyes Jaz gave John. She clearly harboured a secret crush on her handsome, mature boss. Though Hetty was also equally convinced he was too wrapped up in his business and family concerns to notice.

'What was it you wanted to speak to me about?' he asked.

The deep well-spoken vowels sent a vibration through Hetty's body, just as they had in the committee meeting. She'd had to concentrate very hard on Gwen's miserable face to keep herself on track. 'I've had a great response from the food vendors, and I think we'll be able to fill this field and another. And tomorrow I'm going to see Horrocks' Travelling Carnival who I really hope can come, but they need pretty much a whole field to themselves. So this is my plan—'

A wry smile had pulled the corners of John's mouth up and Hetty was momentarily distracted by how much more handsome it made him. His face lost its hard edges and he seemed so much younger and carefree.

Forcing herself to look away, she continued. 'I thought the lower field for the vendors as we agreed, the west field …?' She pointed to another green field filled with tall spindles of grass, and John nodded to confirm she had the right one. 'For parking only. The east field for toilet facilities and the funfair, and the middle field – not the north field'– she rolled her eyes at the ridiculousness of the names – 'for some of the additional food vendors and the mobile film screen where we'll do the movie screening on the Saturday night.'

'I still can't believe we're doing a film screening.'

The 'we' didn't escape Hetty's notice and she enjoyed the way it fell so easily from his mouth. 'Well,' she replied, proudly, 'we really need people to stay at the festival for as long as possible. I've decided rather than charging a pitch fee we'll get a percentage of profits. It gives us the biggest opportunity for a decent return, so we need to give people a reason to travel to us and spend the whole day. The funfair will go some way to ensuring that and attracting families, but a film screening where people can relax with picnic blankets, maybe champagne, is a great way to attract people well into the evening.' He nodded, clearly impressed, and Hetty brushed her short hair over her ear. 'Next year we could even look at camping opportunities, or glamping—'

'Next year?' It was said with a chortle that Hetty couldn't read and she felt an uncharacteristic heat rise in her cheeks.

'Well, if the food festival goes well and we both get what we want, there's no reason we couldn't look into it.' She hadn't mentioned camping to Macie yet. Hetty and Macie had a shared loathing of this particular outdoor pursuit. Neither of them could understand the appeal of sleeping on the ground and were terrified that ants might crawl into their knickers in the middle of the night. Admittedly, it would probably be more traumatic for the ant, but it would leave an emotional scar on them too. People who enjoyed the great outdoors with such wild enthusiasm were always a bit intimidating, and then there was the whole toilet situation. But other people seemed to enjoy it.

Feeling slightly defensive now under his intent gaze, Hetty examined the Ordnance Survey map and kept her eyes from him. Though he wasn't, it felt like John was incredibly close to her and that pure power and heat were radiating off him.

'So, what will there be at the funfair?'

'Funfair-type-things,' she replied sarcastically. Then realising she was being churlish and not in the slightest bit professional, she added, 'A carousel, helter-skelter, ghost train, dodgems and a fun house. Oh, and some of the smaller bits and bobs they have like hook-a-duck and a coconut shy, that sort of thing. I haven't got my list for that, it's in the car.'

John reached up and brushed his right eyebrow with an index

finger. 'I haven't been to a funfair in – well, I don't think I can remember when.'

'Then you should definitely stop by during the food festival.' She chanced a glance and saw him smiling and the next sentence was out before she could stop it, coming from her brain without permission. 'Even better, why not come with me tomorrow to visit Horrocks'?'

'Come with you?' He was almost as surprised at her offer as she was.

Her spine tingled with anticipation and embarrassment. 'I understand if you're busy. It is short notice. But Horrocks' are presently at a country fair not too far from here. I thought you might like to come along and meet them too. If you've got lots to do then—'

'No – no, I'd like to.' He smiled again in that relaxed way that softened his features. 'What time shall we meet?'

'I can pick you up at ten,' Hetty said. Unusually she was having to feign confidence as the thought of being with him unnerved her more than she was used to. It wasn't until after he'd agreed and walked back towards the house she wondered if he'd be able to fit his entire frame in Myrtle. And the thought of the lord of the manor all crumpled up in the passenger seat of her Mini made her laugh out loud.

Chapter 10

Hetty pulled up at the country fair, smiling from ear to ear. John was grinning too, happy to at last remove his knees from his chin. He should have remembered Hetty had a Mini. He should also have remembered her cheeky sense of humour because she'd been hiding a sly smile every time she glanced in his direction which had been quite often. He didn't know if it was just out of amusement, but it made his insides squirm in a very pleasant way.

'Here we are then,' she said cheerfully, her voice ringing with excitement as she unclipped her seatbelt and climbed out.

The country showground was already busy with people and the car park was filling up quickly. As Hetty hurried on into the fair, John watched her go. She had a beautiful hourglass figure made all the more attractive by the skinny jeans she was wearing. Pulling his eyes away, he made a mental note of where they were parked.

The country fair was in the depths of the Kent countryside and while John had admired the scenery as they drove along, he suddenly felt a very real love for his home. Whether it was due to the overpowering smell of manure he wasn't sure, but he much preferred the seaside to the countryside – and Swallowtail Bay had the perfect mix of both.

'Come on,' Hetty called, walking backwards. With her giant sunglasses and short hair, she looked incredibly chic. 'I want to see the pigs.'

'Pigs?'

'Yep. There's a piglet race soon.'

'Please tell me we're not having animals at our event. That would pretty much hospitalise my mother.' Not to mention the extra room it would require and the smells it would create. Not inducive to selling food, he concluded.

She laughed at his joke and it brought a smile to his face, diminishing the stress he'd felt that morning. A loose piece of guttering had swung down and bashed against his mother's window, frightening her half to death and cracking the pane. He'd added it to the ever-increasing list of things that needed fixing. The trouble wasn't so much the list itself but trying to prioritise it. How did you decide what was a priority when everything needed fixing with some degree of urgency?

'Are you looking forward to having this many people at Thornhill Hall?' she asked as they entered a balloon-covered archway into the fairground proper.

'Umm, I'm not really sure,' he answered honestly. Seeing Hetty's confused look, he gave her a little more explanation 'Of course I want as many people there as possible but—'

'You don't fancy venturing into the world of the great unwashed?' He knew she was teasing but her comment hurt. Did she still think he was like that? He'd hoped she might know him better by now. 'Or are you going to hide in your house for the entire weekend with the door barricaded?'

'No, no hiding for me. My mother, though …' He sucked some air in. 'Now, that's a different story.'

'Oh?' A flash of concern passed over Hetty's face. 'Is she not in favour of the idea? I'm sorry if that's causing you any problems.'

'She's always been like it,' John said with a shrug. 'Always against opening up the house to visitors even though it could help us a lot.' Surprised at his own openness, he frowned. 'Anyway, where are these pigs and are we seeing them before or after we meet Mr Horrocks?'

'After. Let's get business out of the way first, then we can have some fun.'

Fun? The term was alien to him these days. Fun was having a day when he didn't have to tackle some minor messy problem. Fun was a day when he could focus solely on his antiques business. Fun wasn't something he came across very often and he wondered if he could even be fun after all this time. Sometimes he felt far older than his years, more like his father's age than his own; too old for fun. But today he was determined to be different. Today, he was determined to forget about the house and its problems and enjoy the sunshine.

They walked past a number of pens containing enormous cows the size of monster trucks and as they lowed and fidgeted, rustling the straw beneath their feet, John and Hetty headed to the funfair. She was busy making notes on her phone as she went, clearly studying the layout of the place and anything else of interest.

'It's missing a bit of atmosphere isn't it?' Hetty said, looking around her. 'There's no music, only lots of loud voices.' A giant shire horse made her jump as it was led past, neighing and shaking its head.

'Wasn't that atmospheric enough for you?'

Hetty narrowed her eyes in mock reproach. 'That wasn't atmospheric, it was terrifying. I had no idea horses could be that big.'

'They're beautiful creatures though.' John admired the animal. It was a working horse, bred for a hard, strenuous life. He felt an affinity with it, slogging away with no hope of an end.

'Can you ride?'

'Why? Because I live in a big house I must be able to ride a horse? Like we all must have gone to Eton and know all the rules to polo.' His voice had taken on that grumpy edge again.

Hetty's eyebrows were just visible over the top of her sunglasses. 'Well, can you?'

'Yes,' he conceded with a grudge.

'Ha!' She pointed at him, and strangely his response was to smile. Normally he'd be curt or even walk away, but with Hetty he couldn't.

'But that's not the point. Lots of people who don't live in big houses learn to ride a horse.'

'Did you do that whole hunting thing?'

He could tell from her tone she didn't approve. Luckily for him, his family didn't either. 'No. Mother couldn't stand anything like that.'

'Good.'

Why did her approval matter so much to him? He wasn't used to feeling like this and it was unnerving.

Hetty paused in front of him, staring at the funfair in awe. He could tell from the way her cheeks had risen as she smiled it was exactly what she was looking for. It was, however, enormous and would definitely take up most of the field they'd allocated for it.

After asking one of the funfair staff for his whereabouts, they located Mr Horrocks, sat on the steps of his own little wooden caravan, sipping at a cup of tea.

'Mr Horrocks, I'm Hetty Colman.'

'Miss Colman,' he replied kindly, holding out his hand. He had a round red face, weather-beaten and thread-veined, and a mop of white hair that made him look like a summery version of Father Christmas. He wore a bright red coat with tails, like that of a circus master, and big black boots.

John felt like all his senses were being assaulted at once. The air was heavy with the smell of boiled sweets; beeps, bleeps and noises came from every direction; and flashing lights were everywhere. Standing in the middle of the funfair with its activity and noise, it suddenly seemed like he'd been living his life in black and white while all around him everyone else experienced glorious technicolour.

Hetty was in her element again, chatting to Mr Horrocks, and John left her to it. They genially discussed details of the set-up, checked documents and exchanged information. Mr Horrocks seemed a very nice man and he took them on a tour of the carnival. It was a very old-fashioned one which seemed perfect for their event, and Hetty was happy with it too, which was enough for John. Strange, given that he always had to know the ins and outs of something before agreeing to it, but Hetty exuded such confidence he trusted her implicitly.

'I think Mr Horrocks is going to be absolutely perfect,' she said when the meeting finished, and they went to find the piglets. 'You were very quiet.'

'I didn't have much to add. You had everything under control.'

'I was worried you were changing your mind about giving me the extra land and having all these extra bits.'

John shook his head. 'If you can make this festival bigger and better, I'd be a fool to say no. And if these extras are going to make us more money …'

Hetty gave a cheeky smile. 'You're right, you would be a fool to say no.'

'Did you think I was one?' He raised one eyebrow, teasing, but unsure if he really wanted to know the answer.

'Did you think me one?' It was a nice evasion tactic, but he could play that game too.

'I asked you first.'

A smile pulled at her lips. 'I admit, when we met that day at Raina's I did think you'd be less reasonable. And I know when I first arrived at Thornhill Hall you thought me nothing more than a charity mugger too big for her boots.'

'Maybe at first.' He grinned, feeling a slight heat on the back of his neck. 'I soon realised my mistake.'

'Good,' she teased, and their eyes locked for a moment. John didn't want to look away, fixed in the warmth of her gaze, but then she dropped her eyes to the ground. 'Come on, let's find the piggies.'

John followed behind, his mind filling with worry. Looking into her eyes had done something to his heart. Something was happening to him and he had a sneaking suspicion he knew just what it was.

***

Hetty kicked her shoes off and curled up on the sofa, a large glass of chilled white wine in her hand, and the TV remote ready to find something worth watching. She had the windows wide open, the net curtains fluttering in the breeze. The voices of people still frolicking on the beach carried gently while the birds sung loudly. As the sun set, illuminating her tiny living room, Hetty reflected on her day with John and the phone call from her mum that had followed half an hour after she got home.

John Thornhill was an enigma. She didn't know him at all and yet, there was an uncharacteristic easiness about him sometimes that came through when she least expected it. He wasn't as stand-offish and uppity as everyone thought. Yes, he'd been like that at their first few meetings and sometimes it came out in conversation, but she felt it was more a defensive reaction. A way of shielding himself. Most of the time now she was seeing a different side to him. He was funny, intelligent and determined. She enjoyed his company. More than that, she looked forward to it and found herself wondering when she might see him next.

Hetty had thought a lot about what Rupert and Lucinda Thornhill had gone through. She could only imagine what it must be like to have your investment fail, potentially taking your home and way of life with it. She'd been terrified when starting her own business, when profits were scarce and money short. If hers had failed, the prospect of selling her two-bedroom cottage and downgrading to a rented one-bedroom flat wouldn't have been a happy one, but for the Thornhills, the thought of losing Thornhill Hall, a huge house that had been in their family for generations, must have been terrifying. No wonder Lucinda Thornhill didn't relish the prospect of having gossipy, sometimes nasty townsfolk in her home, judging and laughing at her family's misfortune.

John also had the most fascinating eyes she'd ever seen. Maybe it was the darkness of his beard that made them stand out more, but they were like those mood rings she'd worn as a kid. They changed colour depending on how he was feeling. Sometimes more blue than green, like a clear summer sky, at other times more green than blue like a stormy sea. That first physical reaction to him hadn't been a one-off. It had grown stronger each time she saw him to the point that, this morning, she found herself glancing over more than she should have as they drove to the country fair. Her pleasant memories of John and their time together, laughing and joking, had all abruptly faded when her mum called.

Daisy had been matter-of-fact, but nervous. Yesterday's meeting with the solicitor had gone well and she had the information she needed but wanted some time to think about it all. She'd been tight-lipped about her reasons for thinking Jeff was having an affair and a terrible seed of doubt had planted in Hetty's mind that maybe it wasn't her dad who'd had an affair but her mum. She shook her head and cast the thought aside. Assumptions and made-up scenarios weren't going to help anyone. It was best to deal with facts. And the fact was, whether her dad had had an affair or not, her mum wasn't happy. For a while now, her dad hadn't been that happy either. And if neither of them were, then maybe divorce was the best thing. She couldn't quite believe it was though. Hetty's stomach had churned all the time they'd been talking. She loved her mum and dad and it didn't matter that she was a woman in her late thirties, she didn't want her parents to get divorced. She wanted them to grow old together, well, older, and be as in love as they had been when she was growing up.

A knock at the door rang out through the silence of the house and with a groan Hetty put her wine glass down and got up to answer it. Her legs ached from a day spent clamouring over turnstiles and around fields, driving here, there and everywhere. All she'd wanted this evening was to watch something mind-numbing, drink her wine and eat an easy one-pot dinner. She un-latched the door and pulled it open, feeling her tongue drop to the bottom of her mouth.

'Ben. What are you doing here?'

He hadn't been at her house in over four months. Not since a very difficult conversation where she'd had to quite forcefully say that there was no going back for them. But crikey, he did look good. Since seeing him she couldn't help but think about all they'd had together and all that might have been. His charisma was almost like an addiction and his funny, flirty personality always drew her in. Confusingly, she couldn't tell if her feelings were real or just nostalgia, remnants of the past popping back up or emotions that had never really gone away in the first place.

Without his apron she could see him properly and it was like she hadn't looked at him in ages. As Ben regarded her from under his eyelashes, leaning against the doorframe with his hands behind his back – a familiar yet striking stance – Hetty's heart gave a double beat.

'Hey, you,' Ben said. 'I just thought I'd drop by and see how you are.'

'Ben.' She shook her head and the confused thoughts inside all smashed into one another, clamouring to be heard. 'What are you doing here?'

'This food festival of yours has got everyone talking.'

'Well, that's as maybe but you can't just turn up on my door-step. You haven't bothered for the last four months. Why now?'

Anger and bitterness were creeping into her tone and she hadn't even opened the box of feelings she'd kept shut for so long. Her already tired muscles tensed.

'I deserve that, I know.' He gave a slight nod of the head. 'And you're right. I've been a coward staying away. But you stayed away too. You haven't come near my shop and I know how much you like my olive and sundried tomato bread.' Ben smiled to show he didn't mean anything by it, and from behind his back he produced a bag full of treats. A wine bottle poked out the top, as did some of his olive and sundried tomato bread. It had been her favourite when they were together.

Damn that man!

'It's a peace offering.'

She was still tempted to say no and slam the door in his face. He'd hurt her and couldn't just walk back into her life like nothing had happened.

'It's a can-we-be-grown-ups-and-maybe-even-friends offering.' From his reaction, the softening in her heart was reflected in her face. 'Come on, Hetty. I know what a crazy little dynamo you are, and how wrapped up in your work you get, I thought I'd bring you some supper. On your own all you'd have managed is shoving a chicken breast in a pot with a tin of tomatoes.'

Hetty tried hard to keep a stern expression but found herself smiling. He was right. She was so tired with how crazy everything had been organising the food festival, and stressed with her mum and dad's crazy situation, the one-pot meal was ready in the kitchen waiting to go into the oven. That he knew her so well was comforting and though her mind hesitated, her body moved to one side to let him in. Ben walked past and into her house, and the familiarity of it hit Hetty with both pain and longing. He knew his way around the cottage and sauntered through to the kitchen. By the time Hetty had closed the front door, her brain telling her body to stop doing things without checking with it first, he was already lifting out plates from the cupboard and cutting the bread. He'd also brought some cherry tomatoes, celery and a jar of piccalilli – her other favourite – and it was the most natural thing in the world that he should be there. She went to the kitchen doorway and watched him for a moment as he talked over his shoulder like they'd never left each other.

'So, how's it going? I heard on the grapevine this is going to be the biggest thing Swallowtail Bay has ever seen. And you' he turned and gazed at her – 'are the talk of the town.'

Hetty crossed her arms over her chest. 'That's not exactly a compliment. It doesn't take much to be the talk of *this* town.'

'No, but no one's been this excited since that the crazy man who lives in his allotment tried to marry his dog.' Hetty giggled. Ben had always been able to make her laugh. When she'd been sad, stressed or tired, he'd be there cracking jokes and it would act like a release. The effects were immediate. She found herself wondering again if he was seeing anyone. 'You look good, Hetty,' he said simply and clearly. 'How's that for a compliment?'

His words hung in the air, loaded with so much more than a simple nicety. They seemed to contain the essence of their relationship, their attraction to one another, the love that was always there but never quite made it to the finishing line. A gentle breeze from the window blew across her neck, taking her back to reality. She couldn't kick him back out now, and taking the olive branch – or olive bread – he was holding out to her was the adult thing to do. 'Let's eat,' she said, making her way into the kitchen to help serve up.

Ben handed her a plate then grabbed himself a wine glass. He placed the bottle he'd brought into the fridge and picked up her open one. 'Top-up?'

'Not yet, thanks, but help yourself.' He poured a hefty measure. The room suddenly felt hotter and Hetty felt the need for air. 'Shall we eat in the garden?'

'Sure.' Taking his glass and plate with him, he led the way outside. The cool air calmed her a little. Not much of a gardener, the few pots she had managed to plant were wilting in the sun where it shone into her little garden, her little patch of paradise. The honeysuckle popping over the fence from next door where they were thankfully more green-fingered, brought with it a gentle, floral scent. Stanley landed and began hoping about for food.

'Stan's still here then,' Ben said, tossing him a small piece of bread.

'Yeah. I couldn't get rid of him if I tried.'

They happily munched, sharing the spread Ben had brought. It was nice to have company. It was nice to have Ben's company and they talked about anything and everything. Ben's business was doing so well he was thinking about starting a second shop in a nearby town and Hetty was happy for him. Perhaps one day she'd get to expand her own business but that was a long way off yet. And that was if she got back the money she'd invested in the food festival and made a profit on top. He didn't mention if he was seeing anyone and Hetty chose not to ask. She didn't want to seem that interested and was finding it hard enough to keep her confused feelings for Ben in check.

'Are you still sure you don't want a pitch at the festival?' she asked, wiping up the piccalilli sauce with a scrap of bread and popping it in her mouth.

'What, with lord of the manor watching over us all?'

Hetty ignored him. 'If you're looking at opening another shop it could be great for spreading the word and gauging possible business.' Not to mention his reputation would bring more people to the festival.

Ben pushed his plate away and lay back against the sofa. 'I've got enough work on my plate without making even more for myself. And we're talking what? Three weeks?'

Hetty nodded as a rush of nerves swept over her. Three weeks really wasn't long to finish all the things she had to do. Was she crazy to do this? If she was, it was too late now. 'Okay, but it's your loss,' she teased.

103

By the time they'd finished eating, the sun was setting and through the open window Hetty could see a sky dotted with white clouds some of them underlined with bright dashes of pink and lilac. It was the most beautiful sky she'd ever seen. She was just about to clear the plates when Ben suddenly sat forward and leaned in towards her. His hand reached out and brushed the corner of her mouth. The feel of his thumb against her lip made her mouth tingle and her breath hitch.

'What did you do that for?' she asked, almost breathlessly.

'You had some piccalilli on your lip.' Hetty went to move her head and look away but Ben's hand remained cupping her cheek. 'Plus, it was a good excuse,' he added, his voice low and loaded. 'Because what I really wanted to do was this—'

Before she could stop him, he kissed her, and a bolt of exhilaration shot through Hetty. A heady feeling of things being oh-so-right but also dangerously wrong. When he drew back, she took a deep breath to control her unsteady heart. It was beating at three times its normal speed making everything seem like a dream.

'I've missed you, Hetty.' She'd missed him too but didn't yet know what exactly that meant for her. 'I'd been missing you anyway, but when I saw you in the bakery on Friday – talking to you again – I don't know, I …' His sentence dissipated in the breeze and his thumb gently stroked her cheek. 'It was like we'd never been apart, and I realised you don't get that a lot. There's something special between us, Hetty. Something a lot of people would kill for. Something worth holding on to.'

'Ben—' Hetty's normally clear mind was muddled and the result was that her senses were too.

'I think we should get back together. That we should try again.'

A million thoughts ran through her head all at once. She couldn't believe he'd just kissed her or the way it had made her feel. Her stupid heart had run straight back to him as if it had never left. But as her brain caught up with the last few minutes, it was telling her it was all too quick and sudden. If she hadn't walked into the bakery would he be here now? And she was angry too. How could he think he could just walk back into her life and turn it upside down? She removed his hand from her cheek. 'Ben—'

'I know you never felt I really committed to you, Hetty, and in a way I didn't. I don't know why.' He cast his hand out as if the words he could find weren't enough but would have to do. 'Because I'm an idiot probably. I didn't want to feel trapped or tied down by a house or mortgage.' He grabbed her hand again. 'But I realise now I do want to be trapped – by you. Since the day you left, I've regretted it. I've thought about you non-stop. You're always on my mind, Hetty, and I miss you more than I could ever put into words.'

As speeches went it wasn't a bad one and it did go some way to abating her anger. Swallowing hard, a part of Hetty wanted him to stay, to hear him speak more about loving and missing her, and she wanted to tear his clothes off and take him to bed, but it was all moving too fast. Everything was moving too fast. She'd stupidly and impulsively taken on the food festival that was now turning her whole life upside down and now Ben was here doing the same. She had to slow down. She was risking everything with her business right now. She had to concentrate on that. If she lost focus – if she got distracted and made a mistake – she'd lose everything. She had to control her feelings and get them back in their little box. 'It's all too unexpected, Ben.'

He gave a nervous laugh. 'I realise it might be for you, but it isn't for me. For me, this has been brewing since we split.'

Brewing. It made her sound like a cup of tea and she resisted the urge to giggle. Hetty knew her brain was entering defensive mode, thinking of silly things because the real stuff was too scary. It meant she wasn't ready to have this discussion. 'Ben I … I can't deal with this right now. I think you should go.'

He didn't argue or even look disappointed as he gently edged away from her. 'Don't worry, I knew you'd say that.'

Did he know her so well that he'd expected this response already? Had he known she'd pull back until she found her bearings once more? Smiling, he stood up and made his way to the door. Hetty followed and in the doorway he paused, turning back to her. 'See you, Hetty. Soon?'

She nodded but couldn't give him an answer verbally. She couldn't trust herself to say what her brain was telling her, and her heart wanted her to pull him back for more. As he strolled off, she closed the door on him, unsure what was happening inside her own body.

After she sat back on the sofa and drained the last of her wine, she started processing the last hour's events. Her body wanted him back, but her analytical mind reminded her of the reason it all ended in the first place. Had he changed? Could he change?

As she stared down into her empty wine glass, Hetty knew there was only one thing to do in this confusing and terrifying situation – throw herself into work and forget all about it. If that was even possible.

Chapter 11

As it turned out, it was entirely possible because just over a week after agreeing to attend the Swallowtail Bay Food Festival, Mr Horrocks of Horrocks' Travelling Carnival realised he had double-booked and pulled out.

Hetty signed off the call with a galloping pulse. 'Of course, I understand, Mr Horrocks. No, please don't worry, these things happen. I'm sure I'll be able to sort something else out.' But once she'd hung up she stared incredulously at her phone like it would hold the answer she needed. A stress headache began to pound in the back of her head, and she puffed out her cheeks. 'Crap.'

She should have known her luck was about to run out. Everything had gone far too smoothly so far. It was bound to happen sooner or later, but why did it have to be something so big? An advertised stall holder pulling out she could handle, but she'd been marketing a funfair. A great big shiny, lots of attractions, beeps and noises funfair. Disaster. This was most certainly a catastrophic disaster.

The doorbell rang, signifying Macie's timely arrival and Hetty ran to it and yanked it open. 'Macie, we have a problem.'

'Oh no. What?' She followed Hetty into the kitchen where she began making emergency coffee.

'The bloody funfair has only gone and pulled out, hasn't it?' Macie immediately stopped making the drinks and turned, her face frozen in panic. Hetty could see she was just as stressed as her cheeks grew pink.

Macie held a coffee pod in her hand. 'Oh my gosh, Hetty. What are we going to do? I'm having palpitations. I'm panicking. Maybe I'm dying. Am I having a heart attack?'

'I will slap you,' Hetty said like a schoolmistress.

'Will you?'

'No, but do calm down.' This was the first major thing that had gone wrong, and though she was certainly feeling the pressure, she would solve it. What other choice did she have? She pulled out a chair for Macie and pointed for her to sit on it. Macie did as she was told. 'First thing, coffee; second thing, cake; third thing, calm down. Then we'll figure out what to do.'

'Do we have cake?' Macie asked in a small voice.

'Always, my young friend. Always.' She got up and pulled a flowery tin from the side and opened the lid. A great big Victoria sandwich oozing jam sat in the middle. Hetty's own heart rate began to slow as the news sunk in. She couldn't change what had happened, all she could do was re-group.

'Right,' Hetty said, grabbing a notepad and pen. 'I'm advertising a funfair and it's key to getting people to stay for more than an hour or two and in attracting families. We *need* to have one.'

'Why has he pulled out? He's not ill, is he? I thought he looked a bit peaky when you showed me his picture last week. You can never tell with old people. He's got the bulbous nose of a secret drinker. Or maybe it's gout. He looked gouty.'

Hetty stared aghast. '*He looked gouty*,' she repeated. 'What on earth are you talking about? He's perfectly fine – at least I hope he is. He said they just double-booked.'

'Oh, right.' Macie's ears were turning red now.

'Were you going to let me hire a secret drinker? Someone who controls rides that kids go on?'

'No,' said Macie, but the way she averted her eyes let Hetty know she hadn't quite thought before she spoke.

'Anyway, you're completely wrong about Mr Horrocks. This is why you pick such bad boyfriends. You're a terrible judge of character.' Macie didn't reply and Hetty gave her a sideways glance. 'If we can't replace the funfair with another funfair, we'll have to think of something else. So, first things first, let's find our original list of possible funfairs.'

Hetty retrieved the list and after ringing around to see who was still available, there were only two left. Hetty made appointments to see both. One was currently a good hour's drive away and the other would be within travelling distance that afternoon when they pitched up at their latest stop. It was going to be a busy day of driving backwards and forwards all over the county for Hetty and Macie. But if the funfairs were a no-go, she'd have to expand the bouncy castle area, get a bigger one and maybe go ahead with the slip and slide. She could handle this. Problems were made to be overcome, she told herself.

Macie, who was perpetually good-natured, had a twinkle in her eye. 'Road trip!' she announced excitedly, jumping up. She knew where everything was in Hetty's kitchen, so she began to gather supplies from the cupboards.

Before long they were loading a wicker basket containing more food than the two of them could possibly eat into the back of the car. Hetty programmed her phone with the address and they set off with the radio on full blast. After exhausting all essential discussion topics within half an hour (their mutual crushes on Aidan Turner, *Love Island* and how much they were looking forward to *Strictly Come Dancing* in the autumn), the smaller roads gave way to wide, busy motorways, and Macie raised the subject of Ben.

'Sooo …' She protracted the 'o' sound in a long, drawn out note. 'What's the deal with you and delicious baker Ben these days?'

'Urgh.'

Macie nodded quizzically. 'Interesting.'

Hetty swung a glance her way. 'I haven't told you this yet because I've been trying to get my head round it, but …' She took a breath as her heart gave an unsettling flutter. 'Ben came round the other night and he sort of kissed me.'

Macie's head turned so quickly she might have injured herself. 'Really? When?'

'Last Tuesday.'

'Oh my great goodness me. You've been sitting on this information for a week! How could you? And I thought I was your bestest bestie as well as your minion assistant.'

'I just needed to—'

'Process it. Yes, I know. So how was it?'

'Urgh.' Hetty sighed and Macie widened her eyes.

'So it was gooood.' She stretched the 'oo' sound again and wiggled her eyebrows.

'It was very surprising and … powerful.'

'And how do you feel now?'

'I don't know.'

'Come on, you can't tell me that old feelings haven't stirred since The Kiss. I can see it in your face.'

'Don't say "The Kiss" in that way. It makes it sound dramatic.'

'From the way you're acting, it was dramatic. A proper knee-trembler, as my old dad would say.'

'Your dad needs to calm himself down.'

'True.' Macie nodded in agreement. 'Maybe that's why his blood pressure's so high.'

Hetty shifted her hands on the wheel. 'Old feelings have stirred and that's exactly the problem. It wasn't that I didn't love him. It was just that he didn't love me enough to marry me or even commit to moving in after nearly ten years together.' Peeking inside this box of feelings was making her decidedly uncomfortable. Her feelings of rejection had faded as her usual confidence

110

returned, but she really didn't want to complicate this already difficult and intimidating task of organising a giant food festival by throwing in feelings she'd prefer not to deal with.

'Did you actually talk about it though? I mean seriously talk. You used to moan at me, but did you tell him what you wanted?'

'I didn't moan at you! I used to confide in a friend.' Macie grinned, clearly glad her teasing was working. Thinking back, Hetty scowled. 'Over the years there were a few fake-serious conversations where I'd throw in things like, "You'd better marry me soon or I'll find someone else," but he always just laughed them off. He never was one to pick up on subtle hints. Then it all came to a head. You remember the almighty row we had where I gave him that ultimatum.'

'Yes I do,' Macie said. 'I think you cried for about three days. I'd never seen you cry before. I thought something terrible had happened to your mum or dad or something. Then when you said it was Ben, I was ready to go round and deck him.'

The mention of her mum and dad reminded her of that whole disaster and she shuddered. 'Do you think he was right that if he was backed into a corner and made to do something, it wouldn't mean anything?'

'He kind of has a point but it's not like he didn't have enough time to get around to it. Ten years is a long time to wait. I'd probably be gone after five.'

'Maybe I should have. I mean even after that I still gave him a few more months. But nothing.' Hetty gave an audible sigh.

'Do you believe him now?'

'The trouble with Ben is he always believes things in the moment he's saying them. It's whether he still means them later that's the problem.'

'Maybe you need to talk to him again.'

'Yeah maybe,' she replied. In the back of her mind she knew Macie was right. The only way she was going to know for sure if Ben was serious was to ask him and that meant opening up the little box of feelings in her head and she wasn't sure that if she did, she'd ever get them all back inside again.

'Can a leopard change his spots, or a baker change his ...' Macie clearly hadn't thought through this analogy and Hetty waited with bated breath to see what gem she came up with. 'Yeast,' she said after a pause.

'Yeast?' Hetty screwed up her face. 'You really need to start thinking before you speak.'

'You know what I mean.'

'I don't know. I really want to believe him. And I suppose it's feasible that he has changed and that our break-up forced him to grow up. Is that possible? I think for now I'm going to focus on the food festival until I actually have time to sort my head out. He hasn't said anything that would make me think things would end differently. I don't even know if he wants a relationship or if he'd just like a quick shag. His texts have been pretty flirty.'

'If he wanted to get back together seriously, what would you say? What does your heart say?'

Behind her sunglasses Hetty rolled her eyes. 'We're not in a BBC costume drama or a Netflix rom-com, Macie. Hearts can't be trusted to make their own decisions.'

'Well, I think he wants proper back together and not just a bit of the old rumpety pumpety.'

'Another one of your dad's?'

Macie grinned. 'Rumpety pumpety? Nope, that's all mine.'

'Wow.'

'And what about John Thornhill?'

Hetty stiffened. 'What about him? He's a business associate, nothing more.'

'He's a very handsome business associate and from what you've said about him lately, not half as bad as we all thought.'

'I don't mix business with pleasure, Macie. Rule number one.'

'I thought rule number one was always go to the toilet before a kids' party started because you definitely won't want to go in there afterwards?'

'That's rule number two.'

Macie turned and looked out of the window. 'You said "pleasure" though. So being with him is pleasurable?'

Hetty felt a heat creep up her neck. 'I meant hypothetically.'

'Of course you did. Oh! Oh!' Macie suddenly waved her arms around like a lunatic. 'I was meant to remind you this morning to call Bob about judging the awards.'

'No worries,' she replied, thinking over the to-do list in her brain. 'I'll ring Bob later. And I'm going to rope in John Thornhill as it's his land. Do you think it would be massively big headed if I do it too?'

'No, not at all. You should definitely do it. You're organising this whole shindig.'

She was actually looking forward to that bit.

They carried on the rest of the journey singing along to the radio with the occasional bit of seat dancing until Hetty pulled off the motorway and onto country lanes. After a short drive, she stopped at a large village green where the funfair was set out. At first glance it seemed okay, and Hetty climbed out, hoping that by lunchtime disaster would be averted.

Unfortunately, that wasn't to be. As she and Macie drew closer, they saw that the funfair looked the part with all the attractions she wanted and pretty lights strung up here and there, but the rides and mechanical bits were making strange creaking noises, even though no one was on them. They sounded old and worn and immediately Hetty felt her shoulders tighten. The owner came strolling over in grubby jeans that were basically held up by string and with a rather large, angry-looking black dog at his heel. Hetty wasn't very good with breeds of dog, all she knew was it was big and not at all like the cute dogs on TV advertising toilet roll. The man commanded the dog to sit with a single bark of the word, which it did, but Hetty was still nervous of approaching, and from the look on Macie's face, so was she.

'Miss Colman? I'm Gid, owner of Gideon Slay's Funfair.' He held out his hand, complete with grubby black fingernails, and Hetty shook it. Although in his late fifties, possibly early sixties, he ran an appreciative eye over Macie then smiled at her lecherously. Immediately Hetty stepped a little closer to her friend.

'How do you do? This is my assistant, Macie.' She deliberately didn't give Macie's surname, worried that this guy, who kept eyeing her lasciviously, might belong in the weirdo-stalker category of men, rather than just the dirty but fairly harmless old perv group.

'So, what do you think then?' He motioned around and the dog gave a loud bark. 'Quiet, Lady.'

For a second, Hetty thought he was talking to her and was about to slap him when she noticed the dog's enormous teeth. She could smell the animal's breath from where she was standing. She quite liked dogs normally but this one was just a bit too terrifying.

'Lovely,' Hetty replied, unsure what else to say. This man was nothing like sweet Mr Horrocks, who'd been politeness itself. Hetty had felt instantly at ease in his company. Not to mention completely trusting of his abilities to stick to the rules and regulations. She hadn't yet been inspired by Mr Slay with his dirty face and impressive lack of teeth. 'Would it be possible to see your health and safety certificates, please?'

The slight hesitation that made him reach down and stroke the dog's head put Hetty on her guard. 'Well, now, I'd have to dig those out, but they're all in order. I promise.' He gave a grin that only made the large gaps where his teeth should have been even more obvious.

Hetty had heard this sort of nonsense before. In fact, the lovely Mr Horrocks had warned her about unscrupulous and lackadaisical operators when they'd met. He'd had all his documents in a folder that he'd given to Hetty before she'd even had to ask for it. No way was she going to entrust this man with little lives at her food festival. To be honest, she wouldn't trust him with a plastic spoon. 'I'm sorry to cause you any problems, but I really need to see them now, Mr Slay. I can't possibly hire you if I haven't seen them.'

'I tell you what.' He rocked back on his heels. 'Why don't I just bring them with me, and I can show you them when we set up?'

Hetty straightened her spine authoritatively. 'No, I'm sorry, Mr Slay. I'm afraid I really do need to see them now and make sure you're working to all government regulations.'

On the quiet of the village green, the sound of metal clinking and grinding filled the air. Mr Slay's face hardened and Hetty had a horrible feeling he was going to set the dog on her. But Mr Slay didn't give any response at all. He just sniffed, turned his back and sauntered off, yanking the lead of the big black dog, who begrudgingly moved off as well.

Hetty gawped at Macie and raised her eyebrows, before they quickly headed back to the car. Once they'd got inside and locked the doors, Hetty sunk back against the seat. 'How scary was that man?'

'Absolutely terrifying,' Macie agreed. 'How does he manage to eat his dinner? He only had three teeth. And that dog! I thought it was going to eat me.'

'Urgh, and when he looked at you all—' Hetty shuddered.

'I know! Super gross. It made me shudder too.' Macie did the same now.

Hetty huffed out a breath. While she was relieved they were back in the safety of the car and weren't hiring creepy Mr Slay, that left only one person on her list of possible replacements. 'What are we going to do if we don't have a funfair, Macie? What can we have instead that isn't going to shout, "Hetty Colman is crap at organising events and can't deliver what she promised."'

Macie's brow wrinkled. 'Why are you being wobbly? Nothing fazes you normally.'

Though her huge sunglasses made her feel like a movie star, Hetty adjusted them nervously, completely lacking a movie star's confidence. 'I know, but this is the biggest thing I've ever done and if the biggest thing I ever do is a complete failure what's that going to do to my business? And I just don't feel that Plan B of extending the inflatables and having the slip and slide will be enough.' In her mind, Hetty listed her other worries *Plus Mum and Dad, and now Ben*, she thought. She hadn't told Macie about her mum and dad yet. She was still desperately clinging to the idea that having some space from each other might make her mum realise how much she loved Hetty's dad and it might all amount to nothing.

With a calm, motherly tone, Macie said, 'Let's just see what this afternoon's one is like, shall we, before we start panicking or worrying about Plan B. They might be amazing. Let's eat something to keep our energy up. I bought some of that delicious cake you pretended to have cooked when I know full well you bought it from the shops.'

Hetty giggled and relaxed a little. Macie was right. One thing at a time. 'I have never once pretended to bake anything. I know my limitations.'

After a fortifying snack they began the drive to their second location. The air-con was cranked up high and more singing and seat dancing ensued. Hetty felt their duet of 'Especially for You' was particularly impressive this time.

Folly's Funfair were still packed up, the games and rides all folded up like giant kids' toys, but the man that greeted them couldn't have been more different to Gideon Slay. He was younger, in his late forties Hetty would have guessed, clean-shaven, with a face that was tanned rather than weather-beaten. He was wearing slightly-too-tight jeans and a crisp white shirt, and carrying an A4 diary and folder as he walked towards them. Hetty immediately approved.

'Hello, there. You must be Miss Colman. I'm George Wade, owner of Folly's Funfair.' They shook hands and Hetty introduced Macie. Mr Wade gave a short, sharp nod towards her, and opened his diary. 'So, you said you needed someone for Friday 23rd through to Monday 26th? The bank holiday weekend.'

'Yes, that's right. Is there any chance you can help us?' She was already impressed with his professionalism and there were no weird creaking noises from the rides this time. Although it was yet to be set up, she could see that all the rides were clean and shiny and well maintained.

Mr Wade flipped open the diary and found the relevant page. 'We're booked to be at another event, but that's with some of the newer rides.' Hetty glanced again at the rides before her and Mr Wade spotted her inquisitiveness. 'I've got some new rides joining us next week. Kids these days want the type of things you get at theme parks so some of the older ones will be retired. That's why I thought I might be able to help. Your event sounded more traditional, so you could have some of those older rides. They're all up to scratch and in full working order,' he reassured her. 'It's just that they don't make the money anymore. The kids like huge drops and rides that swing them up and down and inside out. Even the new fun house is about twice the size with more movable parts.'

'That sounds great,' Hetty replied. 'Especially if all the rides still meet all health and safety requirements.'

'Of course.' He nodded. 'I've got all the maintenance logs in here.' He pulled out the A4 folder that had been nestled under the diary and opened it to show neat and orderly records. 'When we set up we'll put up bunting to give a really traditional feel.' Hetty could have kissed him. 'So, which ones did you have in mind?'

'Well, as you say, traditional ones, ideally. I was thinking the helter-skelter, dodgems, ghost train …'

Mr Wade nodded along then detailed what he could provide,

and discussion quickly moved on to the space available. Relief flooded through Hetty in a powerful wave. No one was going to think she couldn't deliver what she'd promised. They were going to have pretty much everything she'd originally hoped for. Beside her, Macie made notes and with one disaster averted, Hetty crossed her fingers (and everything else she had) that there weren't going to be any more – either professional or personal – before the date of the festival actually arrived.

Chapter 12

'Hey, Dad,' Hetty called as she pushed the front door open. The air was slightly musty but the heavenly scent coming from her carrier bag masked it.

It had been ten days since the weird family dinner and her mum's announcement that she was leaving. Though she'd talked to her dad on the phone, Hetty had put off coming round. Partly because her evenings had been full of work, and partly because after speaking to her dad on the phone and texting each other, he had got so annoyed with her constant checking on him, he'd begun to respond in random emojis. It was a flash of the sense of humour she loved so much about her dad, but she couldn't deny she was worried about the man she'd find.

Her dad had always been a strong figure in her life. He was the one who sorted out problems with the electricity, did all the decorating, fixed things in Hetty's house when they went awry. To know he was falling apart and damaged was more hurtful than she ever imagined it could be. But she couldn't keep hiding away or forcing her feelings down and neither could he. As an only child she didn't have any siblings who could do this for her or share the responsibility, she had to do this herself. It was time to pull on her big girl pants and go and see her dad whether he wanted her there or not.

Stopping off at the best fish and chip shop on her way home from an appointment (a party booking she couldn't turn down but was going to have to squeeze in before the festival), she had bought them both dinner and was going to at least attempt to cheer him up.

'In here,' he called from the living room.

Hetty walked round the living room to find her dad, unkempt and scruffy-looking, slouched in his recliner armchair surrounded by crisp packets and pork pie wrappers. 'Dad, what are you doing?'

'Watching *Pointless*.'

'Okay, but, what's with the sea of detritus?' Her dad loved a beach clean so seeing all this litter around his feet was disturbing. If Jeff ever saw school kids littering, he'd tell them to pick up their rubbish and watch over them sternly while they did as they were told.

'Hmm?'

Hetty rolled her eyes and held up the carrier bag full of delicious-smelling fish and chips. 'I bought dinner. Haddock and chips and mushy peas. What do you think?'

A rather watery smile came to his lips and his eyes misted over a little. 'You're a good girl, Hetty. Whatever happens with me and your mum, at least we got you right.'

'Oh, Dad,' Hetty said, her voice cracking. She walked over to him and knelt down, taking his hand in hers. 'I'm sure Mum will be back soon. Has she said anything to you?'

'Not really. Only that I'm out all the time and I ignore her.'

'Do you?' She asked the question gently and he looked up into her eyes, his full face looking thinner. It was amazing how misery could have such an effect in so small amount of time. He looked drawn and desolate.

'Maybe I did a bit. But I didn't mean to.'

Trying to be subtle she asked, 'You haven't done anything else, have you?'

'Like what?'

That response and the shocked look on his face answered her question. Surely if he'd been having an affair, he'd look guilty or ashamed and try to deny it. That he had no idea what else she might be referring to was enough for her. If her mum had only plucked up the courage to come out and ask him, she might have found that out too. An uncharacteristic annoyance at her mum flared up. Hetty was sure her mum was acting how she thought right, but she couldn't help feeling it was all a bit unfair. Her dad was still looking at her, wide-eyed. 'Never mind. I'll put out the fish and chips while you clean up this mess. Then I'll put the hoover round before I go.'

They ate at the dining-room table, but it felt strangely bereft without her mum there. Even though the last family meal had been strained, it was infinitely more preferable than this silent treatment her dad was giving. It wasn't personal, Hetty knew that. Her dad smiled at her from time to time but clearly couldn't bring himself to say more than just one word at a time. Hetty found herself talking utter nonsense to fill the silence.

'Have you been cooking for yourself?' She scooped up a vine-gary chip and popped it into her mouth.

'Not really. Mrs Hobbs from across the road has been dropping in food parcels every other day. She left me a sausage casserole yesterday and a peach cobbler.'

'Was it nice?'

'Not as nice as your mum's,' he replied glumly.

Hetty gave her dad's hand a squeeze. 'I'm sure Mum will be back soon, Dad. I'll talk to her.'

Jeff suddenly brightened. 'Oh, I meant to tell you. That Marty Sutcliffe who has the breakfast show on the radio goes to the same golf club as me. He spoke to me about this food festival of yours. Asked about an interview.'

'Did he?' Hetty's excitement lightened the mood considerably. It even brought a brightness to her dad's eyes.

'Yeah. He asked if John Thornhill might want a chat about it. I said I'd pass on his number to you.'

'Oh.' Her excitement ebbed a little. She had hoped *she* might be interviewed. But publicity was publicity and the local radio station would be a great way to get word out about the festival. 'I'm sure he'd be delighted.' He wouldn't, but she'd make him.

'I'll get it after dinner.'

'Thanks, Dad.'

'These fish and chips are going down a treat.'

'Good.'

'You will talk to your mum, though, won't you, Hetty?' The bright sparkle that had flittered across his eyes a moment before had faded leaving them dark and gloomy.

'I will, Dad.' Hetty studied a chip and tried to stop her heart from breaking. It wouldn't be a great conversation, but she couldn't keep ignoring this problem, hoping it would go away or that her mum and dad would sort it out themselves. It seemed there'd been a complete communication breakdown. It was ridiculous that after all their years of marriage they'd got themselves in this situation. 'I promise, I'll speak to her on Saturday.'

They finished dinner with her dad a little chattier than he had been when she first arrived. The house was tidy again and Hetty felt reassured he wasn't going to waste away before her next visit. She had another reason to visit John too and the heart-warming effect that thought had on her was more than a little disconcerting.

Chapter 13

John shuffled in his seat and adjusted the headphones. It was incredibly hot in the small radio studio and the two desk fans plus the tall standing fan in the corner were doing nothing to help. All they did was blow the slightly sweaty-smelling warm air around.

How had he allowed Hetty to talk him into this? In reality, he knew exactly how. She'd rung him up with all that calm self-assurance she was blessed with and talked incessantly about the publicity benefits until he'd caved. Of course, he'd pleaded that she do the interview instead, but apparently, they only wanted him, which in his eyes was both stupid and a missed opportunity. Hetty Colman was the poster child for strong businesswomen everywhere. Who better to speak about the food festival than the woman whose idea it had been and had the vision and work ethic to see it come to life?

Glancing at her on the other side of the glass screen, he had an inkling that she was a bit miffed they were asking for him rather than her. She gave him a smile and a thumbs-up, but the smile didn't shine in her eyes like it normally did. She really was extraordinarily pretty. She was standing, confidently holding a folder, and as she chatted to the producer, she pushed up her glasses. It was a small, unconscious action but one that made his chest tighten.

John had told her he'd be happy not to do the interview, but she'd insisted it was too good an opportunity to miss even if they were choosing to speak to the oily rag rather than the engine grinder. John had laughed then and knowing her joking hid a deeper hurt, he'd thought about putting his arm around her, but couldn't quite bring his muscles to work in case she batted him away. His feelings for her were becoming stronger and he wasn't quite sure how to handle them.

'All ready, Mr Thornhill? We'll be on in two minutes. As soon as T'Pau have finished.'

'I really think you should be talking to my …' *Friend? Colleague? Love interest? Wait, what?* John told himself to calm down. He was clearly nervous about the interview. 'I really think you should be talking to Hetty. This was all her idea and she's actually the one who convinced me that—'

'Hang on,' he replied, shooting out a hand. 'We can talk about all of this in a second.'

Marty Sutcliffe, the radio presenter, who had slicked back hair and a weaselly face, pressed some buttons with one hand, while the other still hung in the air, palm facing John. John was very tempted to push it away. The way the man had dismissed Hetty as John's assistant the moment they'd arrived in the studio had annoyed him greatly. Marty began to talk into the microphone in one of those late-night DJ voices.

'Welcome back to Brekky with Marty. That was T'Pau with their classic tune, "China in Your Hand". Now—' Behind the microphone he clasped his hands together. 'I'm sure you guys have heard all about the Swallowtail Bay Food Festival being held over the bank holiday weekend. Well, today, I'm really pleased to be joined by festival organiser, John Thornhill.'

A horrible tingle shot up and down the length of John's spine. He glanced at Hetty, whose forehead was creased as she frowned.

'So, Mr Thornhill – John – or is it Lord Thornhill?' Marty's head was tipped to the side like the microphone was attached to his nose and would fall off if he moved back an inch.

Oh, for the love of … 'Just John,' he said, trying to smile. Hetty had told him you could hear a smile in someone's voice, and he was to smile no matter what. It was incredibly unnatural for John whose face always formed a frown, and he worried it would make him look like a nutter. Whatever the outcome for his face, he couldn't look any crazier than Hetty who was currently reminding him what to do by smiling like a loon and pointing to her cheeks. It had the desired effect though as he swallowed down the laugh she'd brought on.

'John, can you tell me why you decided to open up Thornhill Hall and host a food festival. What made you think of it?'

'I can't take any credit really. It's all down to a local business-woman called Hetty Colman. It was her idea and she who convinced me to host it. We're very excited at Thornhill Hall to welcome everyone, it's going to be a fabulous weekend with lots to see, taste and do.' Hetty had told him to get that line in and he was glad he'd remembered to do it.

As Marty nodded at him, John glanced at Hetty and she gave him another thumbs-up. Now her smile was genuine, and he could feel the warmth through the glass, like a warming sun through a window.

'So,' Marty continued, nose still pressed against the micro-phone. 'Are you hosting the food festival because of the financial stress your father put you all under?'

The question blindsided him, and John felt his hands clench. 'I'm sorry?'

'I mean, it's quite well known that your father, Robert—'

'Rupert,' John corrected. He couldn't believe this man was going to publicly embarrass his father and he hadn't even both-ered to get his name right.

'Yes, Rupert, sorry. It's quite well known that your father isn't exactly gifted with financial prowess.' Marty seemed very pleased at the use of two grown-up words. 'Is it true that this food festival is so you can make some money to save your home?'

John bit down on the inside of his lip, forcing his mouth to stay closed. Every nerve in his body told him to get up out of his seat and walk out. To pull these headphones off and throw them at the smug-faced idiot. For a fleeting second, he wondered if Hetty knew he'd do this and had set him up, but he dismissed the thought immediately; that was just age-old paranoia forcing itself back in. No, he knew she would never do something like this to him. She was honest, upfront – genuine.

When his eyes met hers, it was like a secret signal passed between them. He knew she was appalled too, but the look in her eye was pleading for him to keep it together, even though she glared at Marty Sutcliffe like she wanted to march into the studio and lump him in the chops. But she'd been right that this was a good publicity opportunity and he wouldn't blow it for her by losing his temper. They both needed the food festival to succeed and he wouldn't undo all her hard work now because of some idiot DJ who thought he could make a bit of a splash with his own lukewarm version of a hard-hitting interview.

Taking a deep breath and unclenching his jaw before it cramped, John remembered to smile. 'Swallowtail Bay Food Festival is a fabulous idea that's going to benefit every trader and every resident. The bank holiday weekend always attracts additional tourists and we're hopeful that with the amazing food stalls we've got, people will also enjoy the funfair, the movie night, and the local awards, and have an amazing weekend. There really is something for everyone and at Thornhill Hall, we couldn't be happier to support this event. I really hope to see everyone there.'

To Marty's shock, John stood up and began removing his headphones. John was aware of a slight muffling of his microphone, but quite frankly couldn't have cared less.

'Right – umm – well, thank you, John Thornhill. It's been a

pleasure speaking to you this morning.' Before he'd even finished the sentence, John closed the door softly behind him and led Hetty from the building.

As they stood outside the radio station, a unit on a new industrial estate near Halebury, John watched Hetty pace back and forth. 'I can't believe what an idiot that man was. I mean, who did he think he was, Jeremy Paxman? Why did he think he could speak to you like that? It's appalling. I've got half a mind to go back in there and complain.'

John felt his short-cropped hair beneath his fingers then ran them down his beard. 'Hetty, it's fine. Just forget about it.'

She stopped and looked at him. 'But aren't you annoyed?'

He shrugged. 'Yes, but it happens all the time. It still hurts but I've learned to ignore it.' That wasn't quite true, he did find it hard to ignore it and sometimes things really did get under his skin. He'd done well to not let it this time.

'Does it really happen all the time?'

'More than you'd think. Often when I take on new clients they like to mention it. They've got money to burn and it makes some of them feel better to remind me that I've got none and need their custom.'

Hetty tilted her head to one side. 'That's horrible.'

'It is what it is.'

Hetty angrily jabbed her finger around as she spoke, her cheeks growing pinker from the force of her response. 'You do know that if I'd known he was going to do that I'd have said no to the interview.'

'I know.'

She stopped her pacing and looked up at him. The sun shone on her face, illuminating her creamy skin and he noticed for the first time a faint smudgy blue under her eyes. She'd tried to cover it, but she looked a little more tired today. It wasn't any of his business, but it worried him. Something strange happened then that he couldn't quite understand when he ran over the facts of it later. He took a half-step towards her, closing the space between them. He wasn't close enough to kiss her, though he wanted to. But it was almost as if something was connecting them together, bonding them to each other in some way.

'I'd better get going,' Hetty said quickly. 'I've got an anniversary party to run tonight and I need to get to the venue and set up.'

He took a pace back, the spell broken. 'Sure.'

'I'll be in touch if anything else comes up before the festival, but everything's under control at the moment.'

'I never doubted it for a second.'

As they'd come in separate cars, Hetty waved goodbye and headed off to Myrtle. John watched her go, his heart heavy. He didn't know when he was going to see her again and he didn't like that uncertainty one bit.

Chapter 14

Shielding her eyes from the glare of the sun, Daisy squinted at the dress in the shop window. 'What do you think to this one?'

'It's a bit short, Mum.' The dress, an off-the-shoulder number, would have barely covered her thighs and though her mum still had a great figure, there was only so much Hetty wanted her showing off.

'Yes, I suppose you're right.'

Hetty hated clothes shopping but there hadn't been anything on at the local theatre or the cinema that they wanted to see, so had settled on a trip to Halebury. It had a big shopping precinct and more bars and restaurants than you could possibly ever eat in, even if you lived there and ate out every night. Her loathing of clothes shopping didn't come from the fact her curvy figure was considered plus-size, that didn't bother her in the slightest. She knew perfectly well what suited her and what didn't, and if she was one size in one shop and another size in another, that was the shops' fault, not hers. She couldn't have cared less if something came from a charity shop or a big-name designer. She liked what she liked and wore what she wore. The thing Hetty hated about clothes shopping was the endless traipsing around, going back and forth in the busy precinct, dodging people who were in a rush and getting too hot and sweaty to actually try anything on. She much preferred shopping online and trying things on in her bedroom. 'Plus, it's not exactly everyday wear is it? Are you shopping for something special?'

'No, just seeing what's about,' Daisy answered. Hetty had hoped it might enable her mum to confess something, if she had anything to confess. Now she was sure her dad hadn't had an affair it had raised the question of whether her mum was the one looking to get out of the marriage to start something new with someone else. 'And I don't suppose your dad would notice if I did wear it. I think I could walk downstairs completely naked in nothing but a smile and all he'd do is ask me to put the kettle on.'

Hetty paused at the idea of her mum naked because her brain had conjured up an image she didn't want to see. Realising she had stopped in the doorway, she moved out of the way and mumbled an apology to the family behind her.

It had been two weeks since her mum had moved out. The idea that she'd sought the advice of a solicitor still sat heavily in Hetty's heart and she hoped to learn more about where things stood today. 'I went to see Dad the other day.'

Daisy's head shot up. 'Did you?' Hetty nodded. In a completely unconvincing way, her mum fiddled with some clothes and tried to act like she didn't care. 'How is he?'

'Not great. He misses you. And he doesn't understand what's going on. He seems to be living on pork pies since you left—'

'I didn't want to leave, you know.' Though Daisy spoke harshly it ignited a spark of hope for Hetty.

'Pork pies and food deliveries from Mrs Hobbs.'

'Mrs Hobbs?' The outrage in her mum's voice almost made Hetty laugh. 'What sort of food deliveries?'

'He said she delivered a sausage casserole the other day and a peach cobbler.'

'Oh.' Daisy's shoulders tensed, pulling her straighter.

'Dad said they weren't as nice as yours.'

'I should think not.'

Hetty could tell her words had the desired effect because although her mum was pretending to examine a piece of clothing, there was no way she was actually looking at the tiny body suit in front of her. Especially as it had massive cut away sections that would put a nipple on display if you bent the wrong way.

'Mum, why do you think Dad's been having an affair? You said you had your reasons, but you haven't actually told me what they are. Has he received weird text messages? Have you smelt another woman's perfume? Found lipstick marks?'

Daisy shuffled the clothes on the rail. 'No. But over the last six months he's been out all the time. He hardly stays in the house unless he's in the garden talking to his plants. Honestly, he speaks to his buddleias more than he talks to me. And then there's the so-called golfing.'

'So-called?'

Her mum assessed another dress then almost broke the hanger as she hooked it back up in annoyance. She looked at Hetty, her face filled with hurt. 'Or maybe when he says he's out golfing he's seeing someone else.'

Hetty cocked her head to one side. 'Who?'

'I don't know. Someone.'

'So you have no actual proof and you don't know who it might be?' Hetty asked gently. She didn't want to sound accusatory, but she needed to know what was driving her mum to such a severe course of action that was tearing her dad apart. 'And your reason for thinking it is that he's been out a lot?' Her mum looked up and Hetty quickly said, 'I'm not having a go, Mum. I just want to know what's going on.'

Daisy blinked slowly and took a deep breath. 'He barely notices my existence anymore, love. For the first six months of retirement we were together all the time, visiting places, going for coffee, chatting and now – oh, never mind.' She finished with a sigh. 'I don't want to talk about this now. How are things with you?'

They stood together searching the sale rail, but Hetty couldn't let it drop. 'Please talk to Dad about it. You have to let him know how you feel and what you think because I don't think he's having an affair and I'm pretty sure the idea has never even occurred to him.'

'I have tried to talk to him about ignoring me, but he never listens. He just asks if we can talk about it later because he's watching *Countryfile*.'

'Maybe don't talk to him when *Countryfile*'s on?' Hetty suggested helpfully.

Daisy stopped her examination of a pair of boring beige trousers and narrowed her eyes. 'It was just an example, Hetty.'

'I know. But have you asked him if he's been having an affair? I mean, that's a pretty big deal, Mum. And I honestly don't think he has. He loves you too much.' Daisy stroked the fabric, gently pressing it between her fingers. 'Mum?'

The worst thing about this whole situation was being in the middle. She knew her mum wasn't deliberately making her life difficult, it was the downside of them being able to talk so freely to each other, but it did add an extra layer of guilt to Hetty's already worried mind.

'And if Dad hasn't had an affair, and you've just stopped communicating, he might genuinely not realise how much he's been annoying you.'

'By now he blimmin' well should know.' Daisy suddenly stopped and held her daughter's gaze. 'Now I've walked out he knows I'm not happy and instead of asking me what's wrong and trying to sort it out, he's putting his head in the sand and hoping that one morning I'll just waltz back in and put the eggs on to boil.'

'But Mum—'

'Nope, I don't want to talk about it anymore.' She held up her hand to silence her daughter. 'You're getting me all worked up and I'm hot enough as it is with this weather and my menopause.

I've really looked forward to our shopping trip seeing as you've been so busy. I've hardly seen you. So, let's not talk about it anymore. How are things with you?'

'Oh, fine,' Hetty lied.

Truth be told, she was stressed up to the eyeballs trying to get everything ready for the food festival and her brain just wouldn't stop thinking about the two men in her life. It was all very well when she was busy during the day, desperately trying to get through her to-do list, but in the evening, when she finally kicked back and tried to relax, it was almost impossible to stop her brain from replaying Ben's kiss, or thinking about John. She gave a confident smile to hide her worries.

'I've got the St John Ambulance coming, to be on hand in case anything happens, and I've got a load of volunteer stewards too. People can't wait to get involved which is great, but I've got a lot left to do. What about this one?' she asked as they reached a different rail and she pointed at an entirely inappropriate dress more suited to a member of Little Mix than her middle-aged mum. Daisy eyed it then stared at Hetty.

'I'm not even going to justify that with an answer. I like that navy top for you though. It'll look lovely with your dungarees when it gets a bit cooler.'

'That's what I thought.'

'I'm glad you're not worrying about certain people bad-mouthing the festival,' her mum said, picking up a wrap dress.

Hetty stopped examining the top. 'Wait, what?'

'Didn't you know?'

'No! Who's been saying what?' This was the last thing she needed on top of everything else.

Her mum glanced around and gestured for her to calm down. Her voice must have been rising without her noticing. 'I saw Gwen in town the other day and she was moaning on about it, saying it was never going to work. But we know she's wrong, don't we? You just have to ignore the nasties.'

Hetty was absolutely gobsmacked. She knew Gwen had reservations but to go around moaning about the festival was just mean-spirited. After all, she'd hated it when it was nothing more than a jumble sale at the church hall, how could she hate it now it was going to be something big and massive that would help the whole of the town?

Daisy carried on talking. 'John did well at that interview though, didn't he? I always liked that Marty Sutcliffe but that was all a bit below the belt if you ask me.'

'He did do well. I was very proud of him.'

Hetty had been so upset on his behalf it had scared her. She shouldn't be feeling anything on his behalf, but there he was, in her thoughts more and more. And when he wasn't there, Ben was. Laid-back, chilled-out, cheeky Ben who had been her everything and was the complete opposite of stern, defensive John. Ben who wanted her back – and she was so sorely tempted to go, to feel part of a couple again. To be with the man she had loved so much for so long.

'Come on,' said her mum. 'What are you thinking about? You're screwing your face up like a bulldog sucking a wasp. What's going on in that head of yours?'

'Well, apart from now wanting to tell Gwen exactly where she can stick her scissors, I'm thinking I've got enough on my plate with Be—' She was just about to let slip about Ben but pulled back in time. She desperately wanted to tell her mum about the kiss and that he wanted to get back together, but she didn't think Daisy could cope with the stress right now. And Hetty couldn't face going through all the details.

'With?'

'Business. I was going to say business. Oh, don't worry, Mum. It doesn't matter.' She waved it away, keeping her voice light. 'Just festival stuff. Too boring to talk about now.'

Hooking the dress back onto the rail, Daisy said, 'Come on. I know what we need.'

'And what's that?' asked Hetty. 'A shop that sells clothing for people with waists and thighs and tummies?'

'Prosecco and lunch. My treat.'

'Now, that's a good idea.'

***

After nearly letting slip about Ben, Hetty decided enough was enough. Not normally one to take Macie's – or anyone else's – relationship advice, Hetty took a detour and pulled up on the seafront. Her nerves were wriggling around in her stomach and not even the happy laugh of children on the beach, or the calm lapping of the tide could stop them. Despite her better judgement telling her to go back home, she was here in Swallowtail Bay, walking towards Ben's shop, hoping to talk to him before the end of the day. She did think about stopping by Snip-It's and giving Gwen a good talking-to, but she didn't have time right now.

In a bid to get her mind off men and completely focused on the final preparations for the food festival, she'd decided to ask Ben if he meant what he said. Once she knew that, she could put all the feelings away again until after the bank holiday weekend.

Hetty had already planned the conversation. She'd take Ben to one side and just ask him directly if he meant all that he'd said the other night, trusting her ability to read the reaction in his face. She didn't want to be romantic about this. She needed to stay detached and let her head make the decision rather than her heart. Her heart had told her to stay with Ben in the hope that he would eventually make more of an effort with their relationship and it had never happened. Her heart could definitely not be trusted. Her head was the thing for *this* job.

The aroma of baked bread and sweet, sugary cakes hit her as she entered the shop. It was late afternoon and as expected they were selling the last few things and the place was virtually empty. People came to his shop from the surrounding villages, arriving early in the morning knowing that his best recipes would be sold out by lunch time. He'd often only be open till mid-afternoon, sometimes closing even earlier. She was happy his business was so successful. It was just a shame he hadn't shown the same level of commitment to their relationship. 'Hey, gorgeous,' Ben said, beaming. 'I didn't expect to see you.'

'Hi, Ben. Have you got time for a walk when you're done?' The squirming in her tummy was making her feel sick. His wide, carefree grin brought a sparkle to his eyes. They were so attractive Hetty averted her gaze to a lonely bread roll.

'Sure. Just give me ten minutes, okay?'

'Okay, I'll wait outside.'

Hetty left and sat on the bench a little way down the high street. All around, the town was busy. Even the high street, a few roads back from the promenade, was full of residents hurrying about while tourists took a more leisurely approach to the afternoon. The hum of the sea in the background was still evident over the chatter and laughter coming from the groups of people sitting under the striped awnings of the cafés. Hetty watched pigeons fight for crumbs and counted the clouds in the sky, anything to keep her brain occupied. It was the longest ten minutes of her life. Eventually he came out, his shirt covered in dashes of flour, and she resisted the urge to brush them off. Ben gave her a kiss on the cheek and they strolled back towards the seafront where Hetty had parked Myrtle.

'So, to what do I owe the honour of this invitation? Let me guess, you're ready to let me back into your heart and you want us to go away for the weekend as soon as this food festival of yours is all done?' Stepping in front of her, he gently placed his hands on her waist and drew her in for a kiss.

Caught up in the moment, Hetty let him, then pulled back. She had to stop him kissing her like that. It made the hairs on the back of her neck stand on end. And she didn't want him kissing her in public yet. At least until she was sure they were giving it another go. 'Not exactly, Ben.' She gently pushed him away. 'But I do need to talk to you about what you said the other night.'

They continued walking and were soon on the seafront. The sea breeze blew a gentle whisper onto her face but feeling the heat of the afternoon and the heat of Ben's cheeky grin hinting at all they'd been and done together, Hetty turned to face the sea. Seagulls were noisily chatting overhead and the calm silver water barely moved. Being direct was the best way with Ben – it didn't give him the chance to charm his way out of things – so she said, 'Ben, when you turned up the other night it was …'

'Wonderful? Amazing? Incredible?'

'Confusing. We were so in love, Ben, but you were never ready to take us to the next level. For so long I felt like I was stuck in limbo with you and it broke my heart to leave.' Ben took her hand rubbing it gently with his thumb. He turned her to him and cupped her face, to ensure their eyes met.

'I know how stupid I've been, Hetty. You don't have to tell me.'

'I just really want to believe you, but I don't know if I can.'

'You can, Hetty. You can.' He kissed her again so even her bones felt the intense emotion.

'How will this time be different though? I know you think you mean what you say, you always do when you're saying it, but it's after, Ben—'

'As soon as this food festival's over, I'll show you. I know you don't want to do anything now. I know you inside and out, Hetty. But when this is over, I'll show you the ring I've bought you.'

'You've what?' Ben's hand suddenly felt heavy on her face and her lungs were heavy.

His eyes searched hers. 'I knew you wouldn't believe just words, Hetty. And I don't blame you. But I need you to know how serious I am about this – about you – about us.'

Hetty's heart felt like it was swelling. 'Are you serious?'

'As a heart attack.' She might just have one, the way her heart currently felt. It filled up all the room in her chest and had forgotten how to work properly. 'When we move in together – your place or mine, I don't mind, I know how much you love the cottage – we can start making plans.'

She covered his hand with hers and removed it, feeling the need for space. 'Ben, this is all so much. It's too soon.'

'After ten years?' He laughed. 'That's ironic.'

He had a point, but he'd forgotten about the last six months and she hadn't. Maybe she needed to as well. If their split had been the catalyst for Ben to realise what they'd had, maybe it would just become part of a funny story they told their grandkids. Ben reached his hand up into her hair and eased her towards him for another kiss, but she stepped away. Her body was a whirlpool of emotions all churning round and round.

'Let's go to yours and go to bed.'

'You can go back to your own house, Benjamin, and your own bed. I've got work to do this afternoon. And I really should be getting back now.'

'Fair enough,' he said, stepping forward and kissing her cheek, sending a flutter over her skin. 'But you're killing me, here, Hetty. You know that.'

'You'll survive.' His hands dropped from her hair as she moved to go back to her car.

'You'd better not be spending time with John Thornhill when you could be spending time with me.'

'Don't be silly, Ben,' she replied with a prickle of annoyance. 'I'm just tired.'

'Okay. But as soon as this is all over, we're talking, all right? But I'll wait. For now.'

His words shot into her heart and brain. 'Okay.' The response didn't seem enough, but there was nothing else to say. She climbed into Myrtle and with shaking hands drove straight back to her cottage, her brow furrowing at the car already parked there.

Hetty haphazardly pulled into a space and quickly climbed

out of the car. There was a man waiting on her doorstep and his handsome face broke into a smile as she exited. 'John, what are you doing here?'

After the stress of seeing Ben just now, there shouldn't be any emotion left, but here she was having a reaction to seeing John again. Her breath seized as he turned to face her. Perhaps it was just a sensation leftover from seeing Ben. She hadn't thought she'd see him till the start of the festival. A lot of the organisation that was left required her on her own, negotiating deals, rounding up volunteers, and thanks to his stint on the radio she was inundated with requests to help.

'Ah, Hetty, I hope I'm not disturbing you?' He scratched the back of his head and seemed almost nervous.

'No. Not all, what can I do for you?'

On the doorstep, John shifted his weight from one foot to the other. 'Oh, I was wondering if you'd thought about ...' He hesitated as if he wasn't sure himself what he was doing there. 'Generators.'

Hetty blinked. 'Generators?'

'For the food festival.'

'Yes, I know you meant the food festival.' She hadn't meant to sound rude, but she was incredibly confused. At her sharp tone John dropped his eyes to the ground and guilt stabbed its way inside. Hetty adjusted her glasses. 'Umm, yes I have thought about them. I've got quite a few on order actually. They'll be delivered the Thursday before the festival when we set up. The funfair's providing their own. Sorry, I thought I told you.'

'Ah, yes. I think perhaps you did. Spectacular.' He said it a little too loudly and Hetty was rather surprised by his over-enthusiastic outburst. She spotted a faint pinkness on his neck. 'I should have known you'd have thought of it already. Well, I'll leave you to it. Good afternoon.'

John began to walk back to his car. The easy atmosphere they'd enjoyed together before now had disappeared. He'd seemed so stilted and contained yet not quite as gruff as the man she'd met at first. 'Is there anything else you wanted to ask me, John?'

'Umm, no, that's fine,' he replied, just reaching his car and opening the door. 'Goodbye.'

Hetty slowly unlocked her front door, trying to understand what had just happened. Had he really come all the way down from his big house and into the bay just to ask her about generators? He could have rung, or texted, or emailed. He'd said himself how the Thornhills tried to stay away from town as much as possible. Why hadn't he done any of those things? Her eyes stayed on his car as it wove its way down the busy main road that ran parallel to the sea. Closing the door, she played with the car keys in her hand. Why had he turned up on her doorstep behaving so oddly, and why did she feel like she'd let him down somehow?

Chapter 15

Five days after their last awkward meeting, John stood at the edge of the formal gardens watching the flurry of activity in the four fields Hetty Colman had convinced him to provide. She was a force to be reckoned with and totally unlike any woman he'd ever met. Every time he saw her, he was impressed by her focus, but there was also something warm about her. She was kind of kooky and unusual and he liked that. Over the last few weeks, he'd felt his guard dropping and a strange freedom to relax in her company.

Which was why he'd impulsively turned up on her doorstep last Saturday, wanting nothing more than to chat to her, spend time with her. But as soon as she'd climbed out of her car, nerves fiercer than he'd ever felt before charged up from his stomach, strangling his brain. He'd clammed up, asking a ridiculous question about generators. *Generators!* It wasn't exactly a sexy topic. No wonder she'd looked so utterly confused. And, of course she'd have it all organised. To his utter embarrassment she had mentioned it to him and now it looked like he hadn't listened. And why had he said spectacular in such a weird way? He sounded like a boy going through puberty. He'd never felt such a fool and considering the incident with the landing ceiling, that was saying something. The burn of humiliation rose up the back of his neck and he shuddered at the memory. He was definitely not a spur-of-the-moment kind of guy.

A soft tread signalled the arrival of his assistant and before long, Jaz was at his elbow. She stared out at the fields alongside him. 'Miss Colman seems quite at home, doesn't she?' Slightly taken aback by her words, John glanced over. Her face was tight, and she seemed almost angry, an emotion he'd never seen her express before. 'She's marching about like she owns the place.'

'She needs to be organised and in control, otherwise it'll be chaos. There are a lot of people relying on her to make everything work. Including us,' he added.

Her eyes remained forward. 'She just seems very comfortable on *your* land. Doing whatever *she* wants.'

'It's not quite like that, Jaz. She does have a … natural authority, I suppose.'

'How are you feeling about the weekend?' Her tone was flat and her hands tightened around the notepad clutched to her chest.

'Fine. Nervous, maybe. This could be good for us.' An almost inaudible snort escaped his assistant. He'd never seen her react like this to anyone and some of their customers could be quite a challenge when they wanted to be. 'You really don't like her, do you?'

'Like I said, I don't mind her either way,' she replied with a light-hearted laugh, but John knew her well enough to know this wasn't true. 'I just think she's just a bit over the top.'

John gave a small nod acknowledging her opinion but not necessarily sharing it, and they both stared off into the distance. Suddenly, there it was again – that tension in the air as if someone had put up a wall of concrete between them.

Over the last few weeks their relationship had become, at times, awkward. The whole beard-stroking incident had made John wary that Jaz was getting a little too fond of him. It wasn't that he thought himself a catch and that it was only natural she should fancy him, quite the opposite in fact. He didn't have much to offer anyone. But there'd been moments recently when she'd been what he considered over-friendly, even flirty. In order to keep their relationship strictly business, he'd overcompensate and bark out orders, being too harsh. Now John was worried he'd made Jaz so unhappy she was going to leave.

A few nights ago, he'd had a strange dream in which the ceiling of the study collapsed, pouring in a flood of paperwork and he'd drowned, unable to swim through it to the door. His subconscious was clearly telling him something. He'd woken shivering in the breeze from the open window and felt the light sheen of sweat dry on his torso. Normally, John would have ignored a dream like that, but the next morning he'd convinced himself it was caused by the worry that his and Jaz's steady, business-like relationship was changing, and that she might not stick around if he kept being grumpy. He'd really come to value her and her skills and was determined to get her something as a thank-you for all her hard work, not to mention her dedication to him and his family. He just needed to figure out what.

Jaz once again adjusted her grip on the diary and notepad in her hands. 'You've been dreading this weekend, haven't you?' John repressed the urge to correct her.

'I wouldn't say dreading it. It'll be different, that's all. And it could make us some real money. That hole in the east wing roof really needs fixing before winter. And though I've requested a loan from the bank, they're taking their time to decide.' He glanced back at the house over his shoulder.

'Not to mention that we need to fix the landing ceiling,' she teased.

'Yeah, that too.' He grinned. 'It's Mother who's my main worry this weekend.'

'I'll make sure she's fine. No one should be coming up to the house. And as long as she sticks to the grounds, she won't come across anyone. I'll keep an eye out for any wanderers.' From the corner of his eye he saw her turn towards him.

'Are you sure about working this weekend?' Jaz had kindly volunteered to help with any food festival problems. He really didn't deserve her. 'You really don't have to. I don't expect you to be here.'

'I know I'm paid out of Thornhill Antiques, but I'm *your* assistant.' She met his gaze and gave him an easy smile. She really deserved much more patience than he'd shown her recently. 'If you want me here to help, I'm happy to come. Besides, I was going to book a long holiday to Mexico when things slow down and I need the extra days of leave.'

John chuckled. 'Just mark the dates in the diary. Whenever you want time off is fine. I'm sure I'll manage while you're away. I'll just leave everything in a big pile until you get back.' Her mouth fell open in surprise and she giggled.

John's phone rang in his pocket and he fished it out, scanning the horizon again. In the lower field he caught sight of the statuesque figure of Hetty Colman striding about in bright blue trainers, rather than purple-spotted Wellington boots. She was only wearing jeans and a long T-shirt but with her short-cropped hair and glasses she looked cute. He hadn't thought about romance in a long time. His heart had been too closed off with his own business and then his family's worries. But Hetty entered his thoughts with increasing regularity. The shrill ringing brought him back to reality and he saw it was Felix. For some reason he glanced back at the house again. Felix should have been at work.

'Hey, Felix, everything okay?'

'John, are you in the grounds?' Felix's blunt and to-the-point sentences were so much like John's own, that it irritated him when he heard them, probably because it reminded him of his own failings. This time there was a different edge to Felix's voice, something more – John braced his jaw.

John scanned the windows for Felix but couldn't see him. 'I was watching them set up the food festival. Why?'

'Can you see Father?'

John hadn't seen him all morning. As usual he'd pecked at some breakfast placed in front of him by Lucinda, and then disappeared into the grounds. John was beginning to think it was time they called a doctor. They'd always assumed his father's problems were brought on by stress and worry, but now John was beginning to wonder if it was medical. The thought there might be something wrong with his father's brain made him feel sick. Even worse was the thought they had ignored it for so long. And if it was more a psychological problem, maybe therapy would help. His mother wouldn't want to face either possibility, and John had decided to wait until after the festival to mention it. If he did it now, she'd have a panic attack. She'd been steadfast for a long time, but the strain was beginning to show. John checked around again for sight of his father. 'Umm, no, he's not out this way. He's probably in the secret garden.'

'Get him and bring him into the house, will you? I need to talk to you all.'

'Why? What's happened?'

'Just get him, will you?' Felix was growing bossier and ruder by the day. He'd always had a tendency to take over, but it was getting worse. Right now, his voice was so much the authoritative big brother, John had to bite the inside of his cheek to let it slide. 'I'll speak to you all together.'

'Okay. Fine.' John scowled at his phone and placed it back in his pocket. This was all very odd. Felix should have been at work and he sounded tense. Maybe another bill had come in that John hadn't seen, or perhaps Felix had received a call about one of the final demands. Whatever it was, John needed to find his father and meet them inside.

'Everything okay?' asked Jaz.

'Not sure.' He paused for a moment and peered around.

'That was Felix, wasn't it?' Seeing John's concerned gaze, she moved beside him and laid a hand gently on his forearm. 'Are you sure there's nothing I can do?'

Her touch was like a static shock, triggering a warning in his brain again. 'It's fine,' he barked and as Jaz virtually jumped back, he knew he'd overreacted again. 'Have you seen Father this morning?'

Jaz shook her head. 'Do you want me to look for him?'

'No, I think I know where he is. Can you get some draft responses done to those queries we talked about yesterday and I'll check them later? It'd be good to get those off the to-do list today before the madness descends.' She nodded making a note on her pad. 'I'll find us something nice for lunch as a thank-you.' Jaz's eyes lit up.

Things would be back to normal between them soon enough, he reassured himself as he strode off to the back of the house and the secret garden. He just needed to let her know how valued she was and stop snapping at her all the time.

Walking back through the formal gardens, John noticed how messy they were becoming. The topiary animals were more like *Doctor Who* monsters, and the grass needed a cut. Last year, his father had become so upset about the state of the tall privet hedges John had agreed to hire someone in for a couple of days to straighten them up. He should have seen that as a warning sign that his father needed help. He expelled a deep breath, hoping to exorcise some of the guilt with it.

As he came to the front of the house, John glanced up and took a moment to appreciate its beauty. Sometimes he was so caught up in all the work it entailed he didn't get a chance to really admire it and all it meant. The house had been in his family for generations and, like his parents, he wanted it to stay that way. Even though it was a pain, the wisteria made the house look like something from a fairy tale when it bloomed in spring, and even in the winter the vines wrapped the house like a protective hand. The trouble was, John realised, he only saw Thornhill Hall's faults these days. Too caught up in work of one type or another.

Gravel shifted underfoot as he stepped off the lawn and onto the turning circle, passing the edge where Hetty had parked over a month ago. A spark of excitement started in his chest at the idea of the food festival. He was looking forward to it and hoped he'd get a chance to speak to Hetty again to make up for the weird generator conversation.

Smelling the sweet scent of roses on the air, he entered the rose garden and strolled through it to a high flint stone wall that marked its boundary, and a tall wooden gate. The paving was uneven where the plants were growing underneath and forcing their way up. Another thing they'd have to have fixed if they were ever to open the house to the public or they'd face a lawsuit should someone fall over. So far, there was no sign of his father, but the secret garden had become his sanctuary.

John still loved it as much as he had as a child when he and Felix would play together for hours and hours. There'd been family picnics in the summertime made by his mother. And in the winter, when the colours faded and the weather grew cold, it was the perfect place for him to build dens.

The secret garden was a long oblong, enclosed by the sturdy tall flint stone wall heavily coated in green from the plants that had been left to do what they will. Here and there, specks of the black flint poked out among the different types of flowers. Honeysuckle grew down one end, tumbling into a corner and near the gate where he had entered, roses scrambled towards the floor. In the gaps of the same worn, uneven paving stones, tufts of grass grew upwards, reaching towards the sun. A huge oak tree, tall and magnificent, grew in the corner, providing some welcome shade from the hot summer sun. Rupert was underneath it, on all fours, pruning a plant that had managed to grow behind the great wide trunk. He could see why his father found comfort here. The whole place gave a sense of remoteness and serenity.

'Father,' John called loudly, his voice penetrating the peace and quiet. Rupert looked up and smiled at his son. He had a kind, oval face, wrinkled heavily and pink from the weather. John suddenly noticed that his father's clothes were hanging looser. He hadn't realised his father had lost weight. 'Felix wants us all at the house. He said he needs to talk to us about something.' Rupert stood, his face contorting into a pained and panicked expression, which tugged at John's heart. His poor father had been blamed for so much by all of them and they had been so unfair.

In the immediate aftermath of the fire, when the dire situation became clear, they'd all shouted and screamed at their father. His mother had shrieked and cried. Angered that Rupert had ignored both his and Felix's advice, they too had vented their spleens, leaving Rupert in no doubt that he was entirely to blame for everything. John remembered shamefully that he had even told Rupert that he could never forgive him for the pain he'd caused his mother. Even now, after copious apologies, the shame still reached down his back, burning him.

'Oh, right. Well – I guess I'd better – shall I just—' With jerky movements he stepped one way and then another, finally dropping the pruning shears he'd been holding.

John motioned for him to come. 'I'm sure it's nothing serious, Father. And if it is, we'll deal with it together.' As Rupert reached him, John put his arm around his shoulders and began to guide him towards the house.

'I do hope it's nothing – did he say …'

They exited the secret garden and took the direct route through the rose garden to the back of the house. 'I'm sure it's nothing too serious, Father,' John said again, but he didn't believe it. Felix's tone had been even more offhand than usual.

'I know that I've …' He didn't finish the sentence, letting the words fall behind them as they moved onwards.

'Please, Father, don't worry. I promise whatever it is I'll sort it. Okay?'

They reached the steps and through one of the windows John could see Felix staring out. He smiled, but his brother's face was forbidding. John's worries ramped up a notch and when he led them inside and opened the door to the parlour, Felix was still standing by the large sash window with his back to the room. Lucinda sat primly on the sofa. She'd never been one for jeans and T-shirts and the floral pattern of her dress almost matched the chintzy sofa she was perched on. Rupert went and sat next to her. She took his hand in hers, resting it on her lap.

Taking the air of authority he always did, Felix rolled his shoulders back and marched to the middle of the room. In front of the grand marble fireplace, he said, 'Thanks for finding Father, John.' But the look on Felix's face wiped out all hints of John's good humour and instead his stomach knotted tighter. Felix was grave and stern as the light shone in through the windows highlighting the drabness of the room. 'I wanted you all here because I have something to tell you.'

As Felix tugged down the front of his suit jacket, John checked his hand for a wedding ring, worried that he was going to announce he and Elizabeth were getting divorced. But the ring was still there, and his feeling of dread heightened. It must be about the family's finances. Felix cleared his throat and continued. 'This morning I invested as much of the family's money as possible in the investment my friend told us about.'

Anger electrified John's muscles making him stand. 'You've done what?'

'I think you heard perfectly well,' Felix replied, lifting his chin. 'John, this is a good chance for us to make some real money. You can't always play it safe—'

'How could you, Felix? You knew I disagreed with this. When everything first happened we agreed we'd make decisions together.'

'Well, we couldn't agree in this case, so I made the decision for us both. This is a sound investment. It's all about timing the market. In at the bottom, out at the top.' His hand jabbed the air first low then higher up. 'A lot of profit if we time everything right and I'm confident my friend won't lead us astray. I met with the investment company and I'm confident in them too.'

John ran a hand through his hair and placed one on his hip. Lucinda watched on, glancing now and again at Rupert, whose eyes were cast down. 'It's too risky.'

'I disagree,' Felix said calmly, with a dismissive shrug of his shoulders. 'The profits from this will wipe out a huge chunk of our debt and pay for some immediate repairs.'

'Why did you just ignore my feelings, Felix. What if—'

'It's a timebound investment, John. It's called timing the market for a reason. And time was running out. I couldn't wait for you to think things through, explore every possible outcome, then change your mind.'

As his anger mounted, John paced the room. 'That's not it at all. You knew I wouldn't change my mind. You're so bloody high and mighty—'

'I am not,' Felix announced. 'This is the right decision for the family, John. It's not my fault you're too pig-headed and stubborn to see a good opportunity when it comes up and smacks you in the face. Just because you built your business slowly, taking tiny baby steps, doesn't mean everyone else sees things the same way. Sometimes, when a debt is as big as ours, you have to take big chances.'

John ignored Felix's deliberately provocative comment and turned to his mother to check she was okay. 'Mother?'

But Felix jumped in before Lucinda could answer. 'You know I've done what I think is right, Mother, don't you? And I'm sure this'll be a success.' He was such a suck-up, John thought. It was all right for him, waltzing in and out of the house like it was some holiday home. He didn't have the burden of being here every day. He was lucky enough to have his own life. Lucinda hesitated for a second, her back ramrod straight thanks to her Swiss-finishing-school-perfect posture. She looked tired and fed up. Heavy dark circles had formed under her eyes, and her skin

– which John always remembered as being soft and plump – was now thin and grey.

'Felix if you think this is the best thing for us, then I support your decision.' She turned to Rupert whose eyes had glazed over.

John shook his head incredulously. How could his mother sit there and just agree with what Felix had done? But he wasn't going to shout at her. It wasn't her fault. She'd been born of a generation of upper-class women who left the finances to the men, and though they'd tried to include her after the fire, as their father wasn't able to make decisions anymore, she'd backed away as much as possible. John's eyes fell on Rupert and he tried to gently coax him into the conversation. Rupert had a say in this too, even if he'd made some bad decisions in the past. 'Father, what do you think? You get a say in this too.'

'Oh, well,' he mumbled, and Lucinda squeezed his hand tighter. 'I think we all know that I'm not – that is to say – bad choices – not really my thing anymore.' He chuckled to himself. 'Gardening now.'

An unspeakable sadness filled John's soul. Rupert had been so completely stripped of his confidence and it was all their fault.

'It's far too risky, Felix,' John said again. Maybe there was a cooling-off period, and they could still get the money back, but he knew that chance was slim. If Felix had signed on the dotted line, which they both had the authority to do, there'd be no going back.

'Well, it's done now,' Felix replied. 'And we'll find out soon enough if it was the right decision. I've been told it's a dead cert. I have every confidence this will change our family's fortunes.'

No matter what Felix said, investing the money meant risking losing it; at least if they had it in the bank it was there for part-payments or for when something came along that was more of a certainty. Every spare minute John wasn't working, and a lot of the time he should have been, was spent looking at different business models and opportunities, figuring out how to get the house making money. He'd thought of opening to visitors, selling more land, converting the east wing to a boutique B&B, a million and one different things. And all that hard work had been thrown out of the window by his overconfident, self-important brother.

'*Your* decision is exactly what it is,' spat John. 'If this doesn't work you could have cost us everything, Felix. I hope you know that. If this investment fails—'

'I don't believe it will,' Felix said, almost triumphantly. And John, knowing that if he stayed he'd do something he regretted, marched away, slamming the door behind him.

Chapter 16

Hetty consulted her ground plan and showed the driver where exactly the Portaloos were to go. A mixture of excitement and nerves bubbled in her stomach as she watched the truck move off. She'd made it this far, so all negative thoughts were banished. This event was going to be the best thing Swallowtail Bay had ever seen.

From the moment she'd opened her eyes, excitement and nerves fired her brain and body into life. She'd been up at 4.30 a.m., her mind whizzing about as she mentally double-checked her to-do list, unable to get back to sleep. A pale light had crept in through the sides of the blackout blind, the birds were singing sweetly. After having a cup of tea while curled on the sofa in her dressing gown, Hetty had made sure the big plastic box was full of all her folders, maps, plans, contracts and everything she else she could think of. Once dressed, she'd loaded it into the back of her car along with another box full of cleaning supplies, bin liners, plasters and chocolate bars. This was her much-used emergency box and covered any eventuality she'd come across so far.

Macie had arrived at the cottage at eight, and together they'd driven up to the lower field to get started. The atmosphere in the car had been almost giddy, like they were driving to a party, not preparing for the culmination of four intense, scary and busy weeks. Not to mention emotionally confusing since that evening with Ben and the mention of a ring, and the unsettling tension she felt whenever John was around.

It had been five days since their walk along the beach and his casually dropped bomb that an engagement was on the horizon as well as moving in together. But since that night there'd been no more contact. No flirty text messages. Not like last time. He'd gone strangely quiet and Hetty hadn't had the courage to text him, unsure what to say. She wasn't sure herself how she felt about the situation and didn't want to give him the wrong impression. Sometimes when she thought on it, she was flooded with excitement for the future they might have but then, thoughts of John would creep in. Images of him standing on the doorstep waiting to see her.

When Hetty had pulled up at the large wooden gate to enter the lower field, she was pleased to see they had all been mowed. Soon these empty fields, silent except for birdsong and the ever-present sound of the sea, would be buzzing with the noise of the funfair and full of people. The smell of grass would be replaced by the aromas from all the different types of food they were selling. The thrill of something special had grabbed Hetty again and she couldn't help but smile.

Once the Portaloo man had been sent off, Hetty and Macie studied the detailed timetable they'd made for the weekend. So far, things were going pretty much to plan. From the back of Hetty's car, Macie grabbed two spray cans.

'Right, time to mark out the pitches. Ready?'

Hetty nodded and together they began making little marks where the pitches were, so they could direct people to their spot. Some last-minute additions had filled the few remaining slots, so just as Hetty had hoped, they had a full house.

Time flew by and soon it was mid-morning and the sun was shining brightly above them. It was shaping up to be an incredibly hot, sunny day. Bending down to mark another pitch line, the sun beat fiercely on the back of Hetty's neck and she knew she should have worn a hat. The trouble was she didn't really have a face for hats, and she was far too old to wear a bandanna. As she stood up to stretch out her back and lifted her head to feel the warmth of the sun on her face, she saw John, his mouth contorted to a tight line and his eyebrows knitted together as he strode across a far field. His eyes were firmly fixed on the ground, his hands in his pockets. Her stomach lurched as she worried he was coming to cancel the food festival, but as he stomped on in a different direction it was like he had no idea she was even there. What misfortune could have made his face cloud like that?

Before she'd met him, it was how she always imagined his face would be, but now she knew him a little better it seemed odd. Over the time they'd worked together they'd begun to share jokes and he'd showed that beneath his posh stand-offish exterior there was an altogether different personality. Hetty still couldn't quite figure out what had happened the other night. Had he really come to talk about generators? Surely he'd remembered that was one of the first things she'd organised.

'Right, I've marked up all the ones in Section D,' said Macie, bouncing over. 'What do you want me to do next?'

Hetty continued watching John march away. 'Can you take over my section and I'll be back in a minute?'

'Yeah of course, is everything all right?'

'I just – yeah,' she said shaking her head. 'Just give me a second. I want to catch up with John. Can you keep an eye on the Portaloo guy please?'

'Yeah, sure. That's a bit brave, though, he's got a hell of a face on.'

'The Portaloo guy?' said Hetty, suddenly worried as she tossed her spray can on the ground and jogged towards John.

'No, John Thornhill.'

Hetty just waved. 'I'll be back in five minutes. John? John?' He turned as if her deafening cry had been a faraway echo he couldn't quite find the origin of. His face was such a picture of confusion it was almost as if he'd forgotten all about the food festival. 'Is everything all right?'

'What?'

From anyone else the sharp tone would have made her angry, but his manner indicated something terrible had happened. For him to be quite so furious and distracted it couldn't have been an ordinary, everyday problem. Where he'd been walking head down, his shoulders were slumped forward and he seemed smaller than usual, weighed down by whatever it was. Away from the noise of cars and vans, she could hear the breeze in the tall, uncut grass of the other fields and a cacophony of seagulls carried over from the sea. Hetty kept her tone calm and clear. 'I was just wondering if everything was all right? The food festival isn't causing you any problems at home, is it? You mentioned your mother being concerned about it. I hope we're not disturbing you too much already.'

John unravelled his spine, coming to his full height, and ran a hand through his hair. 'A private family matter. Nothing to do with the festival.' He gave a quick polite smile, but his eyes were still clouded.

'Oh right. I hope no one's ill.'

'No, just money,' he replied distractedly and rubbed his eye with his forefinger. 'It's always money.' He seemed to suddenly realise he was speaking out loud and changed the subject. 'I take it everything's going according to plan this morning?'

'It is,' she said triumphantly – though she didn't want to count her chickens, there was still a lot that could go wrong, even at this early stage. Yet, her excitement at what was to come couldn't be contained. 'So far so good. There's a lot left to do, and the vendors start arriving this afternoon to set up their pitches, as well as the funfair and the people providing the screen for the movie night.' He nodded but didn't offer anything else, so Hetty kept talking, which was strange considering she wasn't normally a nervous talker. 'Are you still okay to do the judging with me and Bob from the Swallowtail Bay business forum tomorrow?'

'Yes, that's fine,' he replied, and his demeanour relaxed. 'I'm looking forward to it.'

'Good. It should be fun. Oh, and I've organised a couple of bands to give some nice background music, and some security staff to be here at night. I'm setting them up a little booth, but I just wanted you to know as it's not something we'd discussed previously.'

'I'm surprised we'll need it, this isn't exactly Glastonbury.'

'No, but I think it's for the best. The funfair will take care of themselves.' They'd offered to keep an eye on the entire site for her but, to be honest, Hetty didn't like giving anyone else such a level of control. 'I just think it'd be good to have someone around the site to give everyone peace of mind. You, me and the vendors. If you could mention it to your family that would be great. I remembered what you said about your mum hiding in the house this weekend.' His eyes widened a little and he seemed surprised she'd remembered or cared. 'I don't want her to worry that there's a burglar about if she sees someone wondering around the fields with a torch in the dead of night.' He nodded but his features had darkened again. 'Are you sure everything's all right?'

John looked up, making confident and deliberate eye contact with her, but underneath the determined set of his features she could see a weakness. Like a fragment of his high and mighty manner had fallen away. 'Do you get on with your family, Hetty?'

Startled by the question she felt her head pop backwards. 'Most of the time. Not always.'

'Do you have any brothers or sisters?'

'No, I'm an only child.' At times, when she was growing up, she'd wished for a sister, but her parents hadn't wanted any more children.

'Lucky you. It's easier that way.' The anger in his tone was undercut by a hint of regret. So it was something with the brother that had caused this expression.

'Is it?' she asked. 'I never had anyone to play with and even now, I don't have anyone to share family problems with.'

'Do you have any?' His manner was blunt as usual, but there was kindness in his eyes.

For a second, Hetty thought about mentioning her mum and dad's separation and that her mum was considering divorce, but she hadn't even told Macie who'd been a friend for years. Again, she wasn't ready to open that box of feelings and risk losing focus on the most important weekend of her life. Hetty answered with a joke. 'Doesn't everyone?'

A small smile lifted the corner of his mouth and a powerful feeling ignited inside her. His eyes had warmed again and were almost as green as the grass beneath her feet. He looked over her shoulder and Hetty turned to see his assistant running from the direction of the house. When she got to John's side, she was decidedly flustered.

'Is it true? I've just spoken to Felix. Please tell me it's not true.' She put a hand on his arm. He gave her a piercing stare and, embarrassed, Jaz removed it. But Hetty could see John's response wasn't because Jaz had touched him but because she was in danger of letting something personal slip. That he didn't want to confide in her made Hetty feel strangely sad.

'I'll be at the house if you need anything. Or call if you want to speak to me—'

'Perhaps,' interrupted Jaz, looking between Hetty and John, 'it'd be easier if Miss Colman called me if anything happens?' John didn't contradict her, just scowled, though whether at Jaz or the problem he was dealing with, Hetty wasn't sure.

'What time is the funfair getting here?' he asked Hetty.

'Any minute now. I'd better be getting back actually. I've got more pitches to mark out before everyone arrives.'

His gaze lingered on hers for a moment. A moment that, from

the look on Jaz's face, was far too long. Hetty was the first to break away and say goodbye before making her way back to the lower field. But as she went, she couldn't stop the pull of her head to glance over her shoulder. She was surprised to see that at that exact moment, he'd done the same and was watching her too.

***

By half past one Hetty was officially knackered. Her back hurt from marking out pitches and the site was beginning to fill up with people. Every now and then she'd hear a dull thud as packages were lowered to the ground, or the scrape of a crate as it was pulled from a van. Laughter and chatter filled the air, overriding the peaceful birdsong that had started their day when it was just her and Macie.

As she gazed around, she could see banners and signs going up in front of pitches and they were transformed from boring trestle tables to colourful attractions. Tom, from the best florist's in town, had made a parking sign for them out of a piece of old wooden board, with letters made of driftwood. He'd also made a sign saying Swallowtail Bay Food Festival which hung from the wooden gate they'd entered through early that morning. Hetty had almost squealed in anticipation.

Spying the funfair, she decided to say hello and properly welcome them to Swallowtail Bay. It would have been great to have Mr Horrocks but Hetty was pleased with the replacements. Folly's was looking good as Mr Wade directed his people as to where everything should go. As rides were set up, like *Transformers* unfurling, a fission of excitement ran down her spine. Their arched sign covered the entrance to their field, painted in bright, enticing colours and someone was hanging bunting between the rides that had already been set up. A large red and yellow helterskelter sat next to the dodgems where the cars were being wiped down and polished to a shine. Between the bigger rides stood smaller ones like the hook-a-duck, the coconut shy and a candy-floss stall. The ghost train had been unhooked from the van and someone was unloading scary adornments, while another hung fake cobwebs everywhere. It was going to be a real draw. Opposite it, and in bright contrast stood the fun house. Its yellow frontage decorated in red spots and strange mirrors made anyone who passed turn into a short, wide, wiggly version of themselves and Hetty swallowed back a laugh as it did the same to Mr Wade. With the bunting fluttering in the breeze, the funfair would look exactly how Hetty had imagined it – traditional and old-fashioned.

'Miss Colman,' said Mr Wade as he approached.

'How are you, Mr Wade? Welcome to Swallowtail Bay. Did you find us okay?'

'Oh, yes, fine thanks. This is a nice spot, isn't it? That's quite a pile up there.' He nodded towards Thornhill Hall.

Hetty felt a little protective towards the place and wondered again what had affected John that morning, and if his day had got any better. Miss Simmons had certainly not been happy to see him speaking to her, but the poor girl was going to have to get over it. 'Yes, it is a lovely house.'

'Bet that costs a bomb to keep going.'

'Yes, I believe it does.' She readied herself to defend any barbs sent the Thornhill's way, but Mr Wade changed the subject. 'This should be a great weekend. You've got a lot of people here. And I saw the ad in the paper.'

'We've had a good take-up. I'm very pleased. As it's been a couple of weeks since I've seen you, is it possible to get an up-to-date record of your health and safety checks? I'm afraid I'm a bit of a stickler for things like that.'

'Of course,' he replied, shoving his hands in his jeans' pockets. Hetty noticed he had faded black jeans ripped at the knee that were more suited to a teenager. Especially as he'd teamed it with another crisp white shirt that had some fashion designer's logo on the pocket. 'I'll need to get them from the van.'

'No problem. I'll give you some time to settle in and get sorted out then pop back for them later if that's okay?' Hetty left them to it. Her legs were aching from all the squatting to mark pitches and her feet were tired. She and Macie had been working themselves into the ground and deserved a break before they started on the next lot of tasks. She found Macie at the chocolatier's stall, chatting happily.

Hetty watched for a moment, taking a swig from her water bottle. Macie had one hip jutted out, her clipboard resting on it and had flicked her beautiful cinnamon-coloured hair back over her shoulder. The stall holder, a handsome blond-haired man with a chiselled jaw and long fingers, seemed very happy to have Macie there. He was sticking some cute fairy lights to the front of his trestle table but kept looking up at her. As he said something funny, Macie's head flung back in a laugh and she gently touched his arm. The woman knew how to flirt, Hetty had to give her that. Even if most of the time she did flirt with the most undeserving of creatures. With time ticking on, Hetty felt a little guilty for interrupting their moment. 'Hey, Macie. Ready for a break?'

'Definitely. Give me five minutes.'

'Okay, I'm going to plonk over there.'

Knowing that seating would be needed here and there for people to eat the treats they'd bought, and to ensure they'd stay around for longer, Hetty had organised hay bales to be dotted around the site. She perched on one near the entrance. The epic flirting continued with Macie now helping the chocolatier stick up his fairy lights. When she came over, she was a little pink of cheek and shifty of eye, regularly checking her watch.

'Making new friends?' asked Hetty.

'Just welcoming the stall holders,' she replied cheekily.

'I hope you're going to give all our vendors good customer service like that.'

'Of course.'

Hetty rolled her eyes and swigged again from her water bottle but spluttered when a van she recognised pulled into the field and a familiar voice called her name. Some of the water dribbled down her chin and she quickly wiped it away with the heel of her hand. Hetty shot a look at Macie who with burning cheeks averted her gaze and stared intently at a cloud.

'Hey, stranger,' said Ben, giving her his wide, confident grin through the open window of his van.

'Ben, what are you doing here?' Her heart thudded hard in her chest.

'Didn't Macie tell you? I agreed to have a pitch.'

'No, Macie didn't tell me.' She stared at Macie who kept her eyes on the sky.

'Well, I thought, this food festival of Hetty's is shaping up to be something pretty special. Do I really want to miss out on all the fun? And I thought it would be a good way to see you too.' He sat back, his grin still firmly in place.

Embarrassment almost made Hetty shudder. She placed her water bottle on the floor then pulled her site plan from the back pocket of her jeans to study it. Refusing to be drawn into any personal chit-chat, she kept her tone professional and cool. 'I can't see *The Bake House* on here.'

'I asked Macie to put it under the name *Baker's Dozen*. That's my new bakery. Well, possible new bakery.' Hetty's eyes scanned the sheet and she found it. She glared at Macie again and Macie, who had been eyeing the plan too, shot her eyes back to the sky. At least she'd had the good sense to put him in the furthest corner of the field meaning anyone coming just for him would have to pass a lot of other stalls first. Hetty couldn't help but be a little proud, even if she could quite happily beat her to death with the laminated site plan. Hetty pointed to his pitch. 'You're over there.'

'Right you are.' With a wink he began to move off. 'See you later, alligator. Oh, and don't be mad at Macie. I only called the other day and swore her to secrecy.'

When he'd gone, Hetty turned to Macie whose eyes were again glued upwards. 'Macie,' she said, calmly.

'That cloud looks like a turtle having a poo.'

'Macie!' She dropped her eyes to Hetty's face, her cheeks burning such a furious shade of pink Hetty couldn't quite bring herself to tell her off. 'You do realise we're surrounded by fields and I could easily murder you and bury you somewhere and no one would ever find you?'

Macie nodded. 'Yes, but then you'd be down one awesome amazing assistant who loves you hugely and—'

'You should have told me.'

'I know.' She bowed her head. 'I'm sorry. It was just that, you said about his kissing you and then there was the whole ring thing, and you were kind of glad he wasn't coming and then you kind of weren't. And then you said you didn't know how you felt about him anymore. And then you said you were going to stay away from him and see if your feelings faded after the festival. And then he turned up finally talking about commitment and rings and you had a complete wobble. And then you said you might be still a bit in love with him and that you didn't know what to do. And then—'

'All right. All right,' Hetty conceded, her hands held up in surrender. She probably had put Macie in a difficult position. Ben had clearly done so as well by going to her for a pitch instead of asking Hetty directly. There was also the worry of having Ben and John near each other when Ben was proving a bit weird and antagonistic about the lord of the manor, but thankfully, Macie hadn't listed that one.

'I just thought if I kept it quiet, you wouldn't worry about him being here on top of everything else. You wouldn't have stopped him coming anyway. You'd have just been worrying about things you couldn't change.'

Hetty smiled. Macie was quite right, she wouldn't have stopped him coming, they both knew what a draw it would be. And If she had known in advance, she'd only have worried about how to be around him and what to say. At least Macie had saved her all that. Hetty's shoulders relaxed down a little. 'So which cloud looks like a turtle having a poo?'

Macie giggled and pointed up. 'That one. Look.'

'Oh, yeah.' Hetty glanced over at Ben setting up. There were still a lot of vendors left to turn up leaving wide empty gaps. What would happen if they didn't show? All her capital had been sunk into this now, there was nothing left to draw on. This had to work or her business would effectively be starting again from scratch. Hetty inspected the turtle cloud and took a deep breath. 'Come on, let's see how everyone's settling in.' She put her arm around her assistant's shoulder. 'Do you think that local vineyard has unpacked yet?'

Chapter 17

Gravel scrunched underfoot as John paced around outside the house. As soon as he got back to the study, he'd called the bank who confirmed the majority of the family funds had been transferred to an investment company. John also asked if they'd considered his loan application yet, but they just mumbled something about it being a different department and lots to consider and that these things can take time. There was a little money left which would cover one more month's re-mortgage payment, as long as they didn't need it for anything else. They really needed to fix the roof before any more rain, but that would have to wait. He'd then called the investment company who said the money had been invested according to Felix's wishes. It was all tied up. Gone.

With a heavy heart, John thanked the customer service agent for his help and hung up. So that was it, there wasn't anything he could do. They'd already re-mortgaged so they couldn't do that again. For the bank it would be like throwing money into a black hole. He just had to hope the loan was approved and that he could convince the family to open the house to public. The loan would cover the changes to get it all health and safety approved, then by opening to the public they'd at least have some income.

How could Felix do this to them? A surge of bitterness threatened to wrap around John. Felix wasn't here all the time. He didn't see the effect on their mother and father the same way John did. Felix was still angry at their father too. John knew from the way he hadn't bothered asking Rupert what he thought of the investment. Could he not see the physical changes in their father? But Felix had his own life and his own house. He wasn't going to lose everything if this investment failed. He hadn't been the one bailing out the family with his own money the same way John had.

John glanced back at the house to see Jaz in the window, the phone pressed to her ear. She'd been dealing with the majority of his work this morning while he'd been trying to figure out what to do next. The only light in the dark was that the food festival was shaping up to be a huge success.

The charismatic Hetty had things running like clockwork already. He'd expected some phone calls from her with last-minute problems, maybe her needing to change the site plan, or use another field because she'd miscalculated the space required. But there'd been nothing and he'd felt more than a little disappointed. He'd have welcomed the distraction of heading down there and the solace of seeing her again. His stomach gave a loud gurgle and John realised it was almost two o'clock and he was starving. As he'd promised her lunch, Jaz must have been hungry too.

Wandering down, he thought he'd take a break and see who some of the vendors were. As he got closer, he could see the west field had a sign in it saying parking, and in the lower field, stall holders were beginning to set up, laying out tables and equipment. Seeing everything they unpacked, he realised Hetty had been right to organise security. Which reminded him, he still needed to tell his family. That would really top off his mother's day. He hopped over a stile into the middle field; all the others had been removed to make walkways. Some techies were beginning to install the big screen ready for Saturday night's film, and

Hetty was standing near them, watching on. She had a clipboard in her hand, and a piece of paper sticking out of her back pocket that emphasised the curve of her lower body. Someone came over to ask her a question and with a smile and a laugh she responded. It was a smile that lifted her full cheeks and plump lips. As soon as they were gone, she grabbed her phone and was head down, busily typing.

John considered staying away and letting her work while he strolled around the site, but he found himself wanting to talk to her. He enjoyed her company and was genuinely interested in the running of the festival. After Felix's news this morning, he needed it to be a success more than ever. With no money left in the bank, his whole family – though they didn't appreciate it – needed each and every stall holder to make a killing.

If he was honest, he also wanted to hear her voice, her laugh, and see that smile up close. John ambled over in Hetty's direction. He'd appreciated her sympathy earlier, though he was still a little cross with Jaz for forgetting herself and talking of family affairs in front of strangers. She knew how the town liked to gossip about them and should have been more discreet. Hetty wasn't the gossiping type and her concern for him had been touching, but still, he couldn't be too careful. 'How's it all shaping up?' he asked.

She looked up from her phone. 'Pretty good, actually. The Portaloos are all in place.' She glanced in their direction. 'I hope we've got enough. A lot of the food vendors have arrived, but I know some aren't coming till tomorrow morning, so I'll be here at the crack of dawn to sort them out.'

'I get the feeling that was going to happen anyway.'

Hetty tipped her head back a little and laughed. 'Yeah, it probably was, to be fair.'

Her laughter acted as a soothing balm to the troubles of the morning. 'I don't suppose anyone has any food to share?' he asked, looking around.

'I think there's one or two who might. I might grab something too, actually. I'm starving. I only had a breakfast bar this morning, I was so excited.'

'I normally just have coffee.'

She put her phone back into her pocket. 'Let me see if I remember. Black, no sugar?'

'Because I'm boring?' He really hoped that wasn't her impression of him.

'Hey, you said it, not me.'

'I like to think of it as strong and already sweet enough.' Was this flirting? He hadn't done that in a long time – a long, *long* time, it felt like. And yet, it felt so easy with her. 'Why don't you join me? We can sit and stare at the blank film screen. Pretend it's showing something good. Actually, what are we showing?'

'*The Goonies*.'

A big wide grin took hold. 'I love that film.'

'Me too,' Hetty agreed. 'Come on then, let's see who's got some grub.'

They strolled around the stalls, Hetty chatting happily and easily to the vendors. John marvelled at the variety. There was everything from Indian street food to charcuterie, fabulous freshly made pizza to locally made pies. Though no one had started cooking yet, his mouth was already watering. And everyone seemed happy to see Hetty. But sideways glances came his way and he tried to ignore them. His hackles were rising again, the morning news making him more than a little defensive, as if everyone already knew. Though, of course, that was impossible. He made a concerted effort to stay relaxed. This was exactly the reason his mother didn't want to open the house to the public, and right now he agreed with her.

'Don't mind them,' Hetty said, when they were once more on their own. 'It's very rare to see the lesser-spotted lord of the manner actually *in* the wild.'

An involuntary deep and throaty laugh escaped him. 'I suppose it is. It's my fault really. I should actually speak to people when I go into town more. I like Swallowtail Bay. I just don't seem to have the time. When I was little, Mother used to take Felix and I to the rockpools and we'd be there all day, searching for crabs and shells.'

'That's sweet. My mum and dad used to bring me down too. To think we could have run past each other as children. But I'm sure being a judge tomorrow will help you get to know everyone.'

John noticed they were strolling along perfectly in time with each other. 'I'm looking forward to it. How will it work?'

'Macie will provide you with a list of all the entries in each category so you can write down your choice. Then I'll check the answers and do the envelopes.'

'And if there's a tie? Or you need a deciding vote?'

'Then I'll call in a third party. Possibly Macie. Does that sound dodgy?'

'No, not at all,' he chuckled.

They were just passing the local artisan cheese maker who was delving about in the back of his van.

'Hi, Clive,' Hetty said. 'How're things going? Got enough room?'

Clive paused from his task, opening boxes and pulling out baskets of homemade crackers in little cellophane bags, each one tied with a cute ribbon and a tag. He edged out of the back of his van, his wide rear shuffling from side to side. ''Ello, 'Etty. Yeah, I'm all good. You?'

'Yep,' she replied with the brightest grin John had ever seen. 'All good so far.'

'How are your mum and dad?'

A slight cloud passed over her eyes and John wondered what that shadow was. 'Oh, they're fine,' she answered. 'Those look lovely.'

Clive straightened up, placing one of the baskets full of crackers on his display table. 'All homemade too. These are black pepper, and these are rosemary and thyme. Go lovely with some of my local blue.'

'Sounds delicious,' John said, his stomach grumbling in response. But rather than enjoying the compliment, Clive eyed him warily.

'Not like the Thornhills to let us do something like this. We thought you preferred not to have us commoners on your land. Your father never did.'

From the corner of his eye he saw Hetty's head move before she glared at Clive. Poor old boy, thought John. Though John wasn't happy at the mention of his father, Clive was right, and he smiled. 'Well, no one's come up with such a good idea before. I was more than happy to help.' Even though he'd said the same thing at the radio interview, Hetty had obviously expected him to snap a harsh retort. She couldn't have looked more surprised if he'd told the old man he liked to dress in women's underwear every Thursday night. Clive's expression hadn't changed except for a tightening at his eyes. The old man went back to shuffling about in his van. Assuming the conversation was finished, they were about to move on when he came out again.

'Here,' he said, handing over a small white box. He then grabbed one of the packs of biscuits, checking the label before placing it on top. John took it, thanking him. 'It's just a few little samples, nothing much. I just thought you might like them.' And with that he disappeared back into his van, his back well and truly turned.

John turned to Hetty, knitting his brows together. Had one of the town's people been nice to him? Hetty was repressing a smile but as they walked on, it spread over her face and a sweet, musical laugh came out.

'You look like someone just handed you a grenade.'

John laughed too and as his stomach muscles jiggled with the force of it. He felt a weight lift from his shoulders and some of the morning's pressure shifted. As he'd expected, being with Hetty was calming the sea of troubles. 'Could he have hidden one in the cheese?' John held his ear near the box. 'I think we're safe.'

Watching Hetty laugh by his side, his heart did a weird squeezing thing. He couldn't remember the last time it had done that from something other than anxiety. 'If you're not too busy, did you want to join me?' He nodded towards the box. 'I'm sure there's enough for two.'

'I'd love to,' she replied, and her bright, wide smile warmed his heart.

They made their way back towards the giant film screen and sat on a stubby patch of grass. If he sat up straight, he could see the sea on the horizon, a long line of dusky blueish-grey. John opened the box to reveal a couple of small cheeses. One was the blue Clive had talked about, the other was a soft Brie-type cheese. In between them were a handful of tomatoes still on the vine. It smelt delicious. Hetty sat and curled her legs underneath her. There really was something enticing about the way she moved her body, the curve of her hips and the confidence with which she stared around, observing the world.

'I think we're going to have to use our hands, there's no cutlery I'm afraid. Unless you've got some?'

'I might have some in my emergency box,' Hetty said. 'But that's back at base camp.'

'Base camp?'

She nodded, her face deadly serious. 'Mine and Macie's HQ. And don't even start teasing me about my emergency box.'

He shook his head. 'I wouldn't dream of it. Even though I am curious to know what's in it.'

Hetty narrowed her eyes. 'Okay, I'll tell you just in case someone comes to you in an emergency. There are plasters, headache tablets, bandages—'

'Bandages?'

'Trust me, bandages are definitely needed. There are about a million pens. Teabags. And lots of chocolate.'

171

'But no cutlery?'

'Not unless there's some in there from last time. But I don't mind fingers if you don't? Picnics shouldn't be eaten with cutlery.'

They sat in the sunshine, eating on the grass as a sea of action bustled around them. Occasionally, Hetty would place some of the cheese in her mouth then let her head fall back, savouring the taste. John watched her, careful to look away when she lifted her head back up. The atmosphere around them was heady from the heat of the sun and the smell of recently cut grass. John's heart gave the same heavy pump it had before. After a few mouthfuls, Hetty spoke.

'Can I ask you something?'

'Sure.' He stuck on a smile, but from experience, questions like this were never good and that made him reticent.

'You seemed surprised when Clive gave you the cheese box. Why? Why do you think everybody hates you and your family?'

John uncrossed his legs and straightened them out, taking a moment to enjoy the warmth of the sun. He didn't want to be defensive with Hetty, not like he was with everyone else. 'Hate's a strong word. I don't think the town hates us and we certainly don't hate them. It's just that …' He ran a hand through his hair and then down over his beard. 'No one likes being the centre of gossip. Do you know my mother used to go into town every Wednesday – to the farmers' market – but after everything went wrong for us, she stopped going. She'd come back almost in tears at the whispers and murmurs muttered behind her back.'

'That's horrible,' Hetty replied. Her expressive face mirrored exactly the pain he felt for his mother when he remembered some of the states she'd come home in.

'People would talk about us like our life was an episode of *EastEnders*. It always seemed to us that, if we lived in town, in a normal terraced house, we'd get sympathy rather than snide comments that we deserved it.'

'You're quite right,' she said, and John was thrown by her

admission. Before he'd been met with arguments if he made such a point.

'Running a house like this' – he motioned back towards his large, undeniably beautiful but costly home – 'is pretty hard. We don't have any money, everything needs fixing, it's cold and damp, and bits of the roof are falling off or in. People think we should be happy and consider ourselves lucky. We are in a lot of ways, I know that, but—'

'But happiness and luck don't pay for roof repairs.'

Strands of Hetty's short blonde hair lifted a little in the gentle breeze and appeared almost silver in the sunlight. She adjusted her glasses and John had a sudden urge to take her hand and wrap his fingers around it, to feel her soft skin as they touched. His throat tightened with a longing to kiss her, but with everything that had happened this morning, how could he? Knowing he had to look away before the feeling really took hold he stared at the remnants of cheese in the box.

Hetty fiddled with the grass. 'Can I ask you another question? If it's not too intrusive.'

'Sure.' For some reason, he didn't mind speaking about this with Hetty. He knew she wouldn't judge him as harshly as others did.

'What actually happened with your dad and your family's money?'

John felt his body react as it always did, with tension gripping his neck and shoulders, but he resisted the urge to hide behind his usual barriers. 'What have you heard?' he asked gently.

'Bits of gossip about vineyards and a fire but I never believe gossip. That's why I wanted to ask you. Feel free to tell me to mind my own business if I'm overstepping, but I promise anything you say will be in confidence.'

He was sure it would be. Hetty had such a clear, no-nonsense personality and seemed so un-flinching and stoic, but there was a gentleness in her eyes and a level of empathy he hadn't credited her with when they'd first met. He'd grown to realise that beneath her self-confidence was a kind and understanding woman.

For the first time, he didn't feel ashamed of his father for getting them into this situation. It was done and they had to deal with it. He'd held on to those feelings long enough, punishing his father without even realising it. 'My father was very fond of wine. Without taking proper financial advice he sunk the entirety of the family's fortune into a vineyard that then burned down, taking us with it.'

'Very concise,' Hetty said, and John gave a pained laugh. 'It must be very difficult for you.'

'It is.' A bubble of silence wrapped around them while outside it the hustle and bustle continued.

'Didn't the insurance cover it?'

'They think the fire happened on purpose – a disgruntled member of staff. That was their reason for not paying out. I mean we didn't have a ridiculous amount of money to start with, but we were pretty secure. Then the fire ruined us. I spend a lot of the time I should be working on my own business trying to figure out how to keep the house going so it doesn't pass out of the family name. That would destroy my mother.'

'How did you guys come to have the house?' Hetty enquired. 'You're not titled, are you?'

'No, we're just normal.' He chuckled. 'My father's great-great-grandfather had a lot of money and when this house came up for sale, I can't remember the reason, he bought it. Just like any other house purchase really.'

'Just an enormous house,' Hetty teased.

'Yes, just a ridiculous house. I often wish he'd bought a two-bed semi.'

Hetty laughed. 'Yes, I bet you do.'

'Did you know in the dim and distant past, the fields all around here used to grow a particular variety of strawberry? I guess it wasn't very profitable either.'

'I didn't know that. I know the bay used to be a huge straw-berry-growing region, but I guess it's a hard profession to make a living from. What sort of income streams have you looked at for Thornhill Hall?'

John changed position, leaning on one hand. 'Various things. Opening a few days a week, turning the east wing into a boutique B&B, grants – you name it.'

'And nothing's viable?'

'Some more viable than others. It's getting the family to agree that's the problem.' And now that Felix had thrown away the last tiny bit of money they had, all these ideas were looking even slimmer. *Bloody Felix.* As John lifted his eyes and surveyed the land, wondering what it would be like to actually say goodbye to all of this, he sickened. Jaz was standing on the edge of the field, a grim expression on her face and her arms crossed over her chest.

'Isn't that your assistant?' asked Hetty.

'Damn.' He jumped up, startling Hetty. *Damn, damn, damn.* He'd completely forgotten he was meant to get them both some lunch and go back to the house. Jaz turned and walked away. From the long, fast strides, he knew she was angry.

Hetty was standing too, looking around for whatever emer-gency had made him behave this way. 'What? What's wrong?'

'Umm, nothing. It's fine.' He picked up the rubbish and strode away. He hated being impolite and if things were different he'd have stayed for as long as possible. But he couldn't drag anyone into his mess of a life. 'Thanks for lunch, Hetty,' he shouted over his shoulder as he raced away. He hated leaving her standing there, her beautiful face marred by the confusion he'd caused. He broke into a run and made his way back towards the house and Jaz.

When he caught up with Jaz he was sweating and out of breath. He had to get rid of the rubbish before he spoke to her, he couldn't show up with this cheese box in his hand, it would just add insult to injury. Shoving the box in a wall of conifers (he'd remove it later), he called her name.

'Jaz! Jaz, wait, please.'

She stopped and turned, the ends of her long brown hair tied in a ponytail, swished over her shoulder. 'Yes, John?'

'Jaz, I'm so sorry. I got caught up talking about the festival and with everything that's happened this morning, I just … I'm really sorry.' She nodded her understanding and went to walk away again. 'Have you eaten?' She didn't turn but shook her head.

'No, not yet. I'll grab something now.'

'At least let me make you a sandwich?'

'It's fine. I'll probably eat at my desk. I've loads to do.'

'Jaz, come on.' He took her arm and turned her around to face him. She looked like she was about to cry, and John couldn't blame her. She'd put up with his grumpiness, with his short temper and with his family, and never once moaned. And now he'd left her high and dry over lunch. Making sure he made eye contact so she could see how much he meant it, he said, 'I really am sorry, Jaz. I've been the worst boss in the world recently and you've put up with me with a smile on your face. I'm sorry I forgot about lunch. I've no excuse other than I'm useless.' Finally, a small smile came to her mouth and the water in her eyes dried. 'I just got talking about the festival and didn't realise the time. I promise I'll make it up to you.'

She studied his face. 'It might take more than just a sandwich to make it up to me.'

John let his hands fall away and he tucked them into his pockets. 'A cup of tea as well?'

Her giggle let him know he'd been forgiven. He just hoped he'd get a chance to catch up with Hetty again before the day was out. He wanted to see a smile back on her face too. But she probably thought he was a complete imbecile now.

Chapter 18

At three o'clock in the morning, Hetty woke up with a fabulous idea. Scrabbling around in the dark she hastily made a note on her phone and through sheer exhaustion managed to fall back asleep. When she woke up again, feeling as bright and sunny as the day, she wondered now why she hadn't thought of it before and couldn't wait to put her plan into action.

Hetty laid down some food for Stanley the seagull and watched him limp around the garden to his little plate. Set-up day had, as expected, been exhausting, but apart from one or two tiny problems, it had gone well. Even Ben's devious arrival hadn't got under her skin as much as she thought it would. The only thing that was bothering her was John and the way her body and mind kept reacting to him.

To her shame, she'd often thought the same as everyone else in town, that he had a great life up at the huge house on the hill and should be thankful for it. People spoke about the family's problems with glee as if they deserved it simply for being richer, but from her conversations with John, she could see his life wasn't one of a spoilt rich kid, annoyed because he'd lost all his privilege, but rather one of survival since his dad's bad decision. A bad decision anyone could have made.

Hetty wasn't surprised he'd become angry at the residents of Swallowtail Bay.

More than ever she was sure his assistant had a crush on him, and that John had no idea about it. Though the way he ran off after Jaz yesterday afternoon was strange to say the least. Still it was doubtful she'd have to see her much – Hetty couldn't imagine assistants at antique firms worked bank holiday weekends.

Full of energy for her new idea, Hetty waited until seven o'clock – that was a reasonable time to call her, wasn't it? – before excitedly making her way to Thornhill Hall. Not the fields this time, but to the house. She wanted to speak to John and share her idea, let him know about the calls she'd already made. Hopefully he'd like the idea too. Though why that mattered, Hetty couldn't quite put her finger on.

Pulling into the turning circle again, she went to the front door, admiring the deep rich wood as she banged the knocker down hard. It was only after the echo circled around the empty gardens and engulfed her from all directions, that she worried that the family might not even be up yet. A smile formed on her lips as the door opened but turned to confusion when she saw Jaz standing on the threshold. From the scowl on her face, Jaz wasn't particularly pleased to see Hetty either.

'Miss Colman, it's very early. Is something wrong?'

'Wrong? Oh, no not at all, I was wondering if I could speak to John?' Hetty walked up another step and Jaz protectively closed the door a little.

'I'm afraid he's breakfasting with the family.'

Breakfasting with the family? Did Jaz think she was some kind of *Downton Abbey* extra or in a Georgette Heyer novel? Hetty bit her lip to stop herself grinning. 'Well, is it possible to grab him so I can have a quick word please? I'm pretty sure he's going to want to hear what I have to say.'

'I'm afraid not.' The corner of Jaz's mouth quivered a little as if she was resisting the urge to smile. Hetty waited for her to say more but Jaz didn't and simply stared in an almost accusatory manner. Hetty straightened at this feeble attempt to intimidate her.

'Okay,' she replied with a shrug, thrusting her hands into her pockets and heading back down the steps. 'That's not a problem. I'll just give him a call on his mobile.'

Suddenly, Jaz stepped forwards. 'John's asked not to be disturbed until at least …' There was a slight hesitation before she finished, 'Ten o'clock.'

Hetty turned and the tinge of pink on Jaz's face, plus the hesitation, made her one hundred per cent sure she was lying. But that was fine. Hetty wasn't going to play silly games. She had too much to do and the person she'd phoned would be arriving soon. 'Okay, I'll call him then. Thanks.' She gave Jaz a smile and made her way back to her car and the parking field – she couldn't keep calling it the west field, people would get confused. Pulling on the handbrake, she watched as a pale early morning sun took its time to move fully into the sky, waiting for the slight chill that made the hairs on her arms stand on end to burn off.

A few vendors who hadn't been able to set up yesterday were arriving too and Macie directed them where to go. Already, different smells were beginning to drift on the air as the food stalls set out their goods and fired up their equipment. Before long, a small van with Snip-It's written on the side drew up into the field and Gwen got out.

'Are you sure about this, Hetty?' Gwen asked, moving to the back of the van and opening the doors. Her face was softer than it had been at the committee meeting.

'Positive,' she replied. 'A pop-up pamper parlour is the final thing our festival needs. I don't know why I didn't think of it before.' And it would stop Gwen bad-mouthing the festival.

'I can't do hair, of course,' Gwen said. But through her usual grumpy tones, Hetty could hear a note of excitement. 'Well, I can braid or put hair up, but I can't wash and dry. I was planning on offering mainly manicures and pedicures. And I printed out some little vouchers if your stewards could give them out? What do you think?'

To think that she'd printed and cut out all these vouchers since Hetty had called at seven, told her everything she needed to know. Gwen hadn't really been against the festival, she'd just wanted to find a way to be involved. 'Sounds great to me. You're over there.' She pointed to the area she'd assigned that morning on her plan and after Gwen had handed over the vouchers, she moved off.

A moment later, Macie came by. 'What's Gwen doing here?'

Hetty was so excited, her hands had a mind of their own and she animatedly waved the vouchers in Macie's face. 'I had this amazing idea at three this morning.'

'Another 3 a.m. idea? I'm getting worried now.' The ideas that came to Hetty in the early hours of the morning could be either completely mental (air-guitar party) or absolutely brilliant (custard pie fight for kids).

'Hey! They've all been great so far.'

Macie cocked her head in silent sarcasm. 'Remember that time you wanted to start a dog show?'

'Okay, fair point. But this is another good one. We're going to have a pop-up pamper parlour. Visitors can get manicures, pedicures, their hair braided – how amazing is that!'

'I love it,' Macie replied. 'How will we promote it thought? We haven't mentioned it on any of the marketing stuff.'

Hetty thought for a moment. 'We'll have to have someone walking around with a loudspeaker – and look, Gwen printed out some vouchers.' She handed the bundle to Macie.

'Wow.'

'I know, right? She's clearly on board with all this now.' Hetty motioned to the entirety of the food festival.

'Awesome. Well, I'll sort out the loudspeaker and give some of these to the stewards.'

'Fab. You're a superstar, Macie. Let the first day commence, hey?' They high-fived in triumph, anticipation, nerves and excitement, because now, it was finally happening. In only two hours' time, at 10 a.m., the gates would open and the first ever Swallowtail Bay Food Festival would begin.

'What're you smiling about?' came Ben's familiar voice. He'd left his staff setting up the stall under the name The Bake House and not his supposed new business. Tying his apron as he went, he strolled over.

'Change your mind?' Hetty asked, nodding towards the sign.

'About what?'

'I thought you said your stall here was going to be in the name of your new business? Baker's Dozen, wasn't it? Change your mind, did you?'

'Ah, well, yeah.' He laughed and Hetty noticed him tapping his foot. He'd always done that when he was caught out. 'You got me. I must admit I just didn't want you to see The Bake House on your list and then tell me I couldn't come. I know you said I could, but your eyes said different.'

He really was infuriating, and she couldn't decide if she was flattered by his deception or annoyed. The look in his eyes was doing things to her insides again. She cleared her throat. 'Right, well ...' She had to concentrate on the busy day ahead of her because this was it. It was make or break time. The day had finally arrived, and she had to be one hundred per cent focused. Ben would still be here when the weekend was over, and she'd deal with her feelings for him then. Until Monday, she'd lock them away in that little box at the back of her mind and treat him like any other vendor. 'Well, have a good day's business,' she said cheerfully and walked off to Macie, leaving him looking perplexed.

'Go get 'em, Hetty,' he called out. She could hear his smile and the affectionate teasing tone that she'd loved so much. She might need an extra padlock on that little box, she thought with a grimace.

At ten o'clock everything was ready. The volunteer stewards had been briefed and were eager and excited in their high visibility jackets, and the lights from the funfair sparkled even in the bright sunshine. A symphony of noise met her as she gazed around at everything she'd drawn together in one place. Well, she and John Thornhill. And there he was in her mind again, all handsome features and deep, resonating voice.

Comical beeps and noises came from the rides, the clinking of pots and pans emanated from the food stalls, all underpinned by a base level of excited murmurs. Hetty raised her eyes and thanked her lucky stars that the sky was cloudless and fine. The sun was a bright yellow orb in a clear blue sky and the slight breeze was warming by the minute. It was a perfect summer's day. The unmown fields that surrounded the festival remained packed with tall flowers growing wild and free. As people walked up from the bay, along the bridleways, they'd see the sea on the horizon, still, calm and unmoving. Was there ever a more perfect place on earth?

'Right,' she said to the assembled crowd already queueing to come in, 'let's open these gates, shall we, and start the inaugural Swallowtail Bay Food Festival.'

A cheer rose up and the large wooden gate was pulled open and those that had walked up from town were let in, while the stewards began to direct a line of cars as to where to park. Hetty greeted everyone cheerfully. Lexi from Raina's Café waved hello and Hetty waved back. She was here with her ex-husband, Will, and their children. No doubt they'd be popping over to Raina's stall to see her. It was definitely one of the most popular places in town, but the good thing with the festival was that everyone had the same size pitch and the same chance of gaining new customers. This weekend was a celebration of her amazing home-town and everyone who was a part of it.

Snippets of conversation met Hetty from those that passed. 'So good to see the festival coming back' … 'as long as it's not all those burger vans you get in lay-bys' ... 'snooty Thornhills – now they know what it's like for the rest of us, being skint'.

At the mention of the Thornhills Hetty looked around for John. *What a shame*, she thought when she realised he wasn't there. It would have done wonders for him and his family if he'd been here welcoming everyone alongside her. Her buoyant mood dipped as worry surged inside. Was he just busy? Or perhaps his absence meant that despite everything he'd said and done, the festival just wasn't as important to him as she'd come to think.

Chapter 19

John held the phone to his ear and pushed his other hand through his hair. 'I don't care what you say, Felix, we still need to look at other possible income streams whatever happens with your investment.' John paced the study, taking long, angry strides but trying to stay calm. The room wasn't really big enough for him to stomp about in in a temper because after four steps he had to turn around and go back again. He'd wanted to be there at the gate this morning, welcoming everyone onto the Thornhill estate, showing them what the family were really like and supporting Hetty. Instead he was having yet another row with his brother over money. As if they both didn't know what the other would say next. John squeezed the bridge of his nose.

'John, I know exactly what I'm doing,' Felix reassured in his superior tone. It was the 'you're the little brother and don't know anything' tone John hated so much. 'All you have to do is wait it out. I know that's hard for you because it means you're not one hundred per cent in control, but you're just going to have to deal with it.'

They were going around in circles again and John flopped into his comfortable leather chair and stared at the wall of books opposite. The door opened a crack and Jaz slipped in. Silently, she placed a mug of coffee down in front of John and took a seat opposite, taking her notepad from the edge of his desk and getting ready to work. 'Look, Felix, if this investment comes off then great, that'll put money behind us and pay off a lot of our debts, but if it doesn't then we'll be back to square one. Exactly where we are now. Actually, we'll be worse off because at least we had a little money in the bank before. We need to start thinking how we can make some money with no capital because you've thrown the last of it away. Why waste time waiting to see what happens with your dodgy dealings when we can use the time to plan for the future, whatever the outcome. You're a finance manager, Felix, even you can't argue with that.'

The line went quiet then his brother huffed. 'Fine.'

'Great.' John's anger subsided a little and he tried to turn the conversation to something more pleasant. 'Are you coming over to the festival?'

'I guess we'll stop by. Elizabeth wants to come.'

Of course Felix didn't want to come because it was John and Hetty's success. 'Well if you do, let me know and I'll come and meet you. There's a great cheese maker I want to show you.' His brother bid a curt goodbye and John tossed his phone onto the desk. 'Jaz, please tell me I'm not as difficult to deal with as my brother?'

'You have your moments.'

He scowled. 'You're fired.'

'No, I'm not,' she replied with a grin.

'You're right, you're not. But only because you type quicker than me.' He was glad they were getting on better, and that so far today there'd been no tension in their relationship. Jaz ran the side of her hand over the clean sheet of paper in front of her.

'John, I'm sorry I spoke out of turn yesterday. I shouldn't have talked about it in front of Miss Colman.'

'It's fine,' he reassured her, eager not to start the day with this discussion.

'It's not. I let you down—'

'Jaz.' He got up and went to the other side of the desk to sit in front of her. 'It's fine.' She smiled and as he stood to return to his seat, his leg accidentally brushed hers. He felt Jaz's eyes on him and hoped she wasn't going to read anything into it.

'Right, let's sort out Mr Crompton's burning need to own a vintage typewriter and then I'm taking a walk around the festival. I was hoping to be there when the gates opened but because he's as pig-headed as me, it took me a lot longer to convince him than I was hoping.'

Jaz nodded to his cup of coffee. 'I made you another coffee. Your first one had gone cold.'

'Thanks.' He took a sip and savoured the strong, rich flavour. Jaz always made it perfectly. She knew exactly how much coffee to put in and never made it too strong or too weak. John noticed her glancing at him as he drunk, seeking reassurance. He really had been a horrible boss to her lately. 'Lovely,' he said, placing it down. There was a gentle tap on the door and John could identify the visitor immediately. 'Come in, Mother.'

'Oh, hello, John.' She seemed surprised to see him there which made him want to laugh.

Lucinda was impeccably dressed in a pale-blue skirt with matching jacket and a cream silk blouse. John could tell she'd dressed extra formally today, worried that some random person might wander all the way from the lower field, up to the house. Should anyone turn up on the doorstep, she didn't want to appear anything other than at her best. 'Everything all right, Mother?'

'Yes, John, but I wondered if you'd seen my book. I can't seem to find it and I'm positive I left it in the parlour.'

'Perhaps our ghost has moved it?'

'Oh, John, don't be silly.'

'Have you checked the kitchen?'

'Good idea. I'll look there next.' She went to leave, but lingered, holding the edge of the door. John knew exactly what was coming.

His mother hadn't lost her book and he didn't believe in ghosts even though tales of the Thornhill spectre went back generations. 'You haven't seen anyone accidentally coming up to the house, have you? Or you, Jaz?' As she said this, she pulled the top of her blouse closer together in a protective gesture. She really was becoming almost as skittish as his father. If it wasn't for her daily walks around the fields and along the clifftops of Swallowtail Bay, she would probably have become agoraphobic.

He took another sip of his coffee before answering. 'It's a long way from the fields up to the house, Mother. And I'm sure Hetty is making sure no one strays or gets lost.' From the corner of his eye he spotted Jaz's look of disdain. Lucinda gave a resigned nod.

'It's just that people can be quite nosey at times. And they might take the opportunity to sneak up to the house.'

'Sneak?' John repressed a laugh. He suddenly had an image of hordes of people hiding behind the topiary.

'You know what I mean.'

'I do,' he replied, reassuringly. 'If it makes you feel better, I was going to take a walk down to the festival in a bit and I'll speak to Hetty to make doubly sure.' The relief on his mother's face was palpable.

'Oh, thank you, dear.' Lucinda backed out of the room, a little flustered at his teasing. 'Don't work too hard and I hope he's looking after you, Jaz.'

'He is,' she said, then fussed with her pen and notepad. Lucinda disappeared through the gap before closing the door softly behind her. Jaz studied the paper in her hand, tapping her pen against it. 'Umm, John, I need to tell you something.'

'Oh, yes?'

She paused, glancing up from under eyelashes, then shooting her gaze back down to the paper. 'Hetty was here this morning at half seven asking to speak to you.'

'Sorry?' John felt his annoyance mount. 'Why didn't you tell me?'

She looked away to the corner of the room. 'You were having breakfast and I—'

'What? Why didn't you come and get me? Jaz, this really isn't on.' Not only did John want to know why Jaz would lie, but he was also suddenly inquisitive as to why Hetty had been there. He remembered the knock at the door and Jaz coming back saying it was just a vendor who needed directing to the field. He was too cross to sit still and stood up and leant on the back of his chair.

'I just thought you needed a break and a proper breakfast before it all kicked off today. I'm sorry. I thought I was doing the right thing.'

How could that have been the right thing? She'd lied to him. And again, a line had been crossed – an unspoken boundary broken. 'But what if there'd been a problem? What if—'

'I did ask, and she said there wasn't, she wanted to talk to you about something else.' Her pleading eyes followed him. 'If there had been something wrong, I'd have got you straight away. It's just that you're hardly eating at the moment and I really thought it was the best thing for you and your health. I'm – I'm sorry.'

The atmosphere in the study became thick and tense. The walls of books felt like they were touching his nose and he had a sudden need to open the window, for the fresh air to blow away the pressure. This whole not trying to overreact thing was exhausting. Making an effort to relax his shoulders, he replied softly, 'Thank you for your concern, Jaz. It means a lot.'

Wrinkles released a little from her brow. He wished his brow was that wrinkle free. Deep lines of worry were being scored into his skin with every passing day. Sometimes he wished one way or another things would come to a head so his family could deal with it and move on. 'Next time, please just come and get me if someone wants to speak to me. Okay?'

She nodded. 'Okay.'

Jaz looked so downcast, he said, 'Listen, why don't you type up those letters and head off early today? Especially as you're back here tomorrow.'

'Are you sure?'

'Yeah, go on. I want you out of here by one o'clock at the latest, okay?'

'Okay, boss,' she replied affectionately, the smile finally returning to her eyes.

After Jaz left, John tried to work and focus on his own business, but before long he was itching to take a break from his desk and see what the festival was like now it was in full swing. In the distance he could hear the noise of the funfair, the chatter of a crowd and the hum of cars. He felt a fool for ever doubting Hetty that it would be a success. Strange, alluring creature that she was. It was definitely time to stretch his legs and get some fresh air.

Outside he felt suddenly cleaner, and took great deep breaths as he left the damp and dusty air of the house behind. Leaving the formal gardens, John grew more and more excited as he drew nearer to the festival. Walking among the crowd, smiles and nods came his way. The cheerful greetings and compliments provided a strange sense of acceptance he'd never had before. Though he studied the crowd, he couldn't see Hetty. He spotted her assistant, Macie, virtually running past him, and he quickly grabbed her attention. 'Hi, excuse me. Macie, isn't it?' She stopped and turned to him with a big grin on her face, clearly enjoying the hubbub, but she was also holding a screwdriver and hammer tightly to her chest like it was made of gold. 'Have you seen Hetty anywhere?'

'Yeah, she's at the Portaloos dealing with an … issue.'

'Should I ask?'

'Oh, it's not what you think. Someone's got stuck in one of the cubicles.'

'Really?' From the state of some of the Portaloos he'd had to use, he knew how awful that could be. 'That sounds terrible.'

'Is everything okay? Do you need me to give her a message?'

'No. I'll come along if that's okay? Just in case I can help.'

As they approached, he saw Hetty speaking calmly to the Portaloo door. A small crowd were already beginning to linger. 'It's all right, Mrs Martin, don't panic. I'll have you out of there in a jiffy. I know you're upset but you need to take long, deep breaths.' She paused, looking disgusted. 'Well, in that case don't take really deep breaths, take medium-sized ones – through your mouth. I know, Mrs Martin, and I'm very sorry it smells like that but there's not much I can do about it right now except get you out, which is what I'm trying to do.' She turned and her face relaxed with relief. 'My assistant's just coming with a screwdriver and hammer. You'll be out soon, I promise. Remember to breathe, Mrs Martin. Okay?'

They stopped by Hetty's side and Macie handed over the screwdriver. Mrs Martin's voice carried through the door and Macie's jaw dropped open. 'Did she just call you a—'

'Yes, I think she did,' Hetty replied cheerfully. If John had been in that situation he'd have been sweating, stressed and probably shouting at Mrs Martin, but Hetty was smiling, almost giggling. 'Hello, John. How are you this morning?'

'Fine,' he answered with a laugh. 'You?'

'Good,' she said and nodded towards the door. 'Just a minor hiccup.' A voice from the other side was mumbling something rude.

'Can I help at all?' He could see she had it all in hand but felt he should offer anyway.

'If you could hold the door on this side, that'd be great. Mrs Martin's got herself locked in and even though I've tried, I can't get the door to unlock from the outside. The hire company's not answering either so I can't get hold of a master key. Mrs Martin says the mechanism's stuck so I'm going to have to take the door off its hinges.'

'That's very clever of you. Ingenious, in fact.'

'Thank you.'

'Done much breaking and entering before?'

Hetty glanced over her shoulder, grinning. 'Only at weekends.' She placed the screwdriver against the pin in the top hinge and, using the hammer, knocked it downwards. After a couple of whacks on the pin it shot out so the first hinge hung away from the doorframe. She then did the same to the bottom one and within a few minutes the door was off both hinges, ready to be removed. John was just about to take it away when Hetty gently placed her hand there, holding it in place. 'Are you decent, Mrs Martin?'

'Of course I'm decent,' a crotchety old voice replied. 'I've been decent for half an hour since I got locked in this blimmin' box of hell. This is why I don't use Portaloos. Especially not for a shi—'

'Right then, Mrs Martin, we'll open the door now, okay? Ready, John?' He nodded and together they removed the door. Mrs Martin emerged, a little unsteady and slightly green around the gills, but apart from that, completely unharmed. Hetty stood up. 'There we go then. You all right, Mrs Martin?'

Having regained her composure under the gaze of the assembled crowd, the older woman adjusted her waistband and lifted her head high. 'Fine, thank you, Miss Colman. Though you might want to get someone to check that lock.'

Without missing a beat, Hetty nodded. 'Will do. Now you go and have a lovely day.' The lady toddled off, head held high, and the crowd dispersed, sniggering and mumbling as they went. 'John, could you hold the door so I can get this all back together?'

He did as he was told, amazed at her skill and at her temperament. How did someone stay so calm under such pressure? 'I'm sorry I didn't make it for when the gates opened. I was hoping to, but my brother called and – well, it took quite a long time to get rid of him.'

'Not to worry,' Hetty replied, banging the top pin back into the hinge. 'I think you'd have enjoyed seeing everyone so excited though.' She did the same to the bottom hinge and stood up. 'People seem to be really enjoying themselves.'

'Apart from Mrs Martin.'

Hetty examined the lock which was quite hard to move but with force she eventually slid it over. 'It is a bit sticky. Macie, could you run and grab the oil from the emergency box and I'll lube it up.' John felt himself grow hot and felt silly for being so prudish.

'Already got it,' she replied, picking something up from the floor. John hadn't even seen it in her arms. Hetty was obviously training her well.

'You're a star,' Hetty said affectionately, spraying the oil onto the lock and trying it again. 'Right. Good as new, but let's get one of the stewards over here to keep an eye on things for an hour. What's next?'

Macie checked her phone where she was obviously keeping notes. 'Ants were attacking Mr Hobbs' jam stall so I swapped him with the soap lady next door. They're fine but you might want to go and have a word with Hobbs. He was a tad stroppy and got in a bit of a flap.'

'Okay.' Hetty wiped her hand over her forehead. The sun was beating down and there was a pinkness to her cheeks from the exertion. She adjusted her glasses and smiled at him.

John's heart pumped harder and faster as he realised he was definitely falling for this incredible woman. He'd never felt anything as strong as this before and it was unnerving. He felt so alive in her company but with everything going on, should he ignore these feelings? On this crazy summer's day he felt carefree and his heart was saying to try, but there was a weight at the back of his mind. A weight of uncertainty caused by his family's fortunes – dragging her into that might drag her down with him.

'Coming with us?' she asked John, and he found himself nodding.

Mr Hobbs waved his tea towel over his stall packed full of different types of jam, but there didn't seem to be an ant in sight. The soap lady kept glancing sideways and tutting then rearranging her display. 'I can't see any ants here, you know,' she said. 'I think he was making a big fuss about nothing. Probably because he wanted the corner pitch.'

'Oh, I'm sure that's not the case,' said Hetty, completely unfazed. 'Is it, Mr Hobbs?' She began to examine the ground for ants, but she couldn't see any now. Either they'd decided soap wasn't really for them and had hidden themselves back underground, or there weren't quite as many as Mr Hobbs had been making out.

'Of course not,' the older man blustered, still waving his tea towel around. 'Look.' Mr Hobbs picked up a jar of strawberry jam and showed them the ant stuck to the bottom. 'This is my special strawberry jam, made with Swallowtail Bay strawberries. I can't sell this now. No one wants jam with dead ants stuck to it.'

This was an indisputable fact that no one could argue with. 'No,' said Hetty. 'That's very true, but at least it's only one jar.'

John leaned in. 'But, Mr Hobbs, you could wipe it off and give it to the soap lady to say thank you for swapping pitches. I'm sure she'd like that, and you seem a very kind and generous man to me.' As John straightened up Mr Hobbs considered his suggestion and winked.

'Good idea.'

Hetty, John and Macie watched on as Mr Hobbs wiped the bottom of the jar with the tea towel and approached the soap lady. 'Here,' he said, turning slightly pinker. 'As a thank-you.'

She took the proffered jar happily. 'Oh, I say. How very kind, Mr Hobbs. Thank you.'

Mr Hobbs slid back to his waiting customers.

'That was a good idea,' Hetty said as they moved off.

John shrugged. 'I do have them occasionally.'

'Well, I'm glad I was here to witness one of them.' Again they made eye contact and John held her gaze for longer, searching her eyes for a hint that she was feeling the same way as him.

'You two make a good team,' Macie added with a slight raise of an eyebrow.

Hetty eyed her and John felt a heat on his cheeks. He'd never been so grateful for his beard before. As Macie began to speak to another stall holder, checking they were okay, Hetty turned to him, her arm brushing against his. 'We do make a good team. And to think I thought you were going to leave everything to me and just take the money at the end of it.'

'It was my original plan. Mainly because I thought that's the way you'd want it.'

She looked confused. 'Whatever gave you that idea?'

'You just seem the type that likes to be one hundred per cent in charge of everything.'

Hetty gave a sly smile. 'I do, but, as this is your land and you're going to get half the blame if things go wrong, I think it's good that you're here too.'

He chuckled, and the words, 'So do I,' were out of his mouth before he could stop them.

The sun passed over Hetty's face, causing her eyes to twinkle. A heavy drumbeat pounded in his chest, echoing off his ribs as the space between them shrunk. Hetty was the first to break the spell and look away as Macie came back over. 'Ready for the next thing?'

'Have I got time for a quick coffee before the next problem?' she asked Macie. 'I'm gasping.'

'Course. Let's grab one from Raina's stall. She makes the best coffee.'

'Have you got time for one, John?' He nodded and the three of them wandered off to get a coffee.

All the stalls were busy, and John was pleased to see that strawberry products were taking pride of place in people's displays. The hum of generators, and the chatter of adults blended with the delighted squeals of children. The grounds of Thornhill Hall had never felt so alive. His every step brought a new smell as he saw the fresh local produce on display: sweet summer strawberries, earthy potatoes, breads, pastries and cookies, everything you could think of was there. A new life had been born into the place.

They approached Raina's stall and the rich, strong aroma filled his nose. He was pleased to see she'd brought some cakes too, including the rich chocolate mousse cake he'd tried at the planning meeting with Hetty. It had been divine, soothing every worldly worry he had. He hadn't known food could do that to you.

'Hi, Raina,' Hetty said, then ordered the coffees.

'You've done a grand job here, Hetty. This is wonderful. I can't believe we're seeing so many Swallowtail Bay residents come out. And it's only the first day.'

'Thanks, Raina,' Hetty replied, waving a hello to the lady at the stall next to Raina's, who owned Old Herbert's Shop on the high street. They went over and Hetty introduced John. Stella had a number of different artworks on display and he felt a tinge of regret for the paintings they'd had to sell to pay for repairs to the house and cover the bills that seemed to come in every day. Stella's dog, Frank, a pudgy King Charles spaniel was getting more than his fair share of fusses from anyone who came near, and as John went over, he couldn't help giving him a good scratch behind his ears.

The coffee revitalised them all, and he, Macie and Hetty laughed and joked about poor Mrs Martin as they stood outside Raina and Stella's stalls.

'Did you hear her?' Macie asked John. 'She called Hetty a—'

'No, thank you, Miss,' Hetty interjected. 'We don't need a repeat of that.'

'I did,' John confirmed to Macie. 'It almost made me blush.'

They all laughed again just as Hetty's phone rang. She pulled it from her pocket but as her eyes scanned the screen, the smile fell from her face. 'Hello, Mum. You okay?'

Watching on, John grew more and more concerned. His brows knitted together as confusion and pain swept her features. She swallowed hard and as the conversation went on, she seemed to get smaller and smaller. He wanted to reach out and take her hand but kept his own firmly in his pockets. She paced away, her head dipped and voice low so he could hardly hear. Macie, he saw, was worried too.

After a long silence, during which Hetty inadvertently came nearer to them again, listening intently to whatever was being said, her voice when she finally spoke was quiet and pained. 'Okay, Mum. I understand. If you're sure that's what you want to do then I guess I have to accept it. How's Dad taken the news? Right. Okay. Bye.'

'What's wrong?' Macie asked as soon as Hetty dropped her phone away. Macie's concern for her friend only heightened John's own.

She looked at Macie, then John, and finally back at the ground. 'My mum and dad are getting divorced.'

Chapter 20

Hetty thrust her phone into the back pocket of her jeans and kept her eyes on the ground. The sun was shining so brightly it seemed wrong. How could it be such a lovely day and something so horrible happen? The sun suddenly seemed too strong, the noises too loud and the smells almost overpowering. While she'd known it was a possibility – a very real possibility – she somehow hadn't let herself believe it would actually come to this.

It had been a couple of weeks since her mum saw the solicitor and she'd hoped against hope that after their shopping trip, when her mum had clearly been upset someone else was looking after Jeff, that she was beginning to change her mind. Well, that had backfired, hadn't it? Maybe Hetty herself hadn't helped matters by shoving her feelings away, refusing to deal with the situation. Perhaps if she'd actually got on with things instead of pretending they weren't happening, her mum and dad would have been forced to talk to each other and be honest. Would this whole thing have been avoided if they had? She was sure her dad wasn't having an affair and her mum still hadn't produced any satisfactory evidence to the contrary. The crux seemed to be that her mum was massively dissatisfied, but they hadn't sat down and actually addressed any of the issues.

Hetty watched the stumps of grass under her trainers flattening underfoot then springing back up. She had to spring back up and get through this weekend. There was far too much riding on it for her to lose focus and make mistakes. She'd just have to do what she'd done about Ben and lock her feelings away to be dealt with when this was all over. Macie and John had been watching her, she knew, but she wasn't going into details now.

'Hetty? Are you okay?' asked Macie, gently touching her arm.

'Hetty?' This time John spoke, piercing her thoughts, pulling her out. His eyes were full of kindness and concern. 'Do you need to sit down, or have some water or something?'

The noise of the day flooded back into her ears and the different smells hit her nostrils: bacon, something sweet, then something spicy. The noise of the funfair filled her ears with tinny, cheerful sounds. She could hear children laughing, people talking, and pots and pans being banged, moved and scraped. She'd worked so hard for this, and it was only Friday. Saturday and Sunday promised to be even better. She really had to stay calm; she didn't want to let herself or John down. John, with his heavy eyebrows that made him look stern, though that was nowhere near the truth of him. Taking a deep breath, Hetty rallied, plastering on a smile. 'No, no. I'm fine. Come on, Macie. I want to check on the funfair and bouncy pirate ship.'

Macie paused. 'Hetty, are you sure you don't need to take a few minutes. This must be quite a shock.'

'It is and it isn't,' she answered quickly, wanting to drop the subject.

'But to tell you now. Today. How—'

'Apparently Mum accidentally told Mrs Jarvis who's coming to the food festival today. Mum didn't want to tell me like this, but she didn't want Mrs Jarvis to mention something first.'

'Okay,' said John. 'But still, why don't we take five minutes just to have a drink and for you to—'

'To what?' Her tone was scornful, harsh even, and as John

pulled back from her, she felt a sudden stab of regret. 'Honestly, I'm fine. There's nothing I can do about it and they've been on the verge for a while. I don't know why I'm so surprised.'

'Because it's your parents,' Macie said, aghast. 'It's like someone suddenly saying a universal truth isn't universal anymore. Like them changing their minds that the Earth is called Earth or something.'

Hetty pressed her lips together. 'I really am fine. Now, let's get on.' Her parents would be the talk of the town. Still, it might take the heat off the Thornhills for a while, she thought sardonically. Hetty pulled herself together though she found it difficult under John's fretful gaze. 'Right, I need to get on and, John, I'm sure you have stuff to be getting on with too.'

'It's fine, if you need me—'

'I don't need anyone,' she said quickly, then wondered where on earth it had come from. 'Guys, honestly, I'm fine. Please stop fussing around me. I just need to work.' She marched away without looking back, worried that John might be watching her. Again, she ignored the growing feeling inside: that she'd let him down.

An hour later, Hetty had sent Macie to the parking field to check everything was fine there. She couldn't handle any more sympathetic glances or her asking if she was okay every five minutes. Feigning this level of cheerfulness was draining enough without Macie adding to it.

Hetty made her way around the food stalls in the lower field trying to decide what to have for dinner. She didn't really care and had lost her appetite completely. She would have quite happily eaten a stale sandwich and cold tea, sure she wouldn't be able to taste anything. All her senses had dulled since her mum's call and despite her best efforts, she couldn't stop thinking about her poor dad. He'd been devastated when Daisy had moved out. Who knew what state he'd be in now, knowing it was definitely over and she was never coming back? A stinging at the back of her eyes meant tears were threatening. Hetty took a long, deep breath and walked on. Somehow, she'd gravitated to Ben's stall. The old, familiar comfort of his presence helped calm her a little. He'd be as surprised as everyone else when he heard about the divorce.

'Come on, you lot, you know this is the best bread in town. And once it's gone it's gone so if you want to buy two, even three loaves, I'd do it now.' A large crowd had gathered around him, which pleased the deli stall next door as they were getting a lot of add-on trade. 'Did you know you can freeze them?' Ben continued, smiling at everyone. 'Oh, you'd like three of these would you, madam? All I can say is you have excellent taste.' Hetty watched on from the corner. Once the crowd had disappeared, he spotted her. 'Hey, Hetty. You okay? You look a bit stressed. That John Thornhill boring you to death going on about his grand house and shooting parties and all that sort of stuff, is he?'

'You shouldn't say things like that, Ben. John's not like that—'

'Oh, so it's John now, is it?' He was teasing but there was a pinch at the corners of his eyes.

'Not now, Ben, please.' Hetty rubbed her forehead. Her brain felt like it was pushing against her skull. 'He's actually okay.'

'That's not what I've heard, and I've heard a lot.'

'Well, he is actually.' An unreadable emotion passed over Ben's eyes but was gone in a second. She knew it couldn't be jealousy. Ben had never been the jealous type. 'And you shouldn't listen to gossip.'

'Why not?' He wrapped a loaf of bread and handed it to a customer with a wink. Hetty marvelled at his ability to make someone feel special and like the only person in the world – the centre of all his attention. 'Sometimes gossip's gossip for a reason: because it's true. I heard his dad's gone loopy-loo and his mum's become a shut-in.' Hetty knew Ben was joking but knowing how his words would hurt John hurt her too. A profound respect for John had been growing steadily in her since their first meeting. She was also a little shocked at Ben. He'd never been this callous when they were together.

'Ben, please. I know you think you're being funny, but it's really not a laughing matter.'

'Come on, Hetty. Where's your sense of humour?' Hetty pressed her temples, feeling a stress headache mounting. Suddenly concerned, he walked towards her and placed a hand on her shoulder. 'Hey, what is it? Come here.' He pulled her away from the stall and into an embrace. She collapsed into him, the smell of his T-shirt soothing her aching head. 'Where's the bubbly little firecracker I'm used to? What's up?' He stepped back and dipped his head to make eye contact.

Hetty squeezed her eyes shut, trying to drive away the pain in her head. 'Mum rang this morning.'

'Daisy-doo? What's she stressing about now?'

She'd forgotten that he called her mum Daisy-doo. Her mum had loved Ben from the start, he'd fitted so seamlessly into their family dynamic with his easy friendliness. *Would John fit in?* she wondered and banished the thought. It's not like he'd ever meet them and be a part of her family. 'Mum and Dad are getting divorced,' she said for the second time that day. And as the words came out of her mouth she felt a tearing in her soul.

'What? Why? When did this happen?'

Hetty shook her head trying to order her thoughts. 'They've been struggling since they both retired. It's like, now they're actually spending time together, they've suddenly discovered they don't like each other very much. Mum moved out a couple of weeks ago.' She didn't mention the supposed affair.

'I can't believe it. I'd have never pegged your folks as splitters. I'm sorry, Hetty. That's tough.'

As unhelpful as that response was, Ben had always been easy to talk to and now she'd started, she was finding it hard to stop. 'But something about it just doesn't sit right, you know?' Ben gazed back unsure what to say. 'I just know that deep down it's not what they want. Mum's voice was all shaky, like she wasn't sure herself but – oh, I don't know. Dad's a mess.'

201

Ben shrugged. 'Let me give you another squeeze.' He did and Hetty felt a few of her troubles slide away. 'How about tomorrow night, for this film thing, we have a picnic? It'll cheer you up. Besides, I've got something for you.'

'Urgh, can't you give it to me now? I don't want any more surprises, Ben.'

'No. I want to tell you tomorrow when we're sitting on a picnic blanket under the stars.' He moved his hand in a semicircle against the bright blue sky for dramatic effect.

'Okay,' Hetty agreed. There was no point arguing and she didn't want to rain on his parade. 'Have you got any of your olive and sundried tomato bread?'

'Sure.' He grabbed her one and wrapped it before handing it over. 'I'll meet you here at six tomorrow, ready for the film night.'

'Okay,' she agreed, only half listening. Her thoughts were a muddle, punctured here and there by images of her mum and dad and, surprisingly, John Thornhill's concerned face. 'Do I need to bring anything?'

'Nope. I've got it covered. Just bring your gorgeous self.'

She tried to focus on the next thing on her to-do list but a niggling in the back of her mind told her that she was right about her mum and dad. Deep down, she knew they still loved each other, if only she could think of a way for them to see it too. But as her heart sank deep within her chest, she worried that it was all just too little, too late.

Chapter 21

After a long day at the festival, Hetty sat in her garden, throwing pieces of bread to Stanley and desperately trying to relax. She'd hoped that sheer exhaustion would force her mind into some kind of meaningless white noise, but it hadn't yet slowed down. In fact, it had sped up. So as well as thinking about Ben and the surprise he had for her tomorrow, her parents' shenanigans, and everything she had to do the next day, she kept seeing John Thornhill's anxious face, watching her as she took her phone call. His concern for her had been overpowering in its intensity. Not intense in that he'd gone on and on, wanting to know what had transpired, but his alarmed expression had caused a worrisome stirring inside her. She'd again felt guilty, like she'd let him down somehow by making him concerned for her. He had enough troubles of his own to think about.

'What have we got on tomorrow, Stanley, do you think, hey? What's first on our to-do list, my limpy seagull friend?'

Stanley hopped about, pecking at the pieces of bread she threw down for him.

'Site check first thing, of course, then we should probably take a look at some of the stalls we didn't get a chance to today.' She was saying 'we' and on any other occasion she'd mean Macie, but in the back of her mind, she saw herself wandering about with John, laughing and joking. She shook her head to shake his lingering shadow away. 'Gwen seemed happy, didn't she? I'm really glad we could get her involved. Do you know, Stanley Seagull, I think her dislike of the festival was simply down to the fact that she and the others put in the work to organise it and everyone thought it was a joke. I'd be quite cheesed off if that was me too, wouldn't you?'

Stanley looked up from his bread and cocked his head to one side as if considering his response.

'What? John would probably say something clever about getting people onside and bringing people together.' She took a deep breath in, the smell of next door's honeysuckle drifting on the breeze. Closing her eyes, she listened to the sea, enjoying the serenity after such a busy day and with the prospect of more busy days to come. Hetty grabbed her glass and took a sip of the cold, crisp wine. It slid slowly down her throat and as it hit her stomach, she relaxed a little more. Staring at her single wine glass she imagined John sitting with her, smiling as she chatted away, them both throwing food to Stanley. She could imagine him enjoying the peace of the seaside cottage, the sense of being closed off from the world that she enjoyed so often here. John's voice seemed to penetrate her thoughts, replaying conversations they'd had through the day, and their trip the fair.

'I hope John makes it to open the gates tomorrow, Stanley. I think he'll enjoy seeing everyone there.' She tossed another crumb from her plate, but Stanley didn't go after it. He watched it land, then turned to her again. 'What's the matter?'

Stanley stared, and under his beady-eyed gaze, she suddenly realised she hadn't mentioned Ben once this evening so far. And it wasn't because she'd locked her feelings for him in a box at the back of her brain, refusing to open it – that tactic wasn't working particularly well at the moment – it was because her brain was jam-packed with thoughts of John. Not massive life-changing thoughts, just imagining everyday tasks they'd complete together, conversations they'd have about this and that. Every time she asked Stanley a question, she could hear what John would reply. It was like he was with her in spirit, and she realised with a sudden jerk of her limbs that her heart liked that idea as much as her mind did.

Completely unnerved by how much she wished he was there, sharing a drink, talking about the boring ins and outs of the day, Hetty took another swig of her wine. Glancing around, she began to imagine what it would be like to have him standing in the kitchen doorway, bringing out more nibbles for them to share. What would it be like living with him? She knew he could laugh and joke but was also caring and kind. Her treacherous mind suddenly presented her with an image of them in bed together, not just rolling around in the sheets – though the very idea made her hot and her body tingle – but both of them propped up reading books, drinking tea he'd brought her in the morning. She somehow knew that he'd be the one to make it, treating her to a lie-in. Ben had always insisted they take turns, though it was more often her turn than his.

Flopping back in her chair, she realised that what was truly unnerving was that these feelings were stronger than anything she had felt for Ben. Even in the beginning of their relationship.

In the warm evening sun, with the gentle shushing of the sea in the background, it suddenly struck Hetty that she was falling for John Thornhill. And falling hard. As grumpy and blunt as he'd seemed at first, there was so much more to him. There was definitely something between them. A spark in the air whenever they were together. An equal partnership of minds and ideals as well as a physical attraction. And it was growing the more they saw each other.

'Oh, Stanley.' Hetty let her head fall into her hands and rested her elbows on the table. 'As if life isn't hard enough right now, I've gone and fallen for the lord of the manor. I knew my heart couldn't be trusted.' But as worrying as all this was, it created a deep sense of 'right' down in the base of her soul.

The seagull flew off, clearly bored of the conversation and the lack of bread it had created, leaving Hetty alone. A smile pulled at her lips as she thought of John, then quickly disappeared. She was having a romantic starlit picnic with Ben in just about twenty-four hours' time and the very idea made her stomach lurch.

After finishing her wine, Hetty went back indoors and watched some mindless television, trying to fill her brain with troubles from the screen rather than her own worrying thoughts. After flitting between several different television shows, attempting to read three different books and even turning on Radio Four to see what they were arguing about now, she called it quits and trudged up the stairs to bed.

Her bedroom was cool where the windows had been open all day and the blinds drawn. Throwing on the shorts and vest top she liked to sleep in, she climbed into her enormous, comfortable bed. The cool crisp sheets slid over her skin and she enjoyed the feel of the cold pillow on her cheeks. Snuggling in, her legs and back ached from the efforts of the day and her mind was finally beginning to stop its incessant whirring. She closed her burning and gritty eyes and listened to the musicality of the pebbles being drawn underneath the water. She waited for sleep to take her, but sleep stayed determinedly away.

Hour after hour she tossed and turned, and the night was torrid and difficult. Even though a cool breeze blew into the room, she felt hot no matter how she lay, or how many covers she kicked off. She tried hanging one leg out but even then, her mind would fill with thoughts of John and her body would grow hot. Occasionally dozing off, Hetty awoke easily with every noise and her thoughts constantly swung between Ben, her parents and John. Images of what it would be like to kiss him with his trimmed beard pressing against her lips flicked on the back of her eyelids. Her body imagined being held by him, feeling his strong arms around her. Then pictures of Ben would float through her mind. He wanted a second chance and Hetty had loved him so deeply for so long.

Were her feelings for John more to do with the excitement of the festival and the sense of being in it together? Were her feelings for Ben more solid because of the past they shared? Or was it that her feelings for Ben were unreal? Merely a reminiscence of time gone by, and though she had yearned for a future with him back when they were together, was that really what she wanted now?

Having given up all hope of sleep, Hetty opened the blind and curtains, and from the comfort of her bed, watched the sun rise, listening to the birds sing their dawn chorus. The sky was a beautiful shade of pink with bright orange flashes here and there, like someone had gone at it with a highlighter and she felt privileged to see it. Ironically, the serenity of the scene helped her doze off and she awoke a little while later, her alarm buzzing. It turned out it had been for some time and she was now running horribly late. Panic hit like a bolt of electricity and she scrabbled around getting ready though she felt tired and worn out and her eyes stung as if someone had thrown sand into them.

As Hetty clipped her fringe back, the thought of seeing John Thornhill after some of the very naughty thoughts she'd had last night filled her with embarrassment. It was as if he'd know from the look on her face she'd thought about passionate kisses and much, much more. Huffing out a breath, Hetty could honestly say that as far as her love life was concerned she'd never been more confused in her life.

Chapter 22

John didn't know about Hetty, but from his perspective, the first day of the food festival had been a huge success. Considering it had been a Friday and a lot of people were still working, it had been far busier than he'd expected. With today being Saturday, he could only imagine how crazy and fun the day was going to be. Again, he'd used the word fun. A word that was virtually nonexistent in his vocabulary before he'd met Hetty Colman.

This morning, he'd arrived at the gate just before ten o'clock, hoping that today he'd be able to greet the visitors and see Hetty before the day began. He'd tried not to think about her all night but the image of her face, broken by her parents' news, was etched on his brain. He'd hated seeing such pain and being helpless to do anything about it.

After checking his watch again, he gazed around once more but Hetty wasn't there. He spied Macie speaking to one of the stewards. 'Hey, Macie, have you seen Hetty anywhere?'

'No, I haven't.' He could tell she was worried too. 'She texted to say she was running late which is weird. She's never late for anything, and she especially wouldn't be late for this if she could help it. Maybe she went to see her parents or something?'

John checked his watch again. 'Well, it's nearly ten o'clock, we're going to have to get the gates open soon. I can't believe there's such a massive queue.' He rubbed the back of his neck, already warm from the sun.

'Hetty knows what she's doing,' Macie said proudly. 'She knew just how to market it and build a buzz. All the flyers and posters have worked well, not to mention your radio interview. You did really well there.'

'Thanks,' said John feeling ridiculously proud at the compliment. If Macie had said that to him, she might have said the same to Hetty.

'I'm so pleased that things have gone well so far. Well, apart from some minor mishaps but they always happen. Once we ran a children's party and this kid had a giant piñata – when he swung to hit it, he completely missed and walloped his mum square in the face.'

John laughed. 'What happened next?'

'There was loads of blood – the kid had broken her nose – the dad saw the blood and passed out and Hetty was straight in there, telling the other parents what to do while she took everyone to minor injuries.'

'Is that why there are bandages in the emergency box?' he asked.

'Yep. Lots of them.'

John's watch ticked to exactly ten o'clock and he nodded at Macie. They signalled to the stewards to open the gate and the awaiting crowd were let in. Day two was starting and John found himself even more excited than he had been yesterday as he was met with smiling faces, kind comments and excited chatter, but Hetty was still nowhere to be seen. All of a sudden, her Mini screeched into the car park and she hurtled out of the car. The shoelaces of her blue spotty trainers were undone, and she was wearing dungarees.

'Hetty,' he called as she rushed past him. She paused and gave him a polite smile, but it didn't carry any of the warmth it had yesterday. 'Are you okay?'

'Yes, I'm fine. Sorry I'm late.' She went to rush off again, but John felt the need to take charge a little. She'd work herself into the ground if she didn't stop and at least have a coffee. Dark circles rimmed her eyes and he knew then she hadn't slept for worrying.

'Wait, wait.' He caught hold of her bare arm before she could dash off again and where his fingers touched her soft skin they prickled. She paused and stared at his hand. Worried her glare meant he'd gone too far, he quickly removed it. 'Are you sure you're okay? Please, let me get you a coffee or something. There are no disasters to solve yet, we think.'

'No, everything's fine right now,' Macie agreed. 'You should definitely have a coffee and a chocolate brownie. I bet you haven't had breakfast.'

Hetty's shoulders slumped a little. 'No, I haven't. Okay then, a coffee would be great, thanks.' She turned to answer an older lady hobbling by who had said hello. As if she hadn't a care in the world, Hetty said, 'Morning, Mrs Bates. Yes, I think we've got another good day ahead of us. Aren't we lucky?' The old lady cast her eyes over John, and he smiled and welcomed her to the festival.

'Good morning, Mr Thornhill. How's your mother? We haven't seen her at the library in a while.'

Hetty glanced towards him and John beamed. That Hetty would even think about how this sort of comment might affect him with all she was handling herself was the most heart-warming thing he'd ever experienced. 'No,' he answered with a grin. 'Unfortunately, I think her to-be-read pile has got so big she's trying to get through that first. I'm sure she'll be back in town as soon as she's caught up.'

'Well, I do hope we'll see her again soon. Please tell her Mrs Bates says hello.'

'I certainly will. I hope you enjoy the festival.'

Mrs Bates hobbled on and Hetty whispered, 'That's not quite true, is it?'

'No, but she was being nice, and I didn't want to dampen her mood.'

'That's nice of you.'

'I am nice,' he replied, leaning in to whisper, wanting to be close to her. 'But don't tell anyone.'

She leaned in too. 'Don't worry, I won't say a word.'

As they strolled on to one of the other coffee vendors (not Raina's this time as they didn't want to seem biased with the awards coming up), Hetty was quiet and answered his polite conversation with one-word answers. They ordered and he handed her a takeaway cup. 'I'm sorry,' she said with a quick glance up at him. 'I didn't sleep very well last night. I should really put these on.' She pulled a pair of sunglasses from the front pocket of her dungarees and brandished them in the air. 'I look a right state.'

'You look beautiful,' he replied without thinking, and when her head shot up all he could see was the beautiful and worried soul behind her glorious eyes. He had an overwhelming urge to cup her face and draw her in for a kiss. Hetty darted her eyes down and she shrugged off the compliment.

'I look like a right old grot bags, but there's another busy day ahead of us and no time for tiredness today.' She had a sip of her coffee. 'All I need is a bucket of caffeine and maybe some choco-late.'

He could tell she was deliberately trying to avoid discussing the phone call she'd received yesterday, burying herself in her work. 'Could you not sleep last night?' She appraised him for a second and then answered.

'I just kept having a million and one weird dreams, so I don't really feel like I slept at all. I missed my alarm this morning, which I can assure you, never normally happens.'

'I believe you,' he replied. 'I was sorry to hear about your mum and dad. If there's anything I can do to help …'

'No, no, all fine, thanks.' She swigged her coffee. 'I'm just pleased we've got another fine day. Tomorrow's forecast is a bit cloudy but it's still saying only two per cent chance of rain, so we'll be fine.'

Knowing the conversation was ended, John tried to lighten the mood. 'What problems do you think we'll be faced with today?'

'We?' she echoed, her eyes having regained some of their normal brilliance. They began to stroll through the stalls. The vendors were already busy with customers and the wide-open spaces were filling with people. The first band Hetty had organised was setting up at the makeshift stage – a patch of grass surrounded by hay bales – but people were already gathering ready to watch.

'Yes, *we*. More Portaloo problems? Do we need to re-stock the emergency box?'

'I can't imagine what else might happen to the Portaloos, but never say never. There's always something that goes horribly wrong. The key is how you handle it.'

'Maybe the Thornhill ghost will make an appearance.'

It was an off-the-cuff remark but Hetty's tone and expression grew lighter than it had been so far that morning. 'Is there really a Thornhill ghost?'

'Not really, but people love the idea. Mother thinks there is and I'm afraid I do sometimes tease her, moving her book and blaming the old spook.' He nodded a greeting at a passing woman.

'And you're how old?'

John grinned. 'The story goes back to when the original family owned the place, before it got sold, the eldest son fell in love with a woman from the town but she was already engaged to another man. The son challenged the man to a duel—'

'There really isn't enough duelling these days, is there?'

'Definitely not. The son shot the other man and killed him, but then the woman decided she didn't want the son either and when she tried to break it off, he killed her and then himself. Weirdly, only the ghost of the son has been seen according to legend.'

'Well, that's cheerful.' Hetty giggled.

'Ghosts don't generally have happy stories.'

'No, I suppose not. Have you ever seen him?'

'No. When I was little, Felix used to tease me about him, making footsteps and echoes and blaming them on the ghost but he never appeared. Is there anything in the emergency box to help if our spectre turns up?' He took a sip of his coffee, the happiest he had been in a long time.

'Umm, no, but I do need to top up the chocolate bars. If he appears, we might be able to distract him with one of those. Everyone likes chocolate, don't they? Anyway, ghosts aside, are you sure you can handle this? You have no idea what's going to be thrown at you in the exciting world of events management. It might just be more than a lord-of-the-manor antiques dealer can handle.'

'I'll have you know'— John began to grin – 'us stuffy lord-of-the-manor antiques dealers deal with all sorts of emergencies on a daily basis.'

'Is that so?'

'It is. I've saved babies, got cats out of trees, helped little old ladies across the road—' He listed them on his fingers.

'Very heroic,' Hetty replied.

'I am. So I'm sure I can handle today.' His hand brushed against Hetty's as they walked side by side. John's head filled with a million things he wanted to tell her but he couldn't read Hetty's expression or see if she felt the same way. He had a feeling that if she felt even a fraction of what he was right now, she'd explode.

After a second of loaded silence he cleared his throat. 'You ready to do a site check?'

'You're getting the hang of this,' she replied, popping on her sunglasses. 'Let's go.'

Chapter 23

Hetty's heart had fluttered apprehensively on seeing John at the gate when she arrived at the fields.

It wasn't just that after starting off so disinterested in the festival he'd really got involved, or that his support over her mum and dad was appreciated even though she didn't want to open that can of worms just now. It was that her epiphany about him had completely and utterly shaken her world and now she had no idea how to act around him.

Everything felt alien, the atmosphere loaded. But John seemed his usual self, his face never betraying a hint of anything. Pushing up her sunglasses, Hetty knew she had to act as normally as she could.

She was pleased to see that as they walked around the site, ticking things off on her checklist, John was genuinely interested in what she was doing, learning from her. The only problem they encountered was the hooks on the little yellow duckies floating around the hook-a-duck game seemed to be a little too bent over. So much so that it would be very difficult to actually hook one. Hetty had spent five minutes straightening them under the glare of the stall holder. Stubbornly refusing to be intimidated, she'd simply smiled at him and strolled away once she was done. Then they'd called at the pop-up pamper parlour to see a chatty Gwen, busy with teenage girls getting fake nails, and younger ones having their hair braided. She even had another member of staff with her.

As it neared lunchtime, and they came back to the lower field filled with food stalls, Hetty was just treating them to a locally made pie when John said, 'Ah, that's my brother,' and broke away to meet him. Hetty held back, not wanting to intrude on a family moment, particularly as the brother had been the cause of John's mood the other day. But then John turned and ushered her forward too. When Hetty saw Jaz with them, she anticipated another odd exchange.

'Felix, thanks for stopping by.' Though he smiled, John's tone was reserved. He reached an arm around the woman next to Felix – presumably John's sister-in-law – giving her a kiss on the cheek and in an easy voice said, 'Lizzy, how are you?'

'Oh, fine, John. Fine. This is all marvellous. Amazing! I can't believe how much you guys have achieved. It's so lovely to see the town all coming together like this and celebrating everything we make and do.' Hetty liked Lizzy immediately.

'It is, isn't it?' he replied, ruffling the hair of the pretty identical twin girls.

'Uncle John!' they protested, and John simply smiled at them as they batted his hand away.

Hetty studied the family dynamic with interest. They were both clearly keeping up appearances, the body language between the two men tense and forced. Felix was a paler, weaker-looking version of his brother. Smaller in stature and bearing with a weak, hardly-there chin. John had clearly inherited all the burly good looks. As suspected, Jaz wasn't happy to see John had been with her and though Jaz hung back, Hetty could feel the glances that came her way.

'So, welcome to Swallowtail Bay Food Festival.' He gestured around him. 'What do you think, Felix?'

'Very impressive,' Felix begrudgingly replied, and Elizabeth bashed him on the arm.

'It's better than impressive. It's ...' Her eyes were bright with enthusiasm. 'Remarkable.'

'I can't take any credit as you know. It's all down to Hetty here. Hetty, this is my brother Felix, his wife Elizabeth and my nieces Louise and Rachel. Jaz you've already met.'

'Hello, everyone,' Hetty replied with a slight nod of her head. Boy, was she glad of the large sunglasses given the dark circles she was currently sporting under her eyes.

John led them to where the first band were playing to a decent-sized crowd. People gathered, sipping drinks from take-away cups or plastic glasses, and resting on the hay bales. The buzz was exactly the same as Hetty remembered it as a child. The two girls, Louise and Rachel, began to dance to the music. Three women danced with their children, throwing some serious moves, and Hetty and John shared a smile. At least they were enjoying themselves, Hetty thought and she had bandages in the emergency box if they needed them. Macie came and stood by her.

'That one looks like she's going to do herself a mischief,' she whispered to Hetty, pointing to a woman throwing some serious shapes.

'She has some moves,' Hetty replied.

John was still talking and beside him Jaz was quiet but hanging on his every word. Hetty decided that as much as she wanted to stay with John, it was time to catch up with Macie and crack on with judging for the awards. 'Have you got the judging sheets, Macie?'

'Yep,' she replied, unclipping the top of her clipboard and pulling out two pieces of paper. 'One for you, one for John.'

'Brilliant, we'll leave him to do his alone and get cracking. John? Sorry for interrupting but can I just give you your judging sheet? I need it by the end of the day.' She stepped nearer to hand him the paper and received a daggers stare from Jaz for daring to interrupt.

'Okay. Where are you going?'

'I'm going to go and get started.'

'Well ...' he hesitated. 'Why don't we go together? I'm sure Felix and Lizzy want to go off and explore the rest of the festival.'

Jaz's face fell as John made no mention of her and Hetty felt for her, even though she was now looking like she wanted to murder Hetty. It had been another brilliant pleasant morning in John's company and she'd even forgotten about her parents for a while. Ignoring Macie's raised eyebrows, Hetty didn't hesitate in her reply. 'Okay.'

John said goodbye to his brother and sister-in-law. 'Jaz, you should take some time to enjoy the festival too.'

'That's fine,' she said, her voice taut. 'I'd rather head back to the house. I've got a lot of work to do.'

'Don't work too hard,' he called after her as she stalked off. Hetty wondered if she should mention that it was clear to everyone but him that Jaz had a crush, but decided it would be too difficult and awkward, especially given how she felt about him. 'So, who's first?'

'First we've got the Baker of the Bay award.' She wanted to get that one over and done with first. With her heart and head a confused muddle of emotions she was desperately trying to ignore, it was better to have the time when John and Ben would be together over and done with.

'Sounds great,' said John. 'Am I going to be as stuffed as I was when we went around and convinced them all to sign up for the festival?'

'I think so,' Hetty replied with a smile, remembering that afternoon.

As they approached Ben's stall, John was quick to notice how busy he was. 'Wow. He's very popular, isn't he?' Hetty nodded and lingered by the side of the pitch.

'Hey, gorgeous,' Ben called when he noticed her.

Not wanting him to make some comment about their relationship in front of John, she quickly responded. 'Hi, Ben. We're here to taste your entry for the Baker of the Bay award. We're doing the judging today.'

His face clouded when he saw John, but he was soon back to his normal, cheerful self. 'Sure thing. Let me get you some samples.' He grabbed a fresh olive and sundried tomato loaf and cut two thick wedges. Placing them on a paper plate with a tiny ramekin of freshly poured olive oil, he brought it over. 'Here you are. The best olive and sundried tomato bread you'll find outside of Italy itself.'

'You're very confident,' John commented. Having grown to know him, Hetty could tell he was being friendly, but Ben didn't take it that way. The crow's feet at the corner of his eyes tightened and his jaw clenched. Ben's usual confidence overrode his annoyance.

'A fact's a fact, mate. Or should I call you Lord?'

Hetty narrowed her eyes at Ben. This wasn't like him. Why was he being so weird with John? Hetty knew full well if she was with Bob from the business forum, he wouldn't be so argumentative. 'Oh, Ben, sorry, I haven't introduced you properly. You remember John Thornhill. John, this is—'

'Nice to meet you, Johnny,' Ben replied, sticking out his hand. John took it politely. 'How do you do?'

'So, is it?'

'Is it what?' Hetty replied, getting a little annoyed with him.

'Lord,' he said, staring at John.

'No, it's just John.' He popped some of the bread into his mouth. As he chewed, Hetty watched his eyes widen as he tasted the flavours Hetty loved so much. 'Wow, this is amazing.'

'Told you,' Ben said gleefully. 'It's Hetty's favourite.'

John looked over and Hetty nodded her agreement, feeling her cheeks burn. 'Thanks, Ben. We've got to move on to the next one now.' With what she hoped was a normal smile, she hurried John away but was aware of Ben watching them as they went. She tried to study his reflection in on-coming sunglasses like she'd seen in the movies, but it was too difficult to make out anything and she was too afraid to turn around and look back at him.

After they'd tasted the rest of the entries for Baker of the Bay, the next stop was at the chocolatier's stall as they moved on to the Maker of the Bay awards. They'd been surprisingly in tune in their opinions though she wouldn't let John tell her for certain who he was voting for.

Hetty scowled as she approached the chocolatier's stall despite it being one of the prettiest with the fairy lights and mouth-watering chocolates. Macie was there, flirting like her life depended on it.

'Hello, you,' Hetty said, as she and John approached.

'Hey, yourself,' Macie replied with a grin and chocolate on her chin. It seemed she was up to her usual tricks.

'Enjoying yourself?' Hetty joked with a slight widening of her eyes.

'Just checking that James is okay.' A faint blush coloured her cheeks obscuring the sprinkling of freckles Hetty thought so pretty.

'James,' said John, stepping forward to shake his hand. Macie stood to the side. 'We're here to taste your entry for the Maker of the Bay award. What have you got for us?'

The tall, handsome chocolatier gave Macie an almost shy glance and picked up a plate. With tiny metal tongs he put two small balls of chocolate on a plate and offered it to John. 'This is one of my favourite flavour combinations. It may sound a bit odd, but it works really well. It's a blackberry and meringue truffle.'

Hetty's mouth was already watering and she and John popped them into their mouths at the same time, while looking at each other. It was a strangely intimate moment and one that made the hairs on the back of her neck raise. Normally when she ate chocolate, really good quality chocolate like this was, she closed her eyes and savoured the flavours, but she couldn't bring her eyes away from John's face. Every inch of her body came alive as she watched him. Like the sun had set her on fire.

Once she'd swallowed and the out-of-body experience ended, Hetty hoped the rest of the afternoon's entries were going to be rubbish because if John carried on doing things like that, she was in real danger of letting her untrustworthy heart run away with her. Her brain could go hang.

Chapter 24

Luckily, some of the other awards entries were pretty average, so Hetty made it through without her body and heart doing things her brain didn't approve of.

As the late afternoon sun began to hang heavier in the sky, Hetty took a moment to appreciate the day. The second day of the festival had gone well. Really well. So well in fact, that she grew more and more nervous of what was going to go wrong. As she'd said to John that morning, something always did. That was how events happened. The disconcerting thing was, not having run a food festival before, she didn't know what it might be. Though there were some clouds here and there in the sky, they were white and fluffy with no hint of grey, so rain was unlikely, but she couldn't shake the horrible feeling that something would go wrong soon.

She was right.

About six o'clock, as the brightness of the day was replaced by a warming golden light, and people made themselves comfortable for the movie, Hetty heard raised voices from one of the fields. Making her way over, she spotted two men on the verge of a fight. They were squaring up to each other and looked like two puffed-up peacocks. At first, she thought it was a joke, but then she heard the language and, with children nearby, knew she had to put a stop to it immediately.

Marching straight into the middle of them despite the threat of a wallop, she placed her hands on her hips and looked them both squarely in the face. 'What on earth do you two think you're doing? And the language coming from you two – in front of children, I might add – would shock anyone. This is completely unacceptable. If you two can't behave yourselves, you'll have to pack up and go home.'

One had the good grace to blush, but the other raised his chin defiantly and brushed his comb-over back the right way. They weren't people Hetty recognised from the bay which meant they were both traders from nearby villages.

'He,' said Comb-over, jabbing his finger in the direction of the other man, 'has been undermining my prices all day—'

'Only because you have too,' the blushing one interrupted. 'Every time I called out a price for my gooseberries you changed yours and called out one that was ten pence lower!'

'Outrageous!' Comb-over replied. 'You started it all by under-cutting my nectarines.'

'Huh! I think you'll find you started all this by commenting on the size of my moolis.'

A sudden thought occurred to Hetty that made her smile. There was nothing in the emergency box to help with this situation and for that, John would tease her. He'd laugh when she told him about this, and then, again, she realised he was popping into her head all the time. Right now, she couldn't decide if she was looking forward to seeing Ben tonight for the picnic or not. She didn't particularly enjoy secrets or surprises and finally discovering whatever it was would be another weight off her mind. For now, she had two disgruntled punters to deal with.

'Right,' she said, turning her head to look from one to the other. 'First of all, you can both come and stand here so I can see both your faces at the same time. I'm not an owl—'

'Hang on a sec,' Comb-over interrupted, but Hetty glared at him and he soon shut his mouth, moving to the ground in front of her she was pointing at.

'Secondly, are you going to start behaving yourselves? How do you think this reflects on your businesses let alone my food festival? Do you think people are going to flock to your stalls after creating this sort of reputation for yourselves? Hmm?' Both traders glanced at each other then looked away, back to Hetty. 'I don't want to kick you out, but I will if I have too.'

'That won't be necessary,' the blushing one said.

'Good. From tomorrow, I'm going to move one of you to the other end of the field so you can't start a fight and swear in front of children. You should both be thoroughly ashamed of your-selves.' Both traders dropped their eyes to the ground, suitably chastised. 'Thirdly, why don't you both go and have a drink in the beer tent and discuss sensibly, like adults, what you'll charge for the last day of the festival because if I have any of this sort of nonsense tomorrow, I really won't hesitate in coming over and packing up your stalls myself.'

With mumbles and nodding heads, they began to clear up, and Hetty left them to it. She'd tell Macie to keep an eye on them tomorrow and the thought of Macie dealing with them brought a huge grin to her face. If they thought she was bad, Macie was even worse. They'd once run an event at the local private school and the snooty headmaster had made a snide comment about canapes. Macie had soon put him straight and the poor chap had been too embarrassed to look at her for the rest of the night.

Amid a slow and gentle breeze from the sea, the sun finished its lazy fall and lit the evening sky with a deep burnt-orange hue. After the incident there'd been a few hours of quiet as those who weren't staying for the film screening left, but the funfair had decided to stay open and the place was still packed. In front of the large screen, families, friends and loved-up couples were busy setting out picnic blankets, arranging and sharing food, and popping open bottles of fizz. Casting an eagle eye around, Hetty could see that many of the bottles and much of the food had been bought from vendors at the festival and a contented smile spread over her face – one that grew even wider when she saw John approaching with a picnic basket.

'Hi,' she said, hoping that he would invite her to sit with him, even though she knew she couldn't accept.

'How was your afternoon?' If he was asking that, he clearly hadn't heard about the fight. Hetty was secretly pleased – she'd been looking forward to telling him herself. She liked the idea of making him laugh.

'You know I said that I couldn't imagine what else might happen?'

'Yes,' he replied, hesitantly.

'You won't believe the problem I had to deal with this afternoon.'

Hetty told John and before long his heavy, deep laugh was surrounding her, lifting her mood. She found the way his eyes scrunched up at the corners particularly attractive. When she'd first met him, she'd wondered if he ever laughed and couldn't imagine him being silly or joking around, but now she knew better. His face had relaxed as she'd told him the story, breaking into a sexy smile.

When they'd settled down and stopped giggling, she motioned to the picnic basket, secretly wondering who he was eating with. 'Are you staying for the film night?'

'Yes, I am. I wondered if you—'

Suddenly Ben was beside her, an arm sliding around her waist. 'Hey, Hetty. You ready?' He jiggled a hessian bag that she could see contained a bottle of champagne, some pots of olives, bread and cheese. She could even spy paper plates and plastic cutlery.

Hetty's heart stilled. 'Ben, hi. Umm, yeah.' Ben gave John a confident – possibly too confident – grin. It wasn't his usual easy smile. It was almost smug.

'Johnny, you sticking around for the film too? Slummin' it with the riffraff?' Internally, Hetty rolled her eyes. After all these years he still hadn't learned to turn his teasing off when the occasion called for it. 'It's going to be a nice evening, I reckon. Even better as Hetty here is going to join me.' He gave Hetty's waist a squeeze.

'Yes, I was planning to.' A look of sadness passed over John's eyes. Had it been her he was going to invite to join him? No, surely not.

'Shall we grab a spot, Hetty? I've been looking forward to this all day.' Ben dropped his hand from her waist and marched off on his own. Words formed in her brain asking John to join them. She didn't want him to leave, but there was nothing she could do. 'Come on, Hetty,' called Ben again, unfurling a picnic blanket and laying it on the floor.

She turned back to John. 'Maybe I'll see you later.'

As she went to follow Ben, a sharp pain stabbed in her chest. She really did like John more than she should and being with Ben now filled her with guilt. She couldn't stop her head turning to glance over her shoulder and see John still standing there. She caught his eye and he gave a small smile then dropped his eyes away. Yet again she felt she'd let him down, hurt him even, and she hated it.

Hetty sat down with Ben on the thick chequered rug, feeling the coarse fibres beneath her fingers. He pulled the tubs out of the bag then laid out different types of bread. He'd gone to a lot of trouble but Hetty couldn't enjoy it as much as she wanted to. She'd felt terrible leaving John standing there alone in the middle of the field. Hetty's throat tightened, stuck with remorse. When she peeked again, he was talking to Jaz, and she felt her brows knit together as he sat down with her. The pop of a bottle forced her head to turn and Ben handed her a glass.

'Do you think John should say a few words before the film starts?' asked Hetty.

Ben scowled. 'Why should he?'

'Well, it's his land and he's helped organise everything.'

'Not as much as you.'

'No but—' Hetty's head began to turn – she just had to see what he was doing now and if he still looked so sad – but then she noticed Ben was watching her. 'He has helped. I just kind of feel he should. It would do wonders for how his family are thought of in the bay.'

'Who cares? They'll never like him.'

'Why do you say that?' Hetty sat up straighter, tension pulling up her spine.

'He's too stand-offish. A bit stuffy. And why should he get all the credit? He hasn't really done anything, has he?' Ben tipped his plastic champagne flute back and drank half the glass in one go. Hetty saw his eyes dart to John and the wink he gave him, pretending to be friendly. 'Look he's chatting up his secretary now.'

'She's his assistant,' Hetty said crossly. 'And there isn't anything between them.'

'Not what I've heard. Anyway, you've done all the organising and problem solving. He's just strolled about as lord of the manor. Why give him any of the credit?'

Because he's a nice man and his family has had a horrible time? she wanted to say but bit the words back. Ben wouldn't understand, but Hetty knew in her gut it was the right thing to do. 'I'm going to ask him if wants to say something.'

'Hetty, wait—' Ignoring Ben's protests, she upped and went over to John.

'Hi, John.'

John was also drinking fizz and was in the middle of pouring a glass for Jaz. There was a hopeful light in his eyes as she approached, and it made her stomach fizz. 'Hetty, hi. Everything okay?'

If Jaz was ever going to turn into a murderer, now was it,

judging by the look she received. 'I'm sorry to interrupt. I know the film's just about to start but I wondered if you wanted to say a few words? I can get them to hold off for a minute if you do.'

'Oh, right.' He ran a hand down his beard, a gesture that was becoming more and more familiar to Hetty. He did it when he was thinking or when he was embarrassed, and she liked it, wishing she knew how the short soft hairs would feel beneath her fingertips.

'I just thought it might be nice to welcome everyone on behalf of your family or wish everyone a good night, that sort of thing. Nothing too big. Just, thank them for coming out and making the festival so successful.'

'Shouldn't you be doing that? You've done all the hard work.'

His words showed Hetty how much Ben had misjudged him. 'I know I could, but I just thought it might help the town get to know you a bit better. If you do have open days in the future, it'll make them more likely to attend and maybe make it easier for your mum to go into town again.'

At the mention of Lucinda, Jaz pinned Hetty in angry eyes, clearly unhappy that he'd spoken to her about his mum.

John slowly nodded. 'Okay, good idea. Shall I do it now?' Hetty nodded and went to ask the technician to hold off, then stood at the back of the crowd. Ben was still trying to coax her back to their picnic spot, but she shook her head. She'd go over in a minute, when this was done, then he'd have her full attention.

When John stood in front of the giant screen, he seemed small and Hetty felt nervous for him. In front of him, smiling faces stared back. A few kids were running about between the groups armed with candyfloss and sweets, but when John cleared his throat, the parents called them back and they sat down.

'Good evening, everyone. My name's John Thornhill—'

'Get on with it,' shouted a boisterous middle-aged man who'd clearly had too much of the local ale. His wife hit him with a baguette, and he quietened down as those around him guffawed.

'Don't worry, sir, I promise I won't take long.' John seemed confident, but Hetty spotted a slight redness coming from the top of his shirt. 'Before we begin the film, I just wanted to thank you all for coming out to the Thornhill estate. Not just for this'– he pointed to the screen behind him – 'but for the whole festival. It's been a huge success so far and it's got nothing to do with me, as much as I would like to take the credit. It's all down to the remarkable Hetty Colman.'

He gestured to her at the back of the picnic area and everyone turned around. As she gave a little wave, Hetty was now the one feeling a burning in her chest that crept up her neck and onto her cheeks. When John began clapping, everyone soon joined in.

'Anyway,' he continued. 'I hope you've enjoyed the food festival and will enjoy the film too. With any luck we'll see you again next year.'

From across the sea of heads John smiled at Hetty. He hadn't said anything to her about next year. In fact, he'd teased her when she'd mentioned it that time in the fields, but she smiled back. Among the applause he walked back to his spot next to Jaz, who gazed at him adoringly. And though Hetty wanted to go and speak to him, to sit with him, eat with him, she knew she had to go back to Ben. Approaching Ben, Hetty was surprised to see his expression was as near to angry as she'd ever seen.

'That's got him some brownie points,' he said, his voice icy as he layered a sundried tomato on some bread and popped it into his mouth. He hadn't stopped eating while she was away. Lucky then, that he'd brought too much food. 'I'm sure the town will fall in love with him now.'

The word *love* made her stomach tighten into a giant knot. It was almost like Ben was jealous of John which was so unusual that Hetty didn't really know what to say or do. She had run off to speak to him when Ben had been looking forward to seeing her this evening and confusion once more raced through her, dulling her mind.

'Is that Macie with the chocolate guy?' Ben asked in between mouthfuls. Hetty looked over to see James handing her a chocolate. 'She'd better eat as much as she can before they split up.'

'Stop teasing everyone for a second, Ben. Please.'

'Why?' Without him realising it, Ben's voice was growing louder. She couldn't remember him being like this when they were together. He'd always said what he thought but Hetty was sure he'd never been so cruel and insensitive. Now though, he seemed gossipy and rude, and Hetty really didn't like it. She could only hope that any minute now he'd realise he was crossing the line from teasing to hurtful. 'Shhh, please, Ben. The film's about to start.'

'Okay,' he said, leaning back and relaxing. He must have just been hungry. He used to get hangry when they went shopping together if she didn't keep his sugar levels up, and with his stall being so busy all day he must be exhausted. Ben handed her a drink just as the theme song started.

They settled down to watch the film, and Hetty was aware of Ben glancing at her from time to time. About halfway through he leaned in. 'This is nice. I've missed you, Hetty.'

So often since they'd split up Hetty had longed for him too. 'I've missed you too.'

'You know, it was my fault we broke up.' Hetty raised her eyebrows and stared over the rim of her glass. 'It was. All my fault.' His cheeky grin made her heart murmur. 'I let you down. I knew you needed more from me—'

'I didn't *need* more from you, Ben. I *wanted* more from you. There's a difference.'

He held up his hand in apology. 'You're right. You wanted more from me and I wasn't ready to give it. But I am now.' He let the words hang in the air as he took a ring box from the hessian bag and climbed onto one knee. Ceremoniously, he opened the box to reveal a bright shiny diamond on a silver band.

Hetty froze to the spot, embarrassed by the murmurs of those nearby, as Ben proffered it to her, holding it in the air as if it were the only beacon of light in a dark and stormy night. Before she could think or speak, he launched himself forward, hooking his hand behind her head, attempting to kiss her passionately. Hetty jerked herself backwards. Confusion filled her brain as she tried to figure out how she felt about this moment, but as she did, her heart briskly informed her it was John she wanted to kiss, not Ben. He pulled away, shocked by her reaction, but rather than burning with passion, Hetty felt cold through to her core.

'Are you proposing to me?' she mumbled, forcing the words out even though her mouth wanted to do nothing more than hang open.

'I am. I know what you're like and that you'd want me to wait, but I just couldn't hold on until this whole festival thing was over.' Ben's expression became suddenly vulnerable. 'Is it a yes?'

Hetty stared between the box and Ben. That tiny box signified not just a proposal but a commitment to spending the rest of their lives together – something she'd wanted for so long, and he'd been unwilling to give. But panic was rising in her chest. *I don't know*, she thought. *I just don't know.*

Chapter 25

John pretended he hadn't seen Ben getting down on one knee, but there was no way he could pretend his heart wasn't aching. Hetty had a boyfriend or now a fiancé. He should have known better than to try to act on his feelings. He'd brought the picnic for her, hoping they could chat and get to know each other better. He had a feeling he'd only scratched the surface and that there was so much more to learn. But now he was having to sit and watch her with someone else. A sure sign it wasn't meant to be, if ever there was one. He didn't need anything else to tell him that for now he should stick to trying to help his family and put his personal life to one side. He'd always done that; first for his business and now for his family. This time would be no different, but even as he thought it, he didn't believe it. The hole in his heart was too big.

When Jaz had turned up and saved him from standing in the middle of a field, holding a picnic basket, looking like an absolute plank, he'd been relieved. They'd sat down together, and he'd seen Ben wink at him. John had turned in disgust and ignored him. If Ben was insinuating there was something going on between him and his assistant, then he had the mind of a Tom cat. John only ever thought of Jaz as his employee, or sometimes like a younger sister.

Keeping his eyes away and doing anything possible to distract himself from the fact that Ben was with Hetty, he said, 'So, Jaz, how old are you again?'

'Twenty-six,' she replied nervously, like it was a trick question.

He popped a sandwich in his mouth. He'd made it himself, even going so far as cutting the crusts off. It didn't look a patch on Ben's Mediterranean feast. Perhaps, in hindsight, he'd been saved another humiliation. 'And what's on the cards for you? You must have plans beyond working for me?' Jaz stopped chewing. 'It's okay, you can tell me, I don't mind.'

'Well …' She spoke slowly at first but as she began to relax, she was more like the Jaz he knew. 'I'd really love to learn more about the actual antiques. I have a history degree and obviously I know the admin side, but I'd love to do something like you do one day.'

'Really?' She nodded and John smiled approvingly. 'Let's see what we can do about that then, shall we?'

'Do you mean it?'

'Of course.'

'I don't know what to say, John.' She sipped her drink. 'You're so kind and supportive.'

'Oh, no I'm not.' He laughed. 'We both know I'm grumpy and moody, but let's have a toast anyway.' He topped up her champagne and she giggled. She'd drunk almost half of hers already from nerves. He was impressed with the depth of her ambition but pleased too. 'I'll do everything I can to help you.' He wasn't sure his business would provide those opportunities, but he'd do what he could and if she decided to move on, he'd be happy for her.

Conversation died as they watched more of the film and dusk fell upon them. John spent most of the time trying surreptitiously to see what Hetty and Ben were doing but apart from that one kiss he hadn't seen any more. As the evening grew chillier, and the myriad of smells died when the food vendors packed up for the night, he watched the stars appear in the sky. Jaz shivered in her thin vest top and John handed her his jacket. She wrapped it around her shoulders and stretched out her legs. Her foot kept knocking against his shin and instead of moving away she edged a little closer, so her arm was now resting against his.

When John went to top up his drink, he realised with a sinking feeling the second bottle of champagne was almost gone and surprisingly, Jaz had drunk most of it, along with most of the first. Jaz was very smiley and her eyes glazed. When her glass fell as she put it down, he knew she was drunk.

She needed to sober up, but what could he do to help? He'd been so determined Jaz would have a good time and see the side of him that so rarely came out these days and now things were unbearably awkward. He checked the picnic basket to see what was left; maybe some food would sober her up. Digging around, all he could find were strawberries and cream. Internally, he groaned. Why couldn't there be a pie or something filling that would soak up some of the booze instead of a flimsy pudding.

Jaz was still smiling at him. 'What's left?' she asked, peeking inside the basket.

'Oh, not much.' He tried to close the lid, hoping to grab something more substantial from one of the remaining food vendors but it was too late.

'Oooh, strawberries and cream. How romantic.' She gave John a look that filled him with fear, knowing he was getting backed into a corner of his own making. He clung tightly to the faint, unrealistic hope that Jaz was just having fun, but there was a look in her eye and a tension in his chest that told him otherwise. How had he not noticed her getting a bit too close over the last month? The strange glances, odd tensions between them, and her picking bits of rubble from his beard when he came through the landing ceiling should have been warning enough. And now she was using words like romantic. John's pulse began to race and a sweatiness crept over him as she tried to feed him a strawberry.

He gave an uncomfortable laugh as the terrifying fruit came towards him and turned his head. It hit his cheek, smearing cream into his beard and he wiped it with his hand. Stifled sniggers grew around him and he looked up to see Hetty watching, though she flicked her eyes away as soon as his met hers. He gently pushed Jaz's hand away, urging her to eat it, which she did, enjoying it like a bad actress in a TV ad.

As the film drew to a close, John relaxed a little and tipped his head back. It was over and he could now get Jaz home, but he'd have to wait until everyone had left. It was a beautiful night. A clear, starlit sky and a large bright moon covered the fields in a pale white shimmer. Looking over at Jaz, he didn't trust that she'd be able to walk without staggering here and there, and he wouldn't let her be the subject of gossip or ridicule. She meant too much to him for that.

Hetty walked past him as he drew his head back up. He'd hoped to say goodnight but when she and Ben drew level, Ben took her hand and pulled her close. John watched them go with a heavy heart. But a spark of hope caused his heart to pump hard when Hetty glanced back. That had to mean something, didn't it?

The crowd departed but John had seen the knowing looks and snide smirks from some of the townsfolk. How many had been aware of what was happening with Jaz? He didn't know, but there was no chance of escaping it now: the Thornhills had embarrassed themselves again.

When at last everyone had gone, John climbed to his feet and held out his hands for Jaz. She took them, and he pulled her upright, grabbing her around her waist as she swayed dangerously backwards. He smiled to let her know he wasn't cross but with terror rising within, she pressed herself against him and planted a kiss on his lips. His mind whirred in panic and his stomach dropped to the floor as he gently pushed her away by the shoulder.

Jaz's eyes, wide and hurt at his rejection, teared immediately.

'Oh my God, I'm so sorry, John. I'm sorry. I just thought – I don't know what came over me.'

'It's fine, Jaz. It's fine, let's just forget about it, okay.' He had hold of her shoulders but worried if he let her go, she'd fall.

Hearing footsteps, John panicked and glanced over his shoulder. His jaw clenched as he saw it was Hetty. She'd stopped mid-stride and was watching him with Jaz. Had she seen her kiss him? Without speaking she went back to where she and Ben had been sitting and picked something shiny off the ground – a set of keys – then headed back to the car park. She must have seen everything. John watched her go with an aching heart and this time she didn't look back.

'Is it me?' Jaz whispered. 'Is it because I'm younger than you, because I don't care, John, I really don't. I—'

'Jaz, stop. It's not – I don't—' *Damn it!* How did he say this without sounding like a patronising idiot? This was all his fault because he relied on her so much. Because he didn't have a life outside of his family and his work. He'd let this situation happen by making Jaz such a large part of his existence. He'd clearly given her the wrong impression of their relationship. 'Listen, I just don't think about you like that. You're great – really great – smart, funny, pretty, but you're more like my sis—'

And with that, Jaz crumpled down and was sick on his shoes. John immediately gathered her long hair into a ponytail and kept it out of her face. Never before had he been more grateful to be in an empty field. In the distance he saw the beam of light from the security guard's torch and knew he had to get Jaz out of here before more gossip about his family resounded through the town. Hetty, no matter what she thought, would be discreet. Scooping Jaz's hair into one hand, John pulled his phone from his back pocket and called a local cab firm.

'I'm sorry mate, all my cabs are booked for this film night thing, but if you're there you could see if someone will share.'

'No, that's fine, thanks for your help though.'

It didn't feel right just shoving her into a taxi. God knew what the taxi ride would do to her and what if she was sick again? Would they even take Jaz if they knew she was vomiting like *The Exorcist*?

'I don't feel well.' She rubbed her eyes like a tired child.

'It's all right, Jaz,' he reassured her. Looking back at the house, he knew it was his only option for her to retain some dignity. Helping her to stand up straight, he hooked her arm around his shoulder and slowly but surely got her back to the house, this time thanking his lucky stars for the many spare rooms in the enormous, crumbling money-pit.

Chapter 26

John sat in the study with the door open so he could see the stairs and Jaz, whenever she managed to descend. He hadn't slept much last night and had snuck out at dawn to cover up her vomit, removing all trace of embarrassment, then coming back to the safety of the study as the sky grew blue.

It had been a beautiful shade of pink as he'd walked the fields and the world around him had been quiet and still with a strong cold breeze. He'd wondered – hoped even – that he might run into Hetty, but of course he hadn't. There was no reason for her to be there that early. Seeing her with Ben should have changed how he felt about her, but his heart and head still longed for her. Tentatively, he sipped his coffee and kept watch on the stairs.

He'd stealthily managed to get Jaz back to the house unseen and plonked her into one of the spare beds, fully clothed. The room was a little dusty, as was the bed spread when he yanked it back with one hand. Not exactly The Ritz, but it was better than nothing. Jaz had fallen asleep within seconds, but he'd still left a glass of water on her bedside along with two painkillers. She would definitely need those this morning.

Already John's neck was prickling with shame and embarrass-

238

ment. Suddenly worried she might quit, John knew he had to stay calm and pretend like nothing had happened or have a quick chat that it was flattering but never to be, and then move on to work. But he worried things had irrevocably changed between them. Hot and flustered, he put his unused pen down and began opening a letter left on his desk by Jaz yesterday. Just when he thought life couldn't get any worse, he scanned the page: the bailiffs were coming. Angrily, John scrunched up the letter and threw it across the room.

Footsteps sounded in the hall, but they were loud and heavy. Not Jaz's. John calmed a little until Felix crashed into the room and shut the door behind him, taking a seat without even being asked. John looked up from his work. 'Felix, I need the door open.' He noticed his brother was looking more and more like their mother every day, his face ashen and drawn. John leaned his elbows on his desk and rubbed his hands over his face. He hadn't ever seen his brother anything other than bossy and in control. There was something defeated about him and dread shadowed John's mind, building heavy in his stomach. 'Felix?'

'I need to talk to you.' His voice had lost its authoritarian edge and carried a weakness that John didn't recognise in the man before him. With a sinking feeling he knew it was a weakness born of regret.

'Okay.' John nodded and tried to say it in a way that showed support for whatever it was. He stopped and pulled back from his work. 'What about?'

Felix rubbed his face again, his fingertips resting in the hollows of his cheeks. 'The investment's tanking.'

John's throat closed over in a rush of panic, but he tried to control it. 'What do you mean "tanking" exactly?'

'I mean …' He stretched the word patronisingly and John took a deep controlled breath. 'It's not going up, it's going down.'

'But that's normal, isn't it? They don't all shoot up straight away. It'll come back up won't it?'

'It'd have to come up a long way to get back anywhere near as much as we put in.'

John felt a prickling around his eyes as they sharpened on his brother and his pulse raced. 'But we'll get some back, won't we? Eventually?'

Felix slowly shook his dipped head, keeping his eyes away. 'I just don't know. We were supposed to see almost immediate returns. It was just about timing the market and selling up when the shares shot up, but that hasn't happened yet, and they've sunk so low I don't even know if they'll get going at all.'

Anger rushed through John's body and he felt the muscles of his legs contract. His chair shot back against the wall and he stood, resting his hands on the dark wood of his desk, feeling it cool beneath his knuckles. 'I knew this would happen. I told you not to do it, Felix, but you just had to, didn't you? You just had to ignore me as the stupid little brother you think I am.'

'At least I was trying to do something, John.' His eyes sharpened, losing their tiredness. 'Which is more than I can say for you. All you do is sit here in your little office with spreadsheets and bits of paper.' John balled his fists and turned, focusing out of the window on the winding arms of the wisteria. 'Don't turn your back on me,' Felix spat, standing too.

'Why shouldn't I turn my back? You did this without my agreement, and now it's all gone wrong – as I feared it would – you come barging in here, asking for help.'

'I haven't asked for help,' Felix replied. John turned to face his brother and Felix lifted his weak chin a little more.

'Then what are you doing here? And you may joke about my spreadsheets and bits of paper, but at least I work through all my ideas seeing what's actually viable and what's not. What could make a real difference to this family and what's a pipe dream. I don't get Mother's hopes up with fantastical solutions that don't happen. All the hours I've spent, Felix, ignoring my own business, working my arse off and now you want me to help solve your problem—'

'It's your problem too.'

'—and dig us out of the mess *you* got us into.'

Felix slid back down into his chair, defeated.

'And I'm well aware it's my problem too.' John leaned his back on to the windowsill, tapping his fingers. His stomach was swirling with anger and fear making him feel slightly sick. 'Are you even sorry, Felix?' It wouldn't change anything, but he had to know. It would help a little. Help him forgive and swallow down this terrifying ball of rage filling his stomach. But his brother, ever pig-headed and defiant, simply snorted.

'Sorry for what? For trying to help my family? No. I'm not sorry for that.' Felix crossed his arms over his chest looking every inch the bossy older brother.

'You took a huge risk without the agreement of your family and you're not even sorry now it's failed and you've ruined us forever?' John met his gaze but still no apology came. Of course his brother wouldn't apologise for not listening to his concerns. 'Why did you have to take it all, Felix? Why couldn't you just use some of it? Why is it always all or nothing with you?'

Felix pounced defensively. 'What would have been the point in that? You play it so safe, John. It blinds you to opportunity.'

'And this turned into a great opportunity, didn't it, Felix? Do you think the bank will approve the loan now? How are we going to even start trying to do something new?' They couldn't even make a token payment to keep the bailiffs away. The consequences of Felix's actions were truly dire and a fierce sense of betrayal consumed him. 'You've completely ruined us.'

John needed him to leave before he said something he regretted. He had to get to work as soon as possible trying to fix this mess – a mess he didn't believe he could fix. He'd have to prepare his

241

parents for the very real possibility that their only option now was selling the house. *Would all their stuff fit into a two-bed bungalow?* he wondered. Probably not. 'Just go home, Felix.'

But Felix didn't move. 'You're so bloody pious, John. You always have been. Always playing it safe – overthinking. Maybe that's why no women ever stick around.' Despite its sting, John let the parting shot slide and Felix pushed himself out of his chair, stomping to the study door and pulling it open.

Jaz was just stepping across the hall. 'Morning, Felix.' Her voice sounded delicate from the hangover she undoubtedly had. Felix didn't answer, and as she reached the study door, he ran his eyes over her, examining her rumpled clothes. John readied himself to defend Jaz if his brother dared to say anything, but he walked off into the depths of the house.

Edging into the room, Jaz looked like she might start being sick again at any minute. John fiddled with some papers on his desk, trying to calm down, wishing he'd kept some painkillers for himself. His brain was going to burst out of his head and the tension in his shoulders was killing his back.

Jaz watched on, then quietly slipped into the chair opposite, rubbing her bare arms.

'John, if you want me to resign, I will.' Her eyes were doe-like and misty with tears. She looked like a Disney character and John couldn't help the feeling that overtook him. He wanted to laugh at the absurdity of his day so far. How could it be only half past ten? He pressed the laugh down, but it still escaped.

Seeing Jaz's mortified expression as he let out a breath, he quickly said, 'No, Jaz, I don't want you to resign. You got drunk and made a mistake, that's all. If I told you all the times I'd done that, we'd be here all day. Besides, it's my fault.'

She dropped her eyes, toying with the hem of her top. 'It's not.'

'It is. You're a great assistant. The best I could ever have hoped for. I don't tell you enough how much I appreciate you and what you do, so when I finally did you misread the signs. I should tell you every day how good you are at your job.'

'John—'

'You're like a little sister to me, Jaz.' He needed her to know exactly how he felt about her to extinguish as kindly as possible any more ideas. 'I want to help you achieve the dreams we talked about last night, but because I care about you as a brother. Okay? Nothing more. But this mess – this mess is on me.'

'John, I—' She was either going to protest, drawing out this already difficult conversation, or tell him how much he meant to her, and rather than make a bad situation worse, he cut her off.

'No more about it now. We've got work to do.'

'Okay.' She nodded, but traces of embarrassment were still colouring her cheeks. 'What did Felix want? He seemed a bit stressed out.'

As his anger at Felix flared and the enormity of the situation sunk in, John collapsed into his chair. He rested his head in his hands and began to work through possible outcomes and solutions. The headache that had started pounding after Felix's news spiked and pain shot through his temples. 'You won't believe me when I tell you. And get ready to barricade the front door.'

Chapter 27

Hetty eyed the gathering clouds with concern. Her weather app had lied – out-and-out lied – telling great big giant fibs. This morning when she'd looked at the screen there'd been a big yellow sun, and it clearly said there was only a five per cent chance of rain, but the bulky dark grey clouds that were completely covering the sky said otherwise. She'd worn jeans with a short-sleeved T-shirt and the hairs on her arms were rising with the chill wind because that's what it was now – wind. Not a breeze – a wind. And a gusty one at that.

'What do we do if it rains?' asked Macie who'd left her hair down today – it was now whipping across her face. She tied it back with the spare hair band she always had wrapped around her wrist.

Hetty took a deep breath and examined the sky once more. Though it was blustery, the wind wasn't blowing the clouds away, they were still mounting, blowing them into a huge patch of grey right over her festival. 'We chuck on our pac-a-macs and try to stop people leaving. At least it's not movie night. That went even better than I hoped.' She thought about John and his speech. She admired his courage, his strength of character and those eyes that made her breath seize. Over these few days more than any of the others, she felt she'd seen his true self; the sense of humour beneath the hard exterior he presented to the world. But then she'd seen him kissing Jaz and the shock had been like a smack in the face. She'd long suspected that Jaz had feelings for John but hadn't thought he shared them. How wrong could she have been? The way he'd looked at her, the way he'd been holding her underneath a beautiful, romantic starlit sky. It had caused a pain unlike any other.

And Ben had proposed. The man she'd loved for ten years but whose lack of commitment had ruined them. Had he really missed her so much that he now realised they had a future together? Or did he feel forced into proposing just to get her back? Was it what he *really* wanted? She'd told him she'd think about it after the festival. She needed time to get her thoughts in order and she couldn't do that right now, especially not with her mum and dad's impending divorce.

As facile as it sounded, Hetty was sure that going from getting under each other's feet, to ignoring each other completely was what had sown the seed of doubt in her mum's mind. That was why she couldn't produce any evidence that Dad had been doing something he shouldn't. But how could she get them to see the person they fell in love with in the first place, rather than the grumpy one they'd been living with for the last year?

Macie, still gazing at the sky, said, 'I reckon if it's just a few showers, we'll be fine.' Hetty agreed, bringing her mind back to the present just as a small, furious-looking woman stomped towards them dragging a little boy by the hand.

'Are you the organiser?' she shouted, even though they weren't very far apart. 'That steward' – she pointed to one of the volunteers who gave Hetty an apologetic look – 'told me you were the organiser.'

It didn't take a genius to know a complaint was coming. 'Yes, I am. I'm Hetty. How can I help?' Though the woman was tiny she looked like she could handle herself in a fight. Hetty glanced down at the little boy but he wasn't paying attention, though his cheeks and nose were a little pink and he seemed a bit upset.

'We've just come from the funfair. My little boy tried ten times to win at the coconut shy but didn't win anything.'

Hetty had dealt with things like this before at kids' birthday parties. When someone thought they should have won just because they'd put a lot of money into a game, but unfortunately things weren't like that. 'I'm afraid that is the chance you take with games like that—'

'But even my husband tried and he hit one square on but it didn't fall over. It didn't even wobble. And he's six foot three and built like a brick shithouse.' Hetty's mind took a moment to catch up with what the woman was saying. Not only was it odd to think of this tiny firecracker with a tall, broad man like she'd described, but if he had hit one of the shies it should definitely have fallen over or at the very least, wobbled. Looking at the woman in front of her, Hetty knew she wasn't exaggerating and that she had a fair point. Tiny pinpricks of concern ran over her skin. Since the hook-a-duck thing yesterday, she'd had a suspicion that Mr Wade wasn't as trustworthy as he first appeared.

'Well, that sounds like something I need to look into.' The woman stared in an I-told-you-so manner. 'I think I'd better go and have a look and just make sure everything's okay. If something is amiss then I sincerely apologise, and I'll get it rectified.'

The woman was a tiny bit mollified but still said, 'Well, I'm coming with you because I want my money back.'

Hetty headed to the funfair trying to make conversation, asking questions about the food and if they'd enjoyed the rest of the festival. The woman softened a little as she chatted but was clearly in too bad a mood to give any praise. Hetty couldn't blame her.

Once there, they were immediately hit by the sweet sickly smell of candyfloss. If it had been Mr Horrocks' carnival, Hetty couldn't imagine having to deal with anything like this, the old man had seemed so professional and trustworthy. She hoped that there'd be a next year they could book him for. She was sure nothing dodgy would go on with his games. Mr Wade clearly didn't run as tight a ship. She spied him looking over, pretending he wasn't watching.

Hetty approached the coconut shy with her head held high, assuming her authority. 'Excuse me, what's your name please?'

'Ya what?'

'What's your name please? I'm Hetty, the event organiser, and you are?'

'Robbie.'

'Robbie. Hello. I'd like you to remove your coconuts for me please.' Not a sentence she'd anticipated saying when she woke up this morning, but still. It was one of the reasons she loved her job.

'Hey?' Robbie was middle-aged with a receding hairline and portly tummy and was not happy about Hetty being there. The wind, Hetty noticed, was strong enough to blow the bunting about, and yet, not a single coconut was wobbling.

Keeping her voice pleasant but authoritative, she said, 'Like I said, I'm the event organiser and I'd like you to remove your coconuts please.'

'Why should I?'

The fact that he became immediately defensive put Hetty on her guard. If he had nothing to hide, he would have laughed it off and done it without question. Those who had been about to play held tightly to their balls and behind them, a crowd started to build.

'Because, Robbie, I want to check you haven't glued them down. This young man and his father tried for a long time to win but not a single one budged. And given your reluctance to do what I've asked, I'm inclined to believe that something isn't quite right.'

The little woman nodded, and Mr Wade came over to join the group. 'Everything all right, Robbie?'

'Nah, it's not, guv.' He pointed at Hetty. 'This woman's accusing me of cheating.'

'Is that right, Miss Colman?' Mr Wade asked turning to her. He was speaking like a headmaster, but his body language was that of bluster rather than authority. 'I'm very disappointed to hear that. Relationships like ours should be based on trust.'

Hetty studied his tanned face. She didn't like it – the situation or his face. She'd thought he was decent at first, but he was definitely looking a bit shifty now and that speech was flannel if ever she heard it. 'If that's how you feel, Mr Wade, then remove the coconuts and I'll happily apologise.'

Robbie slyly nudged Mr Wade and he carried on. 'Is that really necessary? Why don't I just refund this lady her money? And then we can restart the games for these people who are patiently waiting.'

Hetty crossed her arm over her chest, partly to keep warm but mostly through annoyance. 'That would be very nice of you, Mr Wade. But I'd still like to see each coconut lifted up from its little perch. I'll just wait here while it's done. It shouldn't take a second.' She gave her brightest smile.

Mr Wade shifted uncomfortably. He tried to take Hetty's arm to speak to her in private, but she pulled it away. Seeing she wasn't going to go anywhere, he leaned in and whispered, 'All right so maybe a couple of them are stuck down. It's just how these things are.'

'Not at my events, it's not,' she mumbled through gritted teeth. Feeling horribly guilty and responsible for hiring him, Hetty narrowed her eyes. 'I knew something was off yesterday when I saw the hook-a-ducks were all bent.'

'You just don't know how these things work, love,' he said softly. 'It's not a big deal.'

Anger tightened her shoulders and tensed her body. 'How have you stuck them down?'

'With a bit of glue that's all.' He gave her a nudge, thinking she'd come round to his way of doing things.

'And do you have spares?'

'Yes,' he replied nervously. 'But I told you—'

'Now listen to me, Mr Wade, this is what you're going to do.' Hetty wasn't normally quick to anger, but Mr Wade's conning of her customers, potential ruining of her reputation and patronising manner, sparked into life. 'You're going to refund everyone here their money and close this stall for fifteen minutes while you unglue all these coconuts and replace them with actual, normal ones. And if I hear that you've been scamming any more of my customers, I will personally remove one of the aforementioned coconuts, come and find you and insert it somewhere a coconut should never go. Do you understand?'

Mr Wade stood back in shock. She could see he wasn't used to being spoken to like that and he too was getting annoyed. 'What if I just pack up my funfair and leave, hey? What would you do then?' He'd given just the response she was expecting and had already prepared for. Hetty's cheeks were hot from annoyance and finally warm against the gathering wind.

'You do that, Mr Wade, if you want. I'll simply let everyone in the county know that the reason you left was because I wouldn't put up with you cheating my customers. The bouncy castle man has said he can fill the space you leave behind so it's no skin off my nose.' This wasn't exactly true because she hadn't spoken to the bouncy castle man, but Mr Wade didn't know that and Hetty wouldn't be bullied.

Mr Wade tried to out-stare her for a moment but naturally it didn't work. Finally, he huffed. 'Oh, fine then.'

'Marvellous. I'll leave you to it, but I'll be making more regular checks on you from now on.' She turned to the lady who'd accompanied her. 'Mr Wade will gladly give you a refund and a free go when he's done some maintenance on the stall. It shouldn't take more than about ten minutes should it, Mr Wade?' He glared at her before sticking on a smile and turning to the assembled crowd.

'Looks like we've got some sticky nuts, guys and gals. You know what I'm talking about, don't you, sir?' There was a small chuckle from the crowd. 'Give us ten minutes to get everything back to full working order and then you're first, aren't you, young man? Look at those muscles! Going to cost me a fortune, I reckon.'

Hetty left him and began to walk away, shivering in the wind. With that done, she had time for a quick coffee and a few minutes to relax. The ghost train suddenly howled as she passed it and she screeched, making a group of kids giggle. A few tiny patches of blue appeared and disappeared, but the heavy cloud cover remained, growing denser by the minute.

At half past eleven, and with half her coffee drunk, the chatter of the crowd was halted by an almighty rumble of thunder. The heavens opened and fat, heavy drops of rain pounded down with such force they seemed to bounce back up off the ground. Some people hid under the small awnings of the stalls, but worryingly, many were making a dash for the exit and the car park. Hetty threw on her pac-a-mac, knowing she had to do something to keep them there, but apart from a one-woman show complete with singing and dancing, she couldn't think of anything. Plus, her singing and dancing were so bad they'd probably just drive people away rather than make them stay.

Abandoning her coffee, she ran to Macie, who had sensibly chosen the chocolatier James's stall to hide under and he seemed very happy to see her. Ben, Hetty decided, had been wrong. She had a feeling that this time, Macie and her guy would go the distance. There was just something in the way he looked at her.

'What are we going to do?' asked Macie, her face damp and her eyes wide in panic.

Hetty shook her head trying to think. Her brain was working overtime running through different options, casting some aside, revisiting others but nothing seemed quite right. Then John appeared at her side, sodden and in a dripping wet coat. She could smell the fresh rainwater on his skin and had the sudden urge to gently wipe the moisture away just so she could touch him, but he'd probably want Jaz to do that now.

'What are you doing here in this?' she asked, hunkering down and trying to stop water trickling down the back of her neck. She'd hoped it would cool her temper, but her voice was harsh. 'I can deal with this, thank you. You don't need to be here.'

He blinked in confusion. 'I came down as soon as the rain hit.'

'Isn't that the opposite of what a sensible person should do?' Yesterday, she'd have said it in a teasing way but now it carried anger over Jaz. Hearing herself, Hetty realised just how cross she was and how much it hurt to think he was with someone else.

'Heroic, remember?' John grinned, but when she couldn't smile back, an uncomfortable silence formed. 'What can I do?' John finally asked.

'Nothing. Thank you. Can you control the weather?' Hetty groaned at her own petulant response, but she couldn't help it. Instead of feeling like she'd let him down, it now felt the other way around. She knew she shouldn't care about his love life she should only be thinking about her and Ben. 'We'll just wait for it to finish.'

Macie suddenly chipped in. 'Hetty, what are you talking about? It's lashing it down and everyone's pegging it.' Hetty spun, her eyes signalling for her to be quiet. John sighed, and taking Hetty's arm, pulled her to one side and relative privacy.

'Hetty, if this about Jaz and last night—'

'Your business is your business,' she said, folding her arms over her chest. Her pac-a-mac stuck uncomfortably to her skin and raindrops misted her glasses.

'Jaz kissed me,' he said in his usually barky manner. 'Not the other way around. She was drunk and misread our relationship. It's not what you and no doubt everyone else thinks.'

Taking a moment to study his face, Hetty examined his clear, truthful eyes. It had been clear to her that Jaz had a crush on John, and with John inviting her to the picnic she could see how

251

she might have misread the signs. Relief refilled her lungs with air. Rain battered the awning above their heads, tapping a constant fast rhythm that her breath tried to match. 'Okay.'

'Hetty, it's true.'

'I believe you,' she said quickly, and she watched his mouth lift into a grin. A raindrop trickled down the side of his face and onto the corner of his lips. Huddled together they were incredibly close and Hetty's heart tightened with yearning. It was such a huge, tidal wave of emotion it frightened her, and more because deep down, she knew she should be feeling it for Ben.

'Everyone's leaving,' cried Macie, over the unhappy screeches of the crowd. 'What are we going to do?'

'I don't know,' Hetty answered, thinking hard, but nothing helpful was coming out. The pitter patter of rain flooded into her ears and a child shrieked at another almighty crack of thunder. As her brain worked, she remembered she had to change her bed and buy some more kitchen roll but no helpful thoughts to do with the festival emerged. 'There's nowhere to shepherd everyone that's indoors, and there's only the awards this afternoon. The vendors care more about those than the visitors. There's no way they're going to sit through a deluge to see who gets a red rosette Macie made three nights ago.' Frustratingly, she couldn't magic up indoor activities in the middle of an open field. The possibility of rain had been slim with the good summer they'd experienced so far and if there had been rain predicted, she'd thought it would be a shower, not something that required a flood warning. 'We'll just have to encourage people to go to the funfair – that has some under-cover activities – or hope they come back later when this is finished.' She threw her hands helplessly towards the sky.

'Well, that's not likely is it?' said Macie. 'Once people leave, they don't generally come back. And without another film night to bring them here …' She tailed off in disappointment. 'It's all over, isn't it?'

Fear gripped every one of Hetty's internal organs. Everything she had worked so hard for was washing away. Almost a full day's takings would be lost if they couldn't think of some way of keeping everyone there. She'd invested every last penny from her business in this and both she and John needed decent profits, but every raindrop that hit the ground was like a pound coin falling down the drain. How on earth could Hetty reply when all she could think to say was, 'Yes, I think it might be.'

Chapter 28

'I might have an idea,' said John.

Another rumble of thunder shook the sky and the rain intensified. Hetty and Macie both turned to him, eager to hear what he had to say. From his furrowed forehead he was clearly thinking something through. Hetty could almost see the cogs turning and the brain power behind his eyes. But when he spoke, what he had to say was completely unexpected. 'Bring everyone up to the house.'

'What?' Macie said it first and a second later, Hetty repeated the question.

'But your mother doesn't want visitors in the house,' Hetty confirmed, shaking her head in amazement. 'You told me. You said it was an option to get some money in and help your family, but she'd always been dead set against it. Surely she wouldn't appreciate this?'

'Yes, but all that might have to change now.' Hetty cocked her head. 'I'll tell you later. But we both need this festival to be as successful as possible. If everyone leaves that's a whole afternoon's business gone.' John pointed to the remaining crowd. 'Bring them up to the house. We'll say it's open for visitors for today only. No charge, of course. They can look around until the rain stops then we'll encourage everyone back out to the fields.'

'John, there's still a lot of people here and—'

'Oh, Hetty,' said Macie, growing stern. 'Just trust him, will you? Sometimes you have to accept help from people, stop being such a control freak. Honestly, it took you three years before you'd let me order stationery let alone run a party. It's absolutely freezing, I've got water in my knickers and my feet are soaked. Please just take John's suggestion.'

Though she was taken aback by Macie's outburst, she did have a point. 'Are you sure?' Hetty asked John. It was a good idea and the fact that he was trying to save her and the festival by going against his family sent her heart fluttering.

'Positive.'

'Okay then.' Hetty felt her own mind suddenly working again and sprang into action. 'Let's do this. Macie, you tell the stewards. Make sure a few stay here to keep an eye on things but get everyone else ready to shepherd the crowd that way.' She pointed back towards the house, then, rolling her shoulders back headed out into the rain to make the announcement. Her thin pac-a-mac did nothing to shield her from the onslaught and the heavy drops buffeted her skin. Cupping her hands around her mouth so she could be heard above the storm she shouted. 'Don't panic everyone, we have a contingency plan.' She glanced over at John and he smiled at her, encouraging her to go on. 'John Thornhill would like to welcome you all inside Thornhill Hall for one day only, so we don't all drown out here in the rain. If you'd all like to follow the stewards, you'll be in the house in a jiffy.'

John and Hetty raced ahead to lead the crowd. Her shoes squelched in the wet grass. There was a thin layer of mud under foot, but the ground had been so hard and the sun so strong for weeks, there wasn't enough to stick to her shoes.

'Are you really sure about this?' she asked. Her hair pressed against her head and she tried to ruffle it up, but it was so damp it just flopped back down again.

'Like you said, we make a good team. This is my contribution. Do you want my coat?'

'What, and ruin my look? No thanks. We'll be indoors in a minute anyway.'

As he smiled, the warming effect it had on her brought with it guilt and confusion and she looked around for Ben, but he wasn't in the group following them. Behind them, excited chatter filled the air and a sense of anticipation was mounting.

Within a few minutes they were pushing open the heavy front doors of Thornhill Hall. As the horde of soggy people stomped into the grand hall and the grey tiles of the hallway grew slippery, John walked towards his mother who had paused in the parlour doorway, speechless and utterly terrified.

'Don't panic, Mother, it's only for a while until the rain stops.'

'But John—' The pale skin of her long, thin face seemed stretched as her mouth hung open in surprise.

Hetty watched as he gently laid his hands on her shoulders and took her to one side. He spoke so softly she couldn't hear what he said, but eventually Lucinda nodded. The crowd were beginning to fill the large hallway and were huddling into little groups, gazing around at the few exquisite paintings that were left. 'Where's Ben?' Hetty asked Macie. 'I didn't see him coming up to the house.'

'He said he was staying behind at that local brewery's pitch. They've got that gazebo bit, haven't they? Karen's covering The Bake House stall.'

'Oh, right.' Hetty was surprised he'd missed this chance to see inside of Thornhill Hall given the gossip he'd been spouting recently. At first, knowing he wasn't there, it was difficult for Hetty to pinpoint exactly how she felt, but she soon named it as relief.

Jaz came running out from the study and went straight to John. She wasn't sure quite what she expected to see between them but as Hetty watched on, something was definitely different.

Jaz seemed a little less sure of herself today, less protective towards him, and Hetty didn't think it was all due to the hangover. John must have made it clear to Jaz where their relationship stood and Hetty shifted a little closer so she could hear over the chatter. 'John, what's going on?'

'It's raining,' he said with a lightness to his voice. 'So we've brought everyone up here.'

'But your mum – Lucinda – she—'

'It's fine, don't worry.' John glanced around. 'But look, there's too many people to all fit in here. If you could take some people through to the parlour, that would be great. Unless you need to go home?'

'No, I'm fine. I'm happy to help,' she replied.

Hetty felt she should add something. She didn't want Jaz to feel put upon or like she was clearing up Hetty's mess. 'Miss Simmons, this is all my fault,' Hetty said stepping towards them. 'I hadn't planned for this much rain. I thought there might be a shower, but I wasn't prepared for this onslaught from the gods.' A hint of a smile appeared on Jaz's face. 'But if we don't keep everyone occupied, they'll leave and once they've gone, they won't come back. We'll effectively be finished. If you could help us at all – help me – it really would be appreciated.' Jaz dropped her eyes. 'Please, Miss Simmons. I'm sure I can pay you, even if it's in chocolate.'

Jaz glanced at John then gave Hetty a genuine smile. 'It's Jaz. You can call me Jaz.' John nodded approval and went to his mother who was fidgeting around like a startled rabbit.

'Jaz,' said Hetty when he'd gone, 'I really appreciate you helping. The forecast said there was only a five per cent chance of rain.'

'It's no problem, Miss Colman.' Her voice had lost the superior tone it had before and gained a friendly warmth and she headed off, shepherding people into the parlour as she went.

'Do call me Hetty. Please?' Jaz nodded.

'Hetty?' John called Hetty over to meet his mother and she suddenly felt like a girlfriend meeting the parents for the first time, worried about making a good impression. She pushed the thought down, unsettled by how real it made her feelings for John. Slowly, Hetty wandered over. 'Mother, this is Miss Hetty Colman who's organised the food festival. Hetty, this is my mother, Lucinda.'

'How do you do, Miss Colman?' John's mother replied. She had strong, clipped upper-class vowels and Hetty could see a resemblance to John in the kind, worried eyes. Lucinda tipped her hand and gave a delicate handshake.

'How do you do, Mrs Thornhill?'

'Please, call me Lucinda.'

As Hetty stood looking at Lucinda, wondering what on earth they could find to talk about, Mrs Bates hobbled over.

'Oh, Lucinda, where've you been? We've missed you terribly at the library.'

'Mrs Bates,' Lucinda replied with a rictus grin. She was clearly unprepared for people approaching her and asking her questions. Hetty stepped in to save her.

'John mentioned your to-be-read pile was keeping you away from town, Lucinda. Mine is too, but I don't seem to be able to stop buying books.'

John smiled at his mother encouragingly.

'Yes – yes, it has,' she replied, catching on to the lie. 'Every time I finish a book it's like I've made no progress at all.' Her shoulders relaxed a little.

'Well,' said Mrs Bates, 'as soon as you've got through it you must come into town again and see us at the library. I've been keeping a list of books I think you'll enjoy.'

'Have you?' she asked, taken aback.

'Of course, dear.' Mrs Bates patted her gently on the elbow. 'Oh, I'm so glad I came back again today. I only came for more of those marvellous local pies that young man is selling. And to be in Thornhill Hall! What a treat!' The old woman appeared ten years younger with the excitement.

'You have a beautiful home, Mrs Thornhill,' Hetty said. 'When was it originally built?'

'Oh, the main part of the house was built in ...'

As Lucinda began to explain to Hetty and Mrs Bates about the history of the house, a subject on which she seemed very passionate, many of the wet, bedraggled crowd flocked over to listen. Hetty made sure to keep eye contact with Lucinda who, though starting off nervously with a wavering voice, soon fell into a confident stride. She didn't seem to notice the large group now surrounding them.

'Perhaps you'd like to show our guests around the rest of the house, Mother?' John asked. 'Give them a tour? I'm sure they'd enjoy knowing more about our resident ghost.'

Murmurs of appreciation from the crowd surrounded them and Lucinda, who studied Hetty and John with a strange knowing expression, nodded. As she began the tour, pointing at a large elegant portrait in the hallway, she added in stories of the ancestors who'd bought the house and what they knew of before then. She was a natural and likeable tour-guide, Hetty thought, but as the group moved on, she remained behind to speak to John.

'Your mum's a natural.'

John observed her with pride. 'She used to be very confident and outgoing before everything happened. Father too. I'm just hoping this'll remind her of that. We might have no choice but to open the house to visitors from now on.'

Seeing his darkened expression, Hetty asked, 'Has something else happened?'

John sighed and shook off his wet coat, hanging it on a tall coatstand in the corner. Hetty edged off her flimsy pac-a-mac and as John took it from her, she was touched by the gentlemanly gesture. 'Come into the study, where we can talk in private. I'm just going to ask Jaz to start another tour in a few minutes' time with the people in the parlour.'

'That's a great idea.' Hetty waved at Macie then pointed to the study door to let her know where she was going. After speaking to Jaz, he dashed back and held the door open for her, ushering her through first.

Just over a month had passed since she had first sat in the chair opposite his desk, when the idea of the festival was so fresh and exciting. Hetty stared out of the window watching the rain hit the long creeping vines of wisteria, knocking them to and fro. John had saved her today and for that she would always be grateful. He sat down and pushed some papers to the side.

It seemed to take all his energy to move them and Hetty noticed how messy his desk was. Knowing him as she did, she realised it wasn't like her organised chaos, but more a reflection of how in disarray his life was, heightening her concern. He sighed before saying, 'I'm sure you've been wondering what's going on. My brother, Felix, took all the money we had left and made a stupid investment, against my wishes. He thought it would offer quick returns, but the shares have gone further and further down instead of up as he was expecting. Now it's going to take such a long time for them to rise we're not going to make nearly as much as money as he hoped and the money will be tied up for longer as we wait for their value to increase enough to even consider selling them. We might not make any money at all.'

Hetty took off her glasses to dry them. 'I thought investments and shares were a long-term thing?'

'Felix thought he could do what's called timing the market. One of his friends had told him that he could invest in something now when the share price was low because it was expected to shoot up in value. When it did, he'd sell and make money for the family – potentially a lot of money – but it's gone the wrong way. The share price has fallen massively. If we sell now, we'll make a huge loss and if we wait for the price to come back up—'

'You still haven't got the money you need to run the house.'

'No.' He ran his hand over his beard then sighed heavily. 'I applied for a loan but the bank's unlikely to approve that now, and the bailiffs are coming.'

'So, what can you do?' Hetty asked, popping her glasses back on. As shocked as she was, she knew it wouldn't help John to see it.

'I need to come up with ideas we can implement quickly that'll give us some money each month.'

'Like what?'

'I don't know.' He picked up a piece of paper with squiggles and circles on it then tossed it to one side. 'I've worked through so many different options but they're all far too big for us right now. Apart from opening up the house I'm out of ideas.'

'Do you mind?' Hetty asked, picking up the piece of paper. He shook his head as she read through the jottings. He'd been brainstorming. Some ideas were good but required long-term business plans. There was nothing short term and immediate, nothing to give returns straight away. 'I think opening the house is a good idea. And the gardens too. Your other plans are good ones but like you say, they're long-term solutions. If you opened up the house and charged a small entrance fee, I think you'd get a lot of people coming in.' Hetty adjusted her glasses, thinking. 'And we could hold the food festival here again next year but that's a long-term solution too. I'll have a think about it and let you know if I come up with any other ideas. There's got to be something.'

'Thanks, I appreciate it.' John sat back, and in the silence, they listened to the rain hammering against the window pane. It was still coming down heavily and the sky outside was a sheet of steel-grey cloud. 'So, your turn. How are you about your parents?'

'Fine,' she said a little too quickly. He raised one eyebrow. 'I wouldn't want to bore you with all the details.' In reality, the festival wasn't over and she'd promised herself the box of feelings would stay shut until it was.

'It won't bore me. And besides, I've told you about my family's possible financial ruin. And it's still raining. What else are we going to talk about?' Hetty pursed her lips, trying not to smile, but she felt a sense of comfort in his company. 'Are you okay? I can at least ask that.'

Despite all her efforts, she couldn't help confiding in him. 'Yeah, I'm fine. I'm just a bit worried – about my parents that is.' She glanced at his concerned face and decided to press on. 'The crux of it is that my mum thinks my dad's been having an affair and I'm absolutely sure he hasn't. The trouble is, she won't tell me what her suspicions are so I can't disprove them. But when I mentioned our neighbour taking Dad some food, she got all jealous and put-out about it. She wouldn't if she didn't care, would she?' It felt good to be talking it out and not bottling things up. 'They've been married for such a long time and have always been happy. Up until they retired last year. Since then they've just been annoying each other, and I think they need to get some perspective – some space – but not like separated space – just—'

'To find themselves again?'

'Yes!' Hetty exclaimed. 'They just need to connect and stop annoying each other all the time. I love Macie to bits, but she annoys me when we're together 24/7 and I know I annoy her. I think that's why Dad's become golf-obsessed and Mum needs to stop sitting in the house waiting for him to notice her again.'

'So how can you get them to do that?'

'I don't know.' She sighed, shrugging.

'What do they both love?'

'Nothing. The only thing they have in common is me.' The strong wind had begun to blow the darker clouds away, and a tiny patch of blue appeared on the horizon filling Hetty with hope. 'Look,' she said to John, pointing out of the window. 'We should be able to get the food festival back on track soon, I think.'

'Now, there's an idea.' John sat back and tapped his index finger on the desk matching the rhythm of the slowing rain.

'What is?' John's eyes were a bright, clear blue.

'Why not invite your parents here for an afternoon tea? Sometimes being somewhere else stops you thinking about all the boring, everyday things and lets you talk about the big stuff, remember what it's like to be with someone. Remember who they are. We can get supplies from the stall holders and set them up in the secret garden.'

'The secret garden?' Hetty asked incredulous. 'You have a secret garden?'

'We do.'

'A resident ghost and a secret garden. Wow. Where is it?'

'I can't tell you, it's secret.' Hetty narrowed her eyes at him and he laughed. 'It's at the back of the house. My father hides there quite a lot. What do you think?'

After a moment's thought Hetty beamed. 'I think it's a great idea. I'll call them now. Get them to come up this afternoon about four. Actually, I'll ring Mum and Macie can ring my dad. It's probably best to keep this a surprise until the very last minute so neither of them can back out.'

'I'll head outside and give you some peace. I think I can hear the tour party coming back.'

Hetty pulled her phone from her back pocket and unable to stop herself, admired his strong, solid frame as he left. Her mum was surprised to hear from her. She was even more surprised when Hetty invited her to a picnic at Thornhill Hall. She didn't mention the secret garden or her dad coming too, and her mum was quick to agree, excited to see the largest event her daughter had organised so far. With a little more hope than she'd felt for the last few days, Hetty went back into the grand hallway to get Macie to call her dad and saw John staring up at his mother who was descending the stairs, speaking confidently to the crowd behind her. When they reached the bottom, Lucinda ended her talk and everyone clapped and thanked her.

'The rain's easing off, everyone,' Hetty said. 'Shall we make our way back to the stalls? It's the first Swallowtail Bay Food Festival awards this afternoon – our Taste of the Bay awards! I really hope you'll stay for those.'

As Hetty began to usher them outside she saw a smile light Lucinda's face as John hugged her. If there was any luck in the world, this would be the start of something good and hopeful for John and his family. They deserved a break.

The last one to leave, Hetty closed the door behind her, leaving them in peace.

Chapter 29

The odd drop of rain still fell, and one caught Hetty on the forehead. The smell of wet grass rose up from under her spotty trainers. She had her wellies in the car but what was the point of getting them now? Her toes were already cold and wet.

With a quick backwards glance towards Thornhill Hall, Hetty continued towards the vendors. They weren't too badly off schedule for the awards and with Macie's help they'd gather everyone together ready to give out the rosettes. As soon as the awards were over, Hetty could gather up a picnic and find John or Jaz to show her where the secret garden was. Crowds began to linger at stalls again and the air filled once more with noise. She'd give everyone fifteen minutes to get back to normal, then start their first awards ceremony.

Hetty found Macie, as she had expected, at the chocolatier's stall. 'Shall I just get you a seat and plonk it here?'

'Sorry,' Macie replied, her freckles hidden again by a blush. Hetty smiled.

'I'm only teasing, Macie. You're amazing and magnificent and the best assistant in the entire world.' Macie grinned back. 'I'm going to get the rosettes from the car. Can you set up the lectern?'

'Sure thing, dude.'

'Dude? Have you been at the free wine samples again?' Macie gave her a cheeky grin and headed off.

Shaking her head, Hetty headed off to the car, passing Ben on the way. He was perched quite happily on a stool at the local brewery's pitch. As usual he was talking away, cracking jokes and at ease in the company of these relative strangers. 'So the gangster says to the bishop, "I told you if you twist it like that it'll snap clean off."'

Giggles and guffaws exploded out and over them all Hetty heard Ben's loud, expressive chuckle. Imagining his smile, a smile came to her lips too but soon she'd have to decide if her future lay with him or without him. As much as she liked John, he'd not given any sign that he felt the same away about her. Watching Ben now, Hetty wasn't sure if she'd locked her feelings away because she had to focus on the festival, or if it was just easier than thinking about what felt right. Still laughing, Ben's voice carried over again. 'I told you it was a good one, didn't I?'

Hetty stuck her head into the tent. 'Ben, we're doing the awards now, okay?'

'Hetty!' he cried enthusiastically. 'Come and have a drink with me.'

'No thanks, Ben. I'm doing the awards now. You need to come.' He slugged back some beer and nodded absent-mindedly, and she carried on to the car. It didn't escape her notice that as she thought about Ben, the smile John had put there vanished from her face.

When Hetty came back with her box of envelopes containing the winners' names and the rosettes, Macie had set up the lectern in the area the bands used earlier, and a crowd was eagerly gathering. So many people had stayed wanting to know the results, it was a wonderful reminder of the closeness of the Swallowtail Bay community. On the sidelines she saw John, waiting to present the awards, chatting away to a man and a woman with bags full of shopping. He had his hands crossed over his chest looking almost forbidding, but then he threw his head back, laughing at something the man had said. Hetty's heart flipped in her chest but she drew her eyes away and stood behind the lectern, ready to speak.

'Hi, everyone, thank you so much for sticking with us through the rain. It's now time for the first ever Taste of the Bay awards!' There was a great big round of applause punctuated by an excited whoop from Macie. She'd definitely been at the wine stall, Hetty thought with a smile, but she deserved it for working her tail off all weekend. 'And to present the awards we have the gorgeous – I mean generous John Thornhill.'

Internally, Hetty screamed. Her face was on fire and the crowd in front of her were smirking. John was, of course, staring at her like she'd grown a second head. He was so shocked she couldn't read any other emotions in his face. As he approached, Hetty stared at the collection of envelopes containing the winners' names. She had to carry on. It was a slip of the tongue, nothing more. When John stood beside her, his shoulder brushed against hers and embarrassment gripped her once more. After handing over the envelopes, she shuffled over to where Macie was standing, grinning like a loon. 'Don't say a word.'

'Wouldn't dream of it,' she replied. 'But who needs to think before they speak?'

The heat rose in her cheeks again. 'Have you seen Ben?'

'Still in the beer tent,' Macie whispered.

'What? But he's won one of the awards, and I just told him to be here before I got the envelopes.' She couldn't believe he'd ignored her.

John began speaking, introducing the first award and building the excitement. 'I can't tell you how excited I am to introduce our inaugural Taste of the Bay awards. The food was amazing, and it has been wonderful to see so many traders here to celebrate all Swallowtail Bay has to offer. Thank you to you all. When I was judging with Hetty' – he looked over to her and Hetty couldn't take her eyes away from his – 'it was the best afternoon I've had in a long, long time. Truly wonderful.'

Hetty's heart was dancing in her chest. Could he really be implying what she thought he was? It was the first real sign that he felt the same way she did. John turned his eyes back to the crowd.

'Even though this is a food festival, we've also got some non-food awards to give out too to celebrate all the fabulous businesses we've have in Swallowtail Bay. With that in mind, our first award is the Business of the Bay award and I'm delighted to say the winner is ...' He opened the envelope. 'Stella Harris and Old Herbert's Shop.'

Stella's smile was wide and wonderful as she walked up to collect her rosette. Her stall at the festival had been packed with art and glass ornaments and forever crowded. There wasn't really anywhere like it in the bay and she deserved to win.

'What am I going to do about Ben?' Hetty whispered to Macie, clapping as Stella walked back into the crowd, beaming from ear to ear.

'You'll have to accept the award on his behalf.'

'Me? I can't.' Hetty kept her eyes pinned on the ground in front of her.

'Why not?'

Why not? Because it gave the wrong impression of her and Ben's relationship? 'I just can't. Isn't there time to go and get Ben?' Macie shook her head and seeing Hetty's concerned expression, treated the situation with the gravity it deserved.

'Do you want me to do it?' Macie asked Hetty.

John was just building up to Baker of the Bay filling Hetty with terror. 'What if I run and get Karen really quickly?'

'There's no time. Do you want me to go up?'

'No, I suppose as organiser I should go for anyone who isn't here.' Even if it did give John the wrong impression of their relationship.

The crowd applauded as John announced The Bake House and Hetty begrudgingly made her way to the front. Where was Ben? This was a big deal for her, he knew that. And it was a big deal for him too. Yes, his business was flying high and didn't exactly need the accolade, but he should have been there to see if he'd won and to support her. If he'd really meant what he said last night, wouldn't he have been there for her now, putting her first? His relaxed attitude meant he'd missed out on such a special moment – the culmination of Hetty's hard work – and he'd put Hetty in an awkward position having to accept the award on his behalf. People might think they were back together. John too seemed unsure, glancing at her in confusion when she stepped up and thanked him. 'Ben is indisposed, I'm afraid, but I'll make sure the award is passed on to him.'

To his credit John seamlessly carried on with the awards. 'Now onto my personal favourite, Cake of the Bay. There were quite a few entries for this one and it was possibly the one I enjoyed judging the most.' The crowd laughed along. 'The winner of Cake of the Bay is … Raina and her chocolate mousse cake!'

As one of the most popular cafés in town, this one was met with a loud cheer. The awards continued and the winners were met with approval from the crowd. A couple of people seemed disappointed they didn't win, but Hetty took it as a good sign. It showed the Taste of the Bay awards already meant something to people.

After announcing the last one, the Spectacular Strawberry award for the best strawberry product, John said, 'Before we all go, I'd really to thank you all for visiting the festival and I hope you've had a wonderful time. I have to say, that my family has very much enjoyed hosting the festival.' His normally clear voice was carrying more emotion now. 'And to those that visited the house earlier, I hope you found it interesting.' She could read in his face the unspoken words that this might be the one and only time the house had visitors. 'Let's hope we can see you all here again next year. On behalf of myself and the quite remarkable Hetty Colman, thank you.' He glanced at Hetty and the sadness in his eyes made her heart hurt.

The applause from the crowd should have made them both happy, but Hetty could see John was feeling exactly the same way as her. To have achieved so much and for it to have been such a success but with very little chance of repeat was heartbreaking. She wondered where he would go if Thornhill Hall was sold. Would he move down to the bay or further away? The chance of never seeing John Thornhill sent a sharp pain through her body.

'How was that?' he asked, his voice calm and even once more.

'Good,' she replied. 'Very good.' Hetty looked up into his eyes and there was a softness to them. She couldn't turn away, caught in the moment between them as her heart stirred into action, until Macie bounced over.

'That was great, John. Well done.'

'Thanks. How long until your parents arrive?' he asked Hetty.

Hetty quickly checked her watch. 'An hour!' She pressed her hand against her forehead. 'I can't believe the time has gone so quickly.'

'Come on, let's gather some bits and I'll show you where the secret garden is. If you get food, I'll get wine. What do they like, red or white?'

'Red, definitely.'

'I'll get some coffees as well. From Raina's. We can decant it into the nice china. We haven't sold that yet, though it might be next.'

'John, there must be something—'

'Meet you back here in ten minutes, okay?' The look in John's eye told Hetty he wasn't quite ready to discuss things yet.

Fifteen minutes later, Hetty hurried to meet John, laden with everything they might need. The day was warming again as if the storm had never happened, the sky a perfect blue. 'Sorry, I'm late. I got caught by a customer. They loved the house and were hoping it would be open again.'

John smiled sadly. 'Let's get going, shall we?'

Hetty followed John back up through the fields to the front of the house. It all seemed so familiar now. The rain had brought back some of the vibrancy to the wilting green leaves on the trees and the wet gravel of the driveway glistened like jewels. Something white pushed into the hedge caught her eye and she paused. John reached over her shoulder and pulled out the cheese box from their picnic on set-up day. It felt like a lifetime ago. A grin pulled at Hetty's cheeks. 'Should I ask?'

'Probably best if you don't.' He put it behind his back as if to hide it.

They rounded to the back of the house and through the rose garden. Flowers bloomed on either side of her in a myriad of colours, from the palest, most delicate pinks and creams to bold and beautiful reds and yellows. Their smell was intoxicating and heady. Rupert really did have a special gift when it came to gardening. There was something so peaceful about this part of the grounds and Hetty felt lucky to be there. After her blunder in the speech, she worried their conversation would be strained, but John remained the same. They chatted easily until at the back of the rose garden, he stopped at an old wooden gate in a high flint wall.

'Are you ready?' he asked and Hetty was pleased to see that his eyes were shining again. She nodded, unable to hide the smile on her face. He opened the gate and let her through to the most magical space Hetty had ever seen. The high stone walls were covered in blossoming plants and in the centre sat a small metal table and chairs. They were wet from the rain and the cobblestones glistened underfoot. In the corner, birds gathered on a large stone bird bath in the shade of a giant oak tree.

'It's beautiful,' she replied, though the word didn't seem enough. 'Enchanting.'

'I used to come here all the time as a kid. I loved it.' Just then Rupert, John's father, appeared. He almost didn't see them as he ambled in and began gently pinching shoots from one of the plants. 'Hello, Father,' John said. 'This is Hetty.' Rupert gave her a very sweet smile but immediately went back to his gardening. 'She's going to use the secret garden this afternoon for a meeting. Do you mind?'

'Oh no – no, no, no, – not at all.' Again, his smile was so emotive and genuine. 'I'll – you know – potting shed.'

He ambled past them and when he paused in front of John, Hetty gently touched his arm. 'Thank you, Mr Thornhill. I hope it's not causing you any inconvenience.'

'No, dear – and do call – Rupert, isn't it,' he said before shuffling away.

Hetty liked him immediately. When he'd gone, John leaned into her. 'Sorry, he's not been himself since the vineyard thing.'

'It's fine. I thought he was lovely.'

'He umm … changed after it all happened. He's much shyer now.'

'I understand,' Hetty replied. 'Sometimes life can be hard to deal with and we all hide inside ourselves.'

'That's it exactly,' John said with a sudden seriousness.

'He may come out of it eventually,' Hetty offered kindly. John didn't answer but storm clouds had gathered in his eyes turning them from blue to green. 'This place is amazing,' Hetty said to cheer him. 'And thank you for being so helpful with my parents. I realise it's not your problem—'

'I'm happy to help.' His smile sent a tingle through her body. 'I told Jaz about the picnic and she left that box of stuff for you.'

Hetty saw a plastic tub, much like her emergency box, full of plates, a cake stand, tablecloth and a towel to dry everything after the rain. Hetty was impressed at her forethought. 'I'd better get set up, they'll be here soon.'

'Sure.' John went to back away but Hetty didn't want him to leave.

'Umm, where do you think you're going? I thought you were helping me set up.' With a wide grin he began to unpack some of the cakes onto the cake stand. Hetty took to wiping the chairs clean. 'Jaz has thought of everything.'

'She's a very good assistant.'

'She seems it.'

John paused as if considering his words very carefully. After a second, he spoke again. 'I meant what I said earlier, Hetty. She got confused that's all. Got the wrong idea. I don't think I led her on, but I can see how some of the things I did might have been confusing.'

'Like the strawberries?' she asked, remembering seeing Jaz trying to get John to eat one and squishing it into his face.

'Yes,' he replied. 'I don't think I've ever been as terrified by fruit before.'

Hetty tried not to glance over but she could hear the hint of guilt in his voice. There was no denying it anymore, her feelings for John were growing by the second and with them, her decision about Ben became more difficult. Could Ben give her everything she wanted? If he had suddenly come around to the idea of them making a commitment to one another, would it even work? His failure to come to the awards hurt, though her brain knew it would be too painful to analyse exactly how much right now. At the back of her mind, a thought was gathering that he still wasn't reliable and mature.

'So, your boyfriend did well to win Baker of the Bay.'

'He's not my boyfriend,' Hetty replied quickly and began to wipe the wet chairs with even greater force. 'He's my ex. He was supposed to be there to collect the award himself, but he didn't show.' Hetty felt an anger rise in her at the way Ben had let her down. Like he wasn't taking this all seriously because he never could take anything seriously.

'Oh, right.'

Just as Hetty flung out the tablecloth to lay it over the table, Macie ran into the garden, followed swiftly by Jaz. Her lips almost trembled and she was out of breath. 'Hetty, you've got to come back. Quick.'

'What's happened?' Pressure mounted in her chest and her head began to pound. Macie was normally cool, calm and collected, but Hetty could see the fear and panic in her eyes. She was pale and her freckles stood against her white skin and the warmth of her ginger hair. Jaz too was terrified, like the whole house was about to come crashing down around them.

Macie's voice trembled as she finally got the words out and when she did, a coldness hit Hetty's body, sweeping through every bone. 'A child's gone missing.'

Chapter 30

All the air escaped from her lungs in one big, panicked breath. 'When? How?'

John turned to her and she could almost see the pulse in his neck.

'I was just checking on the vendors and I heard a woman scream. I ran over to the noise and she was sobbing.' Macie's voice wobbled as she relayed the information. 'She said her little girl had gone missing. She was calling her name and looking around, but she couldn't see her. I told them to stay where they were in case the little girl came back and that we'd start a search straight away.' Macie sniffed and sweetly, Jaz, who'd been standing next to her, rubbed her back. 'I did try and call, but the signal's so hit and miss up here it wouldn't connect.'

Hetty nodded along, her breathing erratic, and took a moment to regain her composure. Panicking wasn't going to help anyone. 'You've done exactly the right thing, Macie. Well done.' Her brain was now kicking into gear, ordering her thoughts to deal with the problem in the best way possible. 'Right, Macie, Jaz, could you two pair up and search around the food stalls?'

Jaz was quick to respond. 'Yes, of course. Anything I can do to help.'

'Thank you. Macie, let's also get it announced on the loud-speaker, okay?' She turned to John, eager to have him with her during this stressful time. 'John, are you all right to search the funfair with me?'

'Of course.' His rich velvety voice was reassuring, but Hetty could read the worry in his eyes. If this is all the first ever Swallowtail Bay Food Festival was remembered for, there certainly wouldn't be a repeat next year. And that was if they could save the house first.

'What's her name, Macie?'

'Melanie. She's 8, has blonde hair, and is wearing a pink summer dress with pink sandals.' Jaz gave a small smile in Macie's direction, clearly impressed with her.

'Good job, Macie,' Hetty said. 'You've handled this brilliantly already, I'm so proud of you. Now all we have to do is find her.' Macie smiled at the compliment from her boss, but she was clearly as worried as the rest of them. That poor little girl must be terri-fied without her mum and dad. Hetty could see her lost, alone and crying, walking around rubbing her eyes, trying to stem the tears. Why hadn't anyone noticed a little girl on her own and taken her to a steward?

Hetty took a deep breath, trying to control her racing mind. If the kid had gone to the car park, surely one of the stewards would have seen her. There were more of them there. 'I'll call Robbie in the parking field and get him to check there.' She felt a hand on her lower back and turned to see John.

'Don't worry. We'll find her. She can't have gone far.'

They left the peace and tranquillity of the secret garden and raced back through the rose garden. Jaz and Macie dashed ahead together, speaking quickly but calmly, deciding where to start.

'It *will* be all right, Hetty,' John said. 'I promise.' She desperately wanted to believe him and was thankful for his attempts to calm her, but how could he promise something like that? What if something truly dreadful had happened? No, she wouldn't think like that. The chances were the girl had accidentally got separated from her parents and was still in the food festival somewhere. Perhaps she was just strolling about on her own not realising she had everyone worried half to death.

Lucinda appeared as they came to the back of the house and John ran over to her. 'Mother, have you seen any little girls around the house?'

'Little girls?' she asked in confusion then realisation dawned. 'Oh, Lord, has someone got lost?'

'Yes, but we're searching for them now. If a little girl called Melanie comes to the house, ring me straight away. Okay?' Lucinda nodded.

'Thank you,' Hetty added. 'She has blonde hair and is wearing a pink dress and pink sandals.'

'Of course,' Lucinda replied then returned to the house, wringing her hands.

By the time they were back at the food festival, Hetty had descended into silence and barely heard anything John said. John's certainty had been reassuring, but as they headed back, it occurred to Hetty that there were so many more fields than the ones they were using. What if the little girl had got into one of those and become disoriented, unable to find her way back? What if she'd wandered off down one of the bridleways that led back into town? If their search didn't yield any results, they'd have to call the police. And soon.

Macie and Jaz set off in the opposite direction while she and John carried on to the funfair. They rushed past some of the stalls, both looking around, eyes searching for a girl resembling Melanie's description. Nothing.

A ball of fear formed in the base of Hetty's throat so she could hardly speak. 'She isn't here, is she?'

'No,' John replied and Hetty wondered if he really was that calm or if he was just pretending.

The voice of a steward sounded out over the loudspeaker. 'Attention everyone, we've got a little girl separated from her parents, so please could we ask you all to keep an eye out for Melanie. She's 8 years old and is wearing a pink dress and pink sandals. Melanie, if you can hear me, can you make your way to the nearest person in one of the bright yellow jackets. Your parents are waiting for you by the giant movie screen.' The concerned faces of the crowd as they listened did nothing to relieve Hetty's stress. It increased it ten-fold, but at least there were extra eyes looking out for the poor little thing.

As they neared the beer tent, she heard Ben's voice before she saw him. 'I'm pretty sure Swallowtail Bay has a higher than usual ratio of hotties to munters. Don't you reckon, Bill?' Hetty heard him wolf-whistle a young lady as she walked past, then a cacophony of macho guffawing met her ears. She came alongside the entrance of the tent, her pace slowing but her anger rising, to see Ben still sitting on the bar stool, tipsy and enjoying himself thoroughly. His legs were splayed open, an almost empty plastic beer glass in one hand, and a wolfish grin on his face. For a second, he didn't realise it was her, but when he did, his happiness evaporated. Hetty didn't stop, and he slid off his stool and jogged unsteadily towards her. 'Hetty, my darlin' one and only.' She cast a look over her shoulder but kept going. 'Hetty, Hetty, Hetty, Hetty.'

Hetty's heart, already beating rapidly from the speed with which they'd returned to the festival, was now reverberating in her chest with anger. Instead of trying to help her when the rain came, knowing how much the festival meant to her, he'd been plonked in the beer tent. Instead of coming to claim his award, helping her make the festival a success, or more importantly, getting off his bum to help look for a missing child, he'd been sitting here getting drunk. He'd clearly left Karen, the poor member of staff he'd brought with him, alone to deal with the rush of people there would undoubtedly be back at the stall while he lived it up like he didn't have a care in the world. Hetty pushed her words out past the cricket-ball-sized lump in her throat. 'Just go back to the tent, Ben. I'll speak to you later.'

'Hetty, come on.' He grabbed her hand and pulled her round, jarring her shoulder. His breath was heavy with the smell of ale and she wafted a hand in front of her face. His eyes were a little unfocused and she could tell from his exaggerated movements he must have drunk a lot. She tried to wriggle her hand free. 'What? What's with the face? I'm just chillin' out, my beloved.' She turned her head from his smelly breath and from the corner of her eye, saw John shift uncomfortably. 'Hey, have you thought any more about what I said? About marrying me? I think I've got the ring here somewhere.' He finally let go of her hand and patted down his pockets.

Thankful to be free, Hetty began to walk backwards. 'Ben, I really don't have time for this right now. We'll talk later.' Ben pulled a sulky face and tried grabbing her hands again. Hetty felt her temper flaring. 'We'll talk later, Ben,' she said again firmly. She hated the way he never listened when he got drunk. 'I've got to find—' She was going to say a kid but couldn't trust Ben to help in the situation. He'd probably start shouting like an idiot, scaring the girl even more if she was around here.

If she was going to spend the rest of her life with him, she should have been able to tell him anything and rely on him to help her when she needed it. That she couldn't was like a warning flare going off in her mind.

'What's lord of the manor summoned you to do anyway?' Ben eyed John with an unsteady gaze and John turned away, obviously sharing Hetty's view that it wasn't worth the hassle.

'Ben, can you just leave the mardiness for now, please? We really have to go, and time is of the essence.' She began to jog away.

'Oh, bye then,' he said sarcastically. As she glanced back, he was watching her go looking like a sulky child, his lower lip sticking out as he made his way back into the tent.

With Ben drunk and wolf-whistling passing women, talking about munters and hotties, Hetty realised he was no more grown-up now than he had been when they were together. In fact, he might have regressed. He acted before thinking things through, he made snap decisions and just rolled with the consequences. He teased everyone like life was one big joke. The thought that he was now mature and ready to commit was laughable. A giant wave of disappointment hit Hetty but was soon replaced by relief. She couldn't help but feel she'd had a lucky escape realising this now, before she'd accepted his proposal.

Hetty sped up as the fair came into sight, conscious of the few minutes they'd lost in that little exchange.

'Are you okay?' asked John, matching her racing stride.

'Fine. I just want to find this kid.' Fear over the little girl mounted in her stomach once more, and another image of her scared and crying flew into her brain.

The noises and lights of the funfair surrounded them. The smell of the candyfloss turned her stomach. Beeps and whistles from the rides mixed with the cheers and happy screams of the children. Though both she and John peered around, they couldn't see the little girl anywhere in the crowds.

They moved around the different rides, checking the queues at the fun house. John even quickly walked through but she wasn't there. There were so many blonde-haired little girls around. At one point, Hetty thought she saw her, but the crying little girl was running towards her parents having fallen over and was wearing leggings and a top, not a pink dress.

They stared at the dodgems and the flying saucer but no one matching Melanie's description could be found. Everywhere the sounds of laughter and music left Hetty feeling isolated and trapped in this moment of fear. They checked the helter-skelter, Hetty this time climbing up to see if she was inside. When she wasn't, the fastest way back down through the queue was to ride it, and she whizzed down to the whoops of waiting children and the confused looks of adults.

Hetty felt cold inside and out and shuddered. If they didn't locate Melanie in the next ten minutes, they would have to call the police. She called Macie, happy to get through first time. 'Any luck?' Hetty prayed silently.

'No. Nothing. We've checked everywhere. We'll go around again, but I don't think she's here. The parents are getting really worried now.'

'Tell them we'll finish the search here and if we can't find her, we'll call the police.' The ball in her throat grew larger. It would mean the end of the festival, the end of her reputation and possibly the end of her business, but the little girl was more important than any of that. Hetty shoved her phone in her pocket and looked around to see what rides they hadn't checked yet. 'The carousel,' she shouted, in a moment of realisation. 'All little girls love horses, don't they?'

'They do,' John said reassuringly and Hetty felt certain she'd be there. As they began to jog over, John hesitated then asked, 'Did you want a pony when you were little?' He was trying to distract her from her worries, and she wanted to respond, but the air felt heavy in her lungs, making it hard to breath. 'Did you?' John asked again, softly. He laid a hand on her shoulder and Hetty suddenly wanted to grab it and wrap her fingers in his.

'Yes, yes I did.'

'I'm sure we'll find her soon, Hetty,' he said again after a moment of silence. She really wanted to believe him.

They walked around and around the carousel, climbing on and moving between the horses, each one so beautifully painted. Every rider gripped on like the horses were real and smiled at proud parents watching.

'What do we do, John? We've looked everywhere a little girl

might go, checked every ride she'd be allowed on.' Hetty stared around trying desperately to think but all she could imagine was the mother crying with worry and the terrified little girl crying with fear. It wasn't helpful. All it was doing was clogging up her brain and stopping it from working in a logical, detached fashion. But there wasn't anywhere in the funfair they hadn't checked.

John had been staring around but his gaze lingered. 'What about the rides she's not allowed on?' Hetty turned to him. 'Like you said, we've checked all the rides she would be allowed on, what about the ones she wouldn't?'

'But that doesn't make sense, she wouldn't get on them. The attendants would stop her.'

'That's if they're paying attention.'

Hetty thought back to the unscrupulous coconut shy guy and the hook-a-duck, and instantly saw John's point. 'Okay, so what rides would normally be out of bounds?'

'There's not many. You made sure pretty much all of them were family friendly. The only one that I wouldn't let a kid on is the ghost train, if I thought it might be too much.' He turned to it. 'The attendant's paying about as much attention as I do when Mother's talking about cross-stitch.'

Hetty managed a small smile but internally she was praying like mad that the little girl was there. A mother and daughter strolled past, the little girl pulling to be allowed on and the mum shaking her head. All kids loved the thought of being scared until it actually happened. John was right. From a distance she could see the attendant was letting anyone on whatever their age. She felt her temper begin to flare under the pressure and stormed over to him.

'Right, sunshine, I need to get on this ride. It's an emergency.'

'Sorry, love,' the spotty youth replied. 'You'll have to wait your turn. I've got a queue here.' The high-pitched cackle of a witch chilled Hetty to the core. The boy shoved his hands in his pockets and rocked back on his heels, looking smug. Fed up with patronising men and about to lose her temper, Hetty grabbed him by the arm and pulled him to one side.

'Listen to me, you little oik!' She calmed her rising voice. 'I'm the festival organiser and I'm looking for a missing little girl. Pink dress, pink shoes, blonde hair. Are you sure she hasn't got on this ride? Because if I get on and I find her I'm going to report you for not doing your job properly.'

'Well I—' He realised he was in it up to his neck. 'Oh, all right, you can take the next cab.'

'No, no, no,' said John, stepping nearer so he could whisper. 'We need to get on and look around, not ride it. How do we do that?'

'There's a door at the back,' the guy said, looking more and more nervous. 'Here.' He led them to the back of the ride which was also painted with ghosts and ghouls. He unlocked the small door and John climbed in first, ducking his head to fit through. It was so dark Hetty stumbled, falling into him. He reached out a hand and steadied her. She pulled out her phone and put the torch on as John did the same.

Everything was dusty and dark, and it felt eerie being inside the machine, behind the scenery. She could hear the screams of the riders, the booing of ghosts and that same cackle of the witch they'd heard outside. The whirring of cogs and grinding machinery surrounded her and she could smell oil and grease. They wound their way through, following the track. People screamed again as in front of Hetty and John, through the gaps in the scenery, they could see skeletons and werewolves jumping out on them.

In the dark, Hetty walked through a fake cobweb that sent her heart rate skywards. She wiped it off her face. John reached out his hand to guide her and Hetty took it, feeling a wave of calm as their skin touched. She shone her phone around, and the strong beam of light made her feel like she was in a bad horror movie. They entered a graveyard and one of the tombstones flew upwards, making the lady in front of it scream and then laugh.

Hetty moved past John, sure she had seen something and slowly moving her torch again. Over the other side of the track behind one of the tombstones she saw a frilly sleeve of a little girl's dress. Hetty jumped over the track once the cabs had gone past and as she drew nearer, she saw her. The girl was hunkered down, her knees drawn up to her chest, her head bowed. A mass of blonde hair fell forward and her tiny toes were scrunched tight in her pink sandals, her whole body tense. The girl's shoulders juddered from her sobs and Hetty nearly dropped her phone in relief.

'Melanie?' she shouted over the noise and the little girl's head popped up. Her cheeks were wet with tears and her eyes wide with fear. Hetty crouched down in front of her. She felt John's strong hand on her shoulder as he bent down too. 'It's all right, sweetheart. We'll get you out of here.' The little girl sniffed and Hetty took her hands from where they were wrapped around her knees. She felt lightheaded as she stood up, able to breathe again. Melanie's face was wet and snotty, and her legs wobbled, unable to take her weight. As Hetty tried to lead her away, she stumbled. 'Is it okay if I carry you?' Hetty asked and Melanie nodded. As Hetty hoisted the little girl up she felt John's hand in the small of her back, helping to keep her steady.

Together, they made their way back outside and in the fresh air Hetty looked at John. His expression matched hers and he let out a long deep breath. Hetty carried Melanie all the way back to the main field, to her parents. As soon as Melanie caught sight of her mum and dad, she wriggled out of Hetty's arms and ran towards them. The mum engulfed her in a tight embrace and her tears fell onto the mop of wheat-coloured hair. 'Thank you. Thank you so much.'

'You're very welcome,' Hetty replied. John moved away to make a call, presumably to Jaz to stop the search. 'She was in the ghost train.'

'*In* the ghost train?'

Hetty nodded. 'Behind a tombstone.'

The mum studied her daughter. 'What were you doing there? I told you that ride was too scary for you. You hate things like that. You don't even like Halloween.'

The little girl sobbed, her words coming out in sharp exclamations. 'I thought it would be fun.'

'It wasn't though, was it?' the mum said, and Melanie shook her head emphatically before bursting into tears again. 'Perhaps you'll listen to me next time.'

Grateful and relieved, the family went off and a few minutes later, Jaz and Macie were at Hetty's side. Hetty felt giddy from the rush of adrenalin but tired and exhausted as the tension flew from her body. When she saw the hay bale, her body gave way and she flopped down on it, lifting her head to the sky. John explained what had happened and where they'd found the girl.

'Wow,' said Macie. 'You two really do make a good team.' Hetty was suddenly jolted back into the same world as everyone else, able to enjoy the laughter and chatter of the crowd. Macie bent double, regaining her breath. 'Before we do another one of these festivals we're going to have to get in better shape. This one's involved a lot more cardio than I'd expected.'

Hetty giggled and John's laughter filled her ears until her phone rang. It was her mum. 'Hello, dear. I'm at the car park. Where should I go?'

'Umm, I'll come and get you, Mum. Just hang on where you are.'

'Are they here?' asked Macie as Hetty hung up.

'Mum's here. Early as usual.' Hetty threw her hands in the air. 'What else can go wrong today?'

'What do you want me to do?'

Hetty pushed her hand against her forehead, her other wedged on her hip. 'Can you delay Mum somehow? Show her around the festival or something?'

'Of course,' Macie said. 'No problem. I like having a natter with your mum.'

'Why don't I do the same for your dad when he arrives?' offered John. 'I can tell him all about the house and grounds and stuff and bring him to the secret garden separately to make sure your mum and dad don't see each other.'

'Really? You're sure you don't mind?'

'I could bore people for England.'

'You're not boring,' she replied, and there was a fire in his eyes that filled Hetty with excitement. 'Can you both give me twenty minutes to get everything perfect?'

'I can help too,' added Jaz, much to Hetty's surprise. 'I know where everything is in the house so I can grab anything else you need.'

John gave Jaz a wink and turned to Macie. 'Right, you go and get Mum, I'll hang around for Dad. I'm sure Richard III stayed in our house once.'

'Really?' Macie asked.

'No. But he won't know that.'

Chapter 31

'So, this formal garden was designed by ...' John paused and scratched the back of his head. He didn't know any famous historical gardeners. 'Monty Don. It was designed by Monty Don.' Jeff raised his eyebrows. He clearly didn't believe him. 'And over here—'

'Umm, I don't suppose you know where Hetty is?' asked Jeff, kindly. 'I mean this is all very interesting but—' John had heard that teasing before in his daughter. 'But I thought I was meeting Hetty.'

John checked his watch. It had been just over twenty minutes. 'Of course.' He smiled, hoping that Jeff liked him. 'If you'd like to follow me, I'll take you to meet her.'

'I'm sorry about that Marty Sutcliffe,' Jeff said, causing John to pause. 'He goes to the same golf club as me and when he said about the interview, I thought it'd be good. I didn't think he was going to be so rude to you.'

John couldn't believe how nice Jeff was being to him, even though he was a complete stranger. 'No need to apologise, Mr Colman. No need at all.'

'My Daisy never liked him.' Jeff gave a slightly watery smile and John could see how devastated he was by the separation.

When John led him through the rose garden, Jeff slowed to appreciate the flowers. 'These are beautiful,' he said, holding one gently in his fingertips, smelling the delicate fragrance.

'My father does a lot of the gardening now. He really enjoys it.' John's shoulders tensed, readying himself for a knowing look or a jibe, his defences automatically going up. But Jeff simply smiled.

'He has a real gift.'

He did. But he'd also lost himself since the vineyard fire, throwing himself into his gardening as a way of coping, and he and his family had done nothing to help him regain his self-esteem. Maybe they could open the gardens, or John could encourage his father to enter a local gardening competition? And if there weren't any, Thornhill Hall could start one, just like they had the food festival. Anything to bring him out of himself.

'Here we are,' said John, opening the large gate to the secret garden. He could hear Hetty and a voice he didn't recognise which he presumed was Daisy. Standing aside, he let Jeff through.

Hetty and Jaz had hung bunting everywhere and the small metal table had been laid for two. A large cake stand stood in the middle, covered with sandwiches and pretty, delicate cakes. Jaz had found the only decent china they had left, and cups and saucers were laid out. At the foot of the table was a metal bucket packed full of ice and a bottle of champagne.

'Jeff?' Daisy raised a hand to her chest while Jeff looked on confused, but from the glint in his eye, also happy to see his wife. 'Daisy?'

Daisy shot an accusing glance at Hetty. 'What's all this, Hetty?'

'Mum, Dad.' Hetty clasped her hands together in front of her. 'I know you've been having a tough time lately, but I just don't think divorce is what either of you really want so—'

'Darling,' Daisy began, but Hetty held out her hands, asking for her to be quiet just a little longer.

'Mum, I am absolutely positive that Dad hasn't had an affair—'

'What?' Jeff shouted, completely shocked. 'An affair? Who with?

Daisy, you didn't think—' Daisy's eyes shot to the ground and her cheeks turned pink.

As embarrassment took over Daisy's features, John could see that Hetty had been right. The love was still there, but it had become buried under the changes they'd made in their lives.

Hetty continued. 'I know that deep down you both still love each other. I think that because you've both been under each other's feet and haven't had any space, you've forgotten all the things you love about each other.'

Daisy and Jeff glanced at each other. There was a definite chance of getting somewhere as long as neither of them bailed.

Jaz gave a shy smile and made to leave. As she reached John, he caught her arm. 'Thank you, Jaz. For everything.' She returned his grin and for once her face was relaxed and happy. 'Where's the red wine I brought?' he whispered.

'In the picnic basket in the corner. You can't have a romantic picnic without champagne, can you? Well, you can but, you know what I mean.' Embarrassed, she slid out through the door.

Daisy and Jeff were now nearer each other, gazing around in admiration. Her expression had grown softer while Jeff looked like he'd seen his wife's face for the first time. Maybe Felix was right that sometimes last-minute decisions were worth acting on. They couldn't all end the way his investment had.

'Anyway,' Hetty said, beginning to edge away, 'I've made you an afternoon tea and all I ask is that you sit together and have a chat. But the subjects of golf, gardening, baking and other boring everyday stuff is off the agenda, okay?' Hetty motioned for them to take a seat at the beautifully laid table and left to meet John at the gate.

The smile she gave him made his heart beat hard, and he closed the gate softly behind them. Just as he moved away, Hetty grabbed his sleeve and pulled him back. Following her example, he leaned in towards the gate, beginning a whispered protest. 'Hetty—'

'Shhhhh!' She pressed her finger to her lips. They listened hard, but at first could only hear the birds singing and the faint buzz of a few bees as they hovered around the lavender bush behind them. Daisy was the first to speak.

'So …' There was a long pause. 'This is nice, isn't it?' There was a tinkling of china as they helped themselves to some food.

'Daisy, do you really think I've had an affair?' A loaded silence descended. 'And do you really want to divorce me?' Jeff's voice was loud and pained.

'Shhhh!' Daisy said, sounding exactly like Hetty.

John smirked. 'Is that where you get it from?' Hetty frowned as her father spoke again.

'I haven't had an affair you know. I haven't even looked at another woman since the day I met you. I can't believe that after all we've been through over the years, you're going to divorce me because I like golfing and gardening?'

'Ha! You mentioned golfing. You broke Hetty's rules first.' The teasing died and Daisy heaved a great sigh. 'Oh, Jeff, it's not that simple and you know it.'

'What is it then? Don't you love me anymore?'

Hetty batted a bee away and in the silence, John's own heart sounded a heavy rhythm in his chest. He could only imagine what Hetty's was doing. She looked desolate that her idea hadn't worked and went to push the gate open. John took her hand and held it firmly in his. 'Give them time,' he whispered again.

Daisy's clear decisive voice replied to her husband's question. 'Have you really not had an affair?'

'Of course I haven't. Who on earth do you think I've had an affair with?'

'I don't know. Mrs Hobbs? I know she's been bringing you food since I left.'

'Mrs Hobbs? You've gone mad, Daisy. She's a very kind neighbour but—'

'Do you know for the last six months all you've done is moan at me? When I used to get dressed for work every day, you used to tell me how nice I looked. Since I stopped working you haven't paid me a single compliment.'

'Haven't I?' Daisy must have shaken her head. 'I'm sorry,' Jeff replied meaningfully.

'And,' she continued, 'for the first six months we were retired we used to have lovely days out together and go here and there. Then all of a sudden you decided you didn't want to spend a single minute with me without any explanation whatsoever. You could hardly even swing a golf club when you were working and used to moan whenever golf was on the telly interfering with *Countdown*. Now you practise like you're the next Tiger Woods. Well, I hate to tell you, dear, but I think your chances of a golfing career are slim to none at your age.'

John studied Hetty's worried gaze. Was this all going to descend into a row?

'Daisy, I'm sorry. It's about time I told you the truth, isn't it?'

'I think you'd better, and if any other woman is involved after all you've just said, I'll cut off your dangly bits with this dessert fork. And I can assure you it will really, *really* hurt.'

'It's not that,' Jeff said. 'How could I ever want anyone but you, my Daisy?' He sighed and Hetty leaned in closer to the gate, her face so close to John's he could see every single eyelash circling her beautiful eyes. 'I've just been so afraid of getting old—'

'You are old!'

'But not just getting old, *feeling* old. I suppose I became obsessed with my golf swing to try and stay young.'

Daisy spluttered. 'What?'

'You know Karl who retired at the same time as me? He was so happy and then he just got afraid to go anywhere or do anything. He stopped coming golfing, then he stopped going out, and now he won't drive anywhere, not even into town. He's so afraid of the world now. He's become a shell of the man he used to be.'

291

'Really?' Daisy asked. 'Why?'

'I think his world just shrank and he forgot who he was. I just got scared that that'd be me if I was at home all the time. So I made sure I was always busy.'

'And then you got tired and ratty and took it out on me?'

John watched as Hetty rolled her eyes at her mum's directness, and smiled that mother and daughter were so similar. He was still holding her hand and the feeling of her soft skin under his made every nerve come to life.

Daisy spoke again. 'Why didn't you tell me, Jeff?'

'I don't know. I'm sorry, Daisy. I still love you very, very much.'

'Oh, Jeff, you great idiot. I love you too.'

Hetty pulled her hand away and punched the air before running on the spot, silently screaming. John marvelled at the woman before him, and in the silence she looked at him in a piercing gaze that spoke directly to his heart. Retaking her hand, he led her back through the roses. Once they were far enough from the secret garden that Daisy and Jeff wouldn't hear them, John loosened his grip so Hetty could let her hand fall if she wanted to. She didn't.

'You know', Hetty began, crinkling her brow as she thought. 'The secret garden would be a great pre-bookable spot for boutique picnics, maybe romantic evening meals. I can see it now – secret garden dining.'

'That's a great idea.' How was she thinking about saving his family at a time like this? She should be so caught up in her own achievements and relief that she didn't have time. Could he hope she cared about him as much as he cared about her?

'We could even team up and rent it as an outdoor event space for small, intimate gatherings.'

'Could it make enough money to save us?' He wasn't sure if he was asking the question of himself or Hetty. 'Could it—' John stopped, overcome by her concern, her empathy, her intelligence and her beauty. 'Do you know you're absolutely incredible?'

'Am I?' Hetty adjusted her glasses and her eyes darted downwards.

John took a small tentative step towards her, but with a giant leap of faith, he dipped his head and kissed her.

***

Hetty felt the power of the kiss in every cell of her body, right down to her feet. An intense wave of emotion tingled each limb and set her head and heart on fire. She squeezed her eyes shut and kissed John back, feeling completely that this was the right thing to do.

'Wow,' he said when they pulled away from each other.

Hetty's chest rose and fell with a big, magnificent breath. 'Yeah. Wow.'

The delicate smell of the roses filled the sweet summer air as John moved his hands from Hetty's waist and cupped her face to kiss her again. Then he rested his forehead against hers. 'When this is all over, can I take you out to dinner sometime?'

'Hmm?' Hetty mumbled as his hands dropped to her waist again. They were warm and strong and wonderful. She'd had good kisses before, but these had been incredible. Her body trembled under the weight of her feelings as she finally admitted to herself that her heart belonged to him. Ever since she'd started to get to know him, she'd been falling in love. There'd been an immediate attraction, but she'd felt such a loyalty to Ben and all they'd had together, it had taken her a while to realise just how strong it was. Her feelings for John had melted into every fibre of her being until they were a part of her. She loved his steadfastness, his kind, caring nature, everything about him.

'So, what were you saying?'

'About what?' Her voice was faint and sounded far away.

John laughed but held on tight. 'We were talking about business.'

She suddenly became animated again as her heart raced for a different reason. 'Oh yes! I was going to say that if you get the bookings you could then get a business plan together and build an actual restaurant.'

'We could renovate one of the old barns. Or there's an abandoned farmer's cottage we've been looking at selling.' He was sounding like an excited schoolboy but Hetty didn't seem to mind. In fact, she was sharing his enthusiasm.

'Is there?'

'Yeah, that way.' He pointed in the opposite direction of the food festival.

'But in the meantime, if you open the house to visitors, host the food festival each year, and do the secret dining thing, that's a pretty good start. If you convert a barn or a cottage you could run small retreats. I know this place that does yoga and Pilates retreats, and art and creative writing, that sort of thing. You could do day ones too. Or we could start them now.' Her brain was speeding up, thinking about different options. 'For now, you could run them in the summer and use the secret garden and lodge people at the house, but there's so much potential here.'

John threw his head back and laughed, but then he pulled her in for another kiss. 'Shall we check on your mum and dad?'

Hetty slid her hand into John's and they walked back to the secret garden. She could feel his eyes on her, as if checking she wasn't changing her mind. Hetty glanced over from time to time to reassure him. As they neared the gate to the secret garden, Hetty was concerned to see it was open.

Had it all gone downhill after they left and her mum had stormed off in a temper? Or her dad for that matter? But several voices were merging, happy together in genial chatter.

Peaking their heads through, they saw Rupert talking animatedly to Jeff, pointing out flowers and plants. He was standing straighter, and his body seemed stronger.

'I'm so sorry,' John whispered to Hetty already pulling away, worried he'd ruined her plan. 'I'll get rid of Father.'

'No, it's fine. He seems really happy talking to Dad. And look ...' Hetty pointed to where her mum had hooked her arm through Jeff's. She couldn't stop smiling. 'Let's go and say hi too.' Hetty led John in still holding his hand and everyone turned to look at them.

'What's all this then?' asked her dad, crossing his arms over his chest, nudging Rupert who responded with his gentle smile. Hetty looked down at her hand held tightly in John's and giggled as they began talking.

Her mum came forward and Hetty released him, moving to meet her. 'You didn't tell me you fancied the lord of the manor,' she whispered.

'I didn't quite realise it myself, actually, Mum.' But now she had, she felt light and free, like the world was just beginning and it was full of promise and opportunity.

'What about Ben? I always wondered if you two would get back together.'

Hetty thought about the beer tent. He was probably still there. 'Ben is the same as he ever was, Mum. I don't think he's ever going to be ready to grow up and commit. Maybe one day someone special will make him change his mind, but that special someone isn't me. And I'm okay with that.' Her mum gave her hand a squeeze. Hetty hesitated before asking her next question. 'And you and Dad?'

'This isn't easy for me to say, darling, but ...' She sighed and Hetty's heart shot up into her throat. Her plan had been working so well. 'You were right. We did just need to be together again, and actually talk to each other properly. Your dad was scared of getting old! Can you imagine?'

'Really?' Hetty laughed. She wasn't going to say she'd been listening at the gate.

'Yes, how silly. I told him not to be so daft. We've got this old together I'm sure we can manage to get a little older.'

'I'm so pleased for you, Mum.' Hetty wrapped her mum in a hug and felt her dad's arms circle round her as well.

'Thank you for doing this, poppet. You're a very clever girl.'

'Dad, I'm 38.'

'Then you're a clever old girl.'

'Hey!' She punched him on the arm as they released her, glad to see her dad was back to his old self. She noticed John standing a little further away and reached her hand out. He came to her side to take it.

'Now, this one,' said Rupert, bringing a delicate shoot over as if it was a tiny baby bird, 'is a cutting I took from that rose bush there. I think it's going to settle in nicely as long as I look after it properly.'

John stared, aghast at his father's full and complete sentences. Jeff studied the plant as Rupert talked on. 'I haven't seen my father this happy for a long time. He hasn't spoken like that since the fire. Especially to a stranger. I think he likes your dad.'

Hetty smiled. 'I'm so pleased.'

The moment's peace was interrupted as Lucinda came bustling into the secret garden, followed by Jaz and Felix.

'John, John – oh, hello.' She paused on seeing them all there, her manner at once formal, but her eyes were shining with unshed tears. 'I'm so sorry to interrupt, may I just borrow my son for a moment, please.'

John stepped forward. 'What is it, Mother?' His voice had lost the giddy lightness of the last half an hour. Felix stood behind Lucinda, shamefaced, keeping his eyes on the ground. 'Is everything okay?'

'Felix told me about the investment.' Unable to hold them back, a few tears escaped and ran down her thin cheeks. She was suddenly very fragile and delicate and Hetty wanted to go to her too. 'We're completely ruined this time, aren't we?'

John put a hand on Lucinda's shoulder. 'Not quite, Mother. It's not going to be easy, but Hetty and I have a few ideas.'

Hetty stepped forward and he took her hand once more. The way he looked at her made her feel unstoppable, something she'd never felt with Ben, even when things were at their best. Not that she needed the confidence boost, but it cemented their relationship in her mind. 'Hi, Mrs Thornhill – I mean, Lucinda.'

The tears dried a little and Lucinda's expression changed when she saw Hetty. A knowing look came to her eyes. Had she seen some sign of John's feelings when they were together? Or had he talked about her? The thought that he had made her skin tingle.

'The food festival has been a massive success, so that should help you in the short term, but there are a number of different options we can look at too. For now, there's private picnics and boutique dining here in the secret garden. All pre-booked so you know what's happening and when—'

'As well as opening the house to visitors more often,' John added. 'Would you mind, Mother?'

Lucinda considered for a moment. 'No, I don't think I would actually. I rather enjoyed showing everyone around earlier.'

'And then later,' Hetty continued, 'once we've got proper business plans together, we could look at converting one of the cottages so you can host health and well-being retreats.'

Felix frowned. 'Health and well-being retreats?'

But, as usual, Hetty was undaunted; she had that feeling in her gut again, and hairs rose on her arms once more, just as they had at the business forum. 'Yes. They're very popular at the moment. We could run yoga and Pilates ones, art or writing retreats. As well as renting it just as a holiday cottage. I think it could be hugely successful and provide year-round income.'

The scowl fell from Felix's face and he stared at his shoes. 'I'd be interested to see whatever plans you and John firm up. And if you needed collateral for a business loan, Elizabeth and I have already agreed we could use our house.'

John spoke up. 'That's kind of you, Felix but I hope it won't be necessary. Right now, they're just ideas, but we can all sit and discuss them together. I'm sure we'll figure out a way that suits everyone without us losing even more than we have already.'

Felix nodded in reply. 'I'm – I'm very sorry, John, for not listening to your advice. You were right to be cautious. And I'm sorry for what I said.' He held out his hand for John to shake, which he did.

'Apology accepted.' John and Felix went off, heads together as John talked about their ideas.

Lucinda stepped towards Hetty, taking her in a huge hug. 'I knew you'd be good for him as soon as I met you.' She stepped back and Hetty, for once, was unable to speak, taken aback by such a show of emotion. 'I'm just glad he's actually done something about it rather than wasting all his time planning to tell you how he feels but never actually doing it. That boy overthinks everything. It's nice to see him listening to his heart for once.'

Hetty's heart was so filled with joy she could barely speak. John and she were so alike, and she could see a bright and happy future before her, fulfilling and filled with love. John was everything she'd been looking for though she hadn't really known it at the time.

'So, Hetty,' John said, returning, and resting his hands in the curve of her waist. 'I asked you earlier, but you never actually gave me an answer. Would you like to have dinner with me tomorrow night?'

A smile so big it filled her soul spread across her face. 'Yes, I really would.'

And though it would technically be their very first date, she knew him so well it felt like it would be their fiftieth. But then, you had to start somewhere, she supposed.

Epilogue

One Year Later

Hetty turned to John and saw him swallow. He looked so nervous and she bit down the giggle in her throat. 'Do you want me to do it?' she whispered.

'No. No, I can do this. I can do this.' He nodded to himself then cleared his throat. 'Thank you, everyone, for coming to the official opening of the secret garden boutique dining experience!'

A round of applause greeted them from the small select crowd they'd invited to attend this momentous occasion. In the secret garden, with its new glass roof, and in front of a few journalists and all their family and friends, Hetty and John toasted their new business venture.

'It's such a pleasure,' he continued, 'to welcome you all here to celebrate this innovative project with us. We're very happy to be starting an exciting, new, financially stable chapter in the history of Thornhill Hall.'

Secret garden dining had been a huge success. They'd been fully booked and even during the winter people were keen to use the space for romantic dinners. At first, they'd added more tables and chairs, then had a heater installed, and so on and so forth.

And today they were celebrating the installation of the glass roof that would enable them to use the space all year round. It was proving a tremendous income stream for the estate.

Though Hetty still had her own events business and John his antiques, they were now working jointly on the retreats idea and it was already beginning to take off, with some prospective partners visiting today. The help they'd received from Jaz had been amazing and her organisation skills had impressed even Hetty.

Among the guests, their parents sat grinning like idiots. Lucinda, under her huge hat, wiped a tear from her eye and Rupert, in an old suit with grubby fingernails, smiled on. Hetty's second home wasn't exactly solvent but they were making headway and it now looked like it was only a matter of time before they could say for certain the house was safe. John had moved into her tiny seaside cottage. There was no way she could have given it up or left Stanley the limpy seagull to fend for himself, but they were still close enough to Thornhill Hall to be there when things broke, or when holes in the roof appeared, which they still did.

Lucinda and Daisy had also become firm friends and often went shopping together in Swallowtail Bay. Jeff and Rupert were nearly always found trimming the topiary or gardening somewhere else on the estate. John had suggested that some of the land that couldn't be sold was used as an allotment, and the two old men were often there together, chatting while they worked, or could be found on camping chairs with bits of paper, planning their sowing schedules. Golfing was a rare activity for Jeff these days, and as well as having his own activities, he and Daisy made sure they had time together as well.

Macie sat in the other corner, resting her head on James the chocolatier's shoulder. She pretty much lived in his flat now and was extremely happy as their relationship went from strength to strength. Felix and Elizabeth were there too and Hetty had found they were fairly easy to get on with. Felix's dodgy investment had, as John suspected, been incredibly unsuccessful and as yet there hadn't been any returns. The guilt had been hard for Felix to bear, but together they were putting it all behind them. The twin girls shifted in their seats, eyeing up the strawberries on the celebratory cake that was piled high with them in the corner. Tables laden with champagne and bowls of strawberries and cream were available for the guests they had invited, and bunting fluttered in the gentle breeze from the open windows.

The second annual Swallowtail Bay Food Festival had just finished, and it too had been a resounding success. Mr Horrocks' Travelling Carnival had been able to make it this year and with the kind old man at the helm nothing had gone wrong. No children had gone missing and no dubious stall holders had stuck their coconuts to the shies. Ben hadn't attended. He'd been too busy with his new shop in the larger town of Halebury and Hetty wished him well. Their last meeting had been awkward. He'd been apologetic, but Hetty had made it clear that things were over between them and there was no going back. He'd then recovered from her rejection quickly, his easy attitude softening the blow.

Hetty smiled at John and squeezed his hand tightly. She had always trusted her instincts and her instincts told her to hold on tight to this handsome, charming, loyal and kind man. A man who even after a year gave her the kind of kisses that made cartoon stars appear over her head and the world burst into song.

'So, thank you all again for coming. It really means—'

Realising John was *still* talking, and the crowd were beginning to glaze over, Hetty gave a gentle tug on the back of his shirt. Their secret signal that meant he was overthinking and gibbering on.

'What John means is,' she interrupted gently, receiving a loving and appreciative gaze from him while she raised her champagne flute in the air, 'we're delighted to welcome you all to Thornhill Hall!'

If you loved escaping to Swallowtail Bay, don't miss out on the next book from Katie Ginger, *Winter Wishes at Swallowtail Bay*!

Acknowledgements

So here we are, our second visit to Swallowtail Bay! How did you find it? I have to say I have a bit of a soft spot for this story and I'll tell you why ... it was the worst book to write! Seriously, I hated this manuscript so much during my first draft, I would have quite happily burned it. It just didn't want to flow, and my first draft was not living up to the idea I had, or how I saw it all in my head. But thanks to my lovely editor at HQ Digital, Sarah Goodey, and her amazing feedback, this story has actually ended up being one of my favourites! And with a hero who looks like beardy Richard Armitage, how could it not?!

I'd also like to thank some amazing writer friends who always keep me going when times get tough: Lucy Knott (the sweetest person you could ever hope to meet), Belinda Missen, Sandy Barker and Heidi Swain, thank you for your constant support! I feel like I know you all already even though I've never met some of you!

Hi, lovely readers,

How did you enjoy *Summer Strawberries at Swallowtail Bay*? Was John a bit swoon-worthy or what? And how did you like Hetty? I'd so love to know what you thought, and I really can't tell you how much reviews mean to us authors. Not only do they stop us feeling lonely, but they help us find new readers and show our publishers that people are enjoying our work. They are absolutely priceless. So, if you enjoyed your time in Swallowtail Bay, please think about leaving a short review on Amazon or wherever you bought it. And thank you, please, thank you in advance!

If, like me, you enjoy a bit of the old social media malarkey, it would be lovely to connect (that's what the young people say isn't it? Connect?). My website is: www.keginger.com; or I'm on Facebook at: www.Facebook.com/KatieGAuthor. And Twitter at @KatieGAuthor.

See you again soon and happy reading, everyone!
Best wishes,
Katie
xxx

Dear Reader,

We hope you enjoyed reading this book. If you did, we'd be so appreciative if you left a review. It really helps us and the author to bring more books like this to you.

Here at HQ Digital we are dedicated to publishing fiction that will keep you turning the pages into the early hours. Don't want to miss a thing? To find out more about our books, promotions, discover exclusive content and enter competitions you can keep in touch in the following ways:

JOIN OUR COMMUNITY:
Sign up to our new email newsletter: hyperurl.co/hqnewsletter
Read our new blog www.hqstories.co.uk
🐦 : https://twitter.com/HQStories
📘 : www.facebook.com/HQStories

BUDDING WRITER?
We're also looking for authors to join the HQ Digital family!
Find out more here:
https://www.hqstories.co.uk/want-to-write-for-us/
Thanks for reading, from the HQ Digital team